MATT SPIKE
AND THE
Vampire's Curse
BY R.E. SOHL

MATT SPIKE AND THE VAMPIRE'S CURSE

From the case files of Matt Spike, P.I.

By R.E. Sohl

Curious Corvid Publishing

For Cory Stanish who helped dream the dream,
And for Jen Burns who helped shape it

PAST IS PROLOGUE

The vampire held down his latest victim with just one arm, his inhuman strength pinning her to the table as surely as if a two hundred pound weight had been placed on her chest. She kicked at him ineffectually with her legs, and her arms flailed about in a blind panic, occasionally making contact and scratching at him. She sure had a lot of fight in her. Good! It was always so much more amusing when they tried to fight back. He relished the woman's look of confusion and dawning terror. This was always the best part - the anticipation. He'd moved with blinding speed as he'd thrown her onto the bed, she had been so taken aback by this that she hadn't even had time to scream. He could see now that she was about to start.

Can't have that. Don't want the neighbors overhearing anything, he thought as he cupped his other hand over her mouth - his cold, dead hand - making contact with her hot breath. The sensation of that warmth was intoxicating. The warmth of life, true life. Something he could never really experience again, save in these all-too-brief moments before he snuffed it out. It had been far too many days since he had last fed. He was going to enjoy this - savor every last moment of it.

He reared back his head, then flung it forward savagely and tore into the flesh of her neck, ripping through the surface layers and biting deep into her jugular. A tide of crimson gushed and sprayed out from her wounds, painting his pale face like some kind of abstract work of art. His fingers fumbled for her chest, his long nails sinking themselves through her skin as he tore her rib cage open and pulled out her still-beating heart. With a flick of the wrist, he snapped the arteries still connecting it to her dying body. He lifted it to his mouth and bit into it, the blood spilling and spewing from it like an overripe fruit.

"I certainly do hope you've left some for the rest of us, Francis. Anything else would simply be rude, and you *know* how much I despise poor manners," a deep, familiar voice intoned from somewhere behind him. It was a voice he hadn't heard in centuries.

A voice he'd never expected to hear ever again. A voice he'd *prayed* to never hear again. A voice that still tortured him in his nightmares.

Francis lifted his head from his latest feast, the body still twitching occasionally as the last vestiges of life ebbed as swiftly as the blood flowed. Yes, there he was, standing on the other end of the room, looking just as he had the last time Francis had seen him, although his clothes were a bit more contemporary, of course. Curse him! What was he doing here? Why wasn't he destroyed? How had he survived? How had he gotten in here? Had Francis been so intent upon enjoying his latest meal that he hadn't heard him walk in?

Then Francis remembered that he had many powers that the rest of his kind lacked, powers which he had often employed to maintain his fierce grip upon them all. Of course, he could simply teleport himself inside of here, such things were like child's play to one such as him! It was probably how he had gotten away that night, too. How to handle this unforeseen and unfortunate turn of events?

He decided that some serious boot licking was in order. He bowed deeply.

"Master! What an...*unexpected* pleasure this is! I'm so pleased to see that you have survived! I believed that you had perished all those years ago, or I *surely* would have sought you out to humbly offer my meager services. Thank the Dark Mother that you still live! Had I known that you were coming, I would've prepared a banquet more befitting one of your great stature. Of course, you are more than welcome, as always, to partake of this meal, inadequate though it may be."

The Master sniffed disapprovingly. "I'll pass. I'm not interested in your sloppy seconds. Besides, you know that I prefer blondes."

Francis laughed, although in this moment he felt no joy, only an increasing sense of dread. "Yes, I do indeed! May I say that you look very well, sir. The years have been most kind to you."

The Master nodded absently at the attempted flattery. "I am eternal. I persist. Always," he said in a very bored tone, as if such things were as routine and obvious as the nose on his face - because they were.

"Might I ask how you found me?" Francis asked, genuinely curious. He took a bit of pride in his skill at covering his tracks. It was one of his favorite parts of the game.

As if in answer, Francis saw a pair of huge, hairy wolves come slinking forth from the shadowy corners of the room, their eyes reflecting the candle light eerily as they stood on each side of the Master. He cursed himself for not noticing them before.

Outnumbered, he reflected despondently. *There'll be no escape for me this time.* He'd enjoyed his freedom from serving the Master. It had been a good run, but all good things must come to an end, he supposed.

"Ah, of course! You still have some of your loyal bloodhounds by your side. I should have known. Well played, Master! Well played, indeed!" He gave another insincere laugh, hating how nervous his voice sounded as he did so.

"I hardly needed them to find you, Francis. You've become sloppy in your old age. It's a wonder that the Guilds haven't found you and put a stake through your chest and separated that idiotic head from your shoulders yet," the Master hissed.

Francis gulped. Knowing full well how much he'd always prided himself on the meticulous precautions he took to mask his true nature from the rest of the world, he knew that the Master understood exactly how cruelly this particular taunt would land.

"I am confident that with your great wisdom to guide me once more, I shall swiftly learn to better myself in that department, Master. Pray tell me, to what do I owe the honor of this visit? How may I best be of service to you once more?"

"A war is coming. The battle lines are being drawn. Soon, very soon, the day of reckoning will be upon us," the Master said, his eyes staring off into the distance as if he was actually looking into that day right now. Perhaps he was. No one knew the true extent of the Master's powers. It was entirely possible that some form of precognition was a part of them.

"War, sir? Then I am happy to volunteer to fight by your side once more, as I did in days long past," Francis said, his wavering voice betraying his true feelings on the matter. Going into battle on behalf of the Master again was the last thing he actually wanted to do.

The Master turned his terrible gaze upon him, his cold eyes boring into Francis. He smiled icily. "Ever the faithful servant, eh?"

Francis nodded enthusiastically. "That's right, sir! You can always count on me!"

"LIES!" The Master spat the word at him. Francis became even more pale than he typically was, which was an impressive feat considering that he had the complexion of a slab of marble. If he'd still been capable of producing urine, he was sure that he would've pissed himself right then and there.

"You are a faithless servant! To assume so blithely that one such as I had been destroyed by a band of hapless mortals? As if such pitiful creatures were capable of such a feat! No, you were quite content to believe that they had done so - you *hoped* for it, prayed for it probably! For all I know, it was *you* that betrayed me to them! You who robbed me of my treasures! You have made no effort to look for me, to rejoin me! Yet you've had centuries to do so! You, who were once one of my Undying Ones, my elite, my most trusted comrades, are naught but a worthless traitor! " he accused in his deep, booming voice, the words reverberating around the room.

Francis fell to his knees and trembled. *And to think, today had started out so nicely,* he thought regretfully.

"Master! It's not true! I swear it! Take me back and I will help you against these new foes, no matter who that may be!" he pleaded.

"No, I have no need of 'friends' like you - and I cannot leave you to your own pathetic devices, lest my enemies find you and recruit you to their foolish cause. Already, their ranks swell to unacceptably threatening proportions," he noted dourly.

"All the more reason to let me help you, Master! It sounds as if you need all the help you can get! I will die for you, happily, sir!" Francis begged.

"Need? I don't *need* anyone's help! I am the Great Immortal! No, there can be no new warriors to join my side. I can only trust those that never left me. And I cannot risk creating new servants, should they decide to someday betray me as well. The more of our kind there are, the more difficult they are to control. But you *are* correct about one thing."

"Yes? And what is that, sir?" Francis said, as he dared to look up at him hopefully.

"You *will* die for me!" the Master smiled, displaying something close to real joy for the first time since entering the room. As he said the words he drew a sword of pure iron that dangled from his side, which had been concealed by his long coat. In a blur of motion, he sliced off Francis's head. It went flying across the room, bouncing off the wall and landing with a sickeningly wet, plopping sound.

One of the wolves by his side quickly shifted into a form that was something halfway between wolf and human, reached a furry hand into the Master's coat pocket, and drew out a few cloves of

garlic. He hurried over to Francis' head (which still wore a shocked expression), and pried open its jaws, stuffing the garlic inside.

The Master sheathed his sword as he approached the severed head, muttering some arcane words to set it ablaze. He looked over to where Francis's body was lying and repeated the same strange words, engulfing the prone form in flames as well.

He stood there for a moment, watching as the flames licked at the body of his old ally and spread out to other parts of the room, crawling across the floorboards and creeping up the curtains, a look of satisfaction upon his stony features.

"Let this place burn. We've got more work to do," he announced, and with a few more words from some long forgotten language, he and his wolves disappeared from the room with as little fanfare as they had first arrived.

CHAPTER 1:

THE TWENTY FIRST CENTURY BLUES

It was a beautiful summer day in 2005; September 16th, to be precise. Despite being one of the few remaining days of that particular summer, it was still pretty warm outside. Though Matt Spike thought he could already catch the first hints of change in the color of the leaves on the big oak tree that stretched outside the window of his office. Soon, he'd be treated to a riot of autumnal hues - rusty browns, burnt oranges and vibrant yellows. He was very much looking forward to it, as it was a welcome change of pace from the part of New Jersey where he'd grown up - further to the south, which is covered in a dense forest of evergreen pines. Despite its name, 'Pine Barrens,' his native stomping grounds wasn't solely made up of pine trees and it wasn't all that barren either, however it *was* true that it's flora was so heavily dominated by pines that the change of seasons from Summer to Fall had never struck him as all that visually dramatic or awe inspiring until he'd moved farther north. The vegetation up here in New Brunswick was far more diverse than it was in the southern part of the state, and therefore the change of seasons was far more dramatic. Even though he hadn't lived in South Jersey for many years now, the brilliant pageant of colors displayed by the trees up here around this time of year, as compared to those of his childhood home, had never failed to impress him. He hoped it never would. He'd be seriously worried about the state of his soul if the simple beauty of nature somehow no longer nourished and gave him a brief measure of inner peace.

The encroaching arboreal grandeur of the season gave him some degree of welcome respite from the anxieties that tended to consume his mind these days. He wasn't worried so much for himself. He was very fortunate in his personal life: happily married, a father to two great kids, he was financially secure and had a good career where he got to be his own boss. No, what worried him lately was the state of the world. He hadn't always paid much attention to such things. He used to be pretty disinterested in current events and politics. He wasn't sure exactly when all of this had started to change for him. Possibly it was a result of his association with his friend and secretary, Penny, who was always championing one cause or another. Or maybe it was because of his wife, Naomi, who was a history professor at Monmouth College now, and had a PhD to boot. She had originally mainly been interested in ancient history, but when she went for her doctorate, she had decided to focus more on American history, and as a result, she had become far more politically engaged, although to her credit she'd never been quite so adept at sticking her head in the sand as Matt once was.

The more he thought about it, the more it seemed to him that while the strong influence of two of the most important women in his life definitely had something to do with this shift in his attitudes, living through 9/11 had been what truly kicked it into high gear. Despite years of living in the Big Apple, he'd been lucky enough not to lose anyone close to him in the disaster. Nevertheless, that terrible day had been when he first started constantly gluing himself to the news, ever anxious about what might happen next in the hours and days afterwards, and he'd never really stopped watching since. He'd seen the country come together like it never had before in his lifetime, the rest of the world seeming to have sympathy too, only to watch with mounting horror as we pissed away all the goodwill and unique opportunities that short period of unity had offered. He felt that at that moment we should've asked ourselves why we were a target of such violent extremism and reversed course on our often imperialistic foreign policies, but we'd instead chosen to dig our heels in and launch ourselves into not just one, but two pointless wars that were proving to be costly quagmires. It seemed to him that throughout his whole youth we'd been telling ourselves that we'd never get stuck in another fiasco like the Vietnam War, yet here we were doing exactly the same thing and expecting a different result. That was the very definition of madness wasn't it? He was concerned about how we Americans might be trading away our freedoms for the promise of greater security with misguided pieces of legislation like the Patriot Act.

What kind of a world would his kids grow up in now? What had happened to the bright promise of the 21rst century, which he'd always expected would eventually lead America into a kind of utopia, and instead seemed to be devolving into some sort of an authoritarian nightmare? Where the hell was his flying car, goddammit? He'd always believed in the idea that "the arc of the moral universe is long, but it bends toward justice." When he was growing up, he felt that he could find plenty of evidence of this in the world around him, that the human race was gradually making progress towards fashioning a more free and tolerant kind of world, yet he found it harder and harder to find any proof of this in current events. He felt like that fateful day five years ago had been a kind of crossroads for us as a species and we'd taken the wrong path. It was as if we were hurtling full speed towards a dead end and nobody knew how to apply the brakes and reverse course.

Yes, he worried about the future a great deal these days, how could he not? Just last month, the beautiful city of New Orleans, where he'd once vacationed with his family only a few short years ago, had been completely devastated by Hurricane Katrina. Like most of the nation he'd been disgusted by the botched response from the President, who he couldn't believe we'd been stupid enough to give four more years of power. It was all making him lose faith in his fellow man, and the poor choices they often made when they allowed fear to dominate their thinking.

He also felt a great deal of frustration with the fact that he was personally acquainted with some very powerful people who *could* do something to stop this nightmare, yet they refused to do so. About ten years ago he had become involved in the surreal world of a coalition of ancient secret societies called "The International Conference of Guilds". In fact, his partner in his detective agency, Randy, was even a member of one of these Guilds - a hidden order of wizards and witches called "The Temple of the Old Gods". Matt and his wife had even accepted an ongoing job for them, guarding a powerful magical item called the Orb of Sinister, which paid so well that it had allowed him to purchase the palatial home that he now shared with his family.

He supposed that one of the reasons he consumed so much media was because he was urgently looking for some kind of a sign, some glimmer of hope that the Guilds had finally started to take action to save us from ourselves. Yet he knew it was a vain hope. They wouldn't help. Contrary to the feverish delusions of conspiracy theorists, the days when they used their influence to do anything other than to further enrich themselves were long gone. In fact, they were likely benefiting from some of this chaos. Which, by extension, meant that he was too, since he was on their payroll. It was a thought which made him more than a little uneasy. No, they wouldn't help unless there was a direct, immediate threat to all of mankind. Otherwise, they were quite content to maintain the current status quo. He only continued to work for them because he knew firsthand how dangerous the Orb was, and how important it was that it always remain hidden and well-guarded. He was proud to do his part to keep it secure, to know that in some small way, he was helping to keep the world a little safer by doing so.

Maybe the real world had always been this dark and scary, but in his younger days he had just failed to appreciate it, too lost in his fantasy world of pulpy detective novels to notice?

He tried to banish all these grim thoughts from his mind. There was little he could do about it personally, aside from voting for the lesser of two evils when the opportunity arose. Driving himself crazy with worry didn't help anyone, but the world these days was like a bad auto accident - the kind that you couldn't help but look at as you drove past, consumed by a kind of morbid fascination over the whole mess. He tried to focus instead upon the splendid display of the sunlight sparkling on the leaves of the tree outside, and to reflect upon how truly fortunate he was personally, despite the madness that the rest of the world seemed to be slowly descending into.

He was stirred from his attempts to soothe his anxieties with an appreciation for the magnificent natural world beyond his office window by the strident ringing of the phone on his desk. With a sigh, he swung around in his plush, high-backed leather chair to face his big, cherry wood desk. He'd been expecting this call. The man on the other end of the line had already spoken to Penny yesterday and completed the preliminary screening process that he had all of his potential clients go through before he agreed to an interview with them. Normally, Matt preferred to interview a possible client in person - face-to-face - so he could get a good sense of them before consenting to take on their case. He despised doing it over the phone. Too many of the little nuances of a person's character that you could pick up during an in-person meeting were lost.

However, he'd decided to make a rare exception in this instance. For one thing, this client was out of state in Connecticut, which made a face-to-face interview impractical for them at this time. For another, from what little he knew of this case already, it sounded like a pretty desperate situation. Even though he normally preferred to work locally, only occasionally taking cases out of the area if they were in NYC (where he had started his career as a Private Investigator and still kept an office), he had already pretty much made up his mind that he'd be taking this case. Apparently, it involved a missing fifteen-year-old boy. As the father of a boy who was the same exact age, he couldn't help but feel more than a little sympathetic and wanted to do whatever he could do to help out, even if it meant that living out of hotel rooms and operating in unfamiliar territory lay in his immediate future. He couldn't imagine what the parents must be going through. He'd go nuts if anything like that ever happened to his son Joe, or his daughter Autumn for that matter, who would soon be celebrating her 7th birthday on the 22nd, which coincidentally was also the first official day of Autumn that year.

He picked up the phone and lifted it to his ear, relieved to have silenced the insistent ringing, a sound which he always found particularly irritating.

"Matt, I've got that dude from Connecticut, Thomas Scott, on the line for you," Penny's somewhat raspy voice informed him.

"Awesome. Send him on through," Matt said. As he did so, he flipped open a slim file on his desk which contained a copy of the police report and a photo of the missing boy, all of which had been faxed to him earlier that morning.

"Hello, Mr. Spike? This is Tom Scott, I'm Kevin's dad. I want to thank you for taking the time to speak to me about all of this," a deep voice rumbled from the receiver.

"No problemo. Please, just call me Matt. 'Mr. Spike' is *my* dad." It was a common correction he felt obligated to make whenever people called him "Mr. Spike". Technically, it was also untrue; he had changed his last name to "Spike" because he thought it sounded kind of tough and was much easier to pronounce than his original last name.

"Oh, I'm sorry," Tom apologized.

"No offense taken. What can you tell me about your situation?"

"Didn't you read the police report I sent over?" Tom asked, unable to hide a trace of irritation in his tone. Matt decided not to let Thomas Scott's attitude annoy him or to take it personally, he reminded himself that this man was currently under a great deal of stress.

"Yes, I have it right here in front of me, and I've read through it several times already. These things are always written so dryly, though. It's like reading stereo instructions. I prefer to hear about it all directly from the horse's mouth whenever possible," he replied calmly.

"Okay, I suppose that does make sense. Where to begin? Well, my fifteen-year-old son Kevin went missing about a week ago. You see, his mother and I split up about two years back, and she has primary custody of him now, but he spends every other weekend with me. Most of the time he's unsupervised - his mother is a nurse who works long shifts, and when she's not at work, she's often over at her boyfriend's house. Luckily, Kevin's a good kid. He's quiet and mainly keeps to himself, so he stays out of trouble. He has a part-time job at one of the local fast-food places a few days a week. He mostly spends his time at school or work."

He paused to catch his breath. Matt thought he detected more than a hint of resentment when Tom was talking about all the time that Kevin spent unsupervised. The divorce didn't sound particularly amicable; it seemed like there was still more than a little bad blood between Kevin's parents. He hoped that it wouldn't affect their ability to cooperate with him on solving this case. Hopefully they'd be able to set all of that aside to do what's best for their son.

Thomas Scott resumed his summary of events.

"My ex-wife came home last Saturday morning to find no trace of Kevin in the house. No note, nothing, which is unusual; he typically leaves a note on a dry-erase board in the kitchen if he's going out somewhere. His bike, which is how gets around town, was still in the garage. He doesn't have many friends, just a few kids that he hangs out with sometimes. She called all of them and they said they hadn't seen him lately.Then she called me because it was my weekend to spend with him. She was wondering if I'd picked him up much earlier than I typically do, especially since she noticed that the duffel bag he uses when he comes over to my place was missing. Of course, I told her I wasn't planning on getting him until closer to noon. I suggested she call the police. She was reluctant to get them involved, she wanted to wait a little longer and see if he turned up first, so I had to tell her that if she didn't call them, that I would."

Matt grunted slightly. It seemed to him that Tom was desperate to establish himself as being the more concerned - and therefore the superior - of the two parents. Matt didn't have much patience for such shenanigans. His heart went out to Kevin. No wonder the kid had run away. Was this the sort of horseshit that the kid had to put up with? Listening to each parent build themselves up by tearing down the other? Never knowing which one to believe or who was more deserving of his love and loyalty? Although his own parents had never divorced, they had fought a lot when he was growing up, so it was a family dynamic that he was sadly all too familiar with.

"That lit a fire under her ass, and she finally contacted them. They asked a few questions over the phone, and eventually sent a squad car over to the house. The officer asked some more questions, made a few notes, asked for a recent photo of him, then told her they'd be in touch. The missing duffel bag convinced them that he had run away from home, even though he had no reason to. It was three whole days later before she heard anything from them! When they did call, they didn't have any new information for her, they just asked if he'd turned up yet or not. Can you believe it?"

He could. Matt knew that while the procedure on such things varied from one locality to the next, for the most part, police departments didn't invest much effort into looking for teenage runaways. Statistically speaking, most of them *did* return after a few days away from home. They were well aware of this, so they used that fact to rationalize their apathy as a wise way of allocating their limited resources. He would be surprised if they had even bothered to issue an APB for him. The cops reserved most of their actual efforts for cases where there was sufficient reason to believe that foul play was involved, such as a kidnapping or an abduction. They only really pulled out all the stops if the child involved was young. When it came to teenagers, the conventional wisdom was that if they didn't return home, they were at least old enough to fend for themselves. It sucked, but it was just the way it was most of the time.

Thomas Scott had his own ideas about why the police weren't helping them though.

"If you want my two cents, I think that the cops have been too distracted by that whole business with Sylvia McCoy to pay much attention to our situation. We're just victims of bad timing. We're being screwed because our problem happened so close to this more sensational news story that's overshadowing it. I guess it's too routine. Don't get me wrong - what happened to her was a real tragedy - it's just that there's nothing more they can do to help her. But my son still *can* be saved! " he noted bitterly.

He didn't have to explain what he meant by the Sylvia McCoy case. It was so bizarre that it had made the news even a few states away, here in New Jersey. A few days ago, a teenaged girl named Sylvia McCoy had been discovered dead in her home by her parents, who had just returned from a business trip on the other side of the country. It looked as if she had already been dead for several days when her corpse was found. Her body had been mauled by wild animals. Wolves, in fact. There were signs of a forced entry - it looked as though the wolves had actually broken through a window and attacked her in her bedroom. This was very unusual for a number of reasons. First of all, there was no known population of wild wolves in Connecticut, and secondly, it went against their behavioral patterns to be so brazen as to smash through a window and attack a person in their home. It would be an odd thing if it happened in a cabin out in the middle of nowhere, but to have it occur in a densely packed residential neighborhood was even more surreal. And yet, the evidence that this was in fact what had happened was pretty incontrovertible. The bite and claw marks on the body were consistent with that kind of animal. Curiously, there were some small clumps of torn flesh from the wolves themselves found at the scene, as if they had fought each other over their meal. These clumps had been DNA tested and had been conclusively proven to have come from at least two different male, grey wolves. The whole thing was extremely puzzling.

While he was watching a story about the incident on the TV out in the lobby of his office with Randy and Penny a few days earlier, he'd heard Randy mutter something about werewolves under his breath. Matt had assumed he was just making a particularly tasteless joke about it. Matt had seen quite a few strange and impossible things since he first became associated with the secret world of the Guilds a decade ago, but he *refused* to believe that horror movie monsters like werewolves were real. You had to draw the line somewhere, right? Sometimes he felt like his sense of reality could only withstand so many challenges before it crumbled completely like a sandcastle that's been built too close to the tides.

Matt had been quite surprised to receive a call from the same small town where this strange death had happened so recently. He wondered if there was some connection between the two events.

Tom wasn't done yet.

"I mean, my son is somewhere out there right now and there could be a pack of man-eating wolves wandering around town too! You'd think they'd try a little harder to find him before he ends up like that poor girl did!"

Matt felt that the local authorities probably thought it was more important to track down that pack of wolves and get them under control first. As much as he hated to admit it, he couldn't really blame them, either. More than just Tom Scott's son was in danger if they were still roaming around. From what he understood though, so far neither the town's Animal Control officers, police force, nor some local hunters who had joined in the search for the wolves had found any trace of them. One theory that had emerged was that the wolves weren't actually wild, but had been trained like attack dogs - brought to the area and deliberately sent after the unfortunate girl for some reason. It was a strange hypothesis, but it would explain the sudden presence of wolves in a place where they weren't native, their uncharacteristic behavior and their apparent disappearance afterwards. At any rate, Matt doubted that Kevin was in much danger from these wolves. He suspected that neither the boy nor the animals in question were even still in town by this time.

For the first time in a while, Matt decided to chime in. Ordinarily, he liked to let his clients ramble on as much as they wanted when describing what had brought them to him, since they tended to reveal a lot about themselves and the case the longer they talked, but something was bothering him.

"Do you think that there's some kind of link between the two things? Did your son know her at all?" he couldn't help but ask. The question had been driving him nuts since he first realized that they came from the same town.

Tom Scott laughed a cheerless little laugh. "The police called and asked us the same thing after her body was found, which was the last time we heard anything from them. I'll tell you the same thing we told them: as far as we know, they didn't know each other."

"But didn't they go to the same school? Weren't they the same age?" Matt pressed.

"Yes, they went to the same High School, but they aren't the same age. She was a year older than he was. He's a Sophomore, she's a Junior. Like I said, neither I nor his mother can recall him ever mentioning her name to us before."

Matt knew that didn't mean jack diddly squat. His own wife, Naomi, had been a grade above him when they were in High School, but they still knew each other well back then because they were both involved in the school's theatre program. He had lots of other friends that were both under or upperclassmen and women back then, too. He also hadn't made a habit of discussing everyone he knew or knew of with his parents, either. However, he could detect the testiness creeping back into Tom's voice and decided to back off on this line of questioning - for now, at least. He *did* find it interesting that the police had also suspected a link between these events, despite the fact that McCoy's death was obviously the work of wild animals, as improbable as that was.

"I'm sorry, I didn't mean to imply that I really think your son was involved in any of that somehow, it's just part of my job to ask those kinds of tough questions. You've gotta cover all the bases, ya know?" Matt said diplomatically.

"It's okay. It's nice to have someone even *trying* to cover the bases for a change," Tom replied.

Something else had been gnawing at Matt. "If I may ask, why did you decide to contact me and not someone a little closer to home?"

"I saw you on one of those crime shows on TV. My new wife is addicted to those shows. I was impressed with how you found the killer of that kid, Melissa Hollins. 'That's the guy I want! That's who can find my Kevin,' I told her."

Matt winced. He wasn't too surprised by this answer. That case had brought him a decent amount of fame and he'd been interviewed about it for a number of different true crime documentary TV shows. It had brought in a fair share of his business over the last few years, a fact which he felt pretty guilty about. He was plagued with the notion that he was profiting off the tragedy and had refused to give any more interviews about it because of that. But that wasn't the only reason he felt guilty about that case. Melissa Hollins was a kid that he *hadn't* been able to save before she met her end. It was ironic that he was so famous for solving a case which he privately considered to be one of his greatest professional failures. It was another occasion when he had been hired to bring home a missing child, but instead he'd only reunited the family with a lifeless cadaver.

True, in the end he *had* managed to catch the killer, but he'd always wished he'd been able to rescue her before she'd lost her life. He constantly blamed himself for not having done so. In fact, he'd only been able to catch the killer because of his unusual ability to astral project in order to tail his suspects as a disembodied spirit. It was something he'd learned how to do from Randy years earlier. It wasn't something he *liked* to do, either. It felt like cheating. He preferred to use his wits to solve mysteries. However, after finding her dead, he'd become so obsessed with getting some kind of justice for Melissa that he'd finally put all of that squeamishness aside and used every resource available to him to get it, including the supernatural ones. If only he'd just done that to begin with, he wondered if he could've prevented her death? Had his prideful attitude brought about her doom?

Of course, he couldn't tell the police how he'd *really* found the killer, he had to leave out the more fantastic details like his astral projection. Solving that case had made people think he was some kind of a genius; a label he didn't think he deserved. Going on all those shows and discussing the case had made him feel like a fraud. Some people thought he was a hero for his role in bringing in the criminal, who had turned out to be a serial killer, but again this left him feeling terrible. They didn't know how *hard* it had been for him to give the information he'd gathered on the killer over to the police, how he had *struggled* with his own dark impulses to execute the killer himself. It was especially difficult for him to control those feelings once he realized that the killer had other victims, and lots of them. It was something he could've probably gotten away with too, with a little help from his Guild friends. They were good at covering things up and owed him a few favors. Only Naomi, who had once made the mistake of taking a life out of revenge herself, had been able to talk him into backing down and letting the proper authorities handle it.

Yeah, not his finest moment. Definitely not something he liked being reminded of either.

"Well, let's just hope that there's a happier outcome to your son's situation than there was in that case," was all he could say.

"So does that mean that you'll take the case?" Tom asked hopefully.

Matt sighed. "Yes. I usually don't work that far from home, but I definitely want to help. You see, I've got a boy who's the same age as Kevin. I know I'd go crazy if he ever disappeared like that, so I can relate," he confessed.

"I'm very happy to hear that, thank you."

"Don't mention it. Now, I'm going to have to ask you a few more of those tough questions if you don't mind."

"That's fine, I'll tell you anything you want to know if you think it'll help."

"The police seem to be pretty convinced that Kevin is a runaway, but I've been wondering what your take is on all of that. Do you think it's possible that there might be some other explanation? What reason would he have to leave home? Did he seem particularly upset or unhappy the last time you spoke with him?" Matt frowned, realizing that he had just bombarded Tom with three questions at once. He supposed that he'd been holding these questions in for so long that they'd just come bursting out uncontrollably.

"That's exactly what my problem is with this whole thing! It's hard for me to buy the idea that he's a runaway. As far as me or his mother can tell, he had no reason to run away from home. It's not like he's some kind of troubled youth or something. He didn't seem any more upset than usual the last time I talked to him," Tom said exasperatedly.

"Hold on, what do you mean by 'more upset than usual'? What was he usually upset about?"

"You know, the usual teenage stuff. Not being popular enough, not being able to catch the eye of the girl you've got a crush on or being too afraid to make a move when you do. Getting good grades without seeming so nerdy that you're making yourself into a target for bullies. Those kinds of things. You were a kid once and you've got a teenager too, you know how it is. Typical teenager stuff. He also said how he felt a little neglected by his mother since she started dating again. Sure, he's old enough to take care of himself in a lot of ways, but he's still a child too. He needs his mother to be around more, whether he likes to admit it or not."

Matt wondered how much of that was *really* coming from Kevin, and how much of it was just Tom's interpretation of things. Maybe he was trying to create a narrative that his ex-wife was being neglectful so he could get full custody of the boy? Not for the first time, he thought that this tension between his warring parents might've been what *really* drove Kevin away, but of course his parents would be reluctant to see the role they may have played in creating this problem.

"How has he handled the divorce? It can be pretty tough on some kids," Matt said.

"He didn't take it so well at first, but he seems to have adjusted to it. It was almost three years ago now, it's his new normal. In some ways, I think maybe he's happier. His mother and I were always fighting the last couple of years before we finally called it quits. It wasn't good for him to be in that kind of environment. His life is a lot more peaceful now that we're apart," Tom explained.

Matt could sympathize. His own upbringing was marred by constant and nasty arguments between his parents. They even separated a few times in his early youth, sometimes for as long as a year, but they never actually got divorced. They kept getting back together and were still together to this day. Sometimes the fighting was so bad, he had wished they *would* get divorced though. Growing up that way had served as a powerful counterexample - it taught him what *not* to do in a marriage if you wanted it to work, or at least that's how he tried to rationalize it. It was his way of making lemonade out of the pile of lemons he was handed as a kid.

"What about your new wife, how does he get along with her?" Matt inquired.

"They aren't all that close, but they get along well enough. He knows she's not trying to replace his own mother," Tom answered earnestly, in such a way as not to trip Matt's finely honed "bullshitometer".

Okay, so I guess I can cross off having a wicked stepmother as a possible motive, he thought.

"Did she have any kids of her own before marrying you? Do you have new ones with her?" Matt continued to probe. Despite being an only child himself, he knew that dealing with new siblings could be a source of tension for some kids. Matt thought it might be significant that Kevin disappeared on the same day he was scheduled to spend the weekend at his father's house.

"No, she hasn't had any kids yet, but we hope to maybe give him a little brother or sister someday." Tom laughed a little nervously. "We're sure trying!"

"What about with your first wife? Is Kevin your only child with her?" Tom hadn't mentioned anything about having any other children so far, but that didn't mean that they didn't exist. If Kevin's mother really wasn't at home very often and Kevin had to help take care of any younger siblings in her absence, that could be another reason for him to run away from home. Maybe he felt overwhelmed or resentful of having to act as the "man of the house" or a substitute parent when he was still a kid himself?

"No, Kevin's still my first and only kid."

Well, so much for that theory. Matt was disappointed. He'd hoped that if he could figure out *why* Kevin had felt compelled to leave home, it might give him some insight as to where he could have fled. He agreed with the police that he was likely a runaway. If he had been kidnapped, the kidnapper probably would've contacted the family by now, and girls were more likely to be kidnapped anyway. The absence of his overnight bag was a big giveaway that he had run away. Most abductors wouldn't go to such elaborate lengths to conceal an abduction. A new idea suddenly struck him.

"You said that he had a job at a fast-food place in town? Did he have a bank account? Do you have any way of knowing if there's been any recent activity on it?" Most people used ATM cards these days, and if Kevin had been using it, the activity on it would be easily traceable - if he could get the bank to cooperate.

"Sure, he opened a joint account with his mother when he started working. Most of his money goes into savings for college and he doesn't have access to that, but there's a small amount from every paycheck that he is allowed to spend. I don't know if there's been activity on it lately. I'd have to ask her, but she could definitely find out for us."

"Good. Have her look into that ASAP. If you don't mind my asking, how is your relationship with your ex-wife, Margaret? How does she feel about the idea of hiring a private investigator?"

"Normally we're like oil and water - we don't mix. We try to avoid talking to each other as much as possible, except for when we have to because of Kevin. But we've been driving around town a lot together lately, searching for him and we've been getting along okay during those times. She wasn't too crazy about the idea at first, but now that he's been gone for over a week and she can see that the police aren't really doing anything about it, she's come around to the idea. I'd say that she's as eager as I am to get to the bottom of this. I think she kinda blames herself for it."

And so do you! Matt thought. *At least it sounds like she'll be cooperative.* "What about your former wife's boyfriend? How does Kevin feel about him?" he asked.

"He doesn't like him. They don't have anything in common, and he just ignores Kevin. The guy hasn't really made any effort to form a relationship with him. Kevin feels like his existence annoys him. The feeling's pretty mutual - Kevin thinks the guy is a loser and doesn't understand what his mom sees in him or why she spends so much time at his place. I don't feel like he's really done much to help search for Kevin since he's gone missing. It's like he doesn't give much of a damn."

Hmmm, might have to look into him a bit more closely, Matt thought. He had the boyfriend's name already. He'd ask Penny to log into some of the databases that he was subscribed to and see if she could dig up anything suspicious about the guy's background. It was possible that he saw the boy as an unwanted complication in his relationship with the mother. Unwanted enough to eliminate? That all depended, of course, on how seriously he took that relationship and if he was obsessed with the mother. However, Matt also had to keep in mind that Tom obviously didn't like this guy either and that attitude was probably coloring his perceptions of the situation.

"What about Kevin's life at school? You said something about him being worried about being bullied? That he had a crush on some girl? Can you elaborate on any of that? Do you think that could've played any part in this?" Matt was imagining the kid getting sick of being bullied and trying to escape that, or maybe running off with the object of his affection.

Tom laughed. "No, I can't. I was just giving you examples of the sorts of things that kids his age are usually worried about. I didn't mean for you to take it so literally. He hasn't really talked much about any of those specific things to me. The days when he used to tell me all about everything he does in school are long gone. I was just assuming that might be the sort of thing he has to deal with. Kevin is a little nerdy. He still likes to read comics and he's into those creepy Stephen King books. He's not terribly athletic either, but despite all of that, as far as I can tell, he's well-liked enough by most other kids his age. Not cool enough to be considered one of the cool kids, but not weird enough to be a total pariah either. He just sort of keeps to himself and flies under most people's radars."

Again, Matt could sympathize. That had pretty much described his own strategy for safely navigating through the jungle that High School could often be without being eaten alive by the wild animals lurking within. Keep your head down and don't draw too much attention to yourself. Keep your freak flag flying at half mast.

"So he has no girlfriend, then?"

"Not that we know of."

Matt realized he'd have to let go of the rather romantic notion that he had run off because of young love. *Romeo and Juliet, this ain't!* he thought ruefully.

"So what do *you* think happened to him if he didn't run off on his own? Do you think someone took him?"

"That's exactly what I think."

"Is there anyone you know of who might want to hurt him? Do you or your ex have any enemies who might try to strike at you through your son?" Matt asked, knowing it was a long shot.

"Not that I can think of, but it's not how it was when we were kids, is it? There's lots of real sickos out there these days. I guess you probably know that more than most."

Yeah, he sure did know that - firsthand. Matt was once again reminded of the sad case of Melissa Hollins and some of the other truly fucked up things he'd witnessed over the course of his career. Although he wasn't quite convinced that there really were more dangerous people at large now than there had been in the past. All that had really changed, in his opinion, was that we were now more painfully aware of the horrifying reality we'd always lived in. We all knew it was quite possible that the seemingly friendly person next door might secretly be some kind of monster.

"Alright. I think I've got enough to work with for now. I'm going to head up there later tonight. Do you think that you and your ex could meet me at her house tomorrow morning? Maybe around 9am? I'd like to get a look at Kevin's bedroom."

"Sure, I don't see why not. Hell, it's more than those good-for-nothing cops have done so far. They never even asked to search his room for clues."

This didn't particularly surprise Matt. "I'd also like you to have the information that my secretary mentioned to you over the phone yesterday ready for me when I get there." Penny had given him a standard list of information that Matt typically expected his clients to provide when investigating these kinds of cases.

"I'm not sure why you need to see that info about our finances. I assure you that we can afford to pay you," Tom said, clearly annoyed by the idea of disclosing those kinds of details.

"That's not why I need them. Try not to take this too personally, but I need to make sure that none of you have any kind of financial motivation for your son to disappear," Matt told him, knowing that such an honest answer might upset him.

He wasn't wrong.

"You're supposed to be working *for* us, not investigating us!" Tom complained.

"I have to look at all the possibilities before I can start eliminating any. It's called being thorough. Truth is our business. If you don't have anything to hide, you shouldn't feel threatened by that. I have no interest in any skeletons that may or may not be in your closet that don't have anything to do with finding your son. That's my only priority here," Matt tried to reassure him.

He wanted to make sure that Tom understood that even though he might be working for him, he wasn't in the business of helping his clients cover up their misdeeds, nor was he trying to expose them unless it was necessary to do so to resolve the case. He had his own code of ethics and his own methodology when it came to how he operated, and if Thomas Scott didn't like it, then he could hire somebody else. Matt didn't need the money. The Guilds paid him well enough to act as the Guardian of the Orb, he just continued to work as a PI because he enjoyed it and he liked helping people.

"Okay. I'll get those papers together for you. It's not like I'm trying to hide anything, it's just that I like my privacy, that's all," Tom said a little reluctantly.

Matt supposed he could understand that, assuming that was the real reason for his resistance.

"Great, then I'll see you tomorrow morning. Thanks for your time, I'm looking forward to working with you to bring your son home safely. Goodbye for now."

"Goodbye," Tom replied, and Matt hung up the phone.

He let out a long breath, relieved that the conversation was finally over. He wasn't *really* looking forward to working with that man. He had just been trying to remain professional when he'd said that. His impression of Tom was that he was kind of a pain in the ass. He hoped that Kevin's mother might be easier to work with. Again, he had to remind himself how much stress Tom was probably under and he felt a little guilty about judging him so harshly, but only a little. His instincts about people were typically pretty on the money and he knew that he disregarded them at his own peril.

Matt rose from his chair, opened his briefcase which sat on one corner of the desk, and placed the file that contained the rather unhelpful police report inside a small pocket. Then he turned around and pulled aside the tapestry of a Welsh Dragon which hung on the wall behind his desk, revealing a hidden safe built into the wall. He punched in the combination on a keypad with practiced ease and opened it up. Inside was a tiny, cheap-looking plastic statuette of a boy wearing shorts and a cap. The chintzy little novelty item was actually the dreaded Orb of Sinister in disguise. There was a pair of tongs sitting beside it, which Matt now used to pick it up and place it inside the briefcase, which contained a large piece of foam that had a hole in it perfectly shaped to fit the contours of the statuette. Matt closed up the briefcase, put the tongs back inside the safe and swung the tapestry back into place. He didn't like to pick up the Orb by hand; it was formed from countless souls and you could *feel* them when you touched it, which was unpleasant to say the least.

Next, he picked up a long case that sat on the floor beside his desk and opened it. He looked up at the almost comically large sword that was on display on his wall above the tapestry, suspended on a number of thick steel hooks. The red blade was at least four feet long and seemed to be made of a shiny, gem-like material. With a thought, the sword flew off the wall and lowered itself into the case. This was the *Vermilion Avenger,* a sword that was legendary amongst the few people who knew of it. Among them it was notorious as the sword that had shattered Excalibur. Yes, *that* Excalibur. It was the product of another time and place, and made of otherworldly, thought-responsive materials. It had been given to Matt years ago to help him guard the Orb. In the unlikely event that someone traced the artifact to his office and tried to make off with it, Matt could kill them in an instant, with just a thought. It creeped him out, to be honest. He didn't think that something as serious as killing should be so damned convenient and effortless. Matt stepped over to a coat tree and put on his trench coat and trademark fedora (he still got a childish thrill from dressing up like a stereotypical PI) before picking up both cases and stepping out of his office.

As Matt walked out into his waiting room, Penny was there, sitting behind her desk. She was a petite, 26-year-old young woman. Her hair was short and styled into chunky spikes. It was not unusual for it to be dyed any number of bright and unnatural colors, but lately she had let it revert back to its original auburn color. She had a somewhat high forehead and her skin typically had something of an oily sheen to it. She had a pierced nose and eyebrow. A full sleeve of tattoos wound down each arm. She'd been Matt's secretary for about 8 years at this point. She even used to live with him and Naomi, when they had first moved to this area. She was the mastermind of a rock band that was now called The Mystery Smiths, after having previously been known as Lung Collapse for several years. The band had originally been a Ska band, but as that genre of music had tapered off in popularity they had begun to explore other styles of music. At this point, they were more of a proper punk band with some new-wave flourishes. The band had enjoyed some moderate degree of success, but not so much that Penny could quit her day job as Matt's secretary when the band wasn't on tour. Matt thought of her as the little sister he'd never had, and always hired her back on when the tours were over, filling her position with temps while she was gone.

The other occupant of the room was Randy, Matt's partner in the detective business. Randy was tall and muscular, with an olive complexion, a mop of thick, unkempt black hair and a neatly trimmed beard. He wore a pair of equally thick glasses. He was the same age as Penny, and he was her partner too, as the bass player of The Mystery Smiths. He was often also her romantic partner as well. Their relationship seemed to be in a constant state of flux, it was very "on again and off again". Sometimes, it seemed like they were just "friends with benefits", other times it looked like there was something more serious going on between them - which appeared to be the case right now. Matt didn't like to pry into the ins and outs of their relationship. Fortunately, it never seemed to seriously impact their ability to work with each other either in the band or at the detective agency. Randy often told Matt that he considered Penny to be his best friend, despite whatever may or may not be going on between them romantically.

Randy had first met Matt back when he was still based out of Brooklyn. Randy had lived in the same apartment building where Matt's office was located and had been fascinated by the fact that a real live detective was working out of it. He used to hang around the office as a teenager and Matt would pay him under the table to tail suspects and do other odd jobs. When Matt and Naomi moved to New Brunswick, Randy had started going to Rutgers University so he could stay in their lives. Randy was unsure what he wanted to do with himself in college at first, but eventually he decided that he wanted to follow in Matt's footsteps and took some criminal justice courses as the first step towards getting licensed as a PI. As soon as he got his license, Matt had made him his partner and they'd started sharing the caseload.

Not that Randy needed to work, either. Randy had been with Matt on the case where he first became involved with the Guilds and he had been recognized as someone with strong potential to become a powerful wizard by a witch named Wendy, who had recruited him into the Great House of Magic known as the Temple of the Old Gods and trained him in the mystical arts. The Temple of the Old Gods was a very wealthy organization, and all of its full-fledged members were regularly paid with a generous share of that wealth. Many of them reinvested that wealth or used it to start their own companies and became quite wealthy themselves. Randy tended to just give most of it away to his family members or charities. He preferred to maintain as much of his independence as possible and liked to keep one foot firmly planted in our "mundane" world rather than the world of the Guilds. He felt like too many of the other magic users he knew were too detached from the rest of humanity and normal people; they spent too much time living inside their own version of reality. Randy was determined not to end up like them.

At the moment, it looked like Randy and Penny were just sitting around watching Spongebob cartoons on the TV mounted on the wall of the waiting room.

"Ah, hard at work as usual I see," Matt remarked as he entered the room.

"Hey, what can I say? I don't have many things on my plate right now," Randy shrugged.

"Good! Then you won't mind taking over my other cases while I'm out of town for the next few days. Penny can fill you in on them," he announced.

"Slave driver!" Randy shot back with a smile.

"So you took that case after all, huh?" Penny asked.

"Yup. I'm on my way back home right now to go pack my bags. Book me a hotel room for tonight as close as you can get to Shadowbrook, Connecticut. Get me something cheap, but..."

"...not too seedy! Yeah, yeah I think I know the drill by now," Penny finished. She'd never understood Matt's penchant for frugality. He had plenty of money, but he was often reluctant to spend it. It's like he had never adjusted to the fact that he wasn't a starving college student anymore. Naomi was usually able to snap him out of that mindset, but when she wasn't around to remind him that they were pretty well-off financially, he always defaulted to his "el cheapo" setting.

"Send the reservation info and directions to my email, I'll print it out at home," he told her.

"You should just get yourself a Blackberry, then you could pull it up on your phone," Penny suggested for the hundredth time. She didn't know why she kept on bothering, she knew all too well how reluctant Matt often was to adopt new technologies. He had only bought his first cell phone a couple of years ago.

Matt made a face. "Nah, all those little buttons...it's overwhelming!"

Penny rolled her eyes and turned to her computer to begin searching for available rooms in or around Shadowbrook. "You know, you're so old-school that it would almost be charming if it wasn't so inconvenient!" she griped as her fingers flew over the keyboard.

"Be careful out there, Matt," Randy warned.

"What? Are you worried that the big bad wolf might get me?" he teased.

Randy smiled again. "No, it's just a feeling. Hopefully it doesn't mean anything too serious."

Matt raised an eyebrow, but said nothing. Randy had legendary instincts. He operated almost entirely on the basis of his gut feelings. If something about this case was ringing Randy's alarm bells, then he'd better watch his step.

Matt started moving towards the front door, then suddenly whirled around. "Oh, I almost forgot! Penny, see what you can dig up for me online about the mother's boyfriend in this new case."

Penny was far more than just Matt's receptionist, she was quite gifted at using the internet to investigate people using public records and other resources - something that Matt used to have to do in person. It was amazing (and also a little frightening) how much you could learn about a person just from a few quick web searches.

Penny looked up from her screen incredulously. "You've already got a suspect?"

"Maybe. Could be nothing. I think it's worth a look. Just take care of it for me, alright?"

Penny gave him an exaggerated salute, which was her normal reaction to being ordered around so much. He knew that despite her always feeling obligated to make a big show of her reluctance, she actually enjoyed researching things for him.

Matt snorted loudly, which was his normal reaction to her faux insubordination.

"Okay, I'll see you two smart asses later. I'm outta here!"

"Happy hunting!" Randy called after him as the door swung shut behind Matt.

About ten minutes later, Matt found himself pulling up to his large, sprawling home situated on a heavily wooded private drive in North Brunswick. As he walked up to the door, set down his cases, and fumbled for his keys, he could hear his large Golden Retriever, Mike, bark a few times and claw at the door in excited anticipation as he always did when Matt got home. Sometimes Matt felt like he was Fred Flintstone about to get ambushed by an over-enthusiastic Dino.

"Down boy, down!" Matt cried as he pushed open the door and fought not to be knocked over by the large dog jumping onto him and licking at his hands. Matt sighed and set down his briefcase long enough to shut the door behind him and rub Mike's belly. He retrieved the briefcase and moved out of the foyer and into the living room where his kids Joe and Autumn were playing against each other in one of those fighting video games (it looked like the latest installment of the "Tekken" series) on their PlayStation 2. There was a rather large gap of eight years between the two of them, and their common love of video games was one of the few things they seemed to have in common.

"Hey dad!" Autumn called to him. She was something of a daddy's girl, so he wasn't too surprised that she'd been the first one to acknowledge his presence. Aside from the dog, of course.

"Hey yerself, kiddo!" he said, setting down his cases and kissing the top of her head.

He looked over at Joe, and felt a surge of gratitude that he was here, safe at home, unlike Kevin Scott. He gave the kid an awkward hug from behind the couch. On the TV screen, Joe lost his match.

"Thanks for distracting me, Matt! You just made me lose!" Joe whined. Matt wasn't his biological father. He had known Matt since before his mother Naomi was even dating him, so he had gotten into the habit of calling him by his first name, even though Matt had legally adopted him shortly after marrying Naomi.

Autumn laughed. "You can't blame Dad for the fact that you suck at this game!"

"You wish! I'll kick your butt in the next round!" Joe declared defiantly.

"Yeah, nice seeing you too," Matt muttered a bit dejectedly.

"You're home early!" Naomi's voice came calling to him from the dining room. Such was the layout of the living room that he could see her sitting at the table from where he stood. She was going through some of her student's papers. She had her own office in another room of the sprawling house (as did Matt), but she rarely used it, preferring to work at the dining room table where she could keep an eye on the kids. Most of her classes were scheduled in the morning and early afternoon, so she normally got home long before he did these days.

"Well, don't get used to it, I'm only here long enough to pack my bag. I've got a long drive ahead of me," he told her as he moved across to her and gave her a peck on the cheek. He sat himself down in a chair next to her. Naomi was a short, curvy woman with a tanned complexion and long, jet-black hair. Her almost golden brown eyes glittered with perpetual mischievousness.

"So, you decided to take the case after all?" she asked somewhat rhetorically.

"Was there ever any doubt?" He smiled at her lopsidedly.

Naomi took a breath. Of course there wasn't. Matt was a sucker for these missing kid cases. She was a little worried about him. She felt like he was constantly trying to make up for not being able to save poor Melissa Hollins. He could save a million other kids, and it would never close up the hole in his heart that her case had left behind. She understood that, but she didn't think *he* ever would. She just hoped he wasn't setting himself up for another such heartbreak. Even though the Hollins case had happened years ago now, she knew how much it still gnawed at Matt. She had suggested he get some counseling to help him cope with it, but he'd been characteristically resistant to the idea.

"You're not even going to stay for dinner? It's Taco Tuesday!" she said, trying to entice him.

"Taco Tuesday? But today is Friday!" Matt laughed.

"Look buster, I can declare a Taco Tuesday on a Friday if I want to, I've got a PhD now!" she protested.

"As tempting as your tacos sound, I plan on grabbing something to eat on the road. This kid's been missing since last Saturday. Time is of the essence. You know, after the first forty-eight hours that someone goes missing, the chances of finding them alive are cut in half," he said, repeating a statistic he was fond of citing.

"Yeah, yeah, I know, I know! So how long do you think you'll be gone? You'd better be home in time for Autumn's birthday!"

Matt shrugged noncommittally. "That's almost a week from today. I don't plan on being gone for quite that long, but I *will* be gone for however long it takes to find this kid."

She gave him her notorious "look", the terrible Naomi death stare that brooked no further argument. "That's not a real answer. Let me rephrase my question: how many changes of clothes are you planning on packing?"

Matt withered somewhat under her gaze. "I dunno, maybe two or three days worth? Don't worry, I have no intention of missing our daughter's birthday!"

"That's better." Naomi smiled, grateful to at least have some kind of ballpark figure she could work with, and a promise not to miss Autumn's birthday. She patted his hand somewhat patronizingly.

"Why'd you bother to lug that thing inside if you're just gonna leave in a few minutes?" she asked, indicating the two cases.

"I was kinda hoping that you could just guard the Orb for me while I'm gone. I don't feel like hauling all this stuff with me, along with my suitcase," he confessed.

Naomi was more than capable of guarding the Orb of Sinister by herself. Not only did she have plenty of practice using the *Vermilion Avenger*, but she also had a few rather peculiar items of her own which she had accumulated over the years to help her in this task. She owned a magic ring given to her by Randy's mentor Wendy, which created an impenetrable force field around her so long as she wore it. She also had an Angel's flaming sword that could cut through just about anything, destroy the soul of anyone who was struck by it, and fire a net made of energy out of the tip. She usually kept that weapon (with the flames turned off, obviously) on display on the wall of her office at work. She also kept a safe in that same office to hold the Orb. They often alternated their duties guarding it.

"Sure, no problem. But is it really wise to leave the *Vermilion Avenger* here, what with all those wolves running loose up there? You might need it!"

"From what I understand, they haven't found any sign of those wolves yet, and believe me, they've been looking. Besides, I always have my trusty old gun," he said, patting the concealed nine millimeter pistol that was holstered under one arm. Matt actually had no great affection for such weapons, but he recognized the necessity of carrying one in his line of work.

"Honestly, I think I'm just as worried about your mental health as I am about your physical wellbeing right now. Just don't get too carried away with this case. You can't save 'em all, ya know?" she said, reaching out to squeeze his hand. He squeezed hers back.

"I know, but I have to at least try," Matt said seriously, suddenly standing up and pushing in his chair.

Naomi just nodded. He could be infuriatingly stubborn sometimes, but then again, the same thing was true about her.

"I need to go check my email. I asked Penny to book me a room up there and she's supposed to send me the details," he explained, moving off towards his home office. Naomi watched him leave the room wordlessly, a concerned expression hanging upon her face.

As Matt entered his home office, he took the computer sitting on his desk out of sleep mode and logged into it. He clicked over to his work email and was surprised to see not just one, but two new messages from Penny. He sat down and opened the one marked "Hotel Info" in the subject line. He saw that she had booked him a room at the Comfort Inn two towns over from Shadowbrook, which was too small of a town to have any decent hotels within the city limits. A link in the email provided driving directions from his house to the hotel. He clicked on that next and printed out the pages on the printer sitting next to his computer. Penny kept on bugging him to get one of those GPS things so he wouldn't have to rely on printed maps to get where he was going, but there was something about the feeling of having a piece of paper in his hand that Matt found reassuring. He'd been in other people's cars who had a GPS; indeed, Naomi had one in her car, but he found it to be more distracting than actually helpful. It was a neat concept, but he thought it needed improvement. *Lots* of improvement before he'd get one for himself.

Matt next opened the other email she had sent over. It was about Kevin's Scott's mom's boyfriend, a man by the name of Cliff Burr. Matt was astounded by how quickly Penny had managed to put together so much information on the man and summarize it so succinctly in just the short amount of time since he'd left his office. Basically, there wasn't much there that stood out to make him seem like an especially likely suspect. Cliff was a few years older than Kevin's mother and he'd served in the military for a few years, even seeing some action in the 1990-1991 Gulf War. He was a local contractor and a divorcee himself, with full custody of a daughter a few years younger than Kevin. Apparently, his ex-wife had a drug problem and was such a mess that she'd given up all parental rights to their daughter. Not that Cliff didn't seem to have a few issues with substance abuse too, although in his case it was alcohol. He had a couple of DWIs and misdemeanors for public drunkenness, although these were all a few years old. As far as Matt could tell, he'd been keeping his nose clean lately.

No wonder Kevin didn't like him, he probably knew about his issues with the bottle and didn't like the idea of his mom shacking up with a drunk. Matt could empathize, if his own mother had left his father for an alcoholic, he would've had a problem with that idea too at that age - although he liked to think that nowadays he was far more understanding of people's struggles with addiction and less harshly judgemental of them than he had been as a teenager. He'd experienced his own difficulties when he had been wrestling with quitting smoking, although he wasn't sure how much that really compared to having a serious drinking problem or an issue with harder drugs. Matt had never been much of a drinker, nor had he ever really experimented with drugs. He tended to avoid anything that clouded his ability to think straight.

Maybe the responsibility of caring for his daughter had helped sober up the guy? Matt was starting to form an impression of the man as someone who had his demons, but was trying to deal with them as best he could. He could respect that. Maybe he'd been wrong to take Tom's negative statements about him so seriously? Or maybe he wasn't? It was hard to tell just from looking at this colorless data about his life, it told him nothing about the intensity of his relationship with Kevin's mother, and the crux of his suspicions regarding Cliff hinged on that. Also, the fact that he hadn't gotten in any legal trouble lately due to his drinking didn't necessarily mean that he was really sober, maybe he'd just gotten better at concealing it?

In any case he didn't truly think the kid had met with any foul play. He was pretty sure he had run away and his parents were just in denial about it. Hopefully Kevin's ATM transactions would help lead to him and he'd be reunited with his folks soon enough. Yet Matt had to remain open to all possibilities, he knew that it wasn't good to go into an investigation with too many preconceived notions.

He shot off a quick reply to Penny to thank her for all her good work in compiling the information of Cliff Burr so quickly. Then he got up and started the process of putting the Orb away. Just like in his office in New Brunswick, he had a safe built into the wall here that was hidden behind a tapestry. In this case, it was a tapestry depicting King Arthur in the midst of a battle. Once the Orb was secured inside the safe, he opened his other case and mentally pictured the *Vermillion Avenger* floating onto a set of hooks above a suit of futuristic looking armor in one corner of the room. The sword obliged, carrying out his mental commands as it always did.

The armor went with the sword, but Matt hardly had any occasion to actually use it. Thankfully the majority of his cases were quite routine. When the kids were younger and he and Naomi were both less experienced in using the sword, they used to keep it locked up in a broom closet at the other end of this room, which is also where they kept their small stockpile of guns and ammunition. However, they were now a bit more confident with the idea that they could display it safely. Matt told the kids (who knew nothing about the stranger aspects of their parent's lives) that he carried it back and forth with him each day because it was extremely valuable and he was paranoid about someone stealing it. This was even partially true, since the blade was made of a kind of extremely dense diamond not found on Earth, the sword probably was priceless simply because of the exotic materials that it was constructed from.

Matt headed upstairs to pack his suitcase with a few days worth of clothes plus his toiletries before heading back downstairs to say goodbye to everyone. Now that Joe knew that Matt would likely be away for several days, he was much friendlier to him and apologized for his earlier behavior. Naomi had started preparing dinner and made one more last ditch effort to get him to stay for Taco Tuesday. Matt was sorely tempted - Naomi was an excellent cook after all (as evidenced by his ever increasing waistline), but again he declined, citing his desire to hit the road. He had a three hour road trip ahead of him - if he didn't get too hung up in traffic. He had half a mind to stop by the fast-food place where Kevin Scott had worked to grab dinner so he could get a look at the place and maybe ask a few questions, but he doubted he'd be able to hold out that long.

"You remember what I said earlier, Mr. Spike. You can't save them all, and that doesn't make you any less of a good person. Take care of yourself, and don't forget to be kind to yourself too - those are my doctor's orders!" Naomi chided him.

Matt sniffed. "But you're not *that* kind of a doctor!" Which was his expected response to this running gag that had been going on between them regularly since she had gotten her PhD, taking advantage of her newfound status to constantly issue "doctor's orders" to everyone around her.

Naomi smiled at his familiar reply, happy to see him feeling well enough to play along and stick to the script between them.

"And did you remember to pack your toothbrush this time?" she asked in a playful tone. This was another recurring joke they shared. Matt often left his toothbrush at home on vacations.

"Yes, dear," he said in an exaggeratedly weary voice, yet another aspect of their ongoing repertoire.

Matt gave her a kiss and a long hug before placing his fedora back on his head and picking up his bags with a slight groan of effort that was a harbinger of his rapidly approaching middle agedness.

"Don't worry about me, I'm not afraid of the big bad wolf!" He grinned as he headed out the door.

CHAPTER 2:

THE PERPLEXING DISAPPEARANCE OF YOUNG KEVIN SCOTT

Matt arrived at his hotel later than he had anticipated, having run afoul of rush hour traffic and losing even more time when he had finally given into his hunger and stopped to grab a bite to eat. As he had predicted, he had lacked the discipline to hold his hunger in check long enough to sate his appetite at Kevin's place of employment; he'd have to save his trip there for tomorrow. After checking into his room, Matt astrally projected and decided to take an advance look around the town of Shadowbrook. It was always possible that Kevin was still in town and he might spot him while flying around in his spirit body. His past reluctance to use such unique abilities had cost Melissa Hollins her life, and Matt was determined to never make that same mistake again.

However, this astral scouting mission had proven fruitless. At this time of night, the streets of Shadowbrook were practically deserted. It was like a ghost town. Anyone still out on the streets stood out like a sore thumb, but none of them turned out to be Kevin. He didn't spot any wolves prowling around the neighborhood either, for that matter. Shadowbrook itself was a fairly unremarkable place, mostly just a collection of suburban housing developments and strip malls separated by clumps of wooded areas. It reminded him far too much of his hometown back in southern New Jersey, except perhaps even more dull, if that was possible. There didn't seem to be much of anything of interest in this suburban wasteland to occupy or engage the restless energy of the young. Perhaps wanting to escape that monotony had really been why Kevin had run away? After astrally zooming over the depressingly uniform rooftops of Shadowbrook for some time, Matt had ultimately relented and returned to his body, which lay strewn across the hotel room bed like a discarded doll. After all, he had a long day ahead of him tomorrow and he'd need his rest.

The next morning, Matt arose bright and early. It had been quite difficult to drag himself out of bed; astrally projecting was extremely exhausting and he had slept deeply despite not being in his own familiar bed. It felt odd to wake up without Naomi's snoring form by his side. He definitely didn't enjoy being away from home by himself like this and hoped he could wrap this up as quickly as he thought he might.

He caught sight of himself in the bathroom mirror as he lurched inside to brush his teeth and studied himself critically. His blue eyes were dulled with tiredness. His skin was almost sickly pale as he spent far more time inside lately than he would prefer. Still, he supposed he was holding up fairly well for a thirty-five-year-old. He still had all of his sandy blonde hair and there were no signs of thinning. His face was a bit rounder than it had been when he was younger and he was thicker in general, which he blamed on being married to an Italian American woman who lived up to the stereotype of being a good cook who was always pushing the fruits of her culinary labors upon her family. However, since he had been built like a lanky scarecrow before moving in with and eventually marrying Naomi, it was generally a good thing that he had put on a few pounds, although sometimes he worried that his weight gain was starting to get a little out of hand. His face was covered with stubble, as it often was, because he had an aversion to shaving, which he found to be generally unpleasant and annoying, yet he was also confident that he'd look ridiculous with a beard, so he never let things get quite that far.

Matt took a shower, dressed, and rushed down to the lobby to partake of the rather unsatisfying "continental breakfast" that was included with his room. The coffee, which was normally the sacred elixir that he depended upon to revive him, was also substandard. He had been spoiled, he knew, by years of enjoying Penny's exquisite coffee brewing skills each morning at his office. After enduring this disappointing experience, he drove over to the home of Kevin's mother, Margaret, where he was supposed to meet both her and Tom this morning.

Margaret Scott's home was a cute little duplex on a cul-de-sac in a small subdivision of similar such structures located on the edge of one of Shadowbrook's larger tracts of housing developments. The duplexes all looked like they were only a few years old, with a spacious looking garage separating one home from the other. Matt was met at the door by Tom, an imposing, dark haired bear of a man with a thick mustache and cheeks that were permanently pockmarked with the battle scars from his adolescent war with acne. Margaret was waiting inside. She was a frail-looking wisp of a woman who always seemed to be exhausted and nervous. She looked vaguely Hispanic. He wondered what her ethnicity was? He always found people's family histories interesting.

They all sat down together in the living room, with Matt in a reclining chair and Tom and Margaret on the couch. A wooden coffee table separated them.

After all the typical pleasantries had been exchanged, Tom handed Matt a stack of papers.

"Here's those records you asked for over the phone," he said, still a hint of resistance in his tone.

"Thanks. Are the bank records for Kevin's account here too?"

"Yes, I printed it out this morning from the bank's website," Margaret answered, pointing to the top of the stack.

Matt studied it for a few seconds.

"Hmmmm.. it looks like he withdrew everything from checking last Saturday morning at an ATM. There's a fee for using another bank's machine, so he must've used one that belonged to his own bank. Are there many of those in town?" Matt inquired.

"We've just got the one at the local branch on Main Street, it's not that far from here," Margaret told him.

"Within a convenient walking distance of this house?" Matt queried, recalling that Kevin had left his bike at home.

"Yes. He went there all the time," Margaret informed him.

Matt made a mental note to stop by there and see if they'd let him have access to the ATM security footage. There was no guarantee that they would, since he wasn't with law enforcement and they were under no legal obligation to cooperate. He wanted to verify that it was really Kevin who had withdrawn that money and that he hadn't been with anyone else at the time. He had to hand it to the kid though, he was smart; sticking to using cash would make him much harder to track down. Luckily, he only had a little less than $150 on him. It wouldn't get him very far. There was a lot more money in his savings account, but apparently he couldn't access any of that without his parents being present to authorize it.

"What's the public transportation system like around here? Any local bus or train terminals?" Matt asked.

Tom laughed dismissively. "In this place? There's only the one CTtransit bus stop in town. I suppose you could take it to the terminal a few towns over."

And from there he could've gone anywhere that $150 could take him, Matt reflected grimly. Of course, there were other ways out of town, although using public transportation would probably give him the biggest bang for his buck, and more anonymity. He'd ask about the other possibilities anyway.

"I guess there probably aren't lots of taxi companies around either?"

"It's a very small town," was Margaret's only response. Matt took that as a "no". Still, he'd check the phone book in his hotel when he got back there. There had to be *some* that serviced this area, even if there weren't any actually located in town. He'd see if he could stop by whatever ones were around and show Kevin's picture to any drivers that might be around the garage.

Matt had a few questions he'd thought up just for Margaret. He'd have to tread carefully though, she might not like some of them.

"How was your relationship with your son? Did you have any recent arguments or any reason you can think of why he might want to leave home?"

"We've always had a very good relationship," she said, a little too defensively, in Matt's opinion

"He didn't seem especially upset or troubled by anything the last time you saw him?" Matt pressed.

"No, he was completely normal."

Lady, NOBODY is completely normal! Matt had wanted to say, but of course he didn't.

"What about your relationship with Cliff Burr? How did he feel about that?"

"Look, it's no secret that Kevin doesn't approve of Cliff, that's why I don't bring him over here and I always go to his house instead." There was that defensiveness again, twice as strong as before. He couldn't really blame her, he *was* implying that her relationship choices had driven her son away - because perhaps it had in fact done just that.

"Was he concerned that you might marry Cliff?" Matt could imagine how that might make the kid feel uncomfortable in his own home. He was grateful that he had come into his son Joe's life when the kid was still a toddler. He couldn't imagine how awkward it would've been if he had started dating Naomi when Joe was the age he was now.

"No! Cliff and I have both been through a tough divorce recently, we're in no rush to make the mistake of getting married again. We're taking things slow." This certainly wasn't the way that Tom had portrayed things. Spending most of her free time over at some other guy's house sure sounded like she was pretty committed to that relationship in Matt's opinion. Of course, he only had Tom's word that that was what was really happening, which was supposedly based on what Kevin had said to him. It was like a bad game of telephone. Matt noticed Tom shifting uncomfortably in his seat at her mention of "making the mistake of getting married again."

Matt took a deep breath; this next question might really send her over the edge. "Do you think that Cliff could see Kevin as a possible obstacle to his relationship with you?"

"Enough to do something to him you mean? Of course not! It's a ridiculous idea! I already told you, it's not really all that serious of a relationship, despite what *some* people might think." She shot Tom with a venomous look as she said so. If he noticed, he didn't show it.

"I'm sorry. I don't mean to put you on the spot so much with all these questions, I'm just trying to eliminate any suspects who might've wanted to harm Kevin, or to establish a possible motive for him running away." Matt tried to smooth things over, he was afraid he was pushing her too far. "It's all just part of the routine, I assure you."

She nodded her understanding. "It's fine. At least you're taking an interest. You've already done more than the police have done. I'm grateful that you've decided to help us."

Matt hoped he wasn't blushing. He wasn't prepared for the sudden shift in her demeanor.

"I'd like to see Kevin's bedroom if that's okay?"

"Sure, the cops never even bothered to look up there when they came. We've already poked around in there a little, but haven't found anything that seems important. Not even a note! If he went somewhere, he would've left me a note! He always left a note!" She looked like she was going to start sobbing. Matt's heart went out to her. He wondered if Kevin had any idea what his disappearance was doing to his parents? He knew that at this age, kids could be pretty damned self-centered and tended to underestimate just how much their parents really did care.

He followed them up to the bedroom. It was a fairly unremarkable room. There was an unmade bed, a desk and chair with a somewhat outdated PC computer on top of it, and a few plastic shelves with books and the type of white cardboard boxes that comic book collectors kept their back issues in. Posters lined the walls, mostly from sci-fi and superhero movies. There was a dark wooden dresser with a TV and a gaming system on top of it. Several random articles of clothing lay in piles on the floor. It wasn't exactly clean, but it wasn't embarrassingly messy either, at least not by Matt's somewhat lenient standards, although he had a feeling that Naomi would beg to differ if she had been present. Margaret and Tom hovered outside the threshold.

"Do you mind if I go through these drawers?" Matt asked.

"Not at all, it's what you're here for, isn't it?" she said, hopeful that he might find something she hadn't.

Matt had a sudden idea. "Did he keep any kind of diary or journal?"

"Not that I know about," Margaret answered again, dashing Matt's hopes. Of course, that didn't mean that he didn't, just that *they* didn't know about it. He wondered if he might find one on the computer? Maybe he didn't keep a physical copy of one. He'd also definitely be taking a look at Kevin's search history.

"Do you know the password to this computer?"

She gave it to him. Matt sat down in Kevin's chair and powered up the computer. As soon as he was logged in he checked out the recent search history. There wasn't anything that seemed out of the ordinary or pointed towards where Kevin might have been heading. There *were* links to quite a few websites that were obviously dedicated to pornography from the colorful names they sported. Matt smiled a little to himself at this discovery. Typical teenager.

Don't worry, kid. Your secrets are safe with me.

Matt wished Penny was here. If Kevin had done any internet searches that might've given Matt a clue to his whereabouts, he could've deleted them. Matt had no idea how to retrieve that sort of data, but he knew that Penny did. However, since Kevin hadn't even bothered to delete his porn searches, he doubted that he had deleted anything else of much importance. Still, he might have to take the CPU back with him to New Brunswick so Penny could work her magic on it. He asked Kevin's parents if that would be a problem, and was told that it wouldn't be. He promised he would return it to them as soon as he no longer had any use for it.

Next, Matt rummaged through the drawers of the desk, but he didn't find anything significant. There were a few spiral bound notebooks; he skimmed through them, but they were mostly filled with somewhat competent sketches of superheroes and didn't really qualify as proper journals. They didn't really offer much insight into Kevin's inner world. He repeated the same process with the chest of drawers, again with no success. Nothing worth noting was to be found upon the bookshelves, aside from revealing what Matt considered to be Kevin's good taste in horror and fantasy novels and a clear preference for X-Men comics. In a lot of ways, it reminded Matt of his own bedroom from when he was a teen, or Joe's bedroom for that matter. *The more things change, the more they stay the same,* he thought, reflecting upon the truth of that tried and true old maxim.

Matt lifted up the mattress, which was universally a favorite spot for hiding things. That's where Matt used to stash his own "girly magazines" back in the day, before such things were just a few keystrokes away. There wasn't anything to be found there. Under the bed itself were several old pairs of Vans and Chuck Taylor sneakers in a variety of colors. As he shined the small, yet powerful LED flashlight he kept on his key ring under the bed, it illuminated some amorphous shape that was seemingly caught between the wall and the bed frame. With some difficulty, he strained to reach it, pulling it out into the clear morning light streaming through the windows.

Matt gasped as he took a look at what was in his hand.

It was a ripped and torn t-shirt. And it was caked in what looked like brown dried blood. Some of it flaked off onto him as he handled it. It looked like it had been practically soaked in it. Matt quickly noted that most of it seemed to be gathered around the collar. The series of long tears in the shirt almost looked like claw marks.

He held it up for Margaret and Tom to see.

"Do you recognize this?"

"Y-yes! That's Kevin's shirt! I think it was what he was wearing about...maybe two days before he went missing? But what *happened* to it?" Margaret stammered. She was clearly disturbed by the state of the shirt.

"That's what I was hoping you could tell me!"

"I don't know! Is that...*blood* all over it?"

Well it sure ain't ketchup! Matt thought sarcastically.

"I'm pretty sure. I'll have to get it analyzed to be sure," was his far more diplomatic verbal response.

"Can you do that?" Tom asked. Matt nodded.

There were plenty of independent forensics labs he could send it off to, but he decided that he'd probably take advantage of his connections in the Guilds to take care of it for him. There was a group within the Guilds called the "ABC", which was a kind of global police force under their control. They were the organization that had inspired the myth of the "Men in Black". Their main duty was to cover up the activities of the Guilds, but they also sometimes investigated unusual threats to the world. Most law enforcement groups in this country thought The ABC were some shadowy federal agency since they had been given strict instructions to give them whatever they asked for when they turned up, but in actuality they answered to no one but their director, Bronson McDowell.

Bronson happened to be one of Matt's personal friends. Bronson was always trying to recruit Matt to work for the ABC, always to no avail, even going so far as to once offer him the leadership position in the ABC branch closest to Matt's home. Bronson had promised Matt he could call upon the resources of the ABC if he ever needed them. Like using astral projection, it was something he was naturally inclined *not* to do, but when it came to finding missing kids, Matt would always use any advantages he had. The ABC had far more sophisticated equipment at their disposal than any of the conventional forensics labs. They'd be able to analyze something like this with more accuracy and a faster turnaround time. There were branches of the ABC in all fifty states and every nation on Earth. He didn't know where the closest one was, but he could find out easily enough.

"Do you have something like a large ziplock or freezer bag that I could put this in?" Matt asked Margaret. She told him she could go get one and disappeared downstairs. Matt slowly set the bloodied garment down on the carpeted floor, inwardly cursing himself for already contaminating it by touching it. He turned to Tom.

"Is there something you can get me that would have lots of Kevin's DNA on it? Like maybe a toothbrush? I might need it for comparison, to see if this is Kevin's blood on this shirt."

"I'll check in the bathroom," Tom said dazedly, obviously having trouble processing how so much blood could've gotten onto Kevin's shirt, or how it got torn up so badly. Looking for the items Matt had asked for would offer his mind a brief respite from such troubling questions.

A moment later, Tom returned gripping a dark blue toothbrush and handed it to Matt.

"I found this, it belongs to him," he explained superfluously.

Matt carefully placed it inside one of the plastic evidence bags he kept in the inner pocket of his overcoat. He always carried a few of these, but he didn't have one big enough to fit that shirt in, which is why he'd asked Margaret for a bag.

"Thanks. So he didn't pack a toothbrush, huh?" Matt wondered aloud. That might point away from the idea that he left of his own volition - then again he might have been in a rush and simply forgotten to pack it. Matt had made that mistake on quite a few trips himself. Naomi loved to give him shit about it. If he had a nickel for every time he had to buy an overpriced toothbrush from the hotel gift shop he'd have at least a dollar and seventy five cents by now.

"He usually keeps a travel one in his overnight bag all the time," Tom said.

That's a good idea. I should do that. Why the hell didn't I think of that? Matt thought, mentally commending the boy on his dedication to good oral hygiene.

Margaret reappeared with a large freezer bag. Matt took it from her, picked up the t-shirt with a pencil he found lying on the desk, then placed it inside and zipped it shut. The conversation he'd just had about the idea that Kevin had forgotten to pack his toothbrush made him think of something.

"Are there any items from around the house that you've noticed have gone missing since Kevin's disappearance?" he asked Margaret.

She looked thoughtful for a moment before speaking.

"There are a few cans of food missing from one of the kitchen cabinets that I don't remember using. Cans of tuna fish, beans, SPAM and soup, mostly. I didn't think much of it. I just noticed it before I went shopping this week and was taking stock of what I might need to pick up. I just assumed that Kevin had gotten hungry and eaten some of it before...before...well, before whatever happened, happened."

Matt was certain this was no abduction now. Not only had the kid cleaned out his bank account, but it sounded like he'd also taken a small stockpile of food with him. He must've been pretty desperate if he was willing to eat SPAM! Matt's stomach did flip flops at the memory of the taste of the stuff. What kind of trouble had this kid gotten himself into here? Whose blood was all over that shirt?

"You said his bike is still here?" Matt asked Tom. This detail troubled him slightly. Why walk to the ATM or a bus stop when you could ride your bike? Apparently, he rode it everywhere. This one thing made Matt wonder if someone had been driving him around instead.

"Yes, it's still in the garage," Margaret answered for him.

"Can you take me to it?" Matt wasn't sure exactly why he had just asked that question. It wasn't as if he didn't believe them. They had no reason to lie to him about such a thing. However, his instincts told him he needed to see the bike, and he knew from years of hanging around with Randy never to ignore his hunches or gut feelings.

Matt was escorted to the tidy garage, which Margaret didn't seem to bother to use for actually storing her car. In fact, it was almost bare except for Kevin's bike (a red and yellow mountain bike) and a pair of oversized plastic trash bins - blue for recycling and black for regular trash. A few plastic totes stood stacked atop each other in one corner. Matt didn't know quite what he was looking for as he approached the bike, which was standing on its kickstand near one wall. He gave the tires a squeeze, wondering if there was something wrong with the bike and perhaps that's why he hadn't taken it with him. Sure enough, the front tire seemed a bit low when he pressed on it, but he wasn't completely sure about it. To test it further, he sat on the bike's seat and watched as his added weight made the tire flatten out where it met the concrete floor. As he hopped back off and crouched down to inspect the tire more closely, he felt as though Tom and Margaret were watching him with a little bemusement at all of this. Sure enough, Matt felt a long gash in the side of the tire that extended all the way into the inner tube.

Then something caught his eye.

Caught in the spokes of the wheels was a long, matted grey tuft of fur of some sort. Wolf hairs? He hoped not. He didn't want to jump to the conclusion that this fur belonged to one of those wolves if there was a more likely explanation. It could just as easily have come from a dog, or a dozen other kinds of animals. He wasn't sure that even The ABC would be able to get DNA off these hairs unless a follicle was still attached to any of them, but it was worth a try. Matt reached inside his inner coat pocket for one of his small evidence bags and a pair of tweezers and carefully pulled out the hairs and transferred them to the bag, sealing it up and putting it in a different pocket of his trench coat.

As he put the bag away, he spotted a dark brown splotch on the floor near the bike; a few inches from it was another one, and another. Matt twisted his head over his shoulder to follow the trail all the way to the now-closed garage door. He was certain that it was a trail of dried blood. As he stood back up, Matt produced a small digital camera from one of his voluminous coat pockets (which had been enchanted by Randy so they could hold more things than was normally physically possible) and snapped a few quick pictures of the blood trail.

"Do you guys have a dog?" Matt asked as he dropped the camera back into his pocket. He hadn't seen one in the house, but they could always have one in the backyard. He often had to put Mike outside when he was expecting new visitors so he wouldn't have to listen to him barking constantly at the strangers in his domain.

"No," Margaret said in bewilderment. Apparently she hadn't been able to see what he'd put in the evidence bag from her vantage point atop the stairs that led down into the garage, and had no idea why he was suddenly asking about dogs.

"What about Kevin's friends? Do any of them have dogs?"

"Not that I know of. He's really only got two friends that he hangs out with sort of regularly outside of school. I've never really been inside their homes. I don't remember him ever mentioning them having dogs. You'd have to ask them - I gave you their addresses and phone numbers in that stack of papers you asked for. What's this all about? You don't think this has anything to do with that weird wolf attack do you?" she asked in a quavering voice.

Matt *did* think that it was starting to look that way, but he could see how much this idea was upsetting her and he didn't want to alarm her until he had some more evidence. The poor woman seemed nervous enough already. He had to hand it to her, his barrage of questioning regarding dogs, coupled with the blood evidence she'd watched him uncover was obviously starting to lead her to think along the same lines he was.

"No, how could it? He didn't even know that girl." Matt said with a conviction he didn't actually feel. In reality. He was thinking that the torn and bloodied t-shirt, the ripped tire and tuft of fur were all leading him to the conclusion that Kevin had been attacked by one of these wolves while he was riding his bike. Obviously he'd managed to escape somehow, but why hadn't he told anybody about it? His mother seemed pretty sure that the torn shirt was the same one he had worn two days before he disappeared, which would've been last Thursday. He would've had ample opportunity to report the attack if it had happened on Thursday. If he'd been wounded by a wolf, which seemed to be the case, why hadn't he sought medical attention? Why hadn't his mother noticed that he'd been hurt? Maybe she really *was* as negligent as Tom had implied?

Another possibility of course, was that all of this blood belonged to someone else. It wasn't a scenario that Matt liked to entertain. How would someone else's blood have gotten all over Kevin's shirt? Matt couldn't help but wonder if it was really Sylvia McCoy's blood? Her body hadn't been discovered until that following Monday, but investigators weren't sure how long it had been lying there - probably all weekend, maybe longer. Her parents hadn't been able to reach her by telephone since Friday.

So many questions! What the hell was really going on here?

Matt couldn't wait to have the evidence he'd gathered evaluated. He wondered if this small trail of blood drops continued on into the house? He'd have to take another look when he went back inside. He hadn't spotted it before, but then again, even the blood trail here in the garage was made up of small drops that were quite easy to miss. It also could've been purposely cleaned up to cover up something. That shirt he'd found seemed to have been deliberately hidden - albeit rather poorly. Why not just throw it away though, if you had something to hide?

Matt walked back into the house, his head down as he studied the floor. He could make out an occasional spot on the tile floor outside the door that led to the garage. He followed these spots up the carpeted steps and back into Kevin's room, the boy's parents anxiously following hot on his heels. The spots terminated close to the bed. Again, Matt produced his camera and took a few pictures. He looked up at the parents.

"I'm going to have to ask you to not clean up these little spots." He pointed at the floor. "At least not until I can get some of my...associates over here to take samples of them." Matt had decided that he'd see if the ABC could spare a few agents to come to the house and gather up some of the evidence that he wasn't equipped to remove.

"It's blood, isn't it?" Margaret asked with a shudder.

"I think so, probably from that shirt," Matt said, deciding to level with her for once. *Or wounds on his body from under the shirt,* he thought grimly.

"What's happening? We find a ripped and bloody shirt in his room and now a trail of blood? Did someone attack him?" Tom demanded.

"Maybe. But if they did, based on how he was dressed, it looks like it happened a whole day before the last time he was seen," Matt said, looking him in the eye.

He now switched his gaze to Margaret. "Are you *sure* he wore that shirt last Thursday, and not Friday?"

"Yes. The last time I saw him was Friday morning before he left for school, and he was dressed completely differently." Margaret asserted.

"And he didn't act strangely that morning? He didn't seem like he was hurt, or trying to hide something?"

"No. He was a little tired, I had a hard time waking him up to get ready that morning, but he's just like that. Sometimes it takes him a long time to get going." She felt like she was grasping at straws as she said it.

"You didn't see him at all later on in the day last Friday?"

"I worked the graveyard shift at the nursing home that day. I didn't get home until early the following day."

"What do you think this all means?" Tom asked a bit testily.

"Your son might've been attacked by someone." *Or someTHING,* Matt thought, not quite sure even he could believe some of the ideas he was now beginning to entertain. "For whatever reason, he chose to conceal this information, and he might've run away in order to escape his assailant. I can't really be sure yet, I need more information," he added at the last minute, realizing that giving away too many of his thoughts on the matter might further panic them.

"Who would want to attack my son? And why wouldn't he tell me if someone had done something like that to him?" Margaret seemed like she was on the verge of losing it.

So much for not panicking them, Matt thought sadly. *Smooth move, Spike.*

"I don't know, but I promise you I'll find out. Maybe he thought he had it under control and he didn't want to worry you unnecessarily? Or perhaps he felt like he was protecting you from them by keeping you in the dark about it?" Matt theorized, hoping that this idea would calm her down.

"Don't you think we should turn this evidence over to the police? If Kevin's in some kind of danger, on the run from someone, shouldn't they be more involved?" Tom asked in his seemingly perpetually irritable way.

Matt considered it. Since he'd resolved to involve the ABC, he didn't see the need. They made the local law enforcement agencies look like amateurs and could accomplish far more. He couldn't really explain that to Kevin's parents though.

"Not yet, I still need to know more first. Don't worry. I *will* find him." He wasn't faking the resolve in his voice this time. This strong, sincere statement seemed to mollify them, for now at least. Having found out everything he thought he could at the house, Matt said his goodbyes and promised to keep them apprised of the progress of his investigation.

As soon as Matt was back in his car, he pulled out his Guild Communicator. It was a kind of sophisticated satellite phone that was issued to all members of the International Confederation of Guilds. He called an old contact, Agent Dale, who ran the NYC branch of the ABC, and asked if he could get some assistance in collecting blood evidence from the floor of the house and analyzing the evidence he'd already bagged from whatever ABC bureau was closest to Shadowbrook, CT. He'd decided to also have them collect Kevin's PC so they could give the hard drive a once over. No disrespect to Penny's skills, but the ABC would be able to tease information from it that even she couldn't. Agent Dale was quite accommodating, as he knew how close Matt was to Director McDowell. Matt had also done a few jobs for the ABC in the past, helping them out with their own investigations a few times when they had been short-staffed. He usually didn't charge the ABC for these jobs, and Dale was eager to return the favor. He told them he'd send a team to Margaret's house within the hour. Matt asked for the agents to meet him at the fast-food place where Kevin worked at noon so he could turn over the t-shirt and hairs he'd recovered to them.

It was still pretty early in the day and Matt had plenty of time to kill before he had to meet the ABC agents at Kevin's place of employment. He spent the rest of the morning interviewing people. He started with the neighbors, to see if any of them might've seen something unusual last week, or noticed Kevin leave the house last Friday night or early Saturday morning. Nobody had noticed anything out of the ordinary, but Matt discovered that it was quite normal for them to see Kevin riding his bike and coming and going from home at odd hours.

Next up, Matt drove to the homes of Kevin's two best friends, which were conveniently located in the same neighborhood. Again, he didn't learn much aside from the fact that neither of them owned any dogs, or even a cat. Kevin's friends hadn't seen much of him outside of school lately. He now spent much of the time he used to spend hanging out with them at work, and Matt got the impression that the friends were beginning to drift apart. None of them recalled Kevin acting particularly unusually in the days leading up to his disappearance. They reiterated that Kevin didn't know Sylvia McCoy, although he certainly knew *of* her. One of them told Matt that he'd mentioned her coming through the drive-thru window and had thought she'd seemed pretty flirty with him on those occasions, but he'd also thought it could just be in his imagination. Matt learned that Sylvia had been a popular girl whose status in school had been further boosted when she began dating one of the school's star football players, Brad Nelson. Neither of Kevin's friends had any idea who might've wanted to hurt Kevin, or where he could've run off to, although one of them did mention that being a movie buff, Kevin had often expressed a desire to visit Hollywood.

Matt hoped he wasn't trying to go that far away. Kevin definitely didn't have enough cash to get himself to the other side of the nation, but he could always hitchhike, hop on a freight train or get a ride with a long distance truck driver. If he'd done any of these things, he'd be *much* harder to track.

Matt tried to talk to Cliff Burr, but when he stopped by, neither Cliff nor his daughter seemed to be home.

Matt arrived quite early at Kevin's workplace. He did so deliberately so he could interview some of Kevin's coworkers before his noon meeting with the ABC agents. The manager was very concerned for Kevin and happy to cooperate. Matt learned that Kevin only worked a few nights a week, last Thursday night being the last time he had been seen there. He had been supposed to work on Saturday, but he never showed up. The manager let Matt take turns interviewing his employees in his small office, one at a time.

Matt was soon astounded to discover a direct link between Kevin and Sylvia when he interviewed one particularly pimply lad named Doug who often worked the drive-thru with Kevin and seemed to be his closest friend at work.

"I've been afraid to tell anyone about this. I didn't want to get Kevin in trouble. I'm not even sure if it really has anything to do with some of the weird shit that's been happening in this town lately...but holding it in has been driving me nuts! I guess I can tell you, you're not a cop, right? Kev's mom hired you just to find him and that's all?" Doug fidgeted uncomfortably in his seat as he said it.

"That's right. I'm not with the police. I only care about finding out what happened to Kevin and getting him back home. If you know anything that might help me figure this out, it's okay to tell me. It'll be just between you and me," Matt assured him.

"Well the last night I worked with Kev, Sylvia McCoy came through the drive-thru like she always does. She works..." he paused to correct himself. "...she *worked* down the road and liked to grab her dinner here on her way home. She used to flirt with Kev all the time. I teased him about it. This time she slipped him a note with her money when she paid him. He showed it to me, it had her address on it and said something like 'meet me at my house when you get off.'"

This bombshell sent Matt's mind reeling.

"And how did he react to that? Did he say he was going to do it?" he asked breathlessly.

"He couldn't believe it! He thought she was pretty hot. It seemed pretty obvious to me that she was being more than just friendly whenever she showed up - but Kev doesn't always have the best self-esteem, so he didn't think she really liked him like that. I was happy for him, but also a little scared. I reminded him that she was dating a football player and he'd better be careful, if he didn't want to get his ass kicked."

"How did he react to that?"

"He said I was probably right. He was afraid that it could all be some sort of prank, and even if it wasn't, he agreed that it would be too dangerous to mess around with her while she was still seeing Brad. He really didn't want to risk getting his ass kicked over her."

"So you don't think that he ever took her up on her offer? That he didn't go to see her?"

"I don't know. That night was the last time I really got a chance to talk to him. I mean, I saw him in the hall at school the next day, but we were both just trying to get to class on time, so I couldn't get into a conversation with him about it. The impression that I got was that he was too scared to make a move. You don't think he has anything to do with, with what...happened to Sylvia do you?"

Matt turned the question around on him. "Do you?"

"I don't see how. Everyone seems pretty convinced that she was ripped up by some wolves even though that doesn't really make much sense. But it is pretty freakin' strange how Kev went missing right after she passed him that note, and then they found her...well, the way that they found her a few days later. I don't know how or why Kev would want to do that to her, unless he was some kind of a werewolf, but that's just stupid isn't it?"

Matt threw up his hands in surrender to the obvious ludicrousness of such notions. "Hey, you said it, not me."

Doug giggled a little. "Nah, Kev's no werewolf, I've worked with him on enough full moons, I think I'd have noticed if he was. If anyone is, it's Brad Nelson. Maybe you should be checking him out?"

"For what? Bite marks? A pentagram in the palm of his hand?" Matt asked sarcastically.

"Yeah, I guess the werewolf thing is pretty silly, but you'd be surprised how many people at school have been talking about it since they found Sylvia. Some people even swear that they've seen them around," he confessed. Matt could only imagine that the rumor mill at their school was having a field day with the circumstances of the unusual death. He expected it was causing a fair amount of hysteria amongst the kids and they were letting their overactive adolescent imaginations get the better of them.

"They probably only *imagined* that they might've seen something like that. Or maybe they saw the real wolves that are responsible?" he suggested reasonably.

"Yeah, except that normal wolves don't walk on two legs, like the things that've been seen around town do!" Doug replied emphatically.

Matt decided that this conversation was getting entirely too outlandish, so he steered it back towards something more substantial that he could work with.

"Do you really think that this Brad guy wanted to hurt Kevin?"

"I doubt that he even knows who Kevin is, but if he ever found out that he was messing around with Sylvia, or even *thinking* about it - yeah, he'd rip his head off for sure!"

"So he's got a bad temper, huh?" Matt asked. *Maybe I really should be looking into this kid?* he thought, although he was reluctant to do anything that might implicate Kevin in the McCoy case. But so far, Brad Nelson was looking like he could be the only real enemy that Kevin might've had. If he had found Kevin and Sylvia together, he may've attacked Kevin in a rage, and maybe that's who Kevin was running away from? It certainly made more sense than involving fictional supernatural beasts in the scenario. Maybe what happened to Sylvia afterwards was just some kind of freak coincidence? "Correlation does not imply causation", as they say.

"He's a big scary jock. Don't they all have bad tempers?" Doug shrugged. Matt thought that was a little unfair. Sure, he'd known plenty of jocks who were also real assholes in his day, but just as many of them also fell into the "gentle giant" category and were actually pretty laid-back guys. Judging from Doug's reaction though, it seemed like Brad did fit into that latter category very well.

Matt was interrupted from his conversation with Doug by the restaurant manager coming in to tell him that there were two men outside asking for him. Matt figured it must be the ABC agents that he was supposed to meet with. He glanced at his watch - it was precisely noon. These guys were impeccably punctual. It was okay, he really didn't have any more questions for Doug anyway. He thanked him for his time and walked out of the office and into the restaurant where a pair of men in black suits wearing black sunglasses waited for him patiently, looking for all the world like the bad guys from those Matrix movies.

They introduced themselves as Agent Grey and Agent Brown. Matt knew these weren't their real names. ABC agents never used real names. He didn't even know Agent Dale's real name, even though he'd known him for the better part of a decade now. The names perfectly matched their generally dull demeanors. Matt found an out-of-the-way table away from other customers and sat down with the pair. He soon found out that they'd already been to Kevin's home and collected the blood evidence from the floor of the house and garage. They'd even found an additional trail of blood on the other side of the garage doors and traced it into the yard before losing it. They planned to return that night and spray the area outside with luminol, a chemical that causes traces of blood to glow under a black light, to see if they could follow it out further into the yard. Matt hoped that these two goons hadn't spooked Kevin's parents too much with their aloof, robotic manner. He could only imagine how much they'd creep out Margaret if she looked out her window tonight and saw them lurking around in her yard, but he also wasn't about to dissuade them. He wanted to find out what that blood trail led to.

Matt handed over the baggie with the hairs he'd collected and the large bag that held Kevin's bloody shirt, which he had crammed into one of his magically enhanced pockets. He asked them to compare the hairs to those found in the Sylvia McCoy case. He knew that the ABC wouldn't have any problem getting access to those records if they requested them. He also asked them to search the hard drive of Kevin's computer for any indication of where he might've fled to, or any enemies he might've made.

"Will that be all?" Agent Grey asked in his perfectly flat, inflectionless monotone. Or maybe it was Agent Brown? Even though one of them was an African American and the other was a white guy, their mannerisms were so identical that it was still hard to tell them apart.

"No, there's one more thing." Matt lowered his voice to almost a whisper and leaned in towards them conspiratorially. "There's a local kid named Brad Nelson, a high school student, football player, probably in his junior year. I need you to see what you can find out about him. Maybe even have someone watch his house and tail him. But be really discreet about it, I don't want anyone to know that I'm looking into him. I need you to do the same thing for a contractor in town named Cliff Burr."

"Consider it done," Agent Brown (or was it Agent Grey?) said. He rose to his feet, and his fellow agent stood up as well at the same exact time, their movements mirroring each other with an eerie precision. "We'll be in touch - soon." Matt shook both of their clammy hands. He watched them depart and drive off in a black Cadillac as he ordered himself some lunch from the counter. When he went to pay for his food, he was told that it was on the house; the manager thanked him for his efforts to find Kevin, who he hoped was safe, and wished Matt luck in his investigation.

Matt's next stop after lunch was at Kevin's bank. He explained to the manager who he was and asked if he could see the security footage from the ATM in front of the bank. There was a time stamp on the withdrawal that told him exactly what part of the footage he needed to review. Luckily, the manager was cooperative once he called Kevin's mother, who was one of the account holders, and verified Matt's identity with her. Matt was grateful, he didn't want to have to use the ABC to twist their arm into releasing the information he needed. A security officer at the bank was able to pull up the footage Matt needed on a computer in his office.

On the grainy black and white video, Matt watched as Kevin rolled up to the bank on a skateboard. *His parents didn't say anything about a skateboard being missing!* Matt thought testily. He watched as he went through the motions of performing his transaction, shoving the money into a wallet and skating off in the same direction he'd come from. Matt noticed that he had a duffel bag slung over one shoulder throughout the video. This verified that he was the one who had taken the bag. Nobody else appeared to be near him during this entire episode, and there was no sign that he was being coerced into taking the money out. It seemed like a classic case of a teenage runaway. Matt asked if he could get a copy of that portion of the footage. They said that they'd have to check with the corporate office first. Matt nodded his understanding and left his card with them so they could get in touch once their corporate overlords passed down their verdict on the matter.

After leaving the bank, Matt returned to his hotel room and flipped through the phone book looking for taxi companies. He called all the ones in the book (which wasn't many, as Margaret had promised) and asked how many of them would send a driver to Shadowbrook. There was an even smaller number of these. He wrote down the addresses of these cab companies and drove out to them, having to rely on his trusty road atlas to get him there. He showed them a picture of Kevin and asked the drivers who weren't out on a job if they remembered picking the teenager up last Saturday morning. None of them did.

Having exhausted that avenue of inquiry, he then visited the bus depot closest to Shadowbrook. Once there, he showed Kevin's picture to some of the workers. He finally seemed to hit pay dirt when a rather bored, portly gentleman with a particularly ruddy complexion who sold tickets at one of the windows told him he recognized the kid.

"Yeah, I remember that kid. He seemed super distracted and upset about something. He had a really haunted kinda look in his eye, ya know? I know that look, I see it all the time. We get all kinds of runaways like that coming through here. I even asked him what he was running away from, and you know what he told me?" The man, who was talking to Matt on his smoke break, took a long drag from his cigarette before continuing. The smell of the smoke was driving Matt wild with the desire to ask him for a few puffs. Even though he hadn't smoked in years, that desire was always there, like a wolf hiding in the dark, always ready to pounce and ensnare him at any moment.

"No, what did he say?"

"From myself. He was running away from himself. Isn't that a strange thing to say? That's why I remembered him. It was such a crazy answer, don't you think?"

"Yeah, that sure is an interesting response." Matt meant it. Why would Kevin feel like he had to run away from himself? "Do you remember where he bought a ticket to?"

"Wonderland."

"Excuse me?" Matt asked incredulously. What nonsense was this guy talking now?

The man laughed, a dry, wheezy sound. "It's a new amusement park way out in Davenport over on the other end of the state, almost in Massachusetts. I guess a guy like you from out of state wouldn't have heard of it. We started running buses directly over there a few weeks ago. I think I heard about that kid making some kind of trouble on the bus too. You should ask the driver who runs that route, Vinny. He'll be pulling back up here in about twenty minutes."

So that is what Matt did. He waited around the bus depot and tried not to allow himself to become overwhelmed by the negative vibes of the place. He always found them to be the sort of places that were inherently a little depressing. He'd once heard them described in an old episode of *Doctor Who* as "terrible places full of lost souls and lost luggage" - a sentiment that he could heartily agree with. He distracted himself by studying the fares to different places from here and realized that a ticket to Wonderland would've still left Kevin with most of his money. He could've gone much further if he'd wanted to. Why go to an amusement park of all places? He supposed it was a good place to go if you wanted to lose yourself in a crowd. The ticket attendant had said he seemed depressed, maybe he wanted to cheer himself up? He was 15 after all, maybe he was just really bored with life In Shadowbrook and wanted to party and live a little?

Matt shook his head, it just didn't fit very well with the image of the serious, responsible young man that he'd been building up in his mind. And what was this talk of him "making trouble" on the bus? That didn't sound like Kevin either. He was beginning to wonder if the guy he'd been interviewing had misidentified him, then an idea hit him. He asked the station manager if there was video footage from last week that might show Kevin. It turned out that there were in fact some hidden cameras in the station, especially near the ticket windows, in case of a robbery. Matt was lucky that everyone was being so cooperative when they didn't have to be, but then again, people were often eager to help when they found out there was a child missing. Within a few minutes, the tape from the previous Saturday was playing for Matt. After much fast forwarding, he got to a section of it that clearly showed Kevin walking up and buying his ticket, then sitting on a bench still in view of the cameras while he waited for the bus to arrive. Like before, he had his duffel bag, although this time he carried his skateboard slung under one arm.

Not much later, Vinny, the man who had driven the bus to Wonderland, was ushered into the back room where Matt had been studying the video evidence. Matt learned from Vinny that the "trouble" Kevin had made was relatively harmless. Apparently he had fallen asleep on the ride and had suddenly awoken screaming incoherently at the top of his lungs, annoying the hell out of his fellow travelers and earning a strongly worded warning from Vinny, who had been so scared by the unexpected disruption that he'd almost run the bus off the road.

Matt could only wonder what sorts of things might be giving the kid such horrific nightmares.

CHAPTER 3:

HISTORY LESSONS WITH NAOMI

By the time he wrapped up his investigation at the bus depot, it was starting to get a little late in the evening, although the sun was still up. After all, it was still technically summer, for a few more days at least. Matt found a diner nearby and had himself some dinner while he tried to digest the day's events. He could now place Kevin in Wonderland exactly one week ago today. But where had he gone from there? Matt knew that the theme park would have a bevy of security cameras covering it. Once he got up there, he'd try to use that footage to trace Kevin's movements around the park and see if he could pick up the trail again. Maybe he'd interview some of his friends again and see if Kevin had ever expressed any kind of interest in that park or mentioned knowing anyone from that area.

Matt finished up his dinner. Even though he was stingy when it came to himself, he wasn't where other people were concerned, so he tipped his waitress quite generously. He drove back to his hotel, which was in the same town where the bus depot had been so it didn't take him very long to get back. Once back inside his room, he decided to call home and check in with Naomi and the kids. He missed them all terribly and always felt out of sorts without them around. He also found that it helped him to talk over his cases with other people. He especially valued Naomi's input; she was unusually perceptive, and he'd always felt that she was a whole lot smarter than he was - even long before she had the credentials to prove it. One thing he really missed about having her as his secretary was the ability to bounce his ideas about an investigation off of her right away. Nowadays, he typically had to wait until he got home to discuss his cases with her.

He called her on the phone in his hotel room to avoid roaming charges, being the frugal fellow that he was. At first they talked about fairly routine things, like how Naomi's day had gone and how the kids were doing. Autumn briefly jumped on the phone to say hi, and even Joe popped on for a moment to see how Matt was doing, something that was becoming rarer and rarer these days It made him miss them all the more. Eventually, the conversation turned to the status of Matt's investigations.

"Well, I'm happy to hear that you were able to swallow your pride and call in the ABC to help out," Naomi told him.

"Yeah, well, you know that when it comes to missing kids, I don't fuck around - not anymore. Especially since it seems like maybe he left because he thought that he was in some kind of danger."

"Good job tracing him to that amusement park, though. You did that all on your own, without any help from the ABC - just good old-fashioned detective work," Naomi pointed out proudly. She knew that Matt needed this kind of encouragement, since calling in the ABC always felt to him like an admission of failure on some level.

"Thanks for that. Yeah, I'm just praying that the trail doesn't go cold after that. I'm planning on driving up there tomorrow to see what I can find out. Damn! I should've told those ABC spooks to put out some kind of APB on him. Did you know that they can hack into those cameras that they're starting to use in lots of the bigger cities, and even do facial recognition matches on the footage? If he ends up somewhere like that, they might be able to find him pretty quickly. It's downright scary what those guys can do with their technology these days - but undeniably useful when used for a good cause."

"It's no biggie - just tell them the next time you talk to them," Naomi reminded him calmly. "So what's your take on all of this, what do you think is really going on here?"

"I think the most reasonable explanation is that the kid's hormones got the best of him. He decided to go see Sylvia despite the strong possibility of an ass kicking in his future. It's not that hard to believe considering what was in that kid's search history. Let's just say that he has a very healthy sexual appetite."

"Indeed. Never underestimate the power of the booty call," Naomi agreed.

"Then something went wrong, Brad found out, maybe he caught them together? He freaked out and attacked Kevin. Maybe with a knife or something, I dunno. He did a number on Kev's shirt and cut him badly enough to get lots of blood on it, but not deeply enough to seriously hurt him. The kid was so scared by the whole episode that he skipped town. He must've really believed that Brad would kill him. I guess you would believe it too if some guy came after you with a knife!"

"And then Sylvia just happens to get mauled by wolves in her own home shortly afterwards? That's just a total coincidence that has absolutely nothing to do with a jealous boyfriend chasing off her latest boy toy?" Naomi asked skeptically. She wasn't done punching holes in Matt's theories. "Why did Kevin wait a whole day before running away from home if he was so scared? Why go to school the next day where he might run into his tormentor in the halls? Why not just tell his mom or the police what kind of trouble he was in if he was really scared for his life?"

"Well that's easy enough to explain, he didn't want his mom to know that he was hooking up with random girls while she was at work," Matt said dismissively.

"So he'd rather just run away from home than tell his mom what a stud he is and that he's afraid of some crazy jock coming after him?" Naomi was having none of it.

"Maybe he didn't want Sylvia to get in trouble with her parents when the truth came out? Maybe he was mainly trying to protect her?" Matt said defensively.

"I'm sorry, but none of this sounds very convincing to me. None of it explains what happened to Sylvia later on, or those animal hairs you found on Kevin's bike."

"That hair could've come from *any* kind of animal for all I know. It could be completely unrelated to what became of that girl. But just for the sake of argument, if Brad *was* involved in what happened to Sylvia at all...maybe he had access to some kind of attack dogs and he used them on her as revenge for her cheating on him? Maybe he used the dogs on Kevin too, but Kevin managed to get away in one piece because he was on a bike?" Matt ventured, already knowing how silly it sounded.

"Attack dogs? The animals were positively identified as wolves! Whoever heard of trained attack wolves? This kid is just a high school football player he's not, like, someone who can command wolves like Aquaman commands fish! If he has these 'attack wolves', where does he keep them? Why does nobody else know about them? C'mon, dude! You're replacing one crazy-sounding theory with something equally nuts."

"They could've misidentified those hairs. DNA analysis isn't foolproof. Maybe the evidence was contaminated? There isn't much of a genetic difference between a wolf and a dog, it's probably not that hard to misidentify them like that. Or maybe it was a hybrid? A wolf dog. I read once that those hybrids can be very dangerous and have been known to attack people." Matt protested.

"That's a whole lot of maybes. You just don't want to admit that there might really be something to all this talk about werewolves, but I know you. You're thinking about it in the back of your mind. Remember what Randy always says - 'ignore your instincts at your own peril.'"

"No. I draw the line at werewolves! There's no such thing!"

"Says the guy whose partner is a wizard. The same guy who gets paid lots of money to guard an artifact that cancels out magic spells. The guy who can control a giant flying sword with his mind. The guy who's ridden inside a flying saucer countless times. The guy who once fought a headless frost giant from Norse mythology alongside an army of Gods, demons and freakin' Santa Claus himself! Yeah, all that other stuff is *totally* believable, but werewolves? Werewolves! No sir, perish the thought! That's a bridge too far!" Naomi said mockingly.

"Hey now! Just because we've experienced a few strange things over the years doesn't mean that there isn't a more down-to-earth explanation for all of this! "

"A *few* strange things? C'mon, you're not making any sense!"

"Look, I just don't want to take a trip into the Twilight Zone unless I have to. Every time something seems a little out of the ordinary it doesn't mean that there's something supernatural going on. It's my duty to eliminate all the more rational explanations before I start going too far down the rabbit hole of weirdness."

"Rabbit hole? It looks like you're heading to Wonderland regardless, might as well get with the program and learn to embrace the crazy," Naomi laughed.

"Oh! I see what you did there! Funny."

"Didn't know you were marrying a comedian, huh? Sorry, I couldn't resist, you walked right into that one. But I digress. 'When you have eliminated the impossible, whatever remains, however improbable, must be the truth.' I get it, I really do." Naomi recited the line with a hint of weariness in her tone. It was a notorious quote from Sherlock Holmes that Matt had repeated to her countless times. Ad nauseam. It was like his mantra or something. Though Naomi tended to associate the quote more with Mr. Spock than she did with the famous fictional detective, since he paraphrased it once on an old episode of Star Trek that she had watched with her father as a child.

"Exactly. I'm not done eliminating the impossible yet." He was happy that she finally seemed to be understanding his reluctance to entertain the idea that something otherworldly was involved.

He was about to be disappointed, she wasn't giving up so easily. It wasn't in her nature. "Yeah, but my point is that the werewolf thing isn't quite as improbable as you assume. What if I told you that I know for a *fact* that werewolves are real?"

Matt was flabbergasted. "So what you're saying is that you've known that werewolves aren't just some piece of folklore and you've conveniently never bothered to mention any of this to me before?"

"I found out all about them while researching stuff for my *Magna Historia Mundi*. I come across all kinds of crazy facts when I'm working on it. If I tried to tell you about every interesting thing that I learn about whilst doing so, I'd never get anything else done!" Now it was Naomi's turn to sound defensive.

The *Magna Historia Mundi* was a comprehensive history of the world that Naomi was working on writing that included the histories of the Guilds and their roles in helping to shape world history. Some years earlier she had gotten permission from Bronson McDowell to research the histories of the Guilds and he had bestowed upon her the grandiose-sounding title of "Supreme Archivist" so she would have access to the records of the various secret societies that were part of the Guilds. She considered it to be her life's work. She wasn't bothered much by the fact that it would never be circulated outside of the Guilds, she found the work fulfilling in and of itself as it satisfied her own curiosity about how the world got to be in its present state. The title was Latin for "the Great History of the World". Naomi was a proud Italian American and that pride had led her to become an expert on Ancient Rome, as well as quite fluent in Latin. Although she was often informal and irreverent in her personal life, she also had another side to her that could be a little cold, analytical and pretentious, which she expressed more often in her professional life. Her choice of title for her book perfectly captured this aspect of her personality.

"But you know how much I love a good werewolf movie! You never thought to say 'Yo, babe! I just found out that those monsters you're into are real'?"

It was true, some of Matt's favorite horror movies involved werewolves; he very much preferred them to vampires, who seemed kind of lame in comparison. He hated the idea that all of these romantic notions had become attached to the idea of the vampire. What was so romantic about a corpse that walks around draining the blood from the living? It was downright ghoulish! At least werewolves usually didn't have such misguided sentiments tied to them.

"It slipped my mind, I've got a lot of things going on. I'm sorry, okay? I'm trying to tell you about them now, if you'll just shut up for a minute and let me."

"How can I not accept such a sweetly worded apology, my dear lady? By all means, do go on - spin your tale without any further interruption from this uncouth wretch."

Naomi giggled. "You've got a real way with words sometimes, Spike. Okay, so here's the deal. Back in the Long Ago Before Times, during the Great Magic War, there were wizards who created armies of werewolves to serve as their foot soldiers in the war. They created them by outfitting them with magic belts made from a wolf's pelt. When someone wore the belt, it gave them the power to transform into a wolf. All those ancient werewolves were killed off during the war, and the belts were destroyed. Most modern werewolves owe their origin to a renegade wizard called Mortus Locke." The Great Magic War was an ancient conflict between factions of wizards that had nearly destroyed the world. The Orb that Matt and Naomi guarded was a copy of the magic item that had been created to end that war and prevent another such conflict from ever happening.

"What do you mean by 'modern'?" he asked. Matt knew that someone like Naomi had a rather generous interpretation of terms like 'modern' compared to your average person.

"Hey I thought you weren't going to interrupt! I mean like around a thousand years ago. Now where was I?"

"You were telling me about Mortus Locke."

"Oh yeah. So anyways, this Mortus Locke guy rediscovered all kinds of forbidden knowledge that had been suppressed since the days of the Great Magic War. He was obsessed with gaining immortality and he was certain that the secret was to be found in the lost knowledge of those ancient wizards. There was another kind of monster that was created by those wizards as a weapon during that war, there were these powerful, man-eating beasts that were immortal. A few of them survived the war. That old poem Beowulf is about them. Grendel and his mother were some of the last survivors of that race of monsters. Mortus Locke used his magic to conjure up one of these Grendel creatures for himself. His theory was that if he drank the blood from this immortal monster, that he would gain some of its immortality for himself. It worked, too, but unfortunately he also gained the monster's insatiable appetite for human flesh in the process. He went on a rampage to try and satisfy his hunger. He had an inner circle of followers with whom he shared his immortality, specifically so they could serve him for eternity. The vampires that his cultists then went on to create became the first of the modern vampires."

"Oh, so now you're telling me that vampires are for real too?" Matt couldn't believe it. He threw up his hands in surrender to the ridiculous. "But they just suck people's blood, they aren't cannibals."

"The thing is that the hunger for human flesh that Mortus Locke had inherited from the Grendel became more and more diluted with each successive generation of vampires that came into existence. The vamps directly created by Locke still had it, but not quite so bad, but the ones that *they* went on to create were mostly just content to drink the blood of their victims. Anyhow, after a while the countryside was being overrun with vampires, and eventually this attracted the attention of his fellow wizards, who didn't approve of what he was up to and set about trying to stop him. He gave a few of his followers some of those magic wolf belts I mentioned earlier to bolster the number of his forces so he'd have an army of monsters to defend him from the other wizards. When the wizards attacked, they only succeeded in driving Locke and his allies underground. For centuries they roamed across Europe, Asia, and Africa, causing trouble. Most of the stories of werewolves and vampires in folklore come from that period. Wherever they went, they created more vampires and werewolves too, sometimes on purpose, sometimes by accident. That stuff about becoming a werewolf if you're bitten by one is for real, y'know? No magic belt required in that case. The legends about the full moon triggering a transformation are true too, but it only applies to people who are werewolves because they were bitten. The ones who have the belts can change back and forth from human to wolf whenever they want to."

"So don't tell me - this Locke guy is still around, and he's right here in the States now?"

"Oh no. He's been dead since the late 1700's. At least that's the assumption. You see, Locke and his followers had settled in a remote part of England by then. At that time, he had a small army of werewolves under his command, as well as his trusted company of vampire lieutenants. Those vampires, in turn, had vampires that they had created who served them. He used this network of monsters to pillage the countryside. In time, he amassed quite a fortune for himself this way, using a mixture of intimidation and bribes to persuade the local authorities to turn a blind eye to his activities. Eventually, the Highwaymen caught wind of this. The idea that someone else was moving in on their territory like that did *not* sit well with them."

"I'll bet it didn't!" Matt remarked. The Highwaymen were an organization of super thieves that were part of the Guilds. The best way to describe them is a group of "land pirates". They could cripple a nation's economy by using their highly organized methods of raiding the land routes used to transport raw materials and finished goods. They were paid an exorbitant sum of money by the nations of the world to *not* do this.

"So the Highwaymen moved against them. Their histories call it the Great Purge of 1793. Unfortunately, they didn't really know quite what they were getting themselves into. They didn't understand that the band of thieves they were going up against were monsters. This was in the 1700's, so the Highwaymen didn't have the kinds of high-tech weapons that they use nowadays. It was kind of a bloodbath. Some of them escaped though, and notified the rest of the Guilds. It was then that a coalition made up of magic users from the Temple of the Old Gods, the Knights of Pendragon, and the surviving members of the Highwaymen joined forces and attacked. In the end, it seemed like they had triumphed. The werewolves and vampires all appeared to have been slain, but Mortus Locke's treasure was nowhere to be found. As for Locke himself, there was uncertainty that he had really been killed. It had been so long since anyone had seen him in the flesh that nobody really remembered what he looked like. So they couldn't positively identify any of the bodies as belonging to him. These doubts were swiftly quashed, probably for political reasons, and the campaign was declared to be a total success. But every so often rumors still surface of renewed werewolf and vampire activity, and with those rumors comes talk that Mortus Locke might still be out there somewhere. He's become something of a bogeyman - a story that members of the Guilds tell their children to get them to behave. It's been so long since he's been heard from that by now, nobody truly believes that he's still alive, aside from frightened little kids," Naomi finished her tale.

"Wow," was all Matt could say at first. "So you're thinking, what? That Kevin was attacked by a werewolf? And Sylvia was killed by one?"

"Basically. Picture this: Kevin is attacked by a werewolf while riding his bike on Thursday night. He gets away, but he's bitten. He's afraid to tell anyone because he thinks they'll think he's nuts if he says he was attacked by a werewolf. Because he was bitten, he is now a werewolf, so his wounds heal up really fast. By the next day, there's no trace of them at all. That makes it easy for him to dismiss the whole thing as nothing but a nightmare. He goes to school the next day and tries to pretend that everything is okay."

"It *does* make sense, I suppose." Matt hated to admit it. "In a world where werewolves are a real thing, that is."

Naomi carried on. "That's the world you're living in, like it or not. Anyhow, that night, he decides to go see Sylvia, and then...maybe he wolfs out and eats her?"

Matt didn't like that last part very much. He didn't like to think of this kid as a killer. "Why would he do that?"

"He couldn't help it once he turned into a wolf, he wasn't in control anymore - the wolf was. You've seen enough werewolf movies to know that!"

"There's a few holes in your hypothesis. One, I'm pretty sure that there was no full moon last Friday. Two, they found hairs from two different wolves in her bedroom."

"No full moon? Are you sure?" she asked, sounding a little worried now.

"Pretty sure. Do you have your laptop around? Why don't you look it up?" he suggested.

"Yeah, I've got it right here," she said. He heard the sound of her typing through the phone line. "You're right. There isn't a full moon until tomorrow. This might be bad news. The werewolves that use a magic belt to transform can do it at any time, they don't need a full moon. I'm wondering if some of those are in town. One of them bit Kevin, and the next night, a pair of them attacked Sylvia. Maybe the fact that they knew each other really is just a coincidence; it *is* a small town. If they're hunting in a place like that they're bound to attack some people who know each other."

"Well, if tomorrow is a full moon, then we have another problem. If Kevin really is a werewolf now, that means he's going to change tomorrow night. Maybe he ran away because he realized what he is? He decided to get away from his mother and the people he cared about the most before he could hurt them. That's why he told that guy at the bus station that he was running away from himself. What I don't understand is why he'd go to a place like Wonderland with lots of crowds if he doesn't want to endanger other people?"

"You're the detective, you figure it out. That's why they pay you the big bucks, hon. I can't solve all your cases for you, I've got papers to grade." She yawned. It was getting late.

"Thanks a bunch." He smiled. He knew she was trying to get him off the phone now.

"Just promise me you'll be careful if you're going to go hunting werewolves. If those ones who use the belts are around they're especially nasty - they're experienced warriors who are known for being totally ruthless. I think you should have Randy join you up there. It can't hurt to have a wizard on your side. He can bring the *Vermilion Avenger* with him. See, I *told* you you'd need it."

"Will it work against them? Don't I need some silver bullets?" Matt asked worriedly.

"What *doesn't* it work on?" she fired back. Indeed, their sword could cut through just about anything.

"Touché," he agreed.

"From my research, though, I've found that anything made of pure silver will hurt or kill them. It doesn't even have to be silver either. So long as it's a weapon made of a pure enough material, it'll do the job. The diamond blade of the *Avenger* is pure, so it should be just the ticket."

"Well that's good to know. Yeah, I'll think about bringing Randy in on this one. I'm still not *totally* sold on this werewolf angle, but I guess I'm much more open to the idea now than I was before."

"Jesus! You're so stubborn!" Naomi cried in exasperation.

"Tell me about it, I learned from the best!" Matt countered, implying that he had learned it from her, which was blatantly untrue. Matt had always been this hardheaded.

"I'll give you my final arguments for the werewolf hypothesis since you still need a little convincing. Don't forget that the wolves that attacked Sylvia broke into her house by smashing through her bedroom windows. Not only is that sort of behavior extremely uncharacteristic, but it would also take an extraordinarily large and powerful kind of wolf, maybe even a *supernaturally* powerful one to leap through a window like that."

"Dully, noted, Doctor, duly noted," Matt replied dryly.

"Stay safe, dear. I love you," Naomi said.

"I will. Love you too," Matt affirmed as he hung up the phone.

He tried to process this new information. As much as he loved werewolves in movies, that's where he preferred to keep them. He didn't particularly relish the idea of meeting one in real life. He began to get that slightly queasy feeling that he got whenever his tidy little world started to get turned upside down again by the weirdness that all too frequently intruded upon it. Even after all these years, he still never got completely used to it. He almost laughed at the irony of the situation. Once he used to dream of the sorts of adventures he now found himself living through, but now that he was really living through these kinds of scenarios, they just filled him with an overwhelming sense of dread. It was definitely one thing to safely read about or watch a movie that involves fighting monsters for your entertainment - it was quite another thing to actually *do* it. To really be in danger, or watch others be endangered wasn't quite as much fun. In fact it was downright terrifying. In a way though, Matt wasn't quite as frightened at the prospect that he might be fighting werewolves in the near future as he would've been at the idea of going up against a more human maniac like the psycho who had killed Melissa Hollins. Somehow, there was something inherently more disturbing about seeing someone who seemed all too human carrying out such horrors than there was when something that literally looked monstrous was responsible.

Matt didn't quite know *what* he'd do if the boy turned out to be a werewolf, as Naomi suspected. He still couldn't quite believe that he was even seriously entertaining such an idea now, yet his wife had been correct, his instincts *had* been telling him that this possibly fit the facts the best, but he'd fought against the realization. He definitely wanted to make sure that Kevin didn't hurt anyone, yet he also knew that he couldn't possibly bring himself to kill the kid. He'd been hired to bring him home safely and that's exactly what he intended to do. But how could he bring a kid who was a werewolf home to his parents without placing them in terrible danger too? Was there a cure for the curse of the werewolf? He'd have to ask Randy about it. If anyone would know, it would be Randy.

Matt's Guild communicator suddenly made the distinctive, loud pinging sound that indicated that someone was trying to reach him. When he answered it, he discovered that it was Agent Grey on the other end of the connection.

The ABC agent informed Matt of his progress on the case in his typical clipped, precise way. They had already analyzed all the blood evidence Matt had discovered and that they had collected themselves from the floor of the house. Matt never ceased to be amazed by their speed and efficiency. It all turned out to be a match to the DNA on Kevin's toothbrush - it was Kevin's own blood. They had also been able to tease DNA out of the fur samples he'd given them. Matt wasn't sure how they'd managed to pull that trick off since he hadn't seen any intact follicles, but he just accepted that the ABC's more advanced technology made it possible. As he had asked, they had been able to get access to the records from the Sylvia McCoy case and discovered a match to one of the wolves that had invaded her home.

That wasn't all, they had just recently finished spraying luminol on the blood trail in Kevin's yard. They found that it had led to a narrow trail through the woods that bordered his backyard. They had followed the spots of blood through these woods to their source, a part of the trail where a small pool of blood had soaked into the soil. There were numerous scratches on the trees, broken branches and more stray bits of fur, which they had yet to analyze. Obviously it had been the site of some sort of struggle. It wasn't difficult to deduce that this was where Kevin was attacked. The trail through the woods connected Kevin's backyard to the subdivision where Sylvia McCoy lived, only a few blocks from where the trail spilled back out onto a residential street. Had he been on his way to or from her home when he was ambushed?

Agent Grey informed him that they had begun surveillance on the people Matt had asked them to watch, but so far there was no unusual activity to report. Matt wondered if either one of his suspects was leading a double life as a werewolf? Did ABC agents have silver bullets in their guns? He doubted it. Part of him felt like he should warn them to start stocking up on them, but he just couldn't bring himself to say something so outlandish sounding to the straight-laced and serious agent on the other end of the communicator. He thanked Agent Grey for his help and mentioned the APB idea he'd discussed with Naomi, and that he had traced the kid to Wonderland in Davenport. Agent Grey promised he'd get on it right away; he'd inform the agents in that part of the state to keep an eye out for the boy.

Before Matt went to sleep that night, he astrally projected once more, searching the area around Kevin's neighborhood for werewolves. He floated along the path that Agent Grey had mentioned and thought he found the scene of the attack that had been described to him. In the end, he found nothing unusual roaming through the warren of suburban lanes aside from his own ghost-like form. He considered flying off towards Wonderland, but decided against it. He was afraid he'd get lost trying to find it, and he found projecting such long distances to be quite exhausting. If he tried it, he'd likely feel like he had a hangover the next morning. Wizards knew various tricks to avoid that unfortunate side effect of long distance astral projection, but alas, Matt was no wizard.

Matt returned to his body and tried to get a good night's rest, but it was not to be. His sleep was marred by a kaleidoscope of tortured visions of gnashing fangs, tearing claws and shaggy beasts that howled balefully at the silvery disc of the moon....

CHAPTER 4:

MEANWHILE, IN DAVENPORT

That same Saturday, on the other end of the state, the sleepy town of Davenport was lost in its typical late-summer idyll. It was a place even smaller and lost in time than Shadowbrook, which was tiny, but at least had an abundance of the trappings of modern suburban life, such as housing developments and strip malls. Davenport had none of those things; the homes were all old farmhouses, separated from each other by miles rather than a few feet as the homes in Shadowbrook were. There was a smattering of townhouses in what passed for the "downtown" area on mainstreet, which was mostly dominated by the town hall, library, post office and what seemed like entirely too many churches for such a sparsely populated place. The town was named in honor of John Davenport, the 17th century Puritan preacher who was the founder of New Haven, despite the fact that this town was nowhere near New Haven. Supposedly, he had once stayed at an inn here on his way to Boston, although there was no real evidence that this had ever happened.

The only thing of note about the place was that it was now home to an amusement park called Wonderland. Years ago there had been a different park on that same stretch of land, which had sat vacant for decades, the rides slowly rusting away and being covered over by tall grass. The town fathers felt it was quite a coup that someone had finally bought the place and breathed some new life into it. Even so, it was a shadow of its former glory. Only about a third of the area of the old park had been hastily reopened, and it was filled with a haphazard array of wobbly old rides purchased from county fairs and traveling carnivals. There were promises of expanding the park and replacing the somewhat lackluster and generic rides with all new attractions unique to the park, but none of these lofty ambitions had yet to materialize. Despite this, the park still seemed to do pretty good business, even this late into the season it was still drawing substantial crowds of people to the town that otherwise would've never stopped there. It created some new jobs in an area that badly needed them, and gave the local kids something to do aside from tipping over cows.

One of the few still-functioning local farms where anxious teens sometimes crept under the stars in the pursuit of toppling an innocently slumbering bovine was the "Sherwood Farm". It was a small dairy farm that had been there for over two hundred years, owned and operated by the same family. The good people of Davenport would surely be shocked, confused and more than a little terrified if they ever learned that this farm was not only run by the same family that had founded it, but the very same *individuals* who had started it in the final decade of the 18th Century.

You see, Sherwood Farm and the rambling, gothic mansion that sat on its grounds was home to a family of vampires and their loyal human servants, the Brandons.

Would the townspeople understand, if they had any inkling of the truth, that this particular group of vampires was relatively harmless? That they satiated their thirst for the blood of the living by slowly draining the cows that they raised? Never draining any one of them enough to kill them, and rotating which ones they drank from in order to give the beasts a chance to recover before it was their turn again? Long ago, the patriarchs of this farm, William and Elizabeth Sherwood, sickened by the monsters they had become, had turned away from the practice of taking human victims. The blood of animals wasn't quite as intoxicating, but it did the job - and more importantly, it carried with it none of the guilt and shame that had once threatened to drive them to the brink of madness.

William and Elizabeth were not the only vampires to be found within the oaken paneled halls of the great old house. They had an adopted daughter, Allison. As undead creatures, William and Elizabeth couldn't have children of their own. One night while out driving, they had been the first ones to happen across the scene of a grisly automotive accident on a deserted country lane and found a young girl inside one of the cars, desperately clinging to life, but losing her grip on it with each passing second. They'd known what they had to do. The only way to save her was to make her one of them. That had been sixteen years ago. It was the last time they had tasted human blood.

They had taken the girl back to their manor, and in time, they had become a family. The girl had spent a long time grieving the loss of her real parents, then coming to grips with what she was now.

There were times in those first few months when she cursed William and Elizabeth for "saving" her by turning her into a monster - screamed at them, slammed doors in their faces and threatened to reveal what they were to the world outside.

However, slowly but surely, she'd come to accept her new reality and even revel in it. There were things she could do that no human being could, sensations that she could experience that were beyond their understanding. It wasn't so bad, really. She discovered that many of the things people believed about vampires were inventions of fiction. The biggest of these lies was the idea that vampires were killed by the light of the sun. This was an idea that actually came from an old silent movie called *Nosferatu* and had pretty much been copied by everyone since, but it had no basis in reality. It was true, however, that the vampires who hunted humans preferred to hunt at night, using the cover of darkness to aid them in their stealthy attacks. She also felt somewhat more energized under the velvety blanket of stars and moonlight, often taking long walks in the forests. As much as she enjoyed the night, she was grateful that she could still experience the feeling of sunlight on her skin, the beauty of a sunrise and all those other things that fictional vampires often waxed so poetically about missing so badly.

She got quite a kick out of reading stories about vampires and watching TV shows and movies on the subject, they cracked her up with their frequent inaccuracies. One thing that *was* true was that she did not cast a reflection in mirrors, but this only applied to certain *types* of mirrors. It was only true of mirrors that were backed in silver, which was how the majority of them used to be made back in the old days, but hardly any of them had real silver in them anymore. Contrary to popular belief, religious symbols had no effect on her. This idea was a result of the false belief that vampires were creatures of the Devil, or were themselves some kind of a demon. William and Elizabeth had explained to her how vampires had in fact been created by some old wizard who'd wanted to live forever that they had escaped from ages ago. Allison had been quite relieved to learn that she wasn't now some sort of spawn of Satan. Apparently, the mistaken idea that a vampire could only enter a home that they had been invited into was tied to that idea as well. As far as she could tell, it had to do with the belief that a vampire's body was animated by an evil spirit, and evil spirits could only enter the home if they had somehow been invited in.

Another misconception about her kind that cropped up in some of these stories was the idea that vampires could transform themselves into bats, wolves, or mists. All of these ideas seemed to come from the story of *Dracula* and were inventions of Bram Stoker. Even within his novel, Dracula had these abilities not so much because he was a vampire, but because he was a black magician who had been trained in the dark arts of sorcery by the Devil himself. For whatever reason, this little detail never made it into any of the adaptations of the story that she had ever seen, even though she thought it was pretty cool. Allison would've *loved* to be able to do some of the things that Dracula could do, but alas, it was not part of her skill set.

Dracula and *Nosferatu* were not the only stories to distort the reality of vampires. In the 1840's there had been a series of penny dreadfuls called *Varney the Vampire or The Feast of Blood* that had introduced the idea of vampires having fangs to the public. Allison had no fangs, which was another disappointment to her. She thought she'd look pretty dashing and dangerous with a nice pair of them.

Instead, she had to settle for just having immortality, superhuman strength and durability, greatly enhanced senses, and an ability to mesmerize people. It was a kind of "Jedi mind trick" which she rarely used, for ethical reasons, although it was sometimes great fun to be able to mess with people's minds like that. Sometimes when she went out at night, she'd use her great strength to propel herself high up into the air. She could virtually "leap tall buildings in a single bound" like Superman did in those old cartoons from the forties. It was as close as she could come to experiencing the exhilarating freedom of flying. She had to be very careful that nobody ever saw her when she did it though, if William and Elizabeth ever found out that this is what she was doing on those restless nights when she went out walking, they'd have a conniption fit for sure.

The only real drawback to being a vampire (aside from the general ickiness of having to regularly drink cow's blood) so far as Allison could see, was that she was permanently stuck at the age of fourteen biologically. Although she was really thirty, mentally, she still had the same maturity level that she'd had when she first became a vampire. Her brain would never further mature, nor would the rest of her body. Then there was all that she had to put up with to protect the family secret. She hadn't been allowed to go to a normal high school so she wouldn't arouse suspicion, although her new "parents" had hired a private tutor to finish her basic education. They had also used their fortune and connections to create a false identity for her as a niece that was staying with them named Amber Knight, which she had used for those first few years. She still made use of that identity sometimes, using makeup to "age" herself, which she found to be great fun. She was naturally a bit of a theatrical person and enjoyed performing like that Indeed, she had once dreamed of becoming an actress before all such ambitions had been dashed by her vampiric condition. Using makeup to artificially age herself was a skill that had been taught to her by William and Elizabeth, who had to employ it to pretend to be their own descendants on the rare occasions when they ventured into town. As much as she'd like to take credit for having amazing acting talents or being a great master of disguise, she knew that her ability to mesmerize people was really what helped to make her disguise so convincing.

In recent years though, she just mostly kept to the manor house reading books from her extensive collection, losing herself in other people's stories. Was she trying to distract herself from the fact that she'd likely never fall in love or have a family of her own?

Probably.

It was something she didn't like to think about. As much as she dreamed about someday being swept off her feet and finding herself head over heels in love, she knew that it just wasn't in the cards for her anymore -, it was an idea she'd had to give up on. Even if somebody was okay with the very weird fact that she was an undead creature of the night, how would they feel about the reality that she would never age, while they would grow old? Or could never have children of their own with her? Sure, she supposed that she could turn them into what she was, but did she have a right to do that to anyone else? Sometimes she still grappled with the fact that William and Elizabeth had dared to make that decision for her. They had saved her, but also doomed her to this bizarre kind of half life. There were moments when she wished that they had just left her there bleeding in the road to die with the rest of her real family. She also didn't think too much of the way the world had been going these past few decades. Maybe she would've been better off if she hadn't "lived" to see what a mess it was becoming? She definitely wished she hadn't been around to see those god awful Star Wars prequels - although she had to grudgingly admit that the last one that had just come out a few months ago hadn't been *that* bad.

There was another, much darker reason why she had resolved to never make someone else like her, no matter how much they might claim that they wanted it. She'd never tasted human blood before, aside from when she had been force fed it on the night that she had said goodbye to any chance of ever having a normal life. There was a part of her that was afraid that if she experienced it again, she wouldn't be able to control her lust for it. Even though William and Elizabeth hadn't had it for decades, they still visibly struggled with their addiction to it. Even Allison had found herself inextricably drawn to the warmth of the bodies of the living, she felt like she could hear the blood surging through their veins if she stood too close to them, almost tasting the coppery tang of it. On more than one occasion she had caught herself staring hungrily at the nape of their necks and realized that she wasn't hearing a word they were saying to her. How much worse would this become if she actually gave in to such desires, even just the one time? Would she ever be able to stop? She couldn't take that chance. It was one of the reasons why she deliberately limited her contact with the living outside of the few mortals in the Brandon family that she shared her home with.

She had another complication with the possibility of ever finding any sort of romance in her life - what kind of a man would want to be with someone who looked like she did? Certainly nobody her own age would except for some kind of a sicko that was into little girls. This reminded her, unfortunately, that she still found herself attracted to boys who were around the same age that she *appeared* to be, didn't this make her into some kind of a sicko herself? She didn't think so, she felt that if she'd been allowed to keep on growing up, it was something she would've grown out of like normal people do. But she wasn't a normal person, not anymore. She was like an insect trapped in amber, permanently frozen at the age of fourteen - which is why she had chosen "Amber " as her name for the false identity she sometimes employed. The conundrum of the age difference between vampires and the objects of their romantic desires was another thing that the fiction often failed to pay much attention to, probably because it was so inherently problematic. In many of the stories, the vampire and their lover looked like they were the same age, but usually the vampire is old enough to be their great, great, great grandparent! It puts a whole new spin on the term "robbing the cradle".

She hoped that someday she'd find another vampire who seemed to be her own age and who also didn't prey on humans. Sadly, that was something of a pipe dream. As far as she knew, her little family were the last vampires on earth, and the only ones who fed exclusively on animal blood. Did William and Elizabeth understand how fortunate they were that they had each other, that they had been turned into vampires at the same time? She was a little jealous of them and their relationship, to be honest. Even after all these centuries, they somehow still enjoyed a love she was certain she'd never find for herself.

So she strived to distract herself from all of this negativity as best she could. She helped out on the farm during the day, and in her spare time she read voraciously, watched movies, played video games, and listened to music so much that the days, weeks and years melted into each other. She had few connections to the outside world; there were a few friends she talked to in online chat rooms devoted to some of the nerdy fandoms that she tended to lose herself in, and one very special friend who was her only link to the world of other teenage girls, the world that she still couldn't help but feel like she was supposed to be a part of.

This friend was Mary Brandon, the daughter of Charles Brandon, the Sherwood's trusted valet. The Brandon family had faithfully served the Sherwoods for generations. They lived in the manor house with them and were so close that they were all virtually one large family. William and Elizabeth had participated in the raising of so many of the Brandons that they tended to think of them as their own children. The Brandons, in turn, thought of the Sherwoods as benevolent grandparents. Mary had been a newborn when Allison first arrived at the house, and she had watched her grow up. She thought of her as a little sister, although at the age of sixteen, she was now biologically older than Allison appeared to be. A fact that Allison couldn't get used to.

She was, quite frankly, her best friend and confidant, but she feared that they had been growing apart lately. Mary had made some new friends outside of the manor, and spent more and more time away from the noble old structure. In a way, Allison was happy for her friend; she couldn't blame her. Wouldn't Allison do the same thing in her position? Why would she want to spend her time in this maze of dimly lit corridors when she could instead be with new and different friends? After all, they had already spent a lifetime together, wasn't it time to move on? Yet she still couldn't quite accept it, she wasn't ready to let her go. Mary represented her one conduit to normalcy - without her, Allison could easily get lost in the darker shadows of her vampiric nature.

It was with some sadness that she watched from her bedroom window as Mary bounded down the steps of the manor and into the waiting car that belonged to Yolanda, one of Mary's new friends from school. Allison couldn't stand Yolanda or Mary's other new, frequent partner in crime, Brittney. She often referred to the pair as "the Terrible Two". Internally, of course. It wasn't just that she was jealous of them stealing away her friend all the time like this, she genuinely disliked the girls, who seemed snooty and vacuous. She also didn't like the effect that she saw them having on Mary, who appeared to "dumb" herself down around them to better fit in. This was the main reason why she was staying behind tonight, despite the fact that the girls were headed off to Allison's favorite place in the whole world - Wonderland.

She loved everything about it, the dizzying variety of people who walked through its gates and the rides that brought thrills to some and terror to others. Wonderland had been her refuge ever since its construction almost four years earlier. Of course, she was old enough to recall the original park that had been there, and had been much nicer in comparison. Her parents, her *real* parents, had brought her there a few times before her accident and she had some of her happiest childhood memories there. She supposed that was one explanation for her great affinity for the place. She had been delighted to see the park resurrected after sitting idle for so many years, even if it wasn't quite as nice as it used to be. It was just like her - hurriedly brought back from the brink of death, but not quite up to snuff.

She hadn't been there that much this past year; her parents worried about her profusely whenever she was away from the manor for too long. She could understand their overprotectiveness, but she didn't enjoy it. They preferred her to spend her time with them, disturbed by the fact that she tended to spend entire days at the park when left to her own devices. This was true, but how could she expect them to understand that these jaunts were as close as she would ever come to experiencing some kind of normalcy? William and Elizabeth were comfortable with what they were in a way that Allison was not. She supposed that would come to her too in time, although in a way she also feared ever becoming so complacent about her "condition". She wasn't quite ready to surrender what remained of her humanity and fully embrace her vampirism as they had. Going out to Wonderland was her only opportunity to see other people, and maybe even make a few friends in real life. Elizabeth and William wanted her to play a bigger part in the family, but she'd never asked to be a part of the Munsters or the Addams Family! They didn't understand that her trips to Wonderland were her chance to be free, to escape from this gloomy prison, and for a few hours, at least, forget what she really was.

Her family feared the rest of humanity, though. Feared what would become of them if mortals ever discovered their true nature. They stayed out of sight, cringing in their rickety old mansion and contributing generously to the local community in order to cement their reputation as responsible and valuable citizens of Davenport. They expected her to do the same. Yes, she knew all too well how people feared what they didn't understand, but she didn't think that the townspeople would descend upon Sherwood Farm with torches and pitchforks just because she liked to ride a few roller coasters. Sure, there was *some* risk in her going out. Perhaps people would notice that she never seemed to age, or she'd give into the ever present temptation to sink her teeth into someone. So far, though, she'd done a good job of resisting such bloody impulses, and she enjoyed disguising herself to vary her appearance each time she went out. She didn't see what the big deal was. Her parents hadn't forbidden her from going there, but they *had* made her promise to limit the frequency of her visits. So she had resolved to stay behind tonight. The idea of having to put up with Yolanda and Brittney's irritating presence had made it a little easier to come to such a decision.

Charles Brandon, Mary's dad, happened to be walking by the open door of her bedroom and noticed her despondent expression as she watched the girls drive off.

"Staying behind again, huh? You don't look all that happy about it. You should get out there and live a little! You can't spend your whole life with your nose buried in a book," he told her as he paused in her doorway.

It was quite the opposite of what William would've told her, but then again, Charles was more like her cooler, more permissive uncle. He'd been here since before the beginning of her time at Sherwood Farm - the only one out of his siblings to agree to follow in his parents' footsteps as the Sherwood's servant. He'd been married once, to a lovely woman named Georgia who had fallen ill and died years ago. Elizabeth and William had offered to "save" her, too, but Georgia had elected to turn down their offer, wisely, Allison thought. She still missed her, she'd been a good friend to Allison as well. Mary reminded her so much of Georgia.

At this point, Allison was probably slightly closer to Charles in actual years than she was to Mary, despite the fact that he was a balding man in his mid-forties.

"Yeah, well tell that to the lord of the manor. He's perfectly happy to see me rot away up here," she said, turning to face him.

Charles wasn't sure that was fair of her to say, although he could understand her frustration. He was never very comfortable criticizing his employer behind his back. "He's just worried about what might happen to you out there; maybe a little too worried, but it comes from a good place."

"I know, I know," Allison said, flopping down on her bed backwards.

"Besides, I thought he hadn't actually ever said you *couldn't* go out there anymore, he just didn't want you going every day, all day, like you used to do."

"I just don't like the company your daughter's been keeping lately," she admitted as she studied her ceiling.

"Between you and me, neither do I. I kinda wish you'd gone with them to keep her out of trouble. I'm not sure that those girls are such a good influence," he confessed.

"Aha! So now you show your true colors! What you *really* want is for me to babysit Mary for you!" Allison, still lying on her back, waved a finger at him in mock accusation, rather melodramatically, as was her way.

Even though he knew she was just kidding around, the serious-minded Charles still felt a little guilty at her being able to see through him so readily.

"Not 'babysit' so much as 'chaperone'. And for what it's worth, I really *do* worry about you sitting up here by yourself so much. I know how much you like hanging out in that place. You shouldn't let William or a few mean girls stop you from doing what you really want to do."

"You know something, you're right! I *should* go out there tonight," she said, sitting bolt upright suddenly.

"I'll drive you if you want, I'm not busy right now," Charles offered nonchalantly.

"That's okay, I like the walk." It was true, she did enjoy the walk. It also didn't hurt that it wasn't that far from the farm to the outskirts of the park. One advantage of being a vampire was that she could simply leap over the high, chain link fence that separated the old, disused part of the park from the rest of the town. Even though she was well paid for her work on the farm, she rarely bothered to go in through the main entrance and pay for admission. Most of the time she just wandered around the park, people watching or playing the games. If she wanted to ride the rides, she would buy a roll of tickets at one of the booths located around the place for just such a purpose. At Wonderland, you had the option of purchasing a roll of tickets, or buying a color-coded wristband that allowed you onto all the rides for the entire day. In her opinion, the wristbands were overpriced, so she rarely bothered with them. She preferred to save her money to put towards buying more books on Amazon.com.

Charles shook his head at Allison's eccentricities. "Okay, suit yourself. Just don't let anyone see you hopping over that fence, or William will have a cow."

Her eyes widened at the fact that he was on to her game. How the hell did he know that she did that? Mary must've squealed on her. She'd have some words with her later on about that! *You just can't trust anyone these days*, she thought.

"Jumping over a fence? Whatever do you mean? I'll have you know that I'm a law-abiding, model citizen, good sir, and I resent such inflammatory, baseless accusations!" she said in her best attempt at a stuffy, upper class British accent. "Besides," she said, reverting back to her normal speaking voice, "William has a cow every night - literally!"

Charles rolled his eyes at her hopelessly cheesy attempts at humor and started to move off down the hallway again. "Thanks for keeping an eye on Mary for me. I really do appreciate it."

Allison sprang from the bed and ran to her doorway with inhuman speed.

"Hey buster! I'm not doing this for Mary, or for you! I'm doing it for *me!* " she called after his retreating form, only half meaning it. She could see Charles absently waving a single hand as if trying to swat away a fly.

"Yeah, yeah, whatever. Have a good time, just not *too much* of a good time," he replied as he was enveloped by the darkness of the corridor, vanishing into its shadows.

Yes, go to Wonderland she would, for the first time in about a week. She often thought of the park as her own private kingdom: a brightly lit world of pleasure akin to the enchanted lands that she lost herself in when reading her beloved fantasy novels. While Wonderland was no Narnia or Middle Earth, she could always pretend, she could dream. She might not own the place, but it did belong to her spirit. To walk the grounds of that park, strewn with laughing people and spinning, sliding, twisting rides was to know Allison's lively, but often tumultuous soul.

Even when the park was closed, she still loved to go there, to climb and sit upon the inert, lifeless rides and envision the customers happily strolling between the attractions. When it was shut down for the winter, it reflected her own lonely condition. She felt like she was just like those hulking, immobile rides. She was someone who had an endless potential to amuse and delight others, yet was frozen by circumstance. Her capacity to share such delights with others long locked away, just waiting for someone to come along and unleash it. Many were the nights when she would sit around in a deactivated roller coaster car, or leap up to the top of the ferris wheel and contemplate life, or compose in her head some mournful sonnet that would never make it to paper.

But tonight, she would go. She would see her baby shining forth in all of its gaudy, neon glory once again, temporarily banishing her loneliness, giving way to a new universe of possibilities, if only in her mind. She loved seeing her baby alive and vibrant again, the way she longed to be herself.

Maybe tonight. Maybe tonight, she hoped, and resolved that she must never give up that hope.

Her continued sanity depended on it.

CHAPTER 5:

ISOLATION

In the almost pitch-black recesses of Wonderland's crumbling and condemned old Tunnel of Love, Kevin Scott watched the clouds roll by through one of the many holes which peppered the ceiling of the moldering structure. His back was against the rough, uneven faux stone wall as he sat there listlessly, just as he had for several days now. How many days had it been? He'd lost count. Maybe a week? Maybe two? Time really had no meaning to him anymore. He was untethered from the routine of school and work that had defined his existence up until recently, liberated from the tyranny of clocks in a way that he hadn't been since he'd still been wearing diapers. Yet he did not feel free - he was trapped in the prison of his own mind, shackled by guilt in a self-imposed solitary confinement filled with endless self-loathing.

He supposed that he should make some kind of an effort to figure out what day it was, if only so he could try and figure out when the next full moon was set to make its dreadful debut in the skies above him. There had been no full moon on the night when his life had changed forever, but that didn't mean that the stories about it weren't true. He had a duty to get as far away as he could from other people before the terrible change, he so feared came upon him again, unleashing the raging beast within.

Perhaps he had simply traded his slavery to the artificial construct of man's conception of time as embodied by clocks for a new servitude to the deeper, more natural ancient rhythms of the moon and her ever waxing and waning cycles? Would the moon be his new God, then? Forever dictating the details of his miserable new existence to him?

It certainly seemed as if his old God had forsaken him when he condemned him to this curse. What was he now? Was there some kind of demon living inside of him, always itching and scratching to get out? What had he done to deserve this? He had been raised Catholic, but he hadn't really taken much of it very seriously since he'd been a small child. Outwardly, he pretended to be devout to please his mother, but internally he was extremely skeptical, verging on atheism even. Now, of course, he wasn't so sure anymore. He'd seen and experienced horrible, impossible things lately. *He* was a horrible, impossible thing. If such things were real, then maybe *all* of the rest of it was too? God, the Devil - all the ridiculous things that he'd once so smugly dismissed as nothing but the product of mankind's wild imaginings. His assumptions about what was real and what was not had been shaken to their very core.

If this was the case, then maybe he was being punished by God. But *why* exactly had he been cursed like this? Was it because of his doubts, his lack of faith? This made no sense to him either, he knew that there were lots of other people who were far more openly faithless and heretical than he had ever been. Why hadn't they been singled out like he had been? Surely, if this was some kind of divine retribution, didn't they deserve it more than he did?

Maybe he was being punished for how he had sinned with Sylvia? But again, this made no sense to him either. Yes, they'd done *things* together, *sexual* things that technically, in the eyes of the Church at least, they had no business doing with one another, especially at their age, but he knew that countless other people had done far worse. He'd seen it for himself endless times, in all those porn videos he watched online. All of those people weren't being punished like he was, like Sylvia had been. The worst thing that he imagined could happen to them as a result of their sins of the flesh was that maybe they'd catch a disease, or end up with an unwanted pregnancy. They didn't turn into actual monsters. They weren't torn apart by monsters.

No! What he and Sylvia had done wasn't any different from what millions of other people had done together since the dawn of time. It didn't warrant any kind of extra special punishment so far as he could tell. Neither of them were perfect, but they weren't particularly terrible people either. They hadn't *deserved* what had happened to them! He couldn't allow himself to accept that. Nobody deserves this! It didn't make any sense! If it wasn't a punishment from God, then did that mean that life was just completely random and senseless? That anything could happen? One minute, you're riding high on life, sleeping with the girl of your dreams - the next, everything falls apart, for absolutely no reason at all. She's dead and you're some kind of a killer on the run.

A *monster.*

Somehow, this idea, the idea that there was no rhyme or reason to existence, no sense to it at all, was the scariest thing of all. He almost preferred to think of himself as the victim of divine punishment. At least in that scenario, there was some hope of redemption if he could only figure out *what* he had done to so displease God and what he could do to get back into his good graces again. Yet even in the deepest pits of his despair, Kevin was still too fundamentally rational to dare to truly believe that this was what was really going on. No, he was not being punished by God for having sex, and neither had Sylvia been. What had happened to them was just some inexplicable, particularly cruel twist of fate in a blind and chaotic universe and there was no hope for either of them anymore.

She was dead, and he was cursed to keep on living although now he wanted nothing more than to be dead. Lord knows he'd *tried* to kill himself. It was one of the first things he'd done after he'd...realized what had happened, and what he *was* now.

He recalled once more, as he had so often these past few days, the tragic series of events that had led him to where he was now. He constantly and deliberately tortured himself by going over these painful memories over and over again, feeling like he *had* to do it as a kind of penance. Or was his mind simply still struggling to make sense of the senseless? He didn't know. All that he *did* know was that he had no business trying to even dare to think of happier things when he was the one who was ultimately responsible for such an inhuman deed. No, he *had* to dwell upon it. He *had* to make sure that there was no chance for even a moment of respite for him. Sylvia would never have another moment of peace or joy or *anything* because of him, and thus, neither should he. This bizarre curse he now found himself under may have robbed him of the ability to hurt himself physically, but he could still devise ways to punish himself psychologically.

So it was that Kevin cast his thoughts back to when he had first awakened upon that horrible morning, how utterly drained he had felt, as if he'd been asleep for a thousand years, how it had taken a terrific effort to simply open his eyes. In retrospect, perhaps his body had been trying to protect him from confronting the new nightmare reality he was being reborn into, trying to keep him slumbering peacefully in blissful ignorance for as long as possible? He remembered how puzzled he had been to find himself lying naked in unfamiliar surroundings, and the overpowering feeling of revulsion that began to seize him as he first caught sight of what was left of Sylvia, now strewn all across her blood splattered bedroom floor. It was a scene from an abattoir - she was hardly recognizable as ever having been a girl, she was now nothing but a reeking collection of half-eaten organs and gore-streaked bones.

Somehow, he'd had the presence of mind to run into her bathroom and puke into her toilet. The ludicrousness of that reaction made him giggle a little like a madman now that he thought about it. As if adding a little vomit to the already hopelessly messy ruin of her bedroom would've mattered in the slightest? *People are such ridiculous creatures of habit, aren't we? I guess we have nothing but our habits left to cling to when our worlds get turned upside down,* he thought. As he'd clung to the rim of that toilet like it was a life preserver keeping him afloat on a storm-tossed sea, he'd sobbed loudly and uncontrollably as his mind began to bombard him with a flood of images from the night before in a cruel attempt to make sense of what had happened in the other room.

The pictures that exploded into his head in that moment were like a series of snapshots from both heaven and hell. The lovely vision of Sylvia's shapely nude body, the exciting sensation of warmth as her smooth skin met his, the intoxicating smell of her - the artificially fruity scent of her body wash masking the saltier notes of her flesh hiding below it. It all came rushing back to him. Intruding upon these more pleasurable recollections, smashing through them and shattering them were images of a completely contrary nature. Visions of a hulking, inhuman, shaggy form. That form! Huge and hairy, with rows of razor sharp fans and sickly yellow eyes. He couldn't banish it from his mind no matter how hard he tried. He saw it tear into her delicate form, rending, tearing, effortlessly snapping off her appendages, biting deeply into them. Blood cascaded through the air all around the beast, its greedy growls drowning out her screams until there was only the sound of cracking bones accompanied by a sickening slurping noise. He knew what this thing was, he'd seen it before in his mind's eye countless times when he read stories about them, yet nothing he imagined previously could've prepared him for the horror of what they were truly like.

But how could this be? These things weren't real! There was no such thing as a werewolf! Surely, he was insane to even seriously consider such a thing, wasn't he? That had to be it. For some reason that he couldn't fathom, he had done this monstrous thing to her.

He'd invented this fantasy that she'd been attacked by a werewolf because he couldn't face the idea that he was the one who was really responsible for it. He didn't understand *why* he'd done such a thing to her. It didn't seem like the sort of thing he'd ever do to anyone, let alone her. He'd figured that his mind was trying to protect him from that information too, walling off the knowledge of just how deeply crazy he was. He must be some kind of a lunatic, fucking psycho!

Despite this, he still tried to understand it, to put it into some kind of rational frame of reference. He had loved to read horror novels, he liked movies and video games about that sort of subject matter too. He knew that some people believed that kind of violent, dark media could twist the minds of people, especially young people, maybe even making them into killers. He'd always thought that was all a load of bullshit. There was no scientific evidence to back up their claims that he was aware of. It was one thing to read about something, but something quite different to actually *do* it. If anything, he'd always felt like it was much healthier to deal with such negative feelings through fiction, that doing so *prevented* people from acting out these destructive scenarios in real life. Now, how could he be so sure? Maybe they'd been right all along? There was a corpse in the next room that seemed to prove their point.

Why had he done this to Sylvia in particular? He didn't know that either. He didn't *think* he'd been angry with her or had any desire to hurt her. He didn't love her. He knew that much. He *was* attracted to her, obviously, but it wasn't love. At least he didn't think so. Sometimes, he thought that maybe it *should* be. That was probably a product of his religious upbringing still creeping into his head, the idea that you weren't supposed to be doing sexual things with someone unless you were not only in love with them, but also married. He felt like that was a terribly old-fashioned way of thinking, but it had been ingrained in him so heavily that on some level he still couldn't help but feel guilty that he was completely going against such teachings. Part of him *wanted* to be in love with her for those reasons, but the inescapable truth of it was that they really didn't have all that much in common aside from a shared physical attraction to one another. He was ashamed to admit it, but when they weren't making out, he'd found her kind of boring. He'd fantasized about her often. She was the girl of his dreams, but only in a way that went skin deep. He just didn't feel any kind of deep, emotional connection to her, although sometimes he felt like he was obligated to, since they had shared so much together physically. He really *did* want to fall in love with someone someday, but he didn't seriously think that she was the right one for him. She had the body, but she didn't have the sort of personality that he was drawn to, and he wasn't so shallow that things like that didn't matter to him.

She was dating a football player, but he didn't seem to spend much time with her, she was more like a status symbol to him. He spent most of his time practicing or hanging out with his teammates. When they did spend time together, it wasn't very meaningful to her, and she'd confided in Kevin that he was *much* better in the sack than Brad was, which had given him a nice little surge of pride at the time. Yet despite all this, she'd had no intentions of leaving Brad. He was a status symbol for her, too. Being his boyfriend had made her more popular, put her into an exclusive clique with some of the other player's girlfriends. Did he resent her for that? Had Kevin really expected her to leave Brad so they could be together more openly? He didn't think that he had. Sneaking around to avoid Brad and keeping their relationship a secret was a little scary and annoying at times, but to tell the truth, it also added another layer to the excitement of it all.

He supposed that he did feel a little used by her sometimes - that he was good enough for her to fuck, but not good enough to date, not popular enough or rich enough. That was pretty hypocritical of him, wasn't it? Honestly, hadn't he felt the same way about her? She wasn't really what he was looking for in a serious relationship either, she wasn't what he would've considered ideal girlfriend material. She had been pretty clear about setting the boundaries for what was going on between the two of them when he'd first gone over to her house the same night she'd passed that note to him, and he had agreed without any real reservations. They'd take advantage of the fact that her parents were out of town on a business trip that week to have a little fun with each other, and that was all. No calls, no texts, no kissing and telling - no evidence to tip Brad off as to what was going on. No promises to each other and no regrets. Kevin would just come over and they'd see where the night would take them, learning how to enjoy each other's bodies.

It had been good enough that first night for him to want to come back for more the next night. He'd had a proper girlfriend once before, but he'd been younger then and things hadn't gone very far physically. That first night with Sylvia, he'd gone much farther than he ever had before with anyone. He'd finally done some of the things he'd only ever seen in those online videos in real life. The sorts of things he'd been longing to experience for himself. He hadn't been disappointed. Neither had she, apparently, since she invited him back over the next night.

But somehow, that second night, it had all gone wrong. It had started out wonderfully enough and she'd taken his virginity that night, and then...then it became a blur. He supposed he'd killed her for reasons he couldn't comprehend, and invented this bizarre werewolf fantasy as a way to disassociate himself from it. He must be a stranger to his own thoughts and feelings, capable of doing things he didn't even dare to imagine that he was. It was the only explanation that made any sense, even though it felt completely wrong. Had he really been *that* out of touch with what was going on in his own mind? Did he secretly harbor some kind of deep-seated hatred towards Sylvia or women in general that he hadn't been aware of consciously? It seemed impossible, but the ugly truth of it was in the next room over.

He rose to his feet unsteadily, abandoning the safe harbor of the toilet, and forced himself to look at Sylvia's remains one more time, to burn it into his memory. He'd noticed for the first time that her bedroom window was smashed open, the floor littered with shards of broken glass on that side of the room. He wasn't sure how that had happened. For that matter, he wasn't sure how he had managed to have done what he had done to her with just his bare hands and teeth. Yet somehow he had. As unpleasant as it all was, he'd had to make himself face it, if only to steel his resolve for what he'd known he must do next. If he was really some kind of a Jekyll and Hyde, someone who was capable of committing this sort of atrocity, then he had to kill himself while his more benevolent nature was still in control, before he hurt someone else. He didn't want to die, he was scared to die, but he also knew that he couldn't possibly live with what he'd done, or the possibility that he could do it again. He didn't deserve life or happiness or anything anymore, not after what he'd done. The best thing that he could do for everyone involved was to put himself down like the mad dog that he was.

He'd wandered down the hall and into her kitchen, where he saw a block of kitchen knives on the counter and selected the biggest one he could find. He'd stood there for some time, naked in the kitchen, looking at his dull, haunted reflection in the gleaming blade. He'd recalled with a grimace the grotesque collection of body parts that had once been a girl. A girl who had been so beautiful and full of potential and how he had robbed her of all of that for no good reason at all. Finally, he'd found the courage to plunge the blade up under his rib cage, trying to get to his heart.

Nothing happened.

The blade had just bounced off his skin. He took a deep breath, and tried again, stabbing at himself even more savagely this time.

Still nothing.

He tried to slit his own neck.

Nothing.

He sliced at his wrist.

Nothing.

He tried different knives from the same block. All to no avail. None of them even broke the skin.

He gave up on knives. He went into her garage and found a hammer from her father's toolbox. He tried to bash his own head in with it. He could feel the force of the impact pushing his head back, but that was it. Over and over he tried. It was pointless. Somehow, he was not only a murderer now, but apparently also some kind of an invulnerable superman.

Slowly, he came to accept that as impossible as it seemed, he could not be killed. Not with any of the things he could find in this house, at least. Maybe *he* was a werewolf? Maybe the only thing that could ever put him out of his misery now was a silver bullet?

More memories had come to him then, memories of his whole world going red. In these memories, he was carried away by a sudden whirlwind of agony. He watched his fingers merge together and extend out painfully before transforming into huge, wolfish paws. Thick grey hairs burst forth at an alarming rate from every inch of his body. His head twisted and elongated. Teeth capable of rending raw flesh with the efficiency of a katana made their debut. He'd even sprouted a tail! Gone was his voice box, replaced with something that could only emit low, guttural, animalistic growls.

Worst of all was the memory of hunger. An inexplicable emptiness that gripped him, a feral longing unlike anything he'd ever experienced before. An all-consuming, bestial bloodlust that pushed out all other considerations. Could there be any doubt of what he was? It made no sense at all, but there was no other explanation. He was a werewolf. He could remember the transformation now, even if he couldn't recall what had triggered it.

These memories were all such a bewildering jumble. In some of them, he seemed to be outside of his body, watching the wolf as it ripped away at Sylvia, in others, he was in the body of the wolf, and sometimes, he was *fighting* the wolf trying to get him off of Sylvia. It was like he could actually see what surely had to be some sort of a metaphorical, inner struggle as clear as day, like it really happened that way.

If he was a werewolf, then *how* had it happened? *Why* was he one? He didn't remember being bitten by one, he was sure that would've been a memorable enough event. He did seem to recall having some strange nightmares about werewolves after that first night with Sylvia, and when he woke up the next morning he could barely recall how he had gotten home. Maybe something had happened to him on his way home? It didn't seem likely though, he was certain he'd remember if something had.

Maybe he'd always been one? Somehow, maybe he'd inherited this curse. Perhaps the beast had always been lurking inside, biding its time, waiting to come out and ruin everything. Why had it chosen this moment to come out? Had it had something to do with his virginity being lost? Had that orgasmic surge of ecstasy unleashed at that moment somehow summoned forth the devil within? Or had it just been some sort of bizarre coincidence that his first transformation had come about at this particular time? He decided that it was something he'd just never understand. One thing that he *did* think he understood now was that he hadn't borne any ill will towards Sylvia, she had just been in the wrong place at the wrong time. The beast that slumbered inside of him was unimaginably hungry and she had made a convenient meal for the monster. A monster that had been beyond his power to control.

The thought that partially digested parts of Sylvia might actually be inside of Kevin's body right now made him suddenly feel sick to his stomach once more. This time, he managed to keep the urge to throw up under control.

He now knew that he couldn't kill himself, and so long as he lived, he was a danger to others. Should he call the cops? Turn himself in? Of course nobody would ever believe that he was a werewolf, they'd just think he was nuts unless they saw him change in front of them and somehow lived to tell the tale. The knowledge that their son was an insane killer would break his parents' hearts and make their lives miserable. He wasn't sure he could do that to them. He also wasn't sure that any kind of prison or mental asylum could successfully hold him in his werewolf form. So that left him with only one option: he had to run away from home, go into a self-imposed exile somewhere far away from the rest of the human race. Running away would hurt his parents too, but not as much as the knowledge that their child was a killer. They'd still have hope that he was out there somewhere and that maybe he'd found happiness and that they would be reunited. As long as they could hold onto that hope, maybe they'd be okay.

To this end, he'd found his clothes from the day before thrown into a corner of Sylvia's bedroom, somehow tucked away so well that none of the blood from her death had managed to get on them. He'd dressed quickly, daring to look upon the mangled form of Sylvia one last time. Hot tears streamed down his face again.

"I'm sorry, I'm so, so sorry," he whispered hoarsely as he took his leave of the disgusting scene for the last time. He felt terrible at the idea of her parents coming home to find this horrific tableaux in a few days' time, if someone didn't find her before then, but what could he do? The mess was beyond his ability to clean up, and there was no way to make her remains look any more presentable. He didn't want to leave any evidence behind that he'd ever been there, which he would surely do if he tried to clean things up. He didn't want the cops coming after him because of what it would do to his parents if he was linked to all of this. He stepped around her remains, careful not to get any blood on his shoes. He tried to remember all the things he'd touched since being there, and wiped off any fingerprints he may have left behind with the hem of his t-shirt. Hopefully the police would believe that she'd been attacked by a wild animal and wouldn't even be looking for fingerprints, but he decided to take the precaution anyway. He let himself out the back door, locking it behind him.

It was still pretty dark outside, around 5:30 in the morning. His mom wouldn't be home for a few more hours. He'd walked home; unfortunately his trusty bike had gotten a flat somehow and he'd been forced to walk ever since. He took the shortcut through the woods a few blocks away. As he walked the trail, he'd been gripped with a sudden, overwhelming panic unlike anything he'd ever felt before, and found himself running as fast as his feet would carry him along the path. When he'd finally emerged from the trees, he was hyperventilating and his heart felt like it would burst out of his chest at any moment. He couldn't understand why he'd reacted that way, he'd traveled down that trail hundreds of times in his explorations of his neighborhood. He'd just chalked it up to all the stress he was under.

Once in the house, he'd started gathering up things he'd need for his life in exile. This didn't take very long, as he already had a duffle bag packed for the weekend he had planned to spend at his dad's apartment. He added a few more changes of clothes, and a mess kit and sterno cooking set left over from his Boy Scout days along with his trusty Swiss Army knife. He also added a pillow and a few blankets. Next, he raided his pantry, taking as many cans of non-perishable food as he could comfortably carry, and even a few things that he normally wouldn't eat, but would do in a pinch, like SPAM.

He thought about leaving a note for his mom, but he thought the less clues he left behind, the better. He hated making her wonder about him like that, but it had to be that way. He decided that he would withdraw as much of his money as he could from the ATM, then hop on a bus and try to get as far away from here as his money could take him. At the last minute, he remembered that he still had his old skateboard from middle school. He barely ever used it anymore, he'd never really been a very good skater, but it might be useful in helping him get around. The bank where the ATM was located wasn't that far away, but the town's single bus stop was. The skateboard was the last thing he grabbed as he made his way out the door. The first rays of sunlight were beginning to paint the clouds in brilliant stokes of orange and purple. He gazed upon this picturesque sky as it stretched over his home, sadly thinking that he'd never see the place again. Shadowbrook was kind of a boring dump of a town, but it was still his home, the only one he'd ever known, and he couldn't help but love it a little despite himself. With a heave and groan, he shouldered his bulging duffel bag and stepped onto his skateboard, slipping away through the quiet suburban avenues. As he made his way through town, the alleys seemed to grow eyes, the wind whispering accusations in his ears and every sound of the emerging day was like a cry of condemnation.

Even though he was suffering from such powerful bouts of remorse and paranoia, he'd still been able to carry out the first stages of his plan without a hitch. He now had all of his cash safely tucked away in his wallet, and he'd boarded a bus bound for the big depot a few towns over all rather uneventfully. He climbed down the steps of the bus and walked into the station. Behind the counter of the ticket booth was a rotund, red-faced man. When Kevin Scott came up to the ticket window lugging his misshapen duffel bag, the man looked as if he had the kid all figured out. He'd probably seen dozens of runaways like him come through here over the years.

Well, not quite like me, Kevin mused.

He stepped back and looked up to study the schedule above the window for a few minutes, trying to figure out what his next destination should be. For some reason, one destination stood out above all the others: Wonderland. It was ridiculous. He had enough money to get himself much further away. What was he doing thinking of going to some cheesy amusement park? Shouldn't a place packed with crowds of people be the last place he should be going to? Wasn't the idea to get as far away from other people as possible? Yet he couldn't get the idea out of his head. *Something* was drawing him there. Something he couldn't quite bring himself to ignore.

"One ticket for the bus to Wonderland, please," he said, surprised by how rough and weak sounding his own voice seemed to his ears. He was even more surprised to hear himself saying these words. Why was he going there? Even in the best of times, he didn't really like amusement parks all that much - he was too scared to go on any of the rides that went upside down (or even looked like they might) or that took you up too high. This was hardly the best of times either. It wasn't like he was going to go try and enjoy himself after what he'd just done, and knowing what he could do again. The idea of allowing himself to feel any kind of joy or pleasure ever again seemed obscene considering that he had taken that possibility away from Sylvia (who had never done anything but *give* him pleasure) forever. Yet, say it he had. The die was cast, and he felt like he had no choice but to follow through on what his intuition was telling him to do.

The man behind the counter told him the price, took his money and gave him his change and his ticket. Kevin began to turn away when the pudgy man behind the window called out to him unexpectedly.

"Hey kid, what're ya runnin' away from?"

"Myself," came Kevin's melancholy response. It was but a single word, yet spoken with such conviction, such an unsettling mixture of sadness and anger, that it drained all of the color from the fat man's face.

He didn't have long to wait until the bus pulled into the depot. Once onboard, he was relieved to find it mostly deserted, especially in the back, where he chose to sit. At the front of the bus, the driver seemed to be flirting with a pair of girls sitting nearby who were probably a little too young for him. Apart from these three others, he was alone on the bus. Soon, he found himself being lulled to sleep by the spell of the rhythmic roar of the engine and the rolling of the wheels along the smooth surface of the highway.

His dreams had been, perhaps not unexpectedly, particularly pleasant ones. He'd dreamed of Sylvia, lying naked and perfect on her bed, he reached out to touch her shoulder, only to see a rivulet of bright, red blood trickling down from the spot where he had touched her. He looked at that spot and saw that his hand had now been replaced by a claw which was piercing the surface of her skin. She kicked and screamed now, her eyes wide with horror as thick, hairy, sinewy arms held her fast. Inhuman, clawed fingers tightened their terrible grip, causing more blood to come gushing out of her arms. Blood. Through it all, the rich river of red, red blood continued to flow - it spurted, it fountained out, it never seemed to end. Neither did the sound of her frightened cries.

Until they did.

Suddenly, she stopped screaming and looked right at him with dead eyes, her face a shredded ruin with jagged flaps of flesh dangling listlessly off her exposed bones.

"Why did you do this to me, Kevin? Why am I dead, while you're still alive?" she demanded of him.

"I'm sorry, I'm so sorry! I tried to kill myself, I did! But nothing worked!" he tried to tell her, but all he could manage to get out were odd, whimpering sounds where words should be.

"WHY WON'T YOU JUST *DIE???*" Sylvia howled at him, and now *she* was the one clawing at *him*, ripping away chunks of his body with manic ferocity. He watched helplessly as he saw pieces of himself go flying across her bedroom, agony wracking every nerve in his body.

Kevin had woken up screaming.

Then he felt the bus suddenly lurch alarmingly as it swerved violently into the next lane and back out again.

The two girls sitting up front were screaming now, too.

"Holy shit! What the fuck?" he heard the driver exclaim.

The next thing he knew, the bus was pulling over to the shoulder of the highway. The driver stood up and whirled around, pointing an angry finger straight in Kevin's direction.

"What the hell is wrong with you? Screaming like that? You trying to get all of us killed? You scared the shit outta me!"

"I'm sorry. I was having a nightmare, I didn't mean to cause any trouble," Kevin protested weakly.

"Yeah, well I've got half a mind to toss you off this bus! I will, too, if you pull any more shit like that, don't test me! You better just keep quiet for the rest of this ride."

Kevin wondered if all this posturing was supposed to be impressing the girls sitting near the driver. If so, it didn't seem to be working. They both looked terrified by the whole exchange.

"I will be, I promise," Kevin answered.

"Alright. *Fucking little psycho,*" the driver said as he sat back down and returned the bus to the road. The rest of the ride passed by without incident. After the intensity of that nightmare, Kevin hadn't been able to fall asleep again, for which he was grateful.

As he'd walked up to the gates of Wonderland and joined the long queue, Kevin again wondered what he was doing here in Davenport, or even why he'd chosen to come here in the first place. It just didn't make a damned bit of sense! He didn't know how long he'd stay, but it probably wouldn't be for very long. He knew that an amusement park stuffed with people was no place for a boy who could turn into a merciless killer without warning. Everyone else was here to have a good time, but the only thing that he was interested in anymore was finding solitude and repentance. This hardly seemed like the sort of place where he was likely to find either.

He'd paid for a roll of tickets that he had no intentions of actually using and was suddenly gripped by the fear that they'd make him open up his bag and go through it, which would lead to all kinds of awkward questions. Questions that he had no good answers for. Or worse, they'd forbid him from carrying it inside; but he'd soon discover that the security was surprisingly lax here. They didn't even make a fuss about the skateboard he still carried slung under one arm. The only thing anyone said about his bag was when the person who was selling him his tickets let him know that they had lockers he could rent if he didn't feel like carrying it around. She even helpfully pointed out the location of these lockers on the map of the park that she handed to him along with his roll of tickets and change.

I could have an assault rifle or something hidden in a bag this big, and all they care about is giving me a sales pitch for some stupid locker! Kevin thought bitterly. Even though all of this worked to his advantage, he still thought it was pretty shitty of them. Mass shootings seemed to be getting more and more common with each passing year, but the people who ran this place didn't seem to be taking any kind of precautions to make sure their visitors weren't armed. It was like they just didn't give a fuck.

He would see more and more evidence of this irresponsible attitude as he wandered aimlessly around the park, noticing the shoddy state of the rides. He was no safety inspector, but even to him it seemed obvious that this place had to be in violation of half a dozen such regulations. He ignored the obnoxious pleas of the people who ran the various game booths to test out his luck as he walked by them.

Luck? I've used up every bit of it, he reflected humorlessly.

But time would prove him wrong on that account. For in time, his meanderings would lead him to a part of the park that was closed off to the public, although not surprisingly, it was closed off rather incompetently. A low fence separated it from the rest of the park, and there was a gap in the chained off gate that was wide enough for him to squeeze through, even with his bulging bag slung over one shoulder - which is exactly what he'd done once he was certain that nobody was watching. He'd walked on, through the tall grass of the unkempt meadows beyond that gate and past the decaying husks of rides long abandoned. Snapped cables and peeling paint marred these forgotten relics, which were only brightened by the occasional outbreak of graffiti along their surfaces. He'd walked until the ceaseless sound of calliope music was just a distant whine. He'd spotted a bulldozer and a large sign promising the arrival of some new and exciting attractions with a variety of outlandish names. The date that the sign announced that they'd be opening was already two years in the past. The ground didn't even look like it had been broken yet, and judging by the dilapidated state of it, he had no trouble believing that the bulldozer had been sitting there for that long. He wondered why their plans had stalled, they sure *seemed* to be making enough money on this place. He just shook his head. It was one more thing he might never understand, like why he'd been cursed to become a werewolf, or what he was doing here to begin with.

It was then that his eyes alighted upon a cave, but not a cave of rock, one of rusty steel support beams and fiberglass molded to resemble stone. It wasn't very convincing upon closer inspection, and it hadn't weathered very well either. Tiny holes dotted the roof, the result of either age or vandalism. Above it hung a faded sign surrounded by blown out lightbulbs, which had probably heralded the cave as a "Tunnel of Love" or something like that, but was now illegible. More legible signs announced that the structure was condemned.

Condemned? So am I. Looks like I've come to the right place after all, he mused.

The hungry maw of the cave beckoned him to step into its inky depths. He could barely see inside at first, but his eyes adjusted with surprising speed. In fact, once he got used to it, he realized with a start that he could see better in the dark than he could in the light. Apparently, this was yet another side effect of his unusual new condition. With each step he was sure that the entire place would come crashing down upon him at any moment. Hell, a part of him was hoping that is exactly what would happen. If he was buried beneath tons of rubble, then maybe even the sleeping demon inside of him wouldn't be powerful enough to dig out of it and hurt anyone else. As he explored the tunnel, he found a maintenance closet off to one side and with a thud, he dropped his duffel bag to the floor. He hadn't heard another human being since entering this section of the park. Maybe he could camp out here for the night? It offered both the isolation and the shelter he needed.

Nights turned to days and back again, over and over. Kevin made a bed for himself in the supply closet with the blankets and pillow he'd brought with him. He ate, sparingly, from the provisions he'd packed. He would sneak back into the park and fill up a bottle of water he'd used up with more water from the fountains scattered around the place. He even made an effort to maintain some degree of hygiene, bringing a washcloth he had with him into the park's public restrooms, placing hand soap and water on it, and "washing up" in one of the empty stalls. He had no way to clean the few pairs of clothes he had brought with him, but he tried to air out clothes he'd already worn instead of stuffing them back into his bag, in the hope that maybe that would keep them from starting to stink too badly. At night, he'd explore more of the disused section of the park that had become his new home, even discovering a few breaches in the much higher fence that seemed to separate the farthest boundaries of the park from the rest of the town. Occasionally, when he couldn't stand the taste of tuna fish and beans anymore, he'd break down and buy a hot dog or something from one of the numerous concession stands throughout the park, although he tried to limit his appearances inside the part of the park that was still in use; security might be loose here, but it wasn't completely nonexistent either. One night he'd even seen what he supposed was a patrol inside the abandoned section where he lived. He'd watched the pair of security guards for a few tense minutes that felt like hours as they came dangerously close to his tunnel sanctuary before finally moving on, their flashlights sweeping the ground in front of them like miniature searchlights.

Thankfully, in all this time, the monster living inside of him had made no fresh appearances, although with each passing day, Kevin seemed to become more irritated and annoyed by every little thing around him. Each night the moon seemed to be getting bigger and bigger in the night sky too. Was this just a coincidence, or did it mean what Kevin dreaded it meant?

That brings us back to the present moment, as Kevin sat on the floor of the tunnel, done for the moment with flagellating himself by dwelling on the sordid series of events that had first brought him there, he now pondered for the hundredth time what was still keeping him there. He still had a fair amount of money left, despite wasting some of it on those tickets he'd bought that first day and the occasional wiener. He could always get back on the bus and take it to another depot, where he could buy a ticket to get him farther away from civilization. Wasn't that supposed to be the goal? Yet, he felt like he had a pretty good thing going here. The tunnel was drafty, and damp, but if he closed the door of the maintenance closet, he was able to remain dry and warm at night, and nobody ever really came out here. The more he thought about it though, the less sure he was that any of those considerations were what was really keeping him there. It had less to do with logic and more to do with feeling. He just *felt* like he was supposed to be here. That there was something nearby that was calling to him. It seemed crazy, but the whole situation was crazy wasn't it?

In the end, it was fear that finally drove Kevin back to his feet. Fear of what would happen to him on the night of the full moon. He had to find out when the next one was going to happen. He had a plan to deal with the wolf if he chose that moment to reemerge. He'd go into town, buy some chains and padlocks and wrap the chains around himself, binding them with the locks. Then he'd hide the key in his bag, and lock himself in the closet where he slept. Maybe it would be enough to contain his monstrous alter ego? The beast wouldn't be smart enough to use a key, even if he found one, and if the chains were strong enough to hold him, it just might work.

First things first, he had to figure out when the full moon was going to happen. He was scared that it would be soon. The moon was definitely getting bigger with each passing night. In fact last night it looked like it was almost there. He remembered seeing information on lunar phases in a newspaper once, wasn't it somewhere in the weather section? He'd sneak out of the park through one of those holes he'd found in the fence and try and find a store where he could get a look at a paper, then try to find someplace where he could get the other things he needed for his plan to succeed.

So it was that Kevin Scott soon found himself skating along the shoulder of a road that led into the pitiful huddle of low buildings that passed for Davenport's downtown area. It didn't take him long to find a convenience store on a corner in that part of town. It was the perfect place to find a current newspaper. He flipped his skateboard off the curb and into the air, catching hold of it and wedging it under his arm as he headed inside.

He soon found a rack with newspapers stacked up on it. He picked one up and as he flipped through the pages rapidly, trying to find the weather section, he stopped dead in his tracks as his eyes happened across a headline:

SEARCH FOR WOLVES CONTINUES IN SHADOWBROOK

He paused to read the article, his heart beating like a hammer as he did so. He was encouraged to hear that Sylvia's death was being attributed to an attack by wolves, and that there was no mention of him. But why was it "wolves", plural? According to the article there was evidence of DNA from two different wolves found at the scene. How could that be? That had to be wrong! He'd believed those flashes of memory he'd had of fighting another wolf had just been something his mind had manufactured, but maybe there was something more to it? If so, who was this other werewolf and where were they now? What role had they played in Sylvia's death? As he read on, his hands were trembling at the implications of these new revelations. According to the article, despite several eyewitnesses reporting sightings of an unusually large wolf last week, Animal Control had yet to find any trace of the dangerous wild animals.

Unable to fully take in the meaning of this new information at the moment, he decided to refocus his attention on his original goal, and resumed his search for the weather section. When he finally found it, his eyes widened in disbelief as he noted that tomorrow was the night of the full moon! He'd have to accelerate his plan.

"Hey, are ya gonna stand there and read that all day, or are ya gonna actually buy something?" a rough voice called out to him.

Kevin turned his head around and grimaced. The voice belonged to a surly looking old man who stood behind the counter. At that moment, Kevin wanted nothing more than to rip off his head. He could feel the blood rushing to his face, and felt his hands begin to crinkle the paper as they tightened into fists.

What the hell is happening to me? he thought, alarmed by how angry he'd suddenly become, as he fought to get his emotions back under control. With some effort, he forced a smile onto his face. He didn't normally have such violent thoughts. He didn't think of himself as a particularly violent person, yet what he'd done to Sylvia argued otherwise. *No, that wasn't me, it was the beast!* he told himself, but what if that beast was just some repressed part of himself?

"Sure, I was just going to buy this paper," he said as he approached the counter. His eyes fell upon a farmer's almanac on a rack near the counter. That would definitely have lunar cycles listed in it - and not for just the next few days either, but the whole year! He picked it up and placed it on the counter with the newspaper.

"And this too."

As the man rang him up, Kevin worked up the courage to ask him a question.

"What's the closest hardware store around here?"

The man's mood shifted, as he now seemed happy to be asked about something which he obviously considered himself quite an authority on. The man gave him a set of directions laden with references to local landmarks that were meaningless to Kevin, but he nodded as if he knew what he was talking about, not wanting to appear ignorant. He was still able to get the gist of what he was saying; basically, there was a hardware store a little farther down the road. Kevin thanked him and took his change and purchases. The man's kindness in giving the directions just made him feel even more ashamed about how he'd been fantasizing about violently removing his head just a few minutes earlier.

It hadn't been difficult to find the hardware store. Kevin did have some trouble locating the section of the store where there might be chains and he'd had to ask for help, saying he needed something strong enough to prevent a big dog from getting loose. The clerk had looked at him sadly, probably thinking something about how cruel it was to chain up a dog like that. The chains and locks had been more expensive than he had banked on them being, and he was quite sad to see his modest reserve of cash dwindling so quickly. They were also damned heavy, and he had a hard time skating back to the breach in the fence carrying them.

As soon as he was back in his tunnel, he decided to test out his plan. He wrapped the chains tightly around himself, connecting them with the locks. He tried to flex to see how hard it would be to get out of them, they definitely did a good job of restraining him, but he was just a scrawny kid right now. Would they be strong enough to hold the wolf?

They had to be.

He had an extremely tough time maneuvering his hands to get the keys back into the locks, as he'd barely allowed himself adequate room to move them freely enough to do so. For a terrible moment he was afraid that he'd end up stuck like that for good. Eventually, however, he was able to open the locks and remove them, then take the chains off. After some almost comical wiggling, they finally slid down off his body and rattled to the ground.

Now I know how Houdini must've felt! he thought.

For the first time in what felt like forever, Kevin felt something akin to hope for the future. He thought his plan had a decent chance of actually working. He suddenly found himself being drawn back towards the part of the park that was open. He felt restless, and was seized by the urge to go up there and be among people again. Maybe it was the surge of optimism that he felt over the possibility of his plan succeeding? Whatever the case, Kevin was being inexorably pulled out of the safety of his tunnel and towards the lights of Wonderland which were coming to life as night began to fall.

This is crazy! This is irresponsible! What am I doing? I shouldn't be out here around all these people! he thought, yet he was helpless before this impulse that was possessing him.

Kevin wandered around for some time, consumed by a feeling he hadn't experienced since he'd been in the bus station. It was the same feeling that told him to stay here in Davenport, only now it was amplified a hundredfold, pushing and tugging him in different directions. Eventually, he found himself in front of the bright lights and loud noises of an arcade. For reasons that he couldn't fathom he felt compelled to walk inside, certain that whatever it was that he was looking for was sure to be found inside....

CHAPTER 6:

THE GAME

Allison held onto her wig as she leapt over the fence. It was clipped to her hair by bobby pins, but nonetheless, she was always a little paranoid about it flying off her head whenever she performed this little maneuver. She had to wear the wig since William was concerned that people might begin to get suspicious if they noticed this girl going to the park constantly, year after year, who never seemed to age, so she'd decided to vary her appearance on her visits. She wore a variety of different wigs and styles of dress whenever she stepped out. She found the whole thing to be great fun for the most part, although there were a few times when she didn't feel like bothering with all of these theatrics and just being herself. Unfortunately, this was out of the question since her true self "died" sixteen years ago. Her immediate family had died in that car crash, but she still had a few living relatives several towns away; aunts, uncles and cousins who she could never see again. It was a fact which hurt her tremendously. She couldn't appear as herself in Wonderland in case one of these relatives or an old friend from school decided to visit the park. It wasn't too far from her old home and was a popular attraction, so it wasn't impossible.

Because she was planning on rendezvousing with Mary and the Terrible Two, on this particular occasion she had to adopt the persona which they were familiar with from past meetings - that of Allison Knight, the "daughter" of her other alter ego, Amber Knight. According to the elaborate backstory she had constructed for her various incarnations, Allison Knight was staying with the Sherwoods, as her mother had before her, while her mother trotted around the globe doing humanitarian work for Doctors Without Borders. She attended a private school, which was why the girls never saw her at the local regional public high school that they attended. For the timeline of Allison being her own daughter to work, it meant that Amber would have given birth to her when she was 16! This would've made it quite difficult, but not impossible, for her to then go on to become a doctor, but Yolanda and Brittney didn't need to know about these little details that might stretch the credibility of her stories. She supposed that she had taken a small risk by creating a new identity linked to one of her older ones like that. But she figured that there were few people left in town who knew her as Amber Knight anymore, aside from a few of the librarians at the local library branch where she used to work as a volunteer when she was Amber. She doubted that the Terrible Two had ever stepped foot inside that place in their whole lives.

As Allison Knight, she wore glasses which she did not need and a wig of long, flowing red hair. The color of this wig was actually quite close to her natural hair color. Unfortunately, she had dyed her hair a platinum blonde color and cut it quite short prior to the accident that had claimed the life of her family. As a result, her hair, which no longer grew, was permanently stuck like that. The dye had faded a bit over the years, yet still persisted. This shade of red was a bit more vibrant than her original hue, which was more of an auburn color, yet not too far off from it. She also wore some of her old clothes from the period when she had first arrived at Sherwood Farms, clothes that were basically hip back in 1989. Fortunately for her, some of these old styles from the Eighties had become popular again, so she could get away with once again rocking the look that she felt most comfortable in. The downside to this was that it made her feel incredibly old to realize that she's now lived long enough to see these styles go out of fashion, then come full circle again.

As she landed on the other side of the fence, she examined her surroundings. She was in the large, disused part of the park where she liked to hang out during the off season. There was nobody else around, which was not unusual, it was extremely rare for her to encounter anyone else out here. Since she seemed to be alone, she felt that it was safe enough for her to display some more of her vampiric "gifts", so she broke into a run, moving at an inhuman speed that surely would've freaked out anyone who had seen it.

She wasn't sure why she was so eager to get into the park, since she'd have to put up with Brittney and Yolanda. Even though she didn't like them, she was still hurt by the fact that they didn't like her. She was also perhaps a bit offended by this because she had worked extra hard with Mary to figure out how to cover up some of her naivety regarding matters such as boys and current trends when crafting this persona for herself, yet it hadn't helped make her any more acceptable to the Terrible Two. Perhaps the two girls sensed that there was more to Allsion than meets the eye? Maybe they even sensed what she truly was and feared her on some instinctive level?

It was hard for her to believe that they were that perceptive, though. They were very much what she would've called "airheads" back in her day. She didn't think they were very smart, and they seemed to be lacking in individuality and personality. They were almost indistinguishable from one another, both in appearance and attitude. She despised how they swooned over unattainable teen idols and their high-pitched, tittering laughter which usually came at the expense of others, sounded evil to her ears. She hated to be so judgmental towards them; she'd *wanted* to like them, but she couldn't help it: sometimes you just had to call a turd a turd. Was it fair for her to blame them for their immaturity? Weren't they just acting their age? She supposed it just highlighted how little she really had in common with people "her own age" anymore, which was a painful reality for her to confront. Yet hadn't it always been that way? Even before her accident, she doubted that she would've wanted to hang out with girls like them. They were the kind of kids that used to make fun of her in her old school. A bunch of empty-headed slaves to trends that she had no respect for. They were just too self-absorbed and mean spirited to make for good companions.

And here she was, rushing off to go spend time with them! She hoped that Charles appreciated what she was doing for him, he owed her one. As she thought this she knew it wasn't true though, she was really there to be in her beloved Wonderland again, something that not even Yolanda and Brittney's unsettling presence could completely spoil for her. She also hoped that she could act as a counterbalance to their corrosive influence over Mary, something she couldn't possibly do if she'd continued to stay holed up in the manor. The Terrible Two might be infuriating, but she'd just have to try and find a way to ignore their excesses and make the best of the situation.

She gradually slowed her pace until she was again walking as she neared the part of the park that was open, easily slipping into it through the gap in the gate. Allison luxuriated in the freedom of moving about the park, reveling in the display of twisting, spinning rides - the faces of the people that were so alive with emotion.

Alive, she thought melancholically. *Maybe someday I will be again, too?*

Was it really such a vain hope? She thought of her condition as akin to a disease, and for every disease, wasn't there also the possibility of a cure? The trouble was that she didn't know how to go about finding such a cure. Maybe that was the real reason why she had immersed herself so deeply in the study of fictional vampires? Was she hoping to find some kernel of truth in all these made up stories that would tell her how to free herself of this curse? In some of these tales, all that was needed to end the curse was to destroy the "master vampire" - the original vampire that had first started the series of vampires that one was descended from. It was a recurring theme in several of these stories, so she'd wondered if there was any validity to it? But to hear William and Elizabeth tell it, the vampires that had spawned them were all nothing but dust now, yet this hadn't cured them of their condition. She sighed. It all seemed so hopeless sometimes, yet she *had* to cling to the idea that someday, somehow, she would find a way to get back to something more closely resembling a normal life. In the meantime, all she could do was try to enjoy the unique gifts of her inhuman life as best she could.

With this in mind, she stretched out her enhanced senses to take in the glorious life that surrounded her. As she moved through the shadows of a ride that was temporarily closed down for maintenance, she could sense the presence of a pair of young lovers embraced in a secret passion within. She could hear their racing heartbeats, smelled the intermingled scents of perfume and sweat long before her eyes found their forms shrouded in the darkness. She couldn't help but stare a little as she passed them, the intensity of her gaze scorching the huddled pair as they swiftly pulled apart in embarrassment at their discovery. With a rueful smile, she hoped that they understood just how fortunate they were. How she longed to find herself in that sort of a situation someday! Did any of them understand what they really had? The endless possibilities that were open to them which seemed forever closed off to her? Had *she* understood such things before she had lost them? No, you never seem to be able to really appreciate such things until they're gone. That was the cruel irony of existence.

Her continued probing of her environment eventually led her to her quarry. Near a food trailer with the name "King Frank's" emblazoned in neon over it, she heard the familiar, irritating sound of Brittney's laughter...or was it Yolanda's? What was the difference anyway?

"Hey, Al!" Mary called to her as she trotted towards her. The Terrible Two were in tow, both stuffing their faces with hot dogs they'd apparently recently purchased from King Frank's. She watched in disgust as the pair chewed with their mouths open and moving with the speed of a runaway freight train. Yolanda was still giggling about something or other, and began to gag on her wiener. They were probably laughing over how Mary had called her "Al". Her nickname always seemed to induce convulsions of laughter in them, although she doubted that either of them even knew what a convulsion was - the word had too many syllables to be a part of their lexicon. She guessed that "Al" sounded like it was too masculine of a nickname to their unsophisticated ears.

"Mary!" Allison called with genuine glee, despite the pair of cackling, choking demons accompanying the girl. She ran up to her and gave her a brief hug. Mary quizzed Allison about how long she'd been there, and offered to buy her a bite to eat from King Frank's. This was mainly just for show, Allison's body couldn't really process normal human food anymore, as she was basically a magically animated, incorruptible corpse. Eating and drinking her favorite foods was one of the things she missed the most about being truly alive. Whenever she'd tried to eat them in the past, she'd become violently ill and just ended up throwing it all back up. She didn't even try anymore, it simply wasn't worth it.

If Brittney hadn't been so busy gorging herself, she probably wouldn't have missed the opportunity to taunt her friend by asking her if she could afford to buy a hot dog for Allison on her father's salary as a butler. She liked to tease Mary about her father's profession, despite the fact that her own father probably made less than Charles, who was actually quite well paid for his services. They saw something inherently degrading about Charles's servile occupation, not understanding the depth of the true nature of his relationship to the Sherwoods. Allison couldn't understand why Mary put up with them disrespecting her father like that. Was she really that desperate for the newfound popularity she'd won from hanging out with them?

Yolanda announced that she needed to go to the bathroom, and convinced Mary and Brittney to go with her. Allison, of course, no longer had any need to do such things, and even if she did, she didn't see why a trip to the lavatory had to be a group activity. The other girls went to the bathrooms located behind King Frank's, and Allison stayed behind, sitting down at a vacant picnic table nearby to wait for them. She waited. And waited. And waited.

Jesus! What the hell are they doing in there? she thought testily.

They must've been gone for something like fifteen minutes. Finally, Allison could stand it no longer and entered the low, concrete slab of a building that served as the restrooms for this section of the park. She found nothing inside but the pungent stench of human urine, no trace of the other girls.

Great, they ditched me! she thought with disdain, feeling betrayed by the fact that the others had somehow convinced Mary to go along with this.

She considered trying to locate them again. With her enhanced senses, it wouldn't be very difficult.

Ah, fuck 'em! she thought bitterly.

She didn't want to be part of any party where she obviously wasn't wanted. She could have a better time without them anyway, and that's exactly what she would do, to spite them. Sure she had promised Charles that she'd keep an eye on them, but she'd tried hadn't she? Besides, it was inevitable that she'd cross paths with them again sometime before the night was through, then she'd *really* give Mary a piece of her mind! But in the meantime, she could enjoy being free of the Ditzy Duo and the responsibility of babysitting Mary.

Some inner instinct now drove her into Wonderland's large and crowded video game arcade; before she was even conscious of it, she was inside. She exchanged a few of her dollars for tokens and decided to get in a few games of Dance Dance Revolution, which was her favorite game in the whole place. Thankfully, despite the fact that the place was packed, nobody seemed to be playing it at the time. It was all hers!

She moved up through a few levels of the game easily. Because of her great speed and superhuman reflexes, the game wasn't quite as much of a challenge to her, especially in these early levels, as it would be to a normal person. Nonetheless, she enjoyed the workout and the dancing. Truth to tell, she didn't enjoy *all* of the music used in the game, as she was still very hung up on the music of her own era. With each passing year, it seemed to be harder and harder for her to find any new popular music that she really enjoyed.

Ah well, it is what it is, she thought.

All of the sudden, she found herself feeling extremely lightheaded and dizzy. For one terrible moment, she was certain that she would collapse right then and there amidst all the honking, beeping machines being fed their coppery meals by the overenthusiastic patrons of the arcade. As quickly as it has come upon her, the feeling subsided until it was nothing but a dull uneasiness in the back of her head. Not a particularly bad uneasiness, mind you, just a sense that something was up and she needed to keep an eye out for whatever that might be. She recognized this sensation as what Elizabeth and William had explained as a "vampiric sixth sense", although Allison, ever the nerd, preferred to think of it as her "spidey-senses tingling".

According to the Sherwoods, this sense was triggered whenever a vampire was in the presence of another supernatural being. She felt it all the time at home when she was in the company of her fellow vamps, and had learned to ignore it in those instances. There had been a few other occasions when she had experienced it outside of the confines of the manor, like when she had been hanging out in the town's graveyard, doing rubbings of some of the old gravestones and it had been triggered by a ghost she'd encountered there.

Meeting a ghost was always a fascinating experience for her, she could always see them quite clearly, as she herself was permanently stuck somewhere between life and death. Unfortunately, most of the ghosts she had met were pretty shitty conversationalists with no real insights to give her on whatever it is that may or may not lay beyond the veil of death. Most of them were *very* confused about where they were and what was going on around them, and barely seemed to know who they were anymore. Most ghosts had very one-track minds, being hopelessly hung up on their routines. Allison imagined that talking to ghosts was probably a lot like speaking with someone who suffered from an extreme case of dementia and expecting to get a straight answer out of them.

However, this didn't feel like a ghost. Or at least, not *just* a ghost. It felt *different* somehow, like something she'd never experienced before. The distraction of her spidey-senses going off had temporarily thrown her off her game, causing her to lose. She cursed at this latest development as she fished around in the pockets of her shorts for more tokens, quickly scanning her surroundings for whatever it was that had set it off like that. Her spidey-senses were *still* tingling, after all.

That's when she saw him. There was a guy staring at her rather intently off to one side of the game platform. He looked like he was about her age. Her *apparent* age, she corrected herself. His gaze would be almost creepy if he wasn't so dang cute. How long had he been there, watching her like that? She had been so focused on her game that she hadn't noticed him. He was a little taller than she was, which is to say that he wasn't that tall at all. He was a bit on the thin side, with deep brown eyes, and short black hair that had hints of brown and even a little red in it. His skin was a light bronze color and he looked like he might be of Hispanic descent. He had a somewhat long nose, but it wasn't terribly out of proportion with the rest of his face, nor was it unpleasantly pointy or beak-like, but rounded off quite nicely at the end. His lips looked particularly kissable. All in all, she liked what she saw. She probably would've been blushing at the way he was looking at her if she was still capable of such bodily reactions. She didn't sense any ill intent from him in the way he looked at her. In fact, his expression seemed to be hovering on a kind of reverence, although she could also feel an ever present kind of melancholy right below it.

Intriguing, she thought. She liked a good mystery.

Then she saw *her.* There was a ghost there too, standing near him. And what a ghost! This one was a total mess. It was a girl who looked like she was maybe a little older than Allison appeared to be. She could tell that she'd once been quite beautiful in life, but now she looked as if someone had run her through a blender. And she was completely naked to boot. The ghost saw that Allison was looking right at her, and she appeared to be startled by that. The ghost turned away and began to slowly walk out of the arcade, passing right through several of the customers as she made her way out. Even though she was now gone, the buzzing at the back of Allison's head continued, almost as strongly as it had before.

The boy definitely seemed to be what was still triggering her spidey-senses. So it hadn't just been the ghost. But if he was another kind of supernatural creature like she was, then what *was* he? What was up with that gory-looking girl ghost that was hanging around him, and whose presence he'd seemed to be completely oblivious to? She *had* to find out.

Kevin was in awe of her. He had found himself coming to a stop in front of the Dance Dance Revolution game. He was immediately overcome with a sensation he hadn't felt in over a week the moment he laid eyes on her - a feeling of great calm and peace, bliss, even, as he watched, utterly spellbound at this wisp of a girl dancing in perfect time to the prompts of the game. He couldn't believe that she wasn't drenched in sweat, considering the breakneck pace of her movements and how hot and stuffy it was in this place. Was she what he seemed to be being led towards? His feelings told him that she was, although he couldn't understand why. He just knew that all of the sudden, all of the anger and tension that had been bubbling up inside of him for the past several days, threatening to spill out, had evaporated.

She wasn't bad looking either. She had long red hair and a round, pixieish face, with sparkling green eyes. Her skin was deathly pale, which was odd considering that it was still summer. He guessed that she must not get out very much. However, he'd never found pale girls to be sickly or unattractive, in fact they reminded him of those beautiful old marble statues from Ancient Greece. Her style of dress was decidedly old-school, like something from the Eighties, but he kind of liked it, he had always had something of a fascination with the past. He was shocked that her glasses didn't fly off of her face the way she was jumping around. He liked the glasses too. Even though he was smart enough to know that wearing glasses didn't mean that a woman was intelligent (it just meant that she had bad eyesight) he tended to associate glasses with smart women. He preferred his women to be on the brainy side. I was silly, he knew lots of people who wore glasses that were total idiots, but he still couldn't help but be turned on by a woman in glasses. She had a nice, round ass, too, he thought wolfishly. And she sure knew how to move it!

Then he chastised himself. What was he thinking? Sylvia was barely cold in her grave, and here he was, already lusting after another girl! True, Sylvia hadn't *really* been his girlfriend, or even someone with whom he'd been in love; in fact, he'd really barely known her - but it still felt wrong somehow. He had no business thinking of his own pleasure like that. Such pleasures were something that forevermore had to be in his past. He didn't deserve to feel any kind of sexual gratification, or love, or any kind of joy whatsoever. He was a killer. A monster. It was obscene for him to have any of those happy things when he'd robbed Sylvia of the possibility of ever having them again. And she might just have been the first to suffer at his hands. It could happen again. He reminded himself once more how foolish, how irresponsible it was for him to be out there in public, around all these people when he still had no real understanding of what could trigger his transformations. He was a walking time bomb just waiting to explode. He had no business here! What was he *doing*?

Yet he *knew* what he was doing on some deeper level. He was here for her. But *why*? What did that actually mean? Was it something good or something bad that was leading him to her? Was she to be his savior, or his next victim? He was getting nothing but positive vibes from her, but maybe that's because the wolf inside of him was elated at the prospect of finally locating his next meal? Could he really afford to continue to hang around here and find out, for her sake?

Then she took the decision out of his hands.

"Hey! Are you just gonna stand around there all day watching me, or are you gonna get up here and try your luck against me?" she asked as her latest game came to an end and she noticed him looking at her.

His face blanched. He hoped he wasn't creeping her out too much. He now felt twice as guilty as he had before about how he'd been thinking about her butt.

"No, that's okay, really. Sorry if I was staring. You're just so good at this game!" he said nervously, ignoring the fact that there was a part of him which wanted nothing more in the world at that moment than to join her on that platform.

"Thanks! Don't be intimidated by that. I'm sure you've got some nice moves of your own." She smiled at him, and he couldn't help but be struck by what a beautiful smile it was, full of promise.

"No, I couldn't, I uh, don't have any tokens," he said lamely as he started to back away.

She reached out with uncommon speed and caught his arm in a surprisingly strong grip. Her touch was as icy as the cold embrace of the grave.

Cold hands, warm heart, he thought. It was one of those strange sayings that old people were so fond of constantly repeating. It had just popped into his head out of nowhere.

He felt an electric tingle of excitement at the sudden contact, hating himself for it.

"No worries, I've got ya covered, man!" she said as she pulled him up onto the platform before he knew what was happening. He was amazed at how strong she was, especially for such a tiny girl.

Before he could protest any further, she was already putting tokens into the machine, enough for a two player game.

Oh well, might as well go along with it, Kevin thought, although he was actually quite thrilled by the prospect. Mostly because he wanted to spend some time with this girl. She was a little pushy, a little forward, but that was something he liked in a woman. He *did* like this game, too. He'd played an earlier version of it on a vacation at the shore a few years back. He wasn't all that great at it, and would likely make a fool of himself in front of her while trying to keep up, but it didn't seem as if she was going to take "no" for an answer.

"I've got this," he said with a confidence that he didn't actually feel, as the game started up. "I mean, it's basically kind of just like a giant game of Simon, isn't it?"

"Simon? Oh, I *love* me some Simon! I'm surprised you know what that is!" Allison remarked. "Simon" of course, was a handheld electronic game that had been popular in the late Seventies and into the Eighties. It got its name from Simon Says, as it had the same premise: the game would light up a series of colored buttons in a pattern which players had to copy, and the game got faster and more manic as it went along. Kevin was correct to say that Dance Dance Revolution was similar, players had to follow a sequence of arrows that appeared on the screen before them, then step on the corresponding arrows on the dance platform in the same order. As the levels went higher, the dances became ever more sophisticated and fast paced.

"They still make Simon. They just came out with a new version," he informed her. He'd barely spoken to another human being in the past week, he was shocked at how easy it was to talk to her. It was like talking to an old friend, like they'd always known one another.

"Cool. I haven't seen that one yet," Allison replied as she followed along with the instructions on the screen.

Kevin was pleasantly surprised to find that it was quite easy to keep up with the game, effortless even. He'd never been that good at this game in the past, he wondered if this newfound agility was yet another change that his body was going through as a result of the curse he now found himself under? In the past week he'd discovered that he was not only physically stronger, but could also see in the dark almost better than he could in daylight. It wasn't just his night vision that had improved lately, but all of his senses, from hearing to smelling, which was as much of a blessing as a curse in certain situations.

It wasn't long before they began moving up through the levels of the game.

"My name's Allison, in case you were wondering. And you are?" she asked as she continued to dance without missing a beat.

Kevin realized that he couldn't tell her his actual name, which could be plastered on the sides of milk cartons for all he knew, along with his last class picture. He said the first thing that popped into his mind, even though it sounded incredibly stupid to him once he said it out loud.

"The Lone Ranger, at your service, ma'am."

"Oh, a real man of mystery, huh? Now I really *am* surprised that you know who the hell the Lone Ranger is," Allison told him earnestly, as the character had lapsed into obscurity. The world was still several years away from the next failed attempt to revive the franchise.

"I used to watch reruns all the time with my Grandpa. I'm kinda into all that old, retro stuff. It's cool," he explained between dance steps.

Old retro stuff! Ouch! Allison thought, suddenly feeling a little dated herself, until she remembered that even in the Eighties that show had been ancient history. Still, she felt like the kids of her generation generally had a better cultural awareness of the stuff that their parents and grandparents had been into than most of the kids she ran into nowadays did. This guy certainly didn't fit into that mold though, which was nice.

"So, are you gonna give me a silver bullet when this game is over, Kemosabe?" she joked.

Kevin suddenly looked serious at the mention of a silver bullet.

I wish I knew how to get my hands on one, lady! I'd put it in my own head if I could! he thought grimly. Maybe that's why he'd told her he was the Lone Ranger, he wished he was a man with a silver bullet.

"No, ma'am. I'm afraid I'm fresh out of 'em," he said in a cheesy accent that couldn't conceal the sadness beneath his words.

Allison sensed the sudden change in his demeanor and tried to cheer him up.

"See, I told you you had some nice moves! You're going to tire me out at this rate!" she said encouragingly, although she showed no real signs of slowing down and didn't seem the least bit winded. Although Kevin's brow was now heavy with perspiration, Allison's remained maddeningly dry.

"Thanks! You've got some pretty sweet moves yerself, little lady!" he responded, continuing to speak in his shamefully bad attempt at a western drawl.

Her eyes narrowed. "Little Lady, huh? It's a good thing I like you so much - if any one else dared to call me a little lady, I'd deck 'em!" she fired back, then immediately regretted it.

Shit! Did I really just say that out loud? Sometimes, she really didn't have much of a filter.

She decided that a change of subject was in order.

"I'll make you a deal - if you can make it through the next five levels without losing, you've gotta tell me your *real* name!" She could just use her hypnotic powers to force him to tell her, but she really didn't think that using mind control on someone was the best way to start off what she hoped would be a nice relationship.

"Huh. And what do I get out of it?" he asked.

Anything you want! is what she wanted to say, but thankfully she found the self control not to blurt that out this time.

"You will have earned my undying respect." *Emphasis on the "undying" part,* she thought with a smile.

"You've got yourself a deal then, pardner," he told her. Of course he had no intention of telling her his real name, although he certainly *wanted* to, and had the feeling that she was someone he could trust, under more normal circumstances. Unfortunately, nothing about his current circumstances in life could be described as remotely normal. However, he figured it wouldn't be too difficult to come up with a more convincing pseudonym for himself than "The Lone Ranger".

"Just make *me* a deal that you'll stop using that accent!" Allison laughed.

"It's that bad, huh?"

"Yes! Omigod, it's the worst!"

They both laughed now. When was the last time he had laughed? It felt like a lifetime ago.

They blasted through the next few levels in a few minutes. Even when he was dancing to some of the terrible songs in the game, he couldn't help but have a good time in her presence. Being with her felt so natural. For a brief moment he forgot all about his guilt, his shame, his self loathing and fear. For an all-too -hort, shining sliver of time, he was just a normal teenager again, playing a video game with a girl he liked and trying to impress her in his own awkward, decidedly dorky manner.

"So, give it up. What's your real name?" she asked when they got to the level that their agreement had hinged upon.

"Scott Summers," he answered. It was actually the name of a character from the X-Men comics and movies, a character who was actually kind of a dick, but Kevin still liked him anyway.

"What? Like Cyclops from the X-Men? You're shitting me!" Allison replied incredulously.

"No for real, my name really is Scott!" he protested. It wasn't a complete lie, either - it *was* his last name.

"Wait? You know the X-Men?" he asked. He'd goofed up and picked a fake name for himself that she was actually familiar with. Those characters weren't quite as obscure to the general public as they used to be. Why did he have to be such a terrible liar? It didn't bode well for his budding occupation as a fugitive.

"Well, not *personally* of course," she joked. "I started reading the comics after that first movie came out. I've been working my way back, reading collections of the older comics. I'm particularly fond of the Claremont/Byrne era." Her coolness factor in Kevin's eyes had just shot up a little more, if that was possible. He didn't know many girls back home who were into all that geeky stuff that he was into - or at least would admit that they were so readily.

"Yeah, that's some good stuff. The Dark Phoenix Saga, classic," he told her approvingly. *Christ! Where has this girl been all my life? Of course It's just my shitty luck that I'd meet the perfect girl now that I'm some kind of a monster. A monster who has no future. Who has nothing to offer to anyone but pain and death!*

It was around that time that Kevin noticed that their little competition had begun to attract a pretty sizable crowd. Some of them were doubtlessly just people patiently waiting their turn to play, but most of them seemed to be watching because they were astounded by their high score. Some of the people now huddled around the machine would occasionally shout words of encouragement at them. It was entirely possible that they were on the verge of setting some kind of record, for this arcade at least.

Allison had noticed the crowd too. It felt great to her, she thrived on the attention.Occasionally she'd respond to the crowd by saying something like "You ain't seen nothin yet!" or "If you think that's good, you should see what happens when I'm trying!" It would've been boastful grandstanding from anyone else, but she could actually back up her words with real action. The crowd seemed to be eating up her antics.

The crowd had the opposite effect on Kevin. It brought him back down from the natural high of playing the game with Allison and snapped him back to the cruel reality of the situation. He was a fugitive, he couldn't afford to be seen by all these people. It was a shame, he'd really enjoyed his time with Allison, but it had to end eventually. It was painfully obvious, even to someone with his low self-esteem, that she liked him, and the sentiment was definitely mutual on his part. There was no hope of a future with her anyhow, or with anyone for that matter. For her own safety, he'd have to stay away from her. Breaking off the game now and running away from her would probably confuse and disappoint her, but he saw no other way out of it. He didn't want to hurt her, but in this case it was unavoidable. Better to do it now before things got even more intense between the two of them. He hated himself for even leading her on like this to begin with. What had he been thinking?

He turned to her, his face red with exertion and his voice suddenly heavy with emotion. "I've loved hanging out with you, but I really have to go now. I'm sorry!" With those words, he jumped off the game platform, almost colliding with one of the spectators as he did so and began fighting his way through the crowd. He couldn't even bring himself to look at her face as he'd said it, doing so would've made it impossible for him to leave.

"Wait! What?" came Allison's shocked reply. "Jesus! Ditched twice in the same night! Is my breath *really* that bad?" she quipped as she watched the top of his head moving through the congested gaggle of people and out of the arcade. She was so distracted by the unexpectedly dramatic exit that she had stopped paying attention to the game and began to lose as she just stood there watching him leave, her mouth hanging open in bewilderment.

"Who *was* that masked man?" she wondered aloud, unable to resist uttering the customary phrase that people always said as they watched the Lone Ranger ride off into the sunset, even if nobody around her knew what the hell she was talking about.

We didn't even get to put our names in for the high score, she thought sadly as the screen now prompted her to do so. She decided that she wasn't going to let him get away from her that easily. She'd better act now while she still had a decent chance of catching up to him.

"Well folks, I think I've hogged this thing enough for one night, it's about time I let someone else have a chance," she told her equally perplexed group of onlookers as she stepped off the platform. Some of them clapped as she made her way off of it. She couldn't help but make a little bow and blow kisses at some of them. The game had churned out an impressive number of tickets that could be exchanged for prizes during their epic session One of the girls who'd been watching her play gathered them up in her arms and shouted after Allison.

"Your tickets! Don't forget them!"

"Keep 'em!" Allison hollered back. She wasn't going to let such trivialities slow her down, besides, most of the prizes offered here kinda sucked anyway. She had to concentrate on Kevin's scent, considering how much sweat had been pouring off of him during the game, that wasn't terribly difficult. He sort of reeked, but in a nice, manly sort of way. She had no problem tracing his path through the arcade, but it did take her a painfully long time to make it out of the place, as it was entirely too packed in there. Being as petite as she was, she was constantly jostled and tossed around by the people around her. It was almost as bad as being in a mosh pit.

Finally, she made it out of the arcade and took a deep breath of relief, more out of habit than any actual need for air. One of the many strange facts she'd discovered about how her body worked now (or perhaps that should be *didn't* work) was that she had no actual need to breathe. It certainly made trips to the ocean more fun for her, as she could spend as much time as she liked exploring the world under the waves. After allowing herself that one short rest, she began jogging off in the direction of Kevin's smell, guided not only by his scent, but by her spidey-senses, which were still all abuzz. What would she do when she caught up with him? Ask him for his number? Confront him with the knowledge that she knew that there was something supernatural about him?

She really had no idea, all she knew was that she had to find him, she had to understand *what* he was. It was more than that, too. She liked him, she *wanted* him. Although she knew how ridiculous and impractical an idea that was, she still couldn't completely push it out of her mind, couldn't help but fantasize about kissing him, holding him. She'd felt like maybe he'd wanted her too, or was that just her own vanity talking? Well, at least he *had* wanted her, until he'd decided to bolt. She was thinking, no, *hoping* that he'd done that because the crowd had spooked him, and not her. Maybe she had been coming on a little too strongly, she knew that some guys don't appreciate that sort of approach, yet it had seemed to her that he'd been enjoying her attention. Whatever the reason for him running off like he had, no matter what they might mean to each other, she knew one thing: she had no intentions of letting their story end like this.

CHAPTER 7:

TEMPTATION

O nce he was out of the arcade, Kevin had run through the park until he realized *that* might attract unwanted attention as well, so he slowed himself down to a fast walk. He glanced over his shoulder a few times to make sure that Allison wasn't following, feeling equal parts relieved and saddened that she wasn't. As soon as he was away from her, the wonderful feeling of calm and normalcy that he'd been able to recapture in her presence had fluttered away from him. The old familiar feelings of agitation at everything in the world around him came back full force. It was all he could do to stop himself from knocking the people around him to the ground as he tried to make his way past them and back to the safety of his tunnel.

Worst of all, he couldn't stop thinking about her. Was this what love at first sight was like? He didn't know. He didn't think that he'd ever really been in love yet. He didn't believe the whole love at first sight thing anyway, it seemed like far too much of a silly, overly romantic notion to him. Wishful thinking. Real love took time, it took getting to know someone, didn't it? Yet there *was* some kind of a powerful, instant connection that he'd felt with her, and he'd been sure that she'd felt it too. There was no denying that he'd been led to her for some reason. She might even be the whole reason why he was here in Davenport to begin with. But why? He wanted nothing more than to find out, but he couldn't allow himself that luxury. He didn't deserve whatever happiness she might be able to give him, and he was far too dangerous to be around anyone. As hard as it might be, as *impossible* as it seemed to him right now, he'd just have to force himself to forget about her.

Love at first sight! What bullshit! He was in a very emotionally vulnerable place right now - was it really all that surprising that in his current mental state he'd latch onto the first person to show any interest in him like this? Attaching too much importance to her kindness and romanticizing the whole thing? Surely he was confusing his carnal physical attraction to her with something more meaningful? No, she was just some random, silly girl and he was reading entirely too much into the whole situation. He tried to tell himself all of these things, over and over again, but he couldn't make himself *truly* believe them no matter how often he repeated them in his head.

As he typically did when he was feeling upset, he laid himself down and tried to sleep. It was the closest thing he had to an "off switch" for all of his nasty, racing thoughts. He'd never had much of a problem falling asleep, in fact it was something that had always come so easily to him that he sometimes wondered if he was mildly narcoleptic. That night, it was especially easy because he was so worn out from playing the game and the hurried pace of his flight back to the tunnel. Once he was back in the tunnel's maintenance closet, he practically passed out on the makeshift bed he'd made for himself in one corner. Soon, he found himself surrendering to the sweet oblivion of sleep.

Allison followed his trail into the same unused portion of the park that she'd passed through hours earlier and right up to the black entrance of the Tunnel of Love. She smiled slightly at the irony of the trail ending here. She vaguely recalled being too scared to go on this ride as a little kid, even with her parents by her side. Right up to the present day she'd always studiously avoided it during her past explorations of this part of the park. She almost laughed out loud at the irrationality of her fears. What was she afraid of? Monsters lurking inside? *She* was the only monster in this equation. Despite all of this, she still gulped a little as she began to nervously move towards the entrance until she was engulfed by its unremitting darkness.

Was she really the only monster here? He definitely had his secrets. He'd been so evasive about giving out his name. She was sure that he was still lying to her when he'd told her that he was "Scott Summers." She knew that there was something supernatural about this guy, aside from the fact that a ghost might've attached herself to him. Allison sure didn't relish the idea of possibly bumping into that gross looking ghost in this spooky old tunnel. So far so good though, no bloody, naked girls were lurking around in here as far as she could tell. Was he a monster too? Maybe even a vampire like her? Was the ghost one of his victims? Geez, she hoped not. He seemed like too nice of a guy to do something like that to someone, yet Allison knew all too well how difficult it was to control the peculiar sorts of *hungers* that afflicted her kind. She knew that her family was the exception and not the rule when it came to preying on normal humans.

Maybe he'd run off in order to protect Allison from himself? But surely he should've sensed that there was something otherworldly about her too if he truly was a fellow vampire? He didn't *feel* like a vampire to her, but how could she really be sure? After all, the only other vampires that she'd ever met were Elizabeth and William. Maybe there were other types of vampires out there, different breeds who gave off a completely different kind of psychic impression than they did? Of course he might not be a vampire at all. If he was some other kind of monster that she wasn't familiar with, she supposed that she might be putting herself in danger by chasing after him like this. Yet she'd felt no ill intentions coming from him, and she was confident that she was a pretty good judge of that sort of thing. She wasn't going to let the possibility of danger slow her down. She would not surrender to her fear. She'd get to the bottom of this little mystery no matter what.

She could see perfectly in the near total blackness. She felt foolish as she recalled her fear of this old tunnel, it really wasn't that bad. There was nothing at all to be scared of in here. His smell was *very* powerful here, almost overwhelming. It was oddly comforting to her. She could tell that he'd spent a great deal of time here. Funny that she'd never picked up on his presence before, considering how often she passed by this building. They must've just kept missing each other. Or maybe he hadn't been coming here until recently? She followed the trail to a small room off to one side of the tunnel, the door was cracked ajar slightly. Carefully, slowly, she crept up to it, mindful not to make any noise, and poked her head inside.

There he was, lying on the floor in one corner, covered in a few thin blankets. It looked like he was already asleep.

I must have tired him out, poor thing. He must've found our encounter very draining. I DO tend to have that effect on people!

She examined the rest of the room. There was a shapeless duffel bag sitting on the floor near where he slept. A stack of canned goods were arranged against one of the walls, with some kind of a mess kit nearby, along with several cans of something called "sterno - canned heat" and a little cylindrical camping stove. She'd never heard of sterno, but she guessed that was what he used for fuel to cook with. In another corner of the room was a pile of heavy chains. She wondered if they had always been in this room, left over from the days when this ride was still active or not. They looked pretty new, though. She wondered what the heck he was doing with those? As her eyes continued to move around the room, she spied a battered-looking skateboard leaning up against the wall and a copy of the local newspaper with a farmer's almanac sitting on top of it.

It was obvious that the boy was homeless. Probably a runaway. But what was he running away from? She risked opening the door wide enough for her to squeeze through into the tiny room. She squatted down near him, just watching him breathe.

It's just like me to fall for some guy and he turns out to be homeless. Yup, I sure can pick 'em!

Hold on a sec, who said anything about me falling for him? she thought.

She might like him, but she also knew all too well how impossible the idea of *really* being with him the way that she longed to be was. Maybe she shouldn't have flirted with him so aggressively? Hadn't it been cruel to lead him on, tease him with a possibility that simply couldn't be? No, she'd just have to settle for maybe having a nice new friend. A friend who could hopefully relate to her, "monster to monster", in ways that William, Elizabeth and especially Mary couldn't possibly hope to .That was still pretty good, that was something worth striving for, wasn't it? Yet as she watched him lying there slumbering, she couldn't help but dream of what it would be like to be with him romantically. It was hard for her not to reach out and stroke his hair, or his cheek.

There's no law against dreaming, is there? What's the harm? I'm not going to beat myself up for daydreaming about being with a cute guy! Daydreams are all I've got!

Then she recalled how she had initially found the way that he was watching her back in the arcade to be a little creepy. Now here *she* was having lurid fantasies about him while she watched him sleep.

Oy vey! she thought.

She'd just elevated creepiness to a whole new level! How could she possibly explain this if he woke up and saw her? He'd think she was some sort of an obsessive stalker or something for sure! He'd never want to have anything to do with her ever again, and she wouldn't really be able to blame him either! This was crazy!

Another part of herself whispered to her that she was a vampire now - *this* is what they did! She was a dark stalker of the night! He was damned lucky that she wasn't chowing down on his lifeblood right now. As she thought the words, she could hear the constant, rhythmic pounding of his heart, the sweet sound of the blood flowing through his body. She could almost taste it! Her mouth watered for it, she licked her lips at the prospect of making a meal of him. One thing was for sure, he was no vampire - vampires didn't have beating hearts like this, they didn't sweat, they didn't breathe. He might not be a vampire now, but he could become one. She could make him just like she was, then she wouldn't have to be alone anymore. They could be together forever, just like Elizabeth and William....

Stop it! This has gone too far! I need to get out of here, like now! I'm not that kind of a vampire! I've never been that kind of a vampire and I'm not about to become that kind of a vampire now! she thought angrily as she rose to her feet and stumbled back out into the tunnel. She was shaken to the core by how close she'd just come to breaking her rule about never doing to someone else what had been done to her.

That's when she saw her.

The ghost was back. She was standing at the other end of the tunnel, silhouetted against the moonlight, which was passing right through her. Allison knew she couldn't really hurt her, but she still almost jumped out of her skin at the terrible sight of her anyway. Just try walking through a dark, deserted old tunnel at night when the ghost of a girl whose body has been savagely torn to pieces suddenly appears before you and see if you're not at least a little bit frightened by it, even if you *are* a vampire yourself. Allison would've screamed for sure if she hadn't been so shocked by her presence.

But Allison being Allison, she tried to play it cool.

"Oh, there you are. I was wondering when you'd show up again," she whispered, the hoarseness of her voice ruining her pretense of nonchalance. The ghost turned and started to walk away from the tunnel and out into the field beyond.

Shit! Where's she off to now?

"Hey! Hold up!" Allison called after her and began running towards her. Because of her great speed, she was able to catch up with her in no time at all.

The ghost turned and looked at her. She was even more horrible to behold this close up.

"You can see me?" she asked in disbelief.

"Oh sure, sure. I see ghosts all the time. It's no big deal. I'm not quite alive myself, ya know," Allison said, still trying to keep things casual and not stare too hard in horrified fascination at the ghost's ugly, gaping, open wounds. She wasn't really succeeding.

"A ghost? Is that what I am now? Yeah, I guess that *does* make sense," the ghost said absently.

Oh boy, here we go. They're always so damned confused about being dead, Allison thought in annoyance. She'd have to try and get the ghost to focus somehow.

"Why are you following that guy back there?" She figured that there was nothing quite like the direct approach.

"Kevin? I guess I feel bad for him. He tried to save me, he really did. He feels awful about it all. He blames himself, I know he does. He even tried to kill himself. Lots of times. I saw the whole thing. I keep trying to tell him that it wasn't his fault, but he can't hear me for some reason."

Yeah, he can't hear you because you're a ghost! I just told you that! Allison thought in frustration. These damned ghosts were always in such a mental fog. At least now she knew what his real name was.

"Save you from what? What the hell happened to you? No offense, but you look rough, really, really rough."

"I...I can't talk about it! I don't even understand it myself! It all happened so fast! It was so *weird!* No! I can't relive it! I can't! It was so painful!" She was practically shrieking the words.

"Yeah, I can see that. It sure looks like it was!" Allison said, wrinkling her nose in distaste at the ghost's disturbing appearance.

"So painful! So horrible! No! No! I can't! I can't!" the ghost repeated, shaking her head violently. "I *won't!*"

Then she was gone.

Great, Al! Perfect! Make the ghost relive the most traumatic moment of her life! Great plan! No wonder she went away!

"Come back!" Allison shouted. "I'm sorry! We'll talk about something else, anything else! I promise! Don't go!"

But she was alone now, with only the cold fires of the distant stars burning away in the night sky to bear impassive witness to the scene.

Allison started walking dejectedly back towards Wonderland. She didn't know what to do now. Maybe she'd come back here tomorrow and see if she could find Kevin again. Although she was still scared about what she'd almost done to him a few minutes ago, she also felt like she was back in control now, that she wouldn't let something like that happen again. She was still determined to find out what was going on here. What was he? What had he tried (and apparently failed) to save the ghost girl from? Was whatever had ripped her body to pieces still lurking around somewhere? Was that the same thing that Kevin was trying to escape from?

She *had* to know!

Maybe if he was in some sort of trouble, being chased by some other kind of monster, she could help? Maybe she could protect him? She *wanted* to protect him.

In the meantime, Allison decided that she would try and find Mary and her two dimwitted companions. In all the excitement of recent events, she'd totally forgotten that Charles was expecting her to keep an eye on his daughter. It was yet another thing she'd found a way to bungle tonight.

Allison searched the whole park that night, yet she found no signs of Mary, Brittney or Yolanda. For the trail to have gone this cold, it meant that they must've left Wonderland quite some time ago. Finally giving in to the reality of the situation, she returned home, back to the stately old manor that was as much her happy refuge from the world as it was her prison.

Once she was back inside, Mary sought her out to offer an apology for ditching her. She laid all the blame on the Terrible Two, explaining how they'd run off and she'd been forced to go along with them or risk losing them in the crowd. Since Brittney was her ride home, she needed to keep up with her. Normally, Allison would have found such a story to be woefully inadequate to satisfy her. While it was true that Brittney was her ride, she could've always called her dad for a ride home, or just walked since they really didn't live all that far away from Wonderland. At the very least, she should've fought harder to convince the others to go back and find her. However, tonight, Allison let her off easy. She was so excited about the events of the night that she didn't really care very much about how Mary had abandoned her, she just wanted the ear of someone who she could share all the details of her latest escapade with.

So Allison filled her in on everything as they sat on the edge of Mary's bed. Well *almost* everything. She decided it would be best to leave out the part about how close she'd come to biting Kevin. There were some things she couldn't bring herself to share, even with someone she trusted as much as she trusted Mary.

Mary's bedroom was a complex mess. Socks, jeans, blouses and sundry other unmentionables were sprinkled throughout the floor, along with a coating of other assorted items, like old plushies and magazines. Interestingly, interspersed amongst this typical teenage clutter was the odd technical manual, soldering iron, diode or circuit board. Mary's hobby was electronics, a fact that she tried to hide from her friends to avoid their teasing. Mary swore that it was impossible for her to find anything if she tried to keep the room clean, so she didn't bother to do so unless things got so dire that Charles forced her to take care of it. As parents went, Charles was a bit of a pushover, even more so since Mary had lost her mother; it was a rare day when he found the courage to lay down the law with her.

"Naturally, when you find a guy who really interests you, it's one who literally lives in a cave!" Mary teased, shaking her head in disbelief.

"It's not a *real* cave. It's the tunnel of love from the old park," Allison corrected her.

"Oh yeah. I've been there. It's spooky as fuck," Mary told her matter of factly.

Allison's eyes boggled. "*You've* been back in the closed down part of the park?" She didn't think of Mary as being daring enough to go exploring out there.

"Of course! Every kid in this town has snuck into Wonderland at least once. You don't even have to hop over the fence like you do. There must be a dozen holes in that fence if you know where to look for 'em," Mary said, thinking how silly it was that Allison acted as if she owned Wonderland, as if she was the only one who was privy to any of its secrets.

"Just for the record, I do not 'hop' over fences. That's so unladylike. So unsophisticated. I do a *Grand Jeté* over them," Allison clarified haughtily.

Mary typically knew better than to indulge Allison's eccentricities, but her curiosity got the better of her this time.

"What does that even mean?" she asked in confusion.

"It's a ballet term for a particularly difficult type of jump, ya uncultured heathen!" Allison revealed in her own unique style.

"Geez, you *really* do read too many books!" Mary laughed.

"And you don't read enough of them! Aside from technical manuals, that is, and *those* don't count," Allison countered.

"There's more to life than just reading," Mary reminded her.

"Maybe for *you* there is," Allison said a little sadly.

Mary decided to change the subject. She didn't feel like traveling down this road of self-pity with Allison again right now.

"You're going to go back there again tomorrow to find him aren't you?"

"Indubitably!" came Allison's enthusiastic reply.

Mary knew better than to try and talk her out of it. Regardless, she still felt obligated to log her objections on the matter.

"Just be careful. It might be dangerous. You don't know anything about him, or *what* he might really be."

She was worried about the way he had tripped off Allison's sixth sense. Not to mention that he had the ghost of a half-eaten girl following him around, what was *that* all about? Whatever it was, it didn't sound good. Frankly, it sounded like nothing but trouble. Allison thought that she was the one who got saddled with babysitting Mary, but what she didn't understand was that just as often it was Mary who felt responsible for keeping Allison out of trouble.

Mary sighed. She felt like she had failed in that regard tonight. The consequences of that failure could lead to her friend getting hurt somewhere down the road, either physically, emotionally, or both. She often tried to make sure that Allison didn't do too much flirting when she went out to Wonderland. She did this partially to protect her friend (a friend who was really more like a sister to her) from the inevitable broken heart she'd get once she realized that her flirtations couldn't possibly go anywhere, and also to prevent any potential suitors from asking too many questions about Allison - questions which she couldn't ever possibly hope to answer with any degree of honesty. Mary had the same issue with her own attempts to date anyone. She had to keep them at arm's length. She couldn't let them come over the house to spend time with her, and she couldn't really tell them too many details about her home life.

Like any good member of the Brandon family, Mary found herself always instinctively protecting the Sherwood's secrets. It was something she attributed to how she'd been groomed to serve them since birth, like the three generations of Brandons before her. Yet despite all of her father's talk of family tradition, duty and friendship, Mary had no intentions of following in his footsteps. Although she loved the Sherwoods like her own family, she dreamed of escaping to a glamorous life in New York City, Los Angeles, Miami - anywhere but the insignificant little dot on the map that was Davenport. The prospect of spending the rest of her life in this gloomy old house, waiting hand and foot on a bunch of vampires and raising children to carry on the same meager ambition did not exactly fill her with glee.

Unfortunately, she couldn't imagine *how* to escape from this cycle she'd been born into. She really *did* love the Sherwoods, and she didn't want to abandon them. Who would help care for them when her father became too old to carry out his duties? How could they find a replacement for him who they could trust to keep their secrets? She had aunts and uncles who had been raised in the manor and were therefore in on the Sherwood's secrets, but they had rejected the family tradition. Some of them had kids, her cousins - in theory any of them could replace her father, but she doubted that they would be any more eager to do so than she was. Sometimes she felt ashamed for daring to dream about leaving the people that were as much her family as her own flesh and blood were. Yet at the same time, what was so horrible about wanting a better life for yourself? A life that *you* chose for yourself, rather than one that somebody else laid out for you to follow?

Allison was the only person she could trust with such treasonous thoughts. Brittney and Yolanda were good for a few laughs, but the buck stopped there. She couldn't really confide in them the way that she could with Allison. Mary hung out with them because she needed to escape from the drab monotony of the manor every once in a while to lose herself in the world of parties, boys and fun that they could open her up to. She wanted to live a little before she got stuck in another kind of world, the world of bills, responsibilities, and more bills. It was a world that was getting closer to her with every passing day. In her own way, Mary was as cursed by her circumstances as Allison was, and Allison was the only other person who could truly understand that. She was also the only person Mary could trust her true self with, that she didn't feel like she had to dumb herself down to fit in with. Allison would never make her feel like she was weird because she was more interested in tinkering around with circuits than she was in learning new ways to apply makeup or style her hair.

"My dear Mary. I'm *always* careful. Besides, I'm a vampire. There's not much that can hurt me," Allison intoned with an air of cool confidence.

It irritated Mary how Allison seemed to think that being a vampire made her completely invulnerable to harm. It was time she gave her a refresher course.

"Uh huh. Yeah. Nothing much can hurt you. Just stakes, and fires, and garlic, and weapons made of pure metals. Oh! And attacks from other monsters, don't forget about that one!" Mary said, ticking off each vulnerability on her fingers as she listed them. She was familiar with these weaknesses from William's stories of the old days, before he and Elizabeth had come to America and founded Sherwood Farm. Out of all these weaknesses, the garlic always struck her as the oddest. Why garlic? That was just weird.

"Yeah, but at least it's not sunlight, crucifixes, holy water or any of that bullshit!" Allison answered. She was the sort of girl who always had an answer for everything. Not always a *good* answer, but an answer nonetheless.

"Seriously, Al, I'm worried. He's got to be some other kind of supernatural creature, or he wouldn't be setting off your senses like he did." Mary was almost worried enough to tell the Sherwoods about all of this. If there was some other kind of supernatural being running around town, William and Elizabeth were the best qualified to deal with it, yet she knew she wouldn't tell them. She couldn't break the bond of trust she had with Allison like that. They kept too many of one another's secrets. Allison would never forgive her and she couldn't bear to be without her friendship.

"I told you, I didn't sense any bad vibes coming from him. The ghost said that he tried to save her, that means he's one of the good guys. C'mon! This is the most interesting thing to ever happen in this town! You can't possibly expect me to just ignore it!"

Mary knew better than to keep arguing the point, doing so would just further agitate Allison and make her even more resolved to forge ahead with whatever crazy idea she was formulating. She tried to think of something more pleasant. She wanted to be happy for her friend, to feel her excitement, but all she could feel was fear for what the immediate future might hold. Nothing could dismiss the overwhelming sense of dread that was descending over her, as if they were all dangling on the edge of some impending disaster, a disaster which none of them could avoid.

132

CHAPTER 8:

DEATH COMES TO DAVENPORT

Brittney Morgan snapped the leash onto Mr. Fluffy's collar. The dog skipped around in excited anticipation of the coming walk. Even though he was a small dog, Brittney had to fight hard to keep him from yanking her in the wrong direction as she tried to steer him towards the door. He wanted to go out, but he was so wound up about it that he couldn't seem to focus long enough to go in the right direction. Brittney was pretty eager to get out of the house herself. Eager to escape the shouting voices of her parents. They were fighting over money *again.*

It was a common problem in their household. Her mother was a woman of extravagant tastes who enjoyed all the finest things in life and expected her father to provide these to her. He owned the largest used car lot in the county, yet even when business was good, he struggled to give her mother the sorts of things she demanded. Unfortunately, sales had been down lately, making it doubly difficult to satisfy her. It also didn't help that her father liked to squander his money on gambling whether or not times were tight. It was becoming more and more of a problem as the years wore on, and it was something that he steadfastly refused to get any help for. Sometimes, Brittney thought that the only thing keeping them together as a family was herself and her younger brother. She got the distinct impression that her parents were only staying together for the sake of their children, and anything resembling love between them had been lost long ago.

So it was with some relief that she stepped outside to take Mr. Fluffy on his nighttime walk. The sounds of strife and domestic turmoil subsided as soon as she shut the back door behind her, replaced only with the blissful silence of the night. The moon was bright out tonight, almost full. It illuminated her path with its cold, silvery light as she made her way around the side of the large house, down the driveway and into the street. She breathed in the cool, fresh night air as she was yanked forcefully forwards by an overeager Mr. Fluffy.

It was too bad that she'd had to come home so soon. She wished she could've spent more time at Wonderland tonight but her overprotective father had imposed a curfew on her that she found to be particularly harsh. It wasn't that she had any great love for Wonderland, it just beat the hell out of coming home to all of this unwanted drama, and there really wasn't anywhere else in town to hang out. She dreaded the approach of the off season, when she wouldn't even have Wonderland to take refuge in. She couldn't really go to Yolanda's house, as her mother was too much of a neat freak who suffered from some type of OCD condition to ever allow company in the house. She couldn't really go to Mary's house either. Her family's employers, the Sherwoods, also didn't allow company. It was a pity, she would've liked to have been able to explore that rambling old mansion that they lived in. She imagined that it was full of trap doors and secret passageways like something out of an episode of *Scooby Doo*. But the Sherwoods were notoriously private and reclusive. She could count the number of times she'd seen them around town in her whole life on one hand. She considered herself lucky that they were gracious enough to allow her to wait in the foyer of the grand old place sometimes when she stopped by to pick up Mary. It had been all she could do to stop herself from wandering around and checking out the rest of the mansion while she waited for her friend.

Mary was a bit of a weirdo, she thought. She didn't seem to be all that interested in the same sorts of things that most of her other friends were. Brittney had to take her under her wing and educate her on how to do some of the most basic things to help her fit in better at school. She wondered if she had done so out of pity for her, or out of curiosity about the Sherwoods and her connection to them. Her interest in the Sherwood family was probably something she picked up from her mother, who seemed to be particularly envious of their large house and estate. It was clear that her mother wanted to live like the Sherwoods someday, that she was almost obsessed with the idea. Being the richest family in town, the Sherwoods were the yardstick of success by which her mother measured herself and continually found herself to be wanting.

Brittney's interest in the Sherwoods did *not* extend to Allison, however, whom she found to be creepy and annoying.That girl never seemed to shut up, and she couldn't understand half of what she said anyway. It was like she thought that she was *sooooo* much smarter than the rest of them, always using big words and referring to things that were way before her time. She was just a big show off. She wasn't even a *real* Sherwood anyway. Just some distant cousin that they'd been saddled with taking care of while her mother went galavanting across the globe. No wonder her mother had abandoned her, Brittney couldn't blame her. If she ever had a child who was that annoying, she'd try to get as far away from them as possible too! She was glad that they'd managed to get rid of her tonight.

All these thoughts swirled in her head as she led Mr. Fluffy down the quiet, tree-lined road. Where they lived might not be Sherwood Farm, but they still managed to live in style, with lots of privacy. There were few other houses around in this neighborhood, if you could even call it that. She enjoyed the peace and the solitude as it was such a welcome contrast to the ceaseless chaos inside her house. However, she had wandered pretty far down the lane and was beginning to wonder if Mr. Fluffy would ever find a spot good enough for him to bless with the dubious honor of receiving his number one or his number two. Finally, the dog came to a stop and assumed a familiar squatting position.

Number two it is then, Brittney thought as she averted her gaze, determined to give the animal some privacy.

It was then when the Hunter, who had been watching her from afar though the nearby woods for some time now became sure of it: she definitely had the scent of the undead about her, it was carried to his sensitive nose by a sudden gust of wind. It was a weak smell, yet unmistakable. This delicious-looking little thing had been in the presence of one of the bloodsuckers, and recently too. So his instincts *had* been correct. There *were* vampires in this town. Unlike his failure from the day before, when he had been so sure that he had found one, only to instead find a recently abandoned farm, there was no doubt that they were still here, somewhere nearby. The feeling that had driven him all across this unremarkable little state for the past few weeks had really been leading him to this town all along.

He thought about trying to capture the girl, interrogate her to find out where the vampire was, or perhaps he should say *vampires,* since the instinct that had driven him here was so strong that it had to mean that there was an entire group of them nearby. He knew that this group was not *them.* Not the enemy. Whoever they were, they felt different from the enemy. He could tell that much, even from this distance. They also felt somewhat familiar, like someone he'd met long ago, if only he could remember! The scent he was getting now was something new though. It belonged to one that he was sure he'd never encountered in the old days. It was quite possible that this child might not have had any idea that she had recently been in the company of one of the undead. All the ones that had managed to survive for this long without the aid of his Master were maddeningly good at blending in with the humans.

He didn't need her to find the bloodsuckers! He was so close, the signal was so strong, it was inevitable that he'd trace it back to its source. He was so confident of it that he resolved to contact the Master later that night and ask him to join him here. He'd ask him to bring all of the rest of them with him too, since he didn't know how many of the undead were hiding out in this one-horse town. No, this girl was good for nothing but a meal. Besides, he was in no mood for asking questions that she'd likely be too panicked by his appearance to answer anyway. There was no point to it. And it was rude to play with your food like that, wasn't it? His master despised rudeness. Mustn't do anything that might upset the Master.

How long had it been? How many days since he'd last feasted on the tender young flesh of a human? At least a week now. And *that* experience had sadly been cut short by circumstances beyond his control. Such a shame, too. That girl had been particularly tasty, her body still tingling with the delicious energy of her recent sexual escapades as he'd consumed her. It had been sweet, so sweet until he'd been rudely interrupted, forced to leave his meal half eaten, his great hunger unsatiated. He didn't like to think of his failure on that occasion. It was best to forget about it. If his Master ever learned of it, he'd be furious with him and punish him for sure. It was better to banish it from his mind completely, so his Master couldn't rip it out of his head later and use it against him.

Tonight would be different, he was sure of it. He couldn't feel the enemy nearby. If *they* were here in this town too, they were too far away to do anything to him right now. There was nobody to stop him from claiming what he wanted. He would feed tonight, and feed well. Oh yes, he'd feed upon his favorite delicacy until he'd had his fill.

His yellow eyes burned with a desperate desire as he crept silently forth through the underbrush, slinking towards his prey.

"Mr. Fluffy! Stop it! What's gotten into you? Bad dog! Bad!" Brittney shouted as the canine erupted into a chorus of non-stop barking and reared up in the direction of the woods. She strained to keep hold of his leash.

Damn that pathetic little thing! I'll not be cheated out of my meal by the likes of you! the Hunter thought as he blasted out of the murky shadows of the forest and into the air.

He landed right on top of Brittney and immediately began rending the meat off of her forearms as she instinctively brought them up to try and shield her face. She shrieked in terror as he bit deep into her. Her fear released hormones that only served to sweeten the taste of her flesh, yet he knew he couldn't allow her to go on screaming like this. With one particularly cruel twist of his snout, he removed her larynx with practiced precision. The little dog continued to bark and run up to nip at him, then dart away. This was another annoyance he'd have to deal with if he was going to be allowed to enjoy his meal in peace. With some reluctance, he turned away from the girl long enough to snatch up the loyal dog in his massive jaws and snap him in two. With a pained whimper, the creature fell silent. He spat him out. He had no interest in eating such a thing, it was below him to do so.

With astonishment, the Hunter saw that the girl was actually trying to get away. Despite the fact that half of her neck was gone and her forearm bones were clearly visible on both arms, she was meekly trying to crawl on her back away from him. He'd been sure that she should've been too much in shock to manage such a feat, and would die from blood loss any second, yet here she was, feebly struggling to escape.

Such spirit! I like it!

He almost pitied her, but he'd been incapable of such fundamentally human sentiments for centuries now. Even before then, those sorts of feelings had been in short supply in him. It was why the Master had picked him in the first place. Not that he had any memory of that. He had no recollection of life before the Master. It was too long ago. As far as he knew, he had always been the Hunter.

Time to finish the job! he thought greedily as he pounced on her again, ripping and biting with renewed vigor. *This* was what he lived for. She was sweet indeed, yet somehow not quite as delectable as the last one had been. Still, at least this time he could enjoy her fully, he could take his time and truly savor every wonderful bite. Each flavorful morsel. And so he did. Ripping. Slurping. Licking. Gulping away as he was bathed in both blood and moonlight. He continued to gorge himself until he felt as though he might burst, until there was almost nothing left of her but bones, and even some of these he broke open with his powerful jaws so that he could suck the marrow out from them. His depraved appetite knew no bounds as he carried on dismembering and desecrating her form.

It wouldn't be until the next morning when her remains were found on the side of the road by a jogger. Her parents, too distracted by their arguments, had assumed that she'd returned from walking the dog and gone to bed while they'd been fighting, as she had a thousand times before. It wasn't until it was time to get her up for church the next morning that they realized, with a mounting sense of panic, that she wasn't in her bed, or anywhere else in the house. They made a few frenzied calls to the homes of her friends, asking if she'd spent the night there. They called the police, and that's when they first heard about the body that had just been discovered down the road only a few minutes earlier. A squad car was swiftly sent up the street to bring them to the awful scene.

There wasn't much left of her to identify, but they could tell it was her by her hair, and the remains of her clothes, and the pitiful sight of Mr. Fluffy's mangled body by her side. Of course, her parents knew it was her before they'd seen any of these horrible things. They felt it in their bones before they even got into the police car. They could sense that their child was gone, *really* gone, through that unexplainable bond that forever ties a parent to their child. And with her passing, a piece of each of them was also gone forever. Never to return.

The news was slow to spread around town. Brittney's family had requested that her name not be released to the press and so far there hadn't been any leaks. Parallels were immediately drawn to the death of Sylvia McCoy in Shadowbrook just a few days earlier. It seemed obvious that nobody in Shadowbrook had been able to find the wolves because the pack had been on the move, and now they were here in Davenport. Again, this was unnatural behavior for wolves, who were typically not so far ranging, but there had been nothing natural about the earlier attack either. Nobody had any trouble believing that her death had been the work of more than one animal, it simply wasn't possible for one wolf to have eaten that much of her, unless that wolf was unimaginably large. Her body had been discovered before scavengers had any real opportunity to have their way with it, so this *had* to be the work of an entire pack of wild animals. At least, that's what the conventional wisdom was saying. The authorities began organizing a search for the rogue animals, and local hunters were enlisted to assist them.

Brittney's family was too numb with pain to care about any of that at the moment. Having no real idea what to do with himself aside from curl up into a little ball and die, which was unfortunately not an option since he still had one child left to raise, her father began calling back some of his daughter's (his *late* daughter's, he corrected himself, the words sounding strange and foreign in his mind) friends that they had called earlier, when they had been clinging to the vain hope that she was still alive. That's how Mary Brandon found out about what had happened to her friend.

Her father Charles had answered the phone, just as he had when the Morgans had called in search of their daughter only hours before. He put down the receiver slowly, an ashen look upon his face. Somehow, Mary knew what he was going to say before he even began to speak the words to her. She'd seen the same look on his face when her mother had died. She was barely listening as her father tried to explain, as delicately as he could manage to, the condition that the body had been found in, and the theories about wolves being responsible. The whole room seemed to be swimming, collapsing in on her. She swayed unsteadily on her feet and almost fell over. Instead, she flattened her back against the nearest wall and slowly slid down to the floor, hot tears streaking down her face and a strange, low moaning escaping from her throat.

How could she be dead? How could she be gone? She'd just seen her last night! That was only a few hours ago! How could your entire world change so quickly? Part of her wildly believed that the whole thing was some sort of a sick prank, and wouldn't dare to believe it until she saw the body for herself, no matter how horrible they said it looked. It wasn't true. It *couldn't* be true!

"It's not real! She isn't gone! I'll prove it!" she managed to get out between sobs.

Charles looked at her sadly "Oh honey, I wish it wasn't true. Why would I ever make up such a hurtful thing?"

She ignored him, pulling out her cell phone and began manically stabbing at the buttons. She was dialing Brittney's cell number. It went straight to her voice mail.

"Hey, you've reached Brittney's phone. Leave a message - duh!" her prerecorded voice announced sarcastically. The sound of that voice devastated Mary all over again. The phone tumbled out of her hand and onto the carpet and she began wailing all over again, even more loudly this time.

Charles crouched down next to her and put an arm around his daughter. She grabbed hold of it and pulled him in closer. She held onto him tightly, rocking back and forth.

"It'll be okay, it's going to be okay, I promise," Charles repeated to her.

"What *is* all this noise? What is going on here?" came the somewhat imperious voice of William Sherwood, the master of the house, from the other end of the foyer. He was a tall, aristocratic looking man with golden hair. He was followed into the room by his wife Elizabeth and Allison. From the way they were all dressed, it was clear that they'd just come in from working outside with the animals. William held a large mug in his hand, doubtlessly filled with some of the cow's blood that Charles had just finished heating up on the stove for their lunch when he had been unexpectedly drawn into the foyer by the sound of the ringing phone. The Sherwoods never drank directly from their cows, it was too difficult for them to not get carried away when feeding off of a living thing and drain it too much. Instead, they reheated blood that they kept stored in a refrigerator that had been drawn out with a syringe.

William immediately regretted his tone when he saw that Mary was obviously in some kind of serious distress and Charles was trying his best to comfort her.

"Is everyone alright?" he asked a bit more tenderly.

Allison ran past William and hugged Mary as Charles slowly rose to his feet and faced William.

"I'm sorry, sir. You recall how the parents of Mary's friend, Brittney, called here earlier, asking if their daughter was here? Well, her father just called back, and..." His voice broke off, not sure if he could bear to repeat the terrible news again, he also didn't want to upset his daughter any further with the reality of it all.

"Oh my! What's become of the poor child?" Elizabeth asked, already knowing from the way everyone was behaving that it must be something horrible, perhaps even the unthinkable. Elizabeth was like a walking porcelain doll. Her skin was so white it was of an almost luminous pallor, it was a stark contrast to her extremely dark, long black hair and deep crimson lips.

Charles' back stiffened as he gathered his strength to tell the rest. "They say it was a pack of wild animals. Wolves probably, just like in Shadowbrook." Charles knew that his employer had been following the events in Shadowbrook with great interest ever since the story broke.

"Oh no, not again. Not here," William said, then looked at Mary. "I'm truly, truly sorry my dear."

Mary barely acknowledged his words with a nod.

"This is the 21rst century! How in the hell are people *still* getting killed by packs of wolves?" Mary moaned.

William and Elizabeth exchanged a troubled and knowing look.

"Omigod Mary! I can't believe it! I'm so sorry!" Allison told her, still hugging her.

Mary suddenly shrugged off her hug and looked at her suspiciously.

"Are you? Are you *really*? You never liked her! You thought she was an idiot! You were jealous of her! Don't try to pretend that you care now! You're probably happy that this happened!"

Allison was taken aback by the unexpected accusation and the venom in Mary's voice.

"Sure, maybe I didn't like her, but that doesn't mean I ever wanted something like *this* to happen to her! And I know what she meant to you, and I care about you - you've gotta know that!" Allison pleaded with her.

Mary got up and started to walk away from them all.

"Sure. Whatever. Just...just leave me alone for a while, okay? All of you, just leave me alone." She walked up the staircase slowly, like someone in a trance. Allison helplessly watched her disappear up the steps.

William put a hand on Charles' shoulder. "Give her time, she'll come around eventually," he said gently. Charles just frowned and balled his hands into fists.

William looked around the room at everyone else.

"In the meantime, I don't want any of us leaving the grounds," he commanded in a voice that brokered no argument.

"What? Why?" Allison asked, sounding alarmed by the decree. "Wolves can't hurt someone like me!"

"Because we don't think that this is the work of normal wolves," Elizabeth suddenly spoke up.

William shot her a warning look. Elizabeth ignored it and continued.

"They have a right to know what we might be up against!" she told him.

William sighed and looked down. "Why do you always have to make so much damned sense?" he said through clenched teeth.

"It's what wives *do*, dear," she smirked at him.

Allison's eyes narrowed.

"What are you both talking about? What aren't you telling me?" she demanded.

"I have suspected, since first hearing of it, that the killing in Shadowbrook was the work of werewolves. And now, with this most recent tragedy, right here in town, I'm afraid that there is little doubt," William revealed gravely.

Allison and Charles took in the news. They were both familiar with William and Elizabeth's stories of the old days and knew that such monsters had once existed. "Once" being the operative word here. They had always been led to believe that such creatures were a thing of the past.

"Werewolves? I thought you said that they were all wiped out, along with the rest of our kind?" Allison reminded them.

"I had always prayed that was the case, but the truth is that we really don't know for sure. We didn't linger long enough to make sure. We were quite intent on getting out of there with our portion of the treasure before our allies decided to change their minds about the arrangement we'd made," William told them with a note of regret in his tone.

"With the sheer size of the forces arranged against them that day and the element of surprise that we had on our side, you must understand that we didn't see *how* they possibly could have failed to destroy them all. The fact that we haven't seen nor heard any hint of the others for centuries seemed to bear out our hopes," Elizabeth chimed in.

"Until now," Charles said.

"Yes, until now. That killing in Shadowbrook was so peculiar. It had all the telltale signs of a werewolf attack. And now it sounds as if we've had a similar one here. And the...victim was someone who has been to this house on numerous occasions, who has been around our kind and those who are in regular contact with us. It cannot be a coincidence. The werewolves could always sense us from afar. They had an instinct to seek us out. It's what he designed them to do. He used them to track us down, to keep us in line. It's why we never tried to escape before, we knew that he'd always be able to use them to find us. To set them upon us. I've seen what they can do to us. It's horrible, revolting!" As William said it, his deep voice quivered slightly. Neither Allison nor Charles had ever heard him sound like this before, he was typically so confident and commanding. Now he sounded almost scared.

"You don't think that...if it really is werewolves, that they're still working with *him,* do you? That *he* could still be alive?" Charles couldn't bring himself to say the name of his employer's former master, he knew how it upset them to do so.

Elizabeth's eyes looked troubled by the idea. "We sincerely hope that's not the case. But we cannot completely deny that possibility either. If it is *him,* and he knows that we were the ones who betrayed him, who made off with some of his treasure...then I shudder to think what twisted revenge he might've devised for us. Even if it's not him, it's still trouble. Werewolves, acting upon their own volition, would still likely be drawn to us, purely by instinct. They might even come here to the manor itself. We could all be in the most terrible kind of danger."

"So, I hope that you can all now appreciate the rationale behind my decision. Charles, I think it best that you keep Mary from leaving here to go to school for the next few days at least, until we have a better idea of what we are dealing with. There is still a remote chance that these are just wild animals, although I doubt it. Even if they are werewolves, hopefully acting independently, they might just move on without bothering us, especially if they know that there are people out hunting for them, as there surely must be by now." Having realized that he might've frightened them too much with all of this talk, Charles was now trying to downplay the situation somewhat.

"Yes, her dad said something about search parties looking for the wolves. They're even talking about shutting down Wonderland until the wolves have been captured or killed," Charles confirmed.

"Well the only thing *I* can see is that none of you have really been honest about what happened to Mortus Locke and the rest of them!" Allison said angrily. She had no problem saying the taboo name, especially under the circumstances.

"Allie, dear, you must understand that we didn't want to worry you all unnecessarily," Elizabeth said mildly.

Allison rolled her eyes. There was no way that she was going to let these latest developments stop her from going out to look for Kevin today. It was possible, maybe even probable that he was one of these werewolves. It would explain why he set off her spidey-sense the way that he did. She refused to believe that he was working with the rest of them, though. For one thing, he was far too sweet and didn't give her any bad vibes. For another, from what she saw of the pitiful state of his living arrangements, he was on his own, a runaway and not part of any larger group. In fact, he was probably running from them. Allison now realized that the ghost that had attached itself to him was probably the first victim of the werewolves, the girl from Shadowbrook. Kevin must've been bitten while trying unsuccessfully to defend her, and was left for dead. Perhaps they were after him? Looking to finish the job? It could be the real reason why they were in town. If anything, the possibility that werewolves might be lurking around made her even more determined to see him, to warn him that they were here and to protect him from them if she could. Allison could've just quietly resolved to sneak out later on, it certainly would've been the smart thing to do, but she couldn't stop herself from speaking her mind on the matter. If there was one thing she hated, it was being bossed around and treated like she was a kid.

"I'm not some little girl that you can't trust with the truth! And you're not going to stop me from going out if I want to go out! You're not even my *real* father, no matter how much you like to pretend that you are, you can't just order me around like this!" she announced defiantly.

William looked skyward, as if seeking divine intervention. "If you wish to be treated like an adult, then you're going to need to start acting like one," he said wearily.

"How can I? Mentally, physically, I'm forever stuck at this stage of development. My body will never grow older. No matter how much knowledge or experience I try to accumulate, my mind will never *truly* mature either. And whose fault is that? Maybe you should've just left me to die that night with my real family! Maybe you weren't *really* thinking about what was best for me! I think you were only thinking about yourselves! Thinking of how you'd always wanted a child of your own, but could never have one because you're both nothing but walking corpses! You had no right to make me like you!"

They'd heard all of this before, but not in a long time. Allison was sounding just like she had when she'd first come to them again. They had no way of knowing that this was because all those emotions, those regrets had been dredged back to the surface by her longing to be with Kevin, and the knowledge that she couldn't be with him because of what she was, which was ultimately their fault. These simmering resentments had only been amplified by William's latest attempts to lay down the law with her.

Elizabeth wasn't going to be baited by any of Allison's painful remarks, she remained focused on what was most important in this discussion. "Be sensible, Allison! We're only trying to keep you safe. I don't think you fully appreciate the danger we might all be in. One person has already died, and I fear she won't be the last."

"Don't worry about me, I can take care of myself!" she retorted.

"Oh, I doubt that. I *can't* believe it, and I also refuse to ever apologize for taking you into this home, making sure you were educated, cared for, *loved*! For not only saving your life but giving you *eternal* life!" William replied, infuriated by her impertinence, her total lack of gratitude.

"Eternal life? Eternal damnation is more like it! This isn't life! It's just a grotesque mockery of it! A curse! I hope the damned werewolves *do* get me and finally put an end to it all!" She spat the words at him and rushed up the stairs just as Mary had before her only a few minutes earlier.

"Allison! You come back here this instant! This isn't over! So long as you live under this roof you will obey me!" William called to her retreating form. He started to move after her, but Elizabeth blocked him.

"No. Let her cool off. You know how she gets sometimes. How much she hates to be told what to do," she said to her husband.

"I agree. Going after her now will only make things worse," Charles, who had been watching the whole exchange with growing unease, chimed in.

"What's gotten into her all of the sudden? She hasn't spoken to us like that since she first arrived. It's as if the last sixteen years never happened! All the progress we've made towards becoming a family - gone!" an exasperated William said.

"I don't know. Perhaps she's scared? We all are. I keep telling you that we'll always lose out in a popularity contest with her birth family. No matter how many years she spends with us, we'll never be able to replace the bond she had with them," Elizabeth said, gently leading him back towards the kitchen.

For once, William was at a loss for words as he numbly followed her lead.

A few moments later they were all gone except for Charles, who remained there alone, looking lost, worried and utterly helpless.

146

CHAPTER 9:

MATT SPIKE - SUPERSTAR

That same morning, Matt Spike opened his eyes and slowly sat up in the unfamiliar bed of the hotel room. Between the hardness of the mattress and his nightmares, he'd been unable to get much sleep. After lying in bed for some time, he finally decided to stop pretending. Sleep was something that just wasn't going to happen. He reached over and turned off the alarm on the clock sitting on the nightstand so that it wouldn't annoy him later on.

He scratched his butt as he crossed the room and parted the curtains to peek out the window. It was still pretty dark outside, with just a hint of purple on the horizon to betray the coming of the sunrise. Matt sat back down on the bed and picked up the phone, dialing Randy's number. He knew he'd be up now too. Randy typically rose very early to meditate. He usually did so outside no matter what the weather conditions might be. Matt assumed that he did some of his wizard shit to prevent the weather from bothering him when it wasn't agreeable, but he'd never bothered to verify this theory.

When Randy answered the phone, he told Matt that he'd been expecting his call.

"Oh, did your intuition tell you that?"

"No, Naomi called me to give me a heads up on the situation after she got off the phone with you last night. We both agreed that you'd be too stubborn to call me until after you'd slept on it," Randy told him in his maddeningly calm way.

"Ah, my tribe, how well they know me!" Matt smiled.

"You must not have slept very well, or else you wouldn't be up this early. I can't blame you, the prospect of facing werewolves would keep most people up all night."

"Damn, kid! Get out of my head! It's downright spooky sometimes, ya know that?"

"So I've been told," Randy said. If he was offended by Matt calling him spooky, there was no trace of it in his voice.

"Well, since I'm already up, I want to get an early start today. We still have to drive across the state to get to Davenport. The good news is, this isn't a very big state, but I want to get on with it right away all the same. How soon do you think you can get up here?"

"Already on it, boss. I'm driving up to meet you in Shadowbrook as we speak." There was a slight pause as if he was looking at something, because he was. In this case, it was his GPS. Unlike his partner, Randy was quick to embrace new technologies. "Should be there in about two and half hours unless I hit too much traffic." Randy could've done a series of teleportation spells to get himself there, but making more than one such trip back to back tended to make even the toughest of magic users violently sick to their stomach unless they waited a few hours in between spells. Because of this, it was actually faster to drive there. Besides, he had a lot of cargo with him that was easier to transport in the car.

"Don't worry, I have your armor and the *Vermillion Avenger* with me. I swung by your house and picked 'em up last night," Randy said, correctly anticipating Matt's next question.

"Awesomesauce. I'm sorry for making you drop everything else to come up here and help out like this."

"Nonsense. That's what partners are for. There's no way I'd let you face a bunch of werewolves by yourself, if it even *is* werewolves. Also, if I didn't come up there, Naomi was ready to drive up herself and personally kick some werewolf butt on your behalf. I had to talk her out of it, she's pretty worried about you. Anyway, it's no problem for me to join you. I don't have a whole heck of a lot going on right now. If we don't have this wrapped up before this weekend is over, Penny will take care of my other cases for me."

Matt grunted. Penny wasn't a licensed private investigator like he and Randy were. She could work as an investigator in a pinch, under the company's license, but he was uncomfortable having her doing anything other than research, which she excelled at. She was highly intelligent, but she lacked a certain subtlety that Matt preferred in his investigators. She was awful at tailing people or staking out a location without giving herself away. He blamed himself for this, since he'd never taken the time to properly train her. He had never anticipated that his business would grow so much, since it had been such a struggle to get any clients when he first started. Lately, he'd found himself having to delay or even turn down jobs because sometimes he simply didn't have the manpower to devote to them. He *hated* turning down jobs for that reason.

"I really need to hire some more investigators, even if they're just part-timers. Especially with all the business we've been getting lately, I worry about what'll happen the next time you guys go on tour with your band. Then I'll really be up shit's creek! The trouble lies in finding someone who we can trust when the weirdness hits us again like it is right now."

"The weirdness" was what Matt called it whenever he got mixed up in one of these cases that involved something otherworldly, something which seemed to happen to him with alarming regularity. "Alarming regularity" meaning every couple of years or so, which was still far too frequent for Matt's tastes. He was quite certain that other PI's didn't have these sorts of problems.

"We're not making much progress on the new album. It's gonna be awhile before we start touring again, so I wouldn't worry about it too much. As for where to find people we can trust with the weirdness, I'll bet there are some ex ABC agents we could hire, you should ask Bronson."

The reason why Randy wasn't making much progress on his latest album, which was tentatively titled *Zuzu's Petals*, was because he was trying to encode hidden messages in the lyrics which would tell the listeners how to access another dimension. Randy was looking for someone to take on as an apprentice magic user and this was his unorthodox way of finding someone who would be worthy. If anyone else ever entered that dimension, a spell Randy had cast would trigger an alarm letting him know so he could liberate them from it. Randy had to make the clues in his lyrics cryptic enough so that almost nobody would be able to figure them out, yet not so obscure that they were completely impossible to decipher. It was a daunting task. Luckily, Penny, who usually wrote most of the lyrics, was willing to indulge this peculiar idea of his.

"Ex ABC agents? No way! All those guys give me the creeps! You should see the two I met with yesterday. Couple of real stiffs! They probably expect to be paid more than we can afford to pay, too." That was Matt's reflexive tendency to be cheap doing most of the talking.

"It's just a suggestion. They're already familiar with the weirdness, and what they lack in personality they make up for in efficiency," Randy said reasonably.

"Yeah, maybe so. But they already treat us like we're an unofficial branch of their organization as it is. Imagine how much worse it would be if one of them actually joined us."

Randy felt like this was a bit of an exaggeration on Matt's part. There had only been a few occasions when the ABC had reached out to Matt's detective agency, usually to hire them to do surveillance on people in their area. These jobs had turned out to be surprisingly routine. Only once or twice had this led to something stranger. Matt usually did the work for them free of charge, as a professional courtesy. He knew it was important to maintain good relations with them. He could understand Matt's attitude about it to some extent though, as he knew how much Matt prized his independence and often resented any intrusion by the Guilds into his tidy, normal existence. As a full-fledged member of one of the Guilds, Randy, of course, had a completely different feeling about the whole matter.

"That's a two-way street, though, isn't it? I mean, they may hire us for the odd job every now and again, but look at how much help they're giving us on this case."

"Touché, pal. Stop making so much sense. It's infuriating!" Matt laughed.

Randy knew that this was "Mattese" for "Okay, you've convinced me, but I'm not yet ready to give you the satisfaction of knowing that your argument has won me over."

"Well, I'm gonna let you go now. I wanna throw on some clothes and see if I can find someplace that offers a decent breakfast in this dinky little town. The continental breakfast in this hotel is an exercise in masochism. I guess I'll see you in two and half hours."

"See ya later boss."

Matt replaced the phone on the receiver. No sooner had he started to brush his teeth than his cell phone began to ring from the next room. "Jesus! What now?" he complained, but because his mouth was full of toothpaste, it sounded more like "Jeethus! Waaath no?" He hastily spit out the toothpaste and rinsed out his mouth, quickly dabbing the area around his mouth with a small towel before rushing out to answer the phone.

It was Kevin's dad, Thomas Scott,on the other end of the line. Matt had intended to call Kevin's parents and fill them in on what he had discovered so far this morning. He took the opportunity to bring Tom up to speed on the latest developments regarding how he'd traced Kevin to Wonderland and was planning to drive up there today to see where the trail would lead him next.

Naturally, he left out any mention of werewolves.

Then Thomas dropped a new bombshell on him. He told Matt that he'd contacted a reporter at the local TV news station about Kevin's disappearance and this reporter was asking if they could do an interview with Matt in a few hours time to help raise awareness of the case. Matt was reluctant to agree to it. In fact he felt a little bit like he was being used, that they'd hired a semi famous detective like himself mainly to get some publicity for the case. But could he really blame them? Wouldn't he have done the same thing if he had been in their shoes? In the end, he consented to it, even though it might slow down his attempts to get an early start on the road to Davenport. He just hoped they wouldn't try to ask about the Melissa Hollins case, he was through talking about that to the press. The plan was for the reporter and her crew to meet him in the lobby of the hotel; they would film the actual interview outside in the parking lot as they didn't have permission to shoot inside the building.

After his conversation with Thomas ended, Matt got dressed and left the hotel in search of a breakfast more palatable than his last one. He ended up just going back to the same diner where he'd had his dinner the night before, as he'd been pretty satisfied with the quality of the place. He was not disappointed. The breakfast there was a bit on the greasy side, but he sort of liked it that way. The most important thing was that they knew how to make a decent cup of coffee! Good coffee was one of his great pleasures in life, and it was something he'd been deprived of for a whole day. He finally felt properly revitalized now and ready to tackle the next phase of his investigation. He checked his watch and almost spat out his beloved cup of joe. He was due to meet with that reporter in a few minutes. He gulped down the remainder of his coffee (thankfully it wasn't still hot enough to scorch his throat on the way down) and asked for a check. It was a good thing that this diner was just down the road from the hotel, he should be able to get back just in the nick of time.

As Matt pulled into the hotel parking lot, he could already see a news van parked in one of the spots. He hoped they hadn't been waiting long. While he wasn't looking forward to the interview, he also had no desire to appear rude by making them wait around for him like he was some kind of a primadonna. As he entered the lobby and looked around, he didn't see many other people, and none of them struck him as someone who would be on the TV news. Feeling a little confused, he sat in a vacant seat and waited.

He didn't have to wait long before he saw an African American young woman who was quite attractive (albeit in that overly well put together, almost frosty way common to TV news reporters which Matt found slightly intimidating), making her way through the lobby accompanied by a few less well dressed men, members of her crew, Matt guessed. They must've been waiting in the van for him. When it was clear that she was making a beeline directly for him, he sat up.

"Matt Spike?" she asked superfluously. It was obvious that she'd already done some research on him and had recognized him right away.

"Last time I checked," Matt replied with his lopsided grin. He hoped he didn't sound like too much of a smart ass.

"I'm Clarissa Woodrow with WCTX, News Channel 8. Thanks for meeting with us on such short notice." She held out her hand and Matt shook it.

"It's no problem really, especially if it helps us find this kid and get him back home safely. I do have a few ground rules though before we start the interview."

"Really? Such as?"

"No questions about the Melissa Hollins case," he told her seriously.

He could tell that she was taken aback by this. "Why? That's your greatest triumph! You played a big part in catching a notorious serial killer. All the information you gave to the police, your testimony at the trial - it's something to be proud of."

The clear admiration in her voice was killing him a little inside, so was calling that case "a triumph". There was no triumph to be found in finding the dead body of an innocent little girl who had only been a few years older than his own daughter was now.

"No it isn't, I didn't find her quickly enough to save her, did I? Hopefully things will be different this time around. That's why I'd like to keep things focused mostly on the current case."

"Oh, I see. Does that mean that you believe the boy you're looking for now is in some sort of danger too?"

She had picked up on the hidden meaning behind him saying that he hoped things would be different this time around. He had to hand it to her, she was one smart cookie. Matt didn't know which possibility bothered him more: the idea that Kevin might be in danger, or that he might be a danger to others.

"It's a big bad world out there. Any kid that age is in some danger being on their own for this long," he said dismissively, hoping this would deflect any further questions along those same lines.

"Well, if we can't ask about the Hollins case, is it okay if I mention some of your books?" she asked.

"Oh geez. So you know about those too, huh?" Matt turned a little red as he said it.

Matt had penned a couple of mystery novels in the past few years under the pen name Charles Gordon Bennett, a name which he felt sounded sufficiently pretentious, as he found the whole idea of writing, the notion that anyone else would be very interested in your inner thoughts and flights of fancy to be kind of inherently arrogant and pretentious. He'd somehow found the time to write them in between the ever-increasing demands of his job and trying to be a good husband and dad, stealing away moments to do so on his laptop on his lunch breaks and while on long stake outs. They weren't what any sane person would consider literature, just some fun, pulpy potboilers like the detective novels he'd enjoyed reading as a child. So far there were two of them: *Death Rattle* and *Dirt Nap*, with a third one currently in the works. They were very loosely based on some of his previous cases, however he'd steadfastly refused to incorporate anything about the Hollins case into them. Part of this was because of his refusal to profit off of her death, and out of respect for her family. The other reason was that the wounds from that case were still too raw and deep for him to face, although he was aware that writing about it, especially in a fictionalized way, might be cathartic. It was just something he couldn't bring himself to do, so instead, he wrote about everything *but* that case.

His books weren't bestsellers, but they'd been moderately successful and seemed to have a small following. Recently, a few internet sleuths had figured out that "Charles Gordon Bennett" was actually Matt Spike. It had generated a slight buzz, which his publisher had loved since it had generated a slight uptick in sales. The media was enamored with the idea of a PI who was also a mystery novelist on the side, and they'd run a few stories about it with predictable titles like "Murder, *he* wrote" that made him groan with embarrassment.

"Yeah, *Dirt Nap* was da bomb!" Clarissa enthused. Matt didn't know what was more surprising, that she still said things like "da bomb" or that she'd actually enjoyed *Dirt Nap*. He personally considered it to be the better of the two books, but it also seemed to be the less popular one. He wondered if she was trying to butter him up with such flattery? He was sad to report that it was working.

"I guess it's okay if you mention the books, but try not to focus on them too much, okay? I don't want this interview to be more about me than it is about finding Kevin," Matt told her, telling himself that it wasn't because of the flattery, but mostly because he knew his publisher would chew him out when she found out that he'd been on TV and didn't take the opportunity to plug his books. And find out she would, that woman's tentacles extended everywhere!

They all headed outside to do the interview. Matt didn't mind since it was a nice morning. The interview didn't last all that long. Matt was a little alarmed, though, when she mentioned that Kevin had been traced to Davenport. He hadn't expected Tom to pass that on to her. Then again, he'd neglected to tell him to keep it under wraps. He wasn't sure he wanted that information out there publicly yet, in case it got back to the kid that he'd been tracked that far and it caused him to skip town (if he hadn't already) or to cover his tracks more carefully going forward. Matt had almost asked her not to broadcast that part of the interview, then he thought better of it. If people in Davenport knew he'd been in the area recently, they could call in with some important leads. The point of the whole interview was to bring in more leads, wasn't it?

Halfway through the interview, Matt saw Randy's car pull into the parking lot. Randy had hovered on the edge of the cameras, watching throughout the interview. When it was finally over with, he walked over to them.

"Hey, Matt. I didn't know you were gonna be on TV!"

"Yeah, well, neither did I. Clarissa, this is my partner Randy Gruman, he's just come up from Jersey to help me with the case."

"You might wanna interview me, too. I'm a little famous, I'm in a band - the Mystery Smiths. We used to be called Lung Collapse." Randy was always eager to generate some publicity for his side hustle. He didn't want to let the team down.

"I know, but nobody cares. Ska is dead, man." she said as she started to climb into the passenger seat of the news van.

"We're not *just* a Ska band anymore!" Randy protested as she slammed the van's door shut.

"We tackle lots of genres now. We're very versatile," Randy continued, though no one was listening.

Matt put a reassuring hand on his shoulder. "Don't let it get you down kid, we can't all be superstars. Now which car are we taking? Yours or mine?"

The answer had been Randy's car. It had a GPS, and Matt's armor and the *Vermillion Avenger* were already loaded inside. It was now Sunday, and Matt had reserved his room at the hotel until at least Monday morning, so they left his car there.

"These fall leaves are really something else, huh?" Randy commented as they wound their way northwest through the state towards Davenport.

"Yeah, they sure are. I always wanted to drive through New England in the fall. I didn't get much of a chance to see them on the trip up, since it was at night," Matt agreed, as he enjoyed the pageant of colors that now assailed them from all sides.

"So, what do you know about werewolves?" he asked Randy.

"Quite a bit. Never met one before, of course. They're very rare. Considered to be extinct. But I think it's neat that they were real, so I've read up a lot about them in the archives on Elysium." Elysium was the Mediterranean island that was the headquarters of the Temple of the Old Gods, the Guild of magic users that Randy belonged to.

"And you never thought to tell me about this before? Both you and Naomi knew that vampires and werewolves were real, you both *know* how cool I think all that stuff is, and yet you never told me about any of it!" Matt couldn't help but complain again.

"Didn't I? I could've sworn that I did!" Randy seemed genuinely surprised. He often got mixed up when it came to whether he had actually said or done something that he'd definitely intended to say or do.

"You didn't."

"Are you sure?"

"Of course I'm sure! I'd remember something like that! It's kind of mind blowing!" Matt was starting to lose patience.

"Well, sorry about that. I'm sure I *meant* to tell you and just got distracted by something."

"It's okay. But *what* do you know about them?"

"There are three main types. The original werewolves transformed themselves by wearing a mystical belt made from a wolf's pelt. Doing so allowed them to channel the energy of the Great Wolf Spirit, becoming one of its avatars."

"The Great whosit?" Matt asked. Naomi hadn't said anything about that last night.

"It's the living embodiment of the very concept of a wolf in the human collective consciousness. A sort of Wolf God." Randy explained.

"Oh. Okay. Wolf God. Got it."

"These kinds of werewolves can shift back and forth between human and wolf and also a kind of intermediate stage that's part human, part wolf whenever they want to, just by thinking about it, so long as they're wearing the belt. They were used as shock troops in the Great Magic War. Mortus Locke discovered how to access the memories of his ancestors who lived during that time, and recreated the lost secret of how to make these belts. He gave them to some of his followers and used them in much the same way, as his enforcers. I doubt that any of these belts are still in existence."

"Alright. And what are the other two types of werewolves?"

"Those that were created from the bite of a werewolf, and those who are the descendants of those who have been bitten."

"Wait a sec. So it can be passed on to your kids? Like some sort of a, a...disease?"

"Exactly. The curse attaches itself to the astral body and can be passed on to a child who is formed from a parent whose astral body has been tainted by the curse in that way."

"Well, ain't that something!" Matt was astounded by this new information. Turns out that *Teen Wolf* was a surprisingly accurate depiction of lycanthropy. Who would've thunk it?

"So if our boy Kevin really is a werewolf, then he was most likely bitten by one recently. Unless you think his parents seemed like werewolves?" Randy asked half jokingly.

"His dad's kind of an asshat, but I don't think he's a werewolf. I'm pretty sure he was attacked on his bike in the woods a day before that girl got killed."

"You don't think that Kevin did that to her do you? They found hairs from two different wolves, didn't they? Maybe he was fighting the one who killed her?"

"I sure hope that's what happened. I'm really confused about that aspect of things myself. Who knows? What I don't understand is how he could've become one when there was no full moon that night."

"They don't need a full moon to transform.The full moon just means that they *have* to change. Any kind of highly emotional situation can trigger a transformation, you know like with the Incredible Hulk."

"Oh. So I wouldn't like them when they're angry?" Matt joked.

"Yeah. All this full moon stuff only applies to those that have been bitten and their offspring. The ones with the belts have total control over their changes. You know, if Kevin really has been bitten and he's still anywhere close to Wonderland, an amusement park full of people...we might have to...you know we might not be left with any choice but to..."

"Kill him? I know. I'm not sure I can do it. He's just a kid! He's the same age as Joe."

"Then it's a good thing I'm around isn't it?" Randy said firmly. Matt looked at him open mouthed.

"You really think you could do that?" Matt had seen Randy hold his own in a few fights and nasty situations, but he always thought of him as more of a lover than a fighter.

"I think so. If I have to. I'm not about to let you become werewolf chow. Naomi would kill me!"

"Yeah, well, let's just hope that it never comes to that. Is it really so hopeless? Isn't there some cure for his...condition?" Matt was beginning to think that the only thing worse than not being able to find Kevin would be finding him and not being able to do anything to help him.

Randy was silent for some time, deep in thought. Finally he spoke, haltingly at first, as if trying to convince himself of what he was saying.

"It's a very old curse. Ancient magic like that is more potent. It's very tricky. There is *one* person who might be able to do it. There's this guy, a wizard that they call 'The Gooch'."

"The Gooch? Why do they call him that? What the hell is a Gooch?" Matt asked skeptically.

"I don't know. Everyone just calls him that. Anyhow, this guy is a real character. He's the world's foremost expert on curses. He's also a gigolo. He uses his clients to further his research into Tantric Sex Magick. Of course, *they* don't know that. He can usually be found skateboarding around Washington D.C."

"Sounds like a total weirdo."

"He is. Don't let Wendy hear you say that, though. He's one of her oldest friends. He's also an expert on herbal remedies and healing. He's where she gets all of her weed from."

Matt shook his head. Wendy was the witch who had been Randy's mentor and taught him everything she knew about magic. She was also the Pontifex Maximus, the leader of the Temple of the Old Gods, and an unrepentant pothead. He also knew that if someone like Randy agreed that the guy was a weirdo, he must be pretty far out there.

"So this wacko is our best hope to cure Kevin?"

"If anyone can do it, it'll be The Gooch," Randy assured him.

"Great. And how well do you know this guy?"

"Not that well. We've only met a few times. But don't worry, if I call for him, I'm sure that he'll come, as a favor to Wendy."

And it doesn't hurt to do a good deed to help out the future Pontifex Maximus, Matt thought, knowing what a bunch of political schemers these magic users tended to be, and that everyone saw Randy as Wendy's hand-picked heir apparent. Wendy had a daughter of her own, Celine, but the girl seemed to have little interest in magic.

"How will we fight a werewolf? You know, if it really comes to that? Naomi said something about them being vulnerable to weapons made from pure substances?"

"That's right. Silver and iron seem to work the best, but I'm certain the *Vermilion Avenger* will work. As magical creatures, they're also vulnerable to magic and attacks from other magical creatures," Randy affirmed.

They were both quiet for a while, lost in their own thoughts. Matt turned on the radio to break the silence. That's when they heard the news report about Brittney's body being discovered. When it was over they both looked at each other with growing horror.

"Shit! It's already happened again! And right in the place that we're headed to! It *has* to be him!" Matt exclaimed. "We're too late!"

"We don't know that for sure. Maybe it's the other wolf? The one that bit him? He or she could be after him too." Randy tried to calm him down. Matt could instantly appreciate the logic behind Randy's reasoning. Although it felt odd for Matt to attach words like "logic" and "reason" to such a bizarre situation.

"Then it's even more imperative that we reach him first. Put the pedal to the metal, pal! We need to get there pronto!" Matt ordered.

Matt and Randy arrived at the gates of Wonderland in the early hours of the afternoon. Matt had already called ahead on his cell phone and explained their purpose in coming there, so they were ushered into the security office as soon as they identified themselves. The security office was just a cramped little trailer near the front gate. It reeked of the general atmosphere of seediness that permeated the whole place.

To say that Matt was not impressed with Wonderland would be an understatement. The only "wonder" he found in it was why anyone would pay good money to come to this dump. To be fair, Matt's expectations of amusement parks were fairly high. His first experience of an amusement park was Six Flags Great Adventure in Jackson NJ, in fact he had once lived near it as a small child. Great Adventure didn't exactly have the cleanest safety record, but that was concealed under a generous sheen of exciting rides and the *illusion* of quality. It tended to be the yardstick by which he measured most amusement parks, fairly or unfairly. If a place was nicer than Great Adventure, he thought it was awesome, if it wasn't as good, it was a dump. As a teenager, Matt had also once spent a summer working at a place called Fantasy Island on Long Beach Island, which also figured into his estimation of amusement parks. Fantasy Island didn't have very thrilling rides, they were mostly kiddie rides, but they were very clean, well maintained and they had a nice arcade. In contrast, Matt felt like he'd need to get a tetanus shot before getting on any of the rides in this place. The whole thing reminded him of one overly large carnival gone wrong.

The fact that the place was so packed, even on a Sunday near the end of the season, was just a testament to how there was apparently nothing else better to do in this neck of the woods. He didn't voice any of these concerns to the staff, of course, although he did express surprise that they were still open considering the fact that there was supposedly a pack of man-eating wolves still at large. He was told that there had in fact been some debate about opening today, but in the end, they felt that the perimeter of the park was sufficiently safely enclosed, and the crowds would serve to scare away any wild animals.

Matt was uncomfortably reminded of that scene in *Jaws* where the mayor unwisely insists on keeping the beaches open after a shark attack.

At least the security staff at the park were quite friendly and cooperative. Matt asked to review the security tapes from last Saturday, looking for signs of Kevin. Luckily for him, they hadn't wiped that footage yet. He had already estimated the time that Kevin should've arrived at the park that day and he fast forwarded the footage to around that time. He watched Kevin's arrival, carrying that ridiculously large bag of his and his skateboard. He was surprised that he'd been allowed to carry both items into the park, further driving down any respect he had for the way this place was being run. The cameras picked him up several more times that day, mostly wandering aimlessly around the park, until he disappeared. The cameras never detected him leaving.

Interesting.

It was likely that he'd slipped out some back way, but some instinct told Matt to ask to look at footage from the next day. After a while, Kevin eventually turned up again, near a camera outside of the bathrooms, wearing different clothes and without his bag or skateboard. He spent a few minutes inside before re-emerging, only to disappear again. Later on that day, he shows up at the bathrooms again, this time when he comes out, he pulls some empty plastic bottles from his jacket and fills them up with water from a nearby fountain.

This same routine was repeated several times over the next few days. Kevin would show up at the bathrooms in the morning, he'd usually return in the middle of the day and before the park closed at night. Occasionally he'd stop by a food truck and buy a hot dog and a soda or a funnel cake.

"Damn, he sure is punctual, isn't he?" Randy commented.

It was true. He always arrived and left at almost the same time, you could practically set a watch by it. It made finding him on the tapes each day that much easier.

"He's a real creature of habit, that's for sure," Matt agreed.

"I think he just doesn't like doing his number two's in the woods or wherever he's staying," Randy replied.

"I'm not so sure the bathrooms in this joint are much better than the woods!" Matt laughed. The security guy who was helping them go through the footage gave Matt an ugly look.

He shrugged. "Sorry."

Matt realized that a change of subject was in order. "It's obvious that he's exiting and entering the park from somewhere nearby. He keeps disappearing and reappearing from the cameras around the same blind spot. Can you take us to that area that isn't covered by the cameras?" he asked the security guard.

"Sure. Do you want to go right now?"

"Not yet. I want to see how recently he's still showing up in this footage. Can you bring up anything from yesterday?"

The guard loaded the tapes from the day before. It started out predictably enough, but then Kevin returned to the park right as the sun was setting and meandered about for a long time. He entered an arcade and came running out after about two hours. He is next seen briskly walking until he vanishes from the camera in the usual spot.

"Who's that girl?" Randy asked.

"What girl?" Matt had no idea what he was talking about.

"There's a girl who comes running out of the arcade a couple of minutes after he does. Then it looks like she's tracing his steps. She's pretty good at it too. Rewind it and I'll show you."

They did so and Randy pointed out Allison.

"She disappears from the cameras in the same area where he does," Matt noted.

"I've seen her before. Local girl, she's here all the time," the security guard told them. Matt worried that she might be the girl whose body had been found this morning. The news report they'd heard on the ride over said that the police had identified her, but hadn't released her name.

Kevin didn't reappear in the footage from that night, but the mystery girl did about an hour later. They watched her walk around the park for a bit, then leave through the front gate. Matt breathed a sigh of relief as he watched her leave the park. She could still be the girl who was killed, though. The attack on her might've just happened later in the night. He wondered if she had really been following Kevin and what, if anything, was going on between the two of them? He'd observed a lot of unusual activity yesterday, Kevin had deviated from his typical routine far more drastically than he ever had before. What did it all mean?

Randy parted the blinds on the one window in the trailer and peered outside.

"Matt, the sun is starting to go down!"

"Fuck!" Matt exclaimed. He'd lost track of time while they'd been pouring over all of this footage. In their defense, it was an entire week's worth of information, and looking for Kevin in the crowds was often like looking for a needle in a haystack.

"Why is that a problem?" the puzzled guard asked.

"Because it'll be harder to spot him at night," Randy quickly answered

"Do we have anything from today?" Matt asked urgently.

The guard cued up some footage from this morning. Sure enough, Kevin showed up, repeating his daily rituals.

"Bingo! He's still here!" Randy smiled.

Matt looked up at the security guard.
"I think you'd better show us where that blind spot is now."

CHAPTER 10:

FULL MOON FEVER

Allison spent a good deal of time that Sunday sulking in her room. She penned a particularly strongly worded entry in her journal in which such words as "unfair!" and "Helsinki Syndrome?" were underlined several times. Eventually though, her hunger for blood drew her back down to the kitchen where she met Charles, who believed he had persuaded her to apologize to William and Elizabeth, yet in truth, Allison had already resolved to do so. However, Charles seemed so pleased with himself at the idea that his words had helped restore some semblance of civility to a home that was so recently torn asunder by discord that she didn't have the heart to dissuade him from this notion.

Allison found William and Elizabeth working outside; this was still a farm after all, and there was work to be done with or without Allison's help. Apologies didn't come easily to her, and she was pleased that her "parents" had made it into a relatively painless ordeal. She truly *did* regret some of the things she'd said to them, even if it was all true. There was no point in rehashing such ancient history, they were in the situation that they were in and just had to try and make the best of it. She knew that William and Elizabeth did care about her, and she cared about them too, and they were doing what they could to try and protect the family.

She'd been surprised to see that both William and Elizabeth were wearing gun belts, like a pair of gunslingers from the Old West, except that upon closer inspection, these guns weren't the six shooters favored by such cowboys, but flintlocks. They also wore powder horns slung over their shoulders. When she inquired about it, William informed her that the weapons were loaded with silver musket balls. He'd had a great quantity of these made shortly after they'd arrived in the New World, in case any of Mortus Locke's werewolves had pursued them there. After a few decades of living in peace, with no sign of their former oppressors, they'd put the weapons into storage and been so convinced that the danger was over that they'd never bothered to upgrade to more modern weapons.

However, recent events had compelled them to dig them out and arm themselves.

"No way! Do those old things even still work? Doesn't the gunpowder go bad?" she asked incredulously.

Elizabeth laughed and shot at a nearby fence post in answer. "As you can see, so long as you keep the black powder nice and dry it still packs quite a punch!"

"You shouldn't waste ammunition like that," William admonished her.

Elizabeth waved away the complaint with one hand. "Husband, may I remind you that we have several crates full of these silver balls?"

"Here, I want you to keep this one. I'll teach you how to load and fire it. You might need it to protect yourself." Elizabeth handed her one of the two pistols she was carrying. Allison was surprised by the heft of it.

With a little practice, Allison found that she could reload the weapon in about half a minute. She enjoyed firing it although the loud sound and kick of it took a little getting used to. However, she wasn't a very good shot.

"Don't feel too badly, these things aren't particularly accurate unless you get really close," Elizabeth said encouragingly.

"Yes, but the whole point is to avoid getting that close!" William added less encouragingly. "Keep practicing!"

And so she did. By the end of the day, she did think she had improved - slightly. She must've because even William seemed satisfied.

"You're a quick learner, I'll give you that!" he'd commented, which was high praise from someone like him. But would she be able to do so well if there really was a huge, fast moving monster bearing down on her? She had to believe that she would.

Allison was feeling so good that she *almost* confided in them what she knew about Kevin, but she still didn't quite trust them with that sort of information. They seemed to think that all werewolves could only be dealt with one way - with deadly force. It was an argument that didn't convince her, especially where Kevin was concerned.

After she was done practicing with the pistol and doing all of her remaining tasks on the farm, Allison fed again. Charles brought the family their bowls of reheated cow's blood. He and Mary often had (a normal, human) dinner with the rest of them at the table, but Mary was still isolating herself in her room. Allison and the others were quite discouraged when they realized that she was still so upset that she wasn't coming down to join them after Charles announced he was bringing her supper up to her in her room.

Once she'd finished feeding, Allison went up to her room. On the way, she passed Mary's room, the door of which was still firmly closed. She wanted so badly to knock on the door and comfort her friend, but she was afraid that she was still mad at her. Besides, the sun would set soon, and she wanted to make sure that she'd reach Kevin before then, tonight was the night of the full moon. She hastily put on her wig and her glasses again, and concealed her pistol in a purse (it took her several attempts to find one big enough to hide it in, along with her powder horn and ammunition). She had no intentions of using the weapon on Kevin (who she still didn't quite believe was a werewolf anyway), but she might need it in case there were any other werewolves around like William and Elizabeth feared. She opened up her bedroom window and balanced on the small ledge beneath it before launching herself off and landing halfway down the long private driveway that led up to the manor.

She began running down the long path up to the manor at her blindingly unnatural speed. A part of her hated all this sneaking around, breaking her promise to Elizabeth and William to stay inside the safe confines of the manor. At the same time, another part of her was thrilled at the danger of it all. She *had* to get to the bottom of this mystery, otherwise she'd spend the rest of her days wondering about it, wondering what might've happened between her and Kevin if she hadn't been afraid to take a chance. The day she stopped living life on the edge, then she knew she would truly be completely dead inside, just another antique gathering dust inside the manor like the pistol that was currently bouncing around in her purse.

She'd *never* allow herself to become like that! She had to do whatever she could to hold onto some kind of feeling of vitality, even if it meant taking seemingly reckless risks like this....

Sequestered in her bedroom, Mary poked at the plate of dinner her father had brought up to her half-heartedly. She had no real appetite. Losing a friend will do that to you. She still couldn't accept that Brittney was gone. She was filled with guilt and regret over every unkind thought she'd ever had about her. She knew that

Brittney wasn't always the cleverest or kindest person, but she also knew that she had a difficult home life that she'd been trying to cope with, and for whatever reason, she'd always been good to Mary. She'd taken her under her wing and taught her how to fit in. Whatever social standing Mary had at school, she owed to Brittney's decision to befriend her. She wondered if Yolanda knew about the tragedy, and how she was dealing with it? Yolanda hadn't called her or texted her, and Mary was afraid to reach out, afraid to be the first one to break the horrific news to her.

She also really regretted how she'd treated Allison earlier. She saw that she'd taken out her anger at herself over her own conflicting feelings about Brittney out on Allison. That had been unfair of her. She would definitely have to apologize for that and do something to try and make up for it. But in the meantime, she still couldn't quite bring herself to leave her room. The only contact she'd had with anyone since this morning was when her father stopped by to check on her earlier. Even then, she'd only spoken to him from the other side of a closed door. He'd said something about Elizabeth and William wanting her to stay on the grounds of the manor until the wolves had been dealt with, even if it meant missing school for a few days. She didn't know that her father hadn't had the heart to try and explain to her the true nature of this danger at that time. He felt that she had enough on her plate already. Having to deal with the grief of losing her friend was bad enough, no need to add to it the fear of being under siege from a pack of werewolves or maybe even something *worse* than werewolves.

So Mary had tried to escape from her grief, from her self loathing over the fact that a part of her wasn't even sure that she'd really liked Brittney all that much more than Allison did. She ran away from all these feelings by occupying her mind with other things. She had an old TV in her room that had once been in William and Elizabeth's bedroom. They were going to throw it out because it was a combination TV/VCR and only the VCR part still worked. Mary had rescued it, not because she had any particular need for such a thing (all her movies were on DVD) but because she just saw it as a challenge to try and resurrect it. She planned to sell it to the local pawn shop for a few dollars once she had it fixed. She'd pulled it apart a few weeks ago, its electronic guts spilled out over a desk in one corner of her bedroom and there it had stayed, forgotten, even after she had acquired the parts necessary to fix it from her local Radio Shack. Now, she had nothing better to do than to put it back together. It sure beat the hell out of thinking about all of the other things going on in her life right now.

She'd taken a break from it to take a stab at eating something when her dad had brought her dinner up. Now she abandoned any pretense of finishing her food. It just wasn't gonna happen. Despite the fact that her dad was an excellent cook, the food brought her no pleasure, or maybe it was more accurate to say that the idea of feeling pleasure right now, when her friend couldn't feel *anything,* would *never* feel anything ever again, made her feel like shit. Why did she get to still feel things, to have the possibility of enjoyment, when Brittney didn't? What made her so damned special? Who got to decide who lived and died? God? If so, what had Brittney done that was so terrible as to bring down His wrath? Wasn't it bad enough that He'd taken away her mother? Why had He taken away one of her only friends too? Why did He have to be such an asshole?

Feeling another wave of anguish and anger beginning to wash over her, she set down her plate of food on her bed decisively and crossed back over to her desk. It was time to lose herself in mending the broken TV set before such emotions overwhelmed her completely. She began working at a frenetic pace, barely aware of what she was doing, as if in a trance. In no time at all, she had it fully reassembled.

"Damn!" she exclaimed, wiping a bit of sweat from her brow, a little amazed with herself. *Now to test it out,* she thought, and plugged it into a power strip located under her desk, then unhooked the coaxial cable from the back of the TV atop her dresser and pulled it over to the back of the TV she'd just been working on.

As the TV powered up, she saw that the Six O'Clock News was on. She had no desire to watch the news. She didn't have much of an interest in such things to begin with, but right now, she was especially scared of seeing any coverage of Brittney's death. She tried to change the channel using the buttons on the front of the TV. They didn't work. *Great, so not completely fixed,* she thought bitterly. This was supposed to be her moment of triumph, now she'd have to open this thing up again. She fumbled around on her desk until she found the remote control. She aimed it at the TV. Nothing. She opened up the battery compartment and saw that the batteries inside were badly corroded, some of the acid had spilled out onto the contacts. *Even more good news, huh?*

She checked her watch. It was almost seven, she supposed that she could put up with the news for a few more minutes while she looked around on her desk for some fresh batteries and something to scrape off the corrosion on the inside of the remote.

The image of an impeccably well-groomed anchor man smiled at her with false cheerfulness from the other side of the screen while he droned on about death and disaster. Mary glanced at the screen as she started using the tip of a small flathead screwdriver to scrape away at the white, dried up battery acid caked over the contacts.

The box behind the too-perfect anchorman read "Teen Missing in Shadowbrook". This caught Mary's attention because that was the same otherwise obscure town where they'd found the remains of that girl a few days ago. A girl who had been killed by the same wolves they now thought had gotten Brittney. Mary knew all about that case, it was so strange that it had been all that anyone could talk about at school last week.

The teen in question was named Kevin Scott. This further intrigued her since Allison's mystery man was also named Kevin. Then they showed a picture of him. It was his eighth grade graduation picture (Mary had no way of knowing that) which had no doubt been selected, despite being slightly out of date, because it was one of his mother's favorites. The boy in the picture was a dead ringer for the one Allison had described to her. This *had* to be Allison's runaway.

As the report continued, they briefly spoke with a private detective that the family had hired to find the boy. Mary's jaw dropped. The detective was Matt Spike! The same guy who wrote those mysteries that Allison had insisted she read. She'd rather enjoyed *Death Rattle,* but had found *Dirt Nap* to be a little off-putting. She couldn't wait to tell Allison that the boy she was obsessing over was being hunted by one of her favorite authors. Matt's interview was terse and brief. It was obvious that he was trying to stick to the facts of the case, despite the reporter's attempts to get him to talk more about his books. At the end of the interview, they flashed a toll-free number to Matt's office for people to call in case anyone had seen Kevin recently.

However, the most important thing that Mary got out of the interview was that Kevin was last traced to Davenport. Her mind was doing somersaults now. A mysterious boy runs away from the same town where a girl is found a few days later who's been mauled by wolves. He flees to Davenport and now her *friend* ends up suffering the same fate? Was this really the work of wolves, or werewolves? Mary had heard William and Elizabeth's old stories, the stories of their lives before coming to America. From those stories she knew that werewolves had existed at one time. What if this boy Kevin was really a werewolf? Perhaps that's why he'd triggered Allison's sixth sense? It was now obvious to her that the ghostly girl who was following Kevin around was also the girl who'd been killed last week in Shadowbrook.

But hadn't she said that Kevin had tried to save her? Well, maybe he had, but in the process, he got bitten and now *he* was a werewolf too. If that was the case, then maybe he was the one who killed Brittney? Or maybe he'd killed the ghost too. Allison had told her before that ghosts tended to be very confused, especially about their own deaths.

Mary rose from her bed, a relentless fear seizing her thoughts. Kevin Scott was the boy living in the Tunnel of Love. Kevin Scott was no boy, but a monster. A monster who tore young girls to pieces. That had not been the work of a mere boy. He might have killed Sylvia McCoy. He probably killed Brittney. And he would kill Allison too, vampire or not. She recalled how determined Allison was to see him again tonight. William had forbidden anyone from leaving the property, but she knew Allison well enough to know that wouldn't stop her. Hell, she'd probably be more likely to go now just out of spite! Allison intended to go to Wonderland tonight no matter what, right into the arms of a monster! Mary had already lost one friend to this wolf in boy's clothing. She wasn't about to stand by and let it happen again. She wasn't going to allow her last conversation with Allison to be that stupid argument from this morning.

Mary darted from her room and out into the hallway. She saw that the door to Allison's bedroom was slightly ajar. It creaked slightly as it was swayed by a gust of wind. Her heart dropped in her chest. Her body felt the truth of things before her mind could accept it. Through the gap between the door and the doorframe, she could see the source of the wind: the large, single window in Allison's room was wide open. Her friend was gone, likely out that same window. Through the window she could see the sun starting to set over oncoming storm clouds. It was a sight that might have filled her with awe under other circumstances, but now only served to punctuate her panic. The sun was going down. Didn't werewolves like to hunt at night? Wasn't tonight, in fact, supposed to be a full moon?

Mary ran back into her room. What worked against werewolves? Silver! Did she have anything silver? Yes, in fact, she had a sterling silver letter opener in the form of King Arthur's sword Excalibur which had been given to her by Allison as a birthday gift. One merely had to pull the sword from the stone. She found it on her dresser and she placed it inside the pocket of the jacket she was throwing on. It might just be a letter opener, but it was one *sharp* letter opener. It might just do the trick, she just prayed that she wouldn't have to use it, that she'd reach Allison in time.

She thought about telling her father what she feared was happening, of telling Elizabeth and William of the danger that Allison might be in, but she thought better of it. If she was wrong and Allison found out, she'd never forgive her for giving up her secrets like that. No, this was something she had to do on her own.

She carefully peered out of her room and down the hallway. It was as dark and empty as it had been a moment before. She crept out into it as silently as she could, and made her way down the steps and out the back door. Once outside, she headed for an old shed where she kept her bike - she'd get there faster on it. She was old enough to drive, but she didn't have her license yet, as her father hadn't really taken the time yet to try and instruct her. If he had, she might've tried to take his car instead. Soon she was pedaling furiously down the long driveway away from the house and towards the glow from the lights of Wonderland, which were so powerful that they discolored the sky for miles around, yet even they weren't bright enough to keep the spreading gloom of the approaching night at bay forever.

Allison had jumped the fence in the usual spot and made her way straight for the Tunnel of Love. She carefully made her way inside, afraid she might spook Kevin by suddenly showing up like this. What would she tell him when she ran into him? "Hi, remember me from last night? Yeah, I've kind of been stalking you ever since then, I hope you don't mind. Hey, I was wondering - you're not really a werewolf are you? Or if you are, hopefully you're a nice one and not the mean type that likes to rip young girls to pieces? You're also being stalked by a ghost too, and she looks like she's been chewed up and spat back out, which is pretty gross. She also said that you tried to save her, but you know how ghosts are, super moody and confused, so I'm not 100% convinced that she's a very reliable witness. Oh, by the way, I'm also a vampire. I hope that isn't too weird for you. Don't worry, I'm a nice one who just sits around the house reading and sipping cow's blood, even though I'm carrying a gun in my purse which is *definitely* not there in case I need to shoot you. That gun is for the hypothetical mean werewolves that might be after you, I *swear*! So you see, I'm really here to help you. Maybe we could go out on a date or something one of these days when all of this is over?"

Yeah, that would go over *really* well!

Allison reached the little room where Kevin had been sleeping the night before, all of his things were still inside, but there was no sign of him, or the ghost for that matter. Her enhanced senses told her that he had just left recently though. She decided to sit down and wait for him. With it getting this close to sun down, surely he'd return soon? While she waited, she tried to work out what she *would* say to him when next they met. Honestly, there simply wasn't an easy way to explain any of it, all the things she came up with sounded too weird. He might not buy the fact that she was a vampire, but he'd definitely think she was some kind of a psycho. Allison pounded her forehead in frustration with her fist. *Why* couldn't she come up with a good way to explain what she was doing there? It was so frustrating! Eventually, after waiting there in the ever-encroaching darkness for some time, she gave up on the idea of waiting for him. She decided instead to go out and look for him in the park before his trail went so cold that he'd be too difficult for her to track.

Where is that boy? she wondered angrily as she vanished into the crowds in the main part of the park.

The boy in question was currently stuffing his face with his sixth hot dog from King Frank's. Ironically, he was sitting at the same picnic table that Allison had occupied the day before. He had only left the dilapidated sanctuary of the Tunnel of Love about a half hour ago. He had felt awful at the time, as if something deep inside was constantly squirming and pawing at him, yearning for freedom. He knew what it was.

The wolf.

He'd had a sudden crazy idea: perhaps if he filled his belly to the point where he was more than full, the wolf trying to escape from inside of him wouldn't feel the need to hunt for a meal tonight? The meager collection of canned goods he'd been living off of wouldn't be enough to fill him up in that way, and besides, he had to ration what was left. So he'd left for King Frank's Royal Wiener Stand (that was it's full name) and bought six foot long dogs with all the fixings. It had set him back quite a bit, the food in this place was a bit pricey, which was one of the reasons why he tried to avoid the ever-present temptation to buy food from the park. When the transaction was completed, he counted his remaining money with a feeling of guilt. This had *better* work, otherwise he'd just wasted too much of a resource that he couldn't replace.

He still intended to chain himself up, but he wasn't completely sure that would be enough. At least this way, if the wolf did slip his chains, perhaps he wouldn't be motivated to try and hurt anyone. Maybe if he gave himself a good tummy ache, he'd just hang around the tunnel, feeling too sick to venture out any further. Kevin wasn't sure if it really worked that way - if anything that he did to himself in human form would be carried over to his wolf form or not. How his body worked now was a total mystery to him. One thing was for certain though, he was succeeding in making himself ill. He'd enjoyed the first few hot dogs, they were a decided improvement over the SPAM he'd had earlier that day (although the main ingredients were probably the same), but now he had to force himself to continue eating. The meal had gone from a pleasure to a chore with surprising speed.

He tried to distract himself from how difficult it was to continue eating by thinking of other things. He still had that persistent feeling that he needed to stay here in Wonderland, but it really was time to think about moving on while he still had enough money for a bus fare, although there was always the possibility of hitchhiking. Hitchhiking wasn't something he was eager to do, long rides with strangers would create too many opportunities for conversations he wasn't prepared to have right now, and anyone who rode with him for any length of time would be sure to remember him if they saw a news report about him being missing. Bus travel was expensive, but it offered him the anonymity he required. He didn't *want* to leave; every instinct in his body was still screaming at him to stay, yet he knew how irresponsible it was to remain this close to so many people. Maybe he could scout out another place where he could camp out, deep in the woods nearby? Maybe find himself a real cave to shelter in? He could still sneak into the park to use the bathrooms and replenish his water supply if it was close enough. He needed something farther away, but not *too* far. He cursed himself for all the days he'd spent sulking over things in the past which he could never change no matter how much he longed to instead of preparing for his future by searching the nearby wilderness for such a spot.

As he sat there, he looked to the setting sun. It should have filled him with dread, but the sheer beauty of the scene drove away all such thoughts. The sun's dying rays seemed to melt the clouds into varying shades of violet and magenta. Through the pink haze that was cast forth by the sinking orange medallion of the sun, the lights of the park threatened to flicker to life at any moment and chase away the shadows that grew ever longer as shades of blue infringed upon the diminishing pinkness still crouching stubbornly on the horizon.

Glorious! he thought.

Even though he thought of himself as an atheist (although recent events had made him question this stance more than usual), he always found something transcendent in the beauty of a sunrise or sunset. It was like a work of art that a thousand artists working for a thousand years could never duplicate. If there was a God, then He or She was one hell of a painter!

What evolutionary purpose can possibly be served by having the capacity to marvel at such displays? What advantage for my survival does this give me? If anything, it's a huge distraction!

He had always enjoyed this time of day the most. The slow transition from light to night had seemed like a magical event to him when he was a small child. There had been a large, gnarled old tree in his backyard where he had dutifully observed this daily phenomenon. No matter how busy he might be, he would try to take the time to watch the retreat of color from the world as it was replaced by the glow of moonlight. He thought that maybe this transition fascinated him so much because it was an analogy for life itself - a never ending cycle of periods of light and darkness. Although lately his life seemed like one eternal period of darkness, without hope or joy.

At least it had until *she* had come into his life. That intriguing girl he'd met the day before, Allison. She was so lively and free. When he was around her, he felt more comfortable and at ease, like he was finally able to freely express all the feelings he was often too nervous and awkward to put out there. She made it simple for him to get in touch with that more adventurous side of himself that he usually kept buried. It was easy to forget all the things that had been troubling him when he was in her presence. He desperately wanted to find that peace, that sense of balance again, but he knew he had to stay away from her, for her own good. He felt guilty for even daring to think of his own happiness like that. Did he really deserve it, after what he'd done?

No, not me, the wolf, he thought, trying to disassociate himself from the actions of his alter ego.

But the reality of the situation was that where he went, the wolf went too. They were forever intertwined and he could never escape from his dark half. This thought jolted him out of his reverie and made him realize that he couldn't afford to sit around here any longer admiring the sunset and thinking about girls. He was running out of time to get back to the Tunnel of Love and chain himself up. If he didn't get back in time and at least *try* to contain the beast within himself, and someone got hurt again as a result…no, he didn't want to even think about it. It was hard enough trying to live with himself with just one death on his conscience, he didn't want to add any more lives to that dreadful tally.

He forced the last bit of hot dog down into his protesting stomach and emptied his tray into a nearby trash can. He was feeling nauseous after all his eating, and he waddled away as quickly as he could without making himself throw up, away from King Frank's and the cheerful lights of Wonderland and back towards his dark den.

"This is where the camera coverage cuts off," the guard who had been helping out Matt and Randy told them.

Matt nodded. He recognized the surroundings from the videos he'd spent the better part of the afternoon watching.

"Alright. Walk us over to where it picks up again," he ordered, looking around for any places nearby where it looked like Kevin could easily slip in and out of the park.

"Sure," the guard replied dutifully as he led the way.

As they made their way through that section of the park, Matt spotted the gate that led off to the unused part of the park. On the other side, he could make out the massive silhouettes of the rotting hulks of old rides off in the distance.

"Wait! What's over there?" he said, stopping the guard.

"Oh, that's just the old park."

"The old park?" Randy asked.

"Yeah, there was a bigger amusement park here back in the day, before Wonderland. That's what's left of it. The owners keep on saying that they're going to expand Wonderland someday into that area, but they've been saying that for years and nothing's changed," he explained.

Matt looked at the crumbling rides beyond the gate. He couldn't believe how poorly this place was run! Those old rides had to be dangerous and they weren't really doing enough to keep people out of that area in his opinion. He wondered how this place stayed open. He figured that the owners must be regularly greasing the palms of local officials and safety inspectors with bribes. He couldn't contain the disgust that had been rising up in him any longer.

"Jesus Christ! Are you fucking kidding me? There's an entrance to a restricted area full of dangerous old rides and you aren't covering it with any cameras? This place is a joke! What the hell is wrong with you people?"

The guard understood that these guys were supposed to be some sort of hotshot detectives, but he'd just about had enough of them. Who did these foul-mouthed city slickers think they were to tell them how to run this place? And now they were taking the good Lord's name in vain, too!

"Hey man, look, I just work here. I don't make those kinds of decisions," he said, trying his best to remain professional.

"Of course, I'm sorry, I know it's not your fault. You've been a big help, really. I just don't think it's very safe for the customers is all I'm trying to say." Matt felt a little ashamed of himself for losing control like that. This case must be stressing him out more than he was aware of. He hadn't meant to take it out on this poor guy. He was just another working stiff, trying to make a living like the rest of them.

"Do ya think that's how he's getting in and out?" Randy said, trying to refocus everyone's attention on the matter at hand.

"Definitely worth a closer look, I'd say," Matt replied as he continued to stare off beyond the gate.

"If you really think he's hiding out back there, shouldn't we call the cops or something?" the guard asked. These jokers weren't even real police. He didn't understand why the owners were bothering to give them this level of cooperation.

"No. We want to bring him back home, not scare him away. If he sees a bunch of cops bearing down on him, he'll run for sure. We can handle it from here," Matt said decisively and began to move towards the gap in the gate. "I think this gap is big enough to squeeze through."

Randy caught his shoulder. "Hold on, before we go in there after him, maybe we should go back to the car and get some of our *special equipment*."

"Special equipment?" a bewildered Matt asked. He was so focused on getting to Kevin that he didn't pick up on Randy's implied meaning.

"You know...the *Vermilion* kind?" Randy clarified.

Understanding dawned on Matt's face and he felt like an idiot.

"Yeah, good idea pal." Matt wasn't about to face a werewolf without any weapons that would actually work against one, although he hoped he'd have no occasion to use it.

The guard really thought that these two were off their rockers now. What kind of special equipment could you possibly need to find a teenage kid?

"Thanks for all your help, we're gonna go back to our car for a minute. Just let us back into the park when we come back," Matt said, then he dashed off before the guard could even respond, with Randy struggling to catch up.

Why is this place so packed on a Sunday - and right after they found a dead body not too far away? I guess nobody wants to let a little thing like murder spoil their chance at a good time, Matt thought cynically as he and Randy tried to fight their way through the crowds as quickly as they could.

Matt hoped that they could get to Kevin before any of these people wound up like that poor girl that had been found this morning. Randy had talked about trying to put Kevin to sleep with a spell, but he wasn't sure if it would work on a werewolf. If it didn't, he'd promised Matt that he had a few more magical tricks up his sleeve that might allow them to contain Kevin until he could resume his human form again. In either case, it made sense for Matt to properly arm himself before going after Kevin, he couldn't depend on Randy to be able to protect both of them and neutralize Kevin safely at the same time. Matt figured he could sneak in his sword under his trench coat by having it hover behind his back. It was a trick he'd used a few times before. Maybe he could even put on a few pieces of his armor and hide them under his coat too, if he kept it buttoned up?

Randy finally caught up with Matt, but then he saw something as they made their way towards the front gates that made him freeze in his tracks. It was that girl from last night's security footage - the one who had appeared to be chasing after Kevin. She looked like she was chasing someone again, darting and weaving through the crowd as if pursuing some unseen signal.

Randy got a strange feeling as he watched her. There was something unnatural about her, but he couldn't quite put his finger on exactly what that was. Maybe if he'd ever met a vampire before, he would've recognized her as one, but he hadn't. All he knew was that her aura, which he couldn't see on the video, was all *wrong* somehow. For a moment, their eyes locked from across the throngs of people. The girl scowled, then she was off again.

"Hey Matt!! It's that girl! The one from the video!" Randy called to Matt, who was already several feet ahead of him. He paused for a moment and was annoyed to see that Randy had fallen so far behind him again.

"That's great! I'm glad she's not sitting in some werewolf's intestines right now, but we're running out of daylight. We don't have time to go chasing after a lead that might just be a dead end! C'mon! Try to keep up, dude!" he replied testily.

"But..." Randy started to protest, then realized Matt was right, the sun was almost completely down, and they hadn't even gotten to the car yet. If it wouldn't have attracted so much attention, he would've just teleported them to the car. With a sigh of resignation, he moved off after Matt.

Mary Brandon pushed her way through the jungle of sweaty human bodies that was Wonderland at night. Allison was nowhere to be seen, and Mary was starting to fear that Kevin had already gotten to her. She felt the reassuring weight of the cold metal of the letter opener in her jacket pocket. If he hurt Allison, if he'd been the one who'd killed Brittney....well, she knew what she *had* to do. She was terrified, but right now she was far more angry than scared. She moved in the direction of the old park. She'd snuck into the park from that direction, but had been too frightened to go straight to the Tunnel of Love earlier, hoping that Allison would look for him in the arcade or elsewhere in the park first. It wasn't a very rational idea, it made far more sense that Allison would immediately go to the place where she knew he was staying. Now Mary was beating herself up because she realized that she'd only decided on that course of action because she'd lost her nerve as she passed by the Tunnel of Love on the way into the park. Doing so might've cost her precious minutes. It might've doomed Allison.

I won't make that mistake again! she promised herself as she slipped her hand into her jacket pocket and her fingers closed around the handle of the silver letter opener with a steely resolve.

Within a matter of minutes, Mary was at the entrance to the Tunnel of Love. She took a deep breath as she took a tentative step forwards into the inky throat of the tunnel. The only light was the relentless glow of the full moon. She was all too aware of what that might mean. From somewhere in the gloom ahead of her, she heard the sound of shuffling feet. Every instinct in her body screamed at her to run away from there right now, as fast as her feet could carry her, but she stood firm and held her ground.

She fought down a lump in her throat and called out. "Allie? Allie, tell me that's you!" she pleaded hopefully. Her voice suddenly sounded unusually small, frightened and foreign to her own ears.

A hulking shape reared up, outlined against the darkness before her.

She screamed, but the only answer was a hungry growl....

CHAPTER 11:

REVELATIONS

Allison bolted down the black maw of the tunnel with as much speed as she could muster. Near the other end, she could hear an inhuman snarl followed by a frighteningly familiar shriek. Allison hadn't known what to expect when she reached the other end of the tunnel, but it certainly wasn't this! Dressed in the tattered remains of Kevin Scott's clothes was a vaguely human creature, and across from it, cringing up against the wall was Mary, brandishing the Excalibur letter opener Allison had given her for her birthday!

Of course, it's made of silver! That's my smart girl! But what's she even doing here?

The monster in Kevin's clothing actually seemed to be growing before her very eyes, becoming taller, hairier and more wolfish by the second. One of its oversized, bestial paws lashed out savagely at Mary. She screamed and ducked, avoiding its claws by only the merest fraction of an inch, the claws slashing through the air with a horrible whistling sound as they passed over her head.

Now Mary did a little slashing of her own, marking out a diagonal line from the beast's shoulder down to its stomach with the silver letter opener's glimmering blade. The creature howled as much in astonishment as in pain and staggered back a few steps clutching at its bloody chest.

Mary saw Allison come running up out of the corner of her eye and lunged over in her direction.

"Allie, *do* something!" she shouted as she reached her. She had come here to save Allison, and now she found herself asking Allison to save her! She tried to thrust the letter opener into her hand.

Allison shook her head. "Keep it. I've got something better," she told her as she pulled her pistol out of her purse and took aim at the creature.

Allison quickly appraised the scene spread out before her: the monster was now lying against the false rock wall of the tunnel, blood gushing from its wound. She thought she could discern the ghosts of Kevin's features in the beast's face, a face she had studied so intently just the night before.

So it IS him! As the realization dawned on her, she felt herself lowering the pistol barrel towards the ground without even thinking about it consciously.

To her utter astonishment, it began to speak.

"Help...me," it rasped through lupine teeth as another painful looking series of changes overtook it. The mouth twisted and elongated into a muzzle, making the head appear even more animalistic.

"C'mon Al! Either shoot it or let's get the hell out of here before it attacks again!" Mary urged. But Allison didn't hear her, she was already staring into those barely human, yellowish eyes, searching for some vestige of the young man hiding within.

"Alllll..." Mary pleaded uselessly, then her mouth dropped open in disbelief as she understood what Allison was attempting.

"It won't work! We've gotta go! We need to tell the Sherwoods what's been going on!" She grabbed onto Allison's arm and started tugging on it, but it was like trying to pull down a statue. Then she looked over at the Kevin-thing. She couldn't believe her eyes, was it her imagination, or did he seem to look a little more human now? Was it really working?

Allison continued looking into those eyes, exerting all of her will upon the beast.

C'mon, Kevin! Come back to me! You can do it, I believe in you! She tried to bore the words into his mind.

Paws separated back into fingers, coarse animal hairs receded, yellowish eyes cleared until they were brown upon white, the human eyes of Kevin Scott. The change continued on in reverse, in defiance of the moonlight that flooded the tunnel. Knife-like teeth shrank back down to normal proportions, it went on and on until the wolf was gone and Kevin Scott sat propped up against the wall of the Tunnel of Love, splayed out like a discarded toy bleeding from shoulder to belly button, dressed only in rags.

Allison collapsed suddenly into Mary's arms and she barely caught her in time, like a corporate trust exercise gone horribly awry. She gently guided her to the ground. For some time they all just sat there on the floor of the tunnel, breathing hard and staring at each other with a mix of mutual astonishment and fear.

"What...what...are you? How did you *do* that?" Kevin gasped.

"Little old me? I'm just your friendly neighborhood vampire, Mr. Summers." She smiled at him, flashing her pearly whites.

Kevin laughed. It was the hollow, broken laugh of a mad man.

"Vampires! Sure! Of course! Why the hell not?" He threw up his hands in resignation. "It makes about as much sense as anything else in my life does lately! If you're a vampire, then where are your fangs?" he asked suddenly. He hadn't seen any sign of them when she'd just smiled at him a moment ago.

"Fangs? That's only in stories. Don't believe everything you see in the movies."

"If you don't have fangs, then how do you, you know…" His voice trailed off.

"Get the blood out? With my regular teeth I imagine. It's probably not very pretty." Allison wrinkled her nose in distaste.

"Don't you know? What the heck kind of vampire are you anyway?"

"The nice kind that doesn't run around feeding on people! We live on a dairy farm and we own some cattle. We only drink cow's blood, and even then we take out just a little at a time with syringes and store it for later use. William says that if we feed directly off of a living thing, it's too easy to get carried away and we might drain it until it's dead. You probably have no idea how expensive it can be to replace a good cow."

"Shit. That was waaaay too detailed of an explanation. I guess you *really* are a vampire, plus you did that weird trick you just did somehow."

"It's a kind of hypnosis. Mind control. Kind of like a Jedi Mind Trick from Star Wars. It's one of my vampiric gifts. We're supposed to use it to lure in our prey and chill them out long enough for them to let us bite them. I use it to calm down the cows before I stick 'em with a needle. Or on people who piss me off. I just used it to will you back into being a human. It was a long shot, but obviously it worked out. You're welcome, by the way."

"Thanks. My mind tells me that this isn't happening, but my bloody chest tells me otherwise! Was that thing made of silver? It's nice to know that really works. I guess not everything in the movies is bullshit, huh?"

Allison crawled forwards to examine the wound, making a mighty effort not to suck it, and Kevin, dry. What would happen if you turned a werewolf into a vampire? Was that even possible? Would they end up being a strange hybrid of the two creatures? She had so many questions, but as fascinating as it might be to know the answers, she thought better of trying to find out. She probed the wound with her fingers, making Kevin wince slightly in the process, then she faced him with her prognosis.

"It's not very deep. It should just scab over by the morning."

"I wouldn't mind if it *was* fatal. I'm not sure I can go on living like this, you saw what I almost did to your friend here." He waved a hand lazily in Mary's direction.

"Sorry about that, for what it's worth. When I change…it's like I'm all instinct, like I'm on autopilot and someone else is doing most of the driving. I tried to eat a bunch of food so I'd be too full to attack anyone, I tried to chain myself up and lock myself in but that didn't work out so well…." He pointed back towards the little room where he slept. The door was now hanging halfway off the hinges and Allison could see a few broken links of chain on the floor, shining in the moonlight. Well, now she knew what he'd been doing with those chains in his room. She kicked herself for not figuring that out sooner.

Mary ignored his apology. "Did you kill Brittney?" she asked coldly. With a start, Allison realized that Mary was eying the antique pistol that she'd dropped when she'd almost fainted. Allison quickly snatched it up and shoved it back into her purse before Mary could grab it.

"Who's Brittney?" Kevin asked innocently. Mary's eyes narrowed, she wasn't sure she was buying his "oh, poor me, I wish I could just die" routine.

"Her friend. They found her body this morning, she'd been torn apart by wolves, just like that girl in Shadowbrook last week," Allison informed him.

"Oh, I'm sure he knows all about that girl in Shadowbrook, don't you *Kevin Scott?*"

"What? How do you know my real name?" an astonished Kevin asked, still not sure who this other girl was. Was she another vampire like Allison?

"It was all over the news. Your parents even hired a detective to find you and guess what? He already knows that you came to Davenport too! So, did you do it? Are you the one who's been killing all these girls just like you almost killed me?" Mary's voice was getting louder as she said each word, she was working herself into a fury at the thought that the person responsible for Brittney's death might be right here, casually sitting across the room from her.

Kevin looked away, unable to face her. "I...I think I did kill Sylvia. I can't really remember it very well, only bits and pieces. It's all jumbled up. But I'm sure that I didn't kill your friend, tonight is the first time that I've changed since...since that night with Sylvia."

"Yeah. Right. Why should I believe you? Either way, you're too dangerous to be left alive. By your own admission, you can't control yourself when you change! Give me that gun, Al, let's put this dog down already and go home!"

"You wanna kill me? Go right ahead! I won't try to stop you! Believe me, I've already tried! I've tried knives and hammers, but nothing would work! Nothing even so much as put a scratch on me until you did tonight! If you've got something in that gun that'll do the job, then just go ahead and do it! I have nothing left to live for! Don't you realize that I've been doing nothing but wishing that I was dead this whole time? I just lie here in the dark all day pretending that I am dead, praying to a God I don't even really believe in for my own death!"

Something about the way he said the words, the sheer conviction behind them, moved Mary a little, in spite of herself.

"Whoa, whoa, whoa! Everybody let's just try and all calm the fuck down for a minute, okay? *Nobody* is shooting or stabbing anyone tonight! Let's all get that through our heads! There's been enough killing going on around here lately, don't you think? Let's just all take a chill pill and try to figure this out," Allison said, physically getting between the two of them and snatching the letter opener from Mary so quickly she didn't register that it had happened until it was already gone from her hands.

"You didn't have to do that! Don't you understand? I *want* her to finish me off," Kevin told her.

"Oh please, quit it with the death wish stuff already. It's boring. Besides, you're far too cute to kill."

Mary buried her head in her hands. "Great! Now she's openly flirting with the werewolf..." she mumbled.

Kevin couldn't help but smile a little at the compliment. "It's just my luck isn't it? The most lively girl I've met in ages, the one who makes *me* feel alive again, isn't even really alive herself! Oh, the irony!"

Allison would have blushed if she was still capable of such fundamentally human reactions. She wasn't totally sure if that was a compliment, but she decided she'd take it as such.

"Hey man, 'alive' is just a state of mind." She smiled back. Then she looked seriously at the two of them.

"Look, Mary, I really don't think Kevin here was responsible for what happened to Brittney. I was with him last night, remember? I watched him while he was sleeping."

"You did?" Kevin was surprised. He didn't quite know what to make of this latest tidbit of information. Why was she watching him sleep? It was kind of sweet, but...also a little weird.

"Uh, yeah. I realize how creepy that sounds, sorry. I followed you back here after you ran off. I have a kind of psychic sixth sense that goes off when I'm around other supernatural beings and you were ringing all of my alarm bells, so I was really curious about what you were."

"Oh." Kevin sounded a little hurt. He was thinking that she saw him as just a mystery to solve and nothing more, despite her saying that she thought he was cute a minute ago.

"So? You weren't with him all night. He could've changed and attacked her after you left," Mary pointed out defiantly.

"Yeah, but you see how his clothes get all messed up when he changes? I was here earlier looking for him and I didn't see any ripped up clothes like that lying around in his room. Also, there's a bunch of other stuff you're ignoring. Like how they found hairs and blood from two different wolves at the crime scene in Shadowbrook, and how the ghost told me that he tried to help her."

"Ghost! What ghost? Don't tell me there's a ghost now too! My life has become a Halloween holiday special!" Kevin griped.

"Oh yeah. That first dead girl, Sylvia, is it? Her ghost is totally attached to you," Allison told him bluntly.

Kevin's eyes widened in alarm "What??? Is she here right now?" He sat up and looked all around the tunnel.

"No, I haven't seen her since last night. She seems to come and go randomly."

"And you actually *talked* to her? What did she say?" Kevin was desperate to know. He'd had nightmares about Sylvia's ghost, her ghost accusing him and attacking him. Was all of that simply a figment of his imagination, or was she really trying to get her vengeance on him?

Allison shrugged. "Not much. She freaked out and disappeared when I tried to get any real details out of her about how she died, but it should make you feel better to know that she doesn't blame you for what happened to her. Like I said, she seems to think that you tried to stop it somehow. If anything she feels sorry for you, she knows you tried to kill yourself."

Kevin slumped back against the wall, like all the wind had just been knocked out of him. He was utterly and completely flabbergasted by this news.

"*She* feels sorry for *me?*" He shook his head in disbelief.

"Yeah, but aren't you the one always telling me how confused ghosts are?" Mary fired back, trying to hold onto some of her skepticism and hatred for Kevin despite the fact that a part of her was being slowly won over by the genuineness of his reactions to each fresh revelation.

"But those other ghosts I've met...they're all really old ghosts that have been dead for a long time. This ghost was different. I have a theory that the 'fresher' a ghost is, the more coherent it is. It's like...maybe a spirit starts to degrade if it spends too much time outside of a body while on this plane? She was traumatized, but she still seemed to have all of her faculties," Allison explained.

Mary just made a dismissive sound.

"Listen, that's not my only theory. I think there's another werewolf. Remember there was hair and blood from *two* wolves. It's pretty obvious that Kevin is on his own here, isn't it? I think that the other werewolf is the one that *really* killed Sylvia. Maybe Kevin tried to fight it and that's how he got bitten? And now he or she is here in Davenport too! Maybe they're trying to find Kevin for some reason, or maybe they were drawn here because they can sense that there are vampires in town? I don't know. But I think that's the same werewolf who killed Brittney. If I'm right, then it's out there right now! If it really is after Kevin, it might be headed here as we speak! So we'd better all get back to the manor pronto where we've got more guns and we're not all so exposed."

"One part of your theory should be easy enough to prove. Just ask Mr. Loverboy over here how he became a werewolf to begin with!" Mary said, trying her best to remain stubbornly unconvinced.

"I don't know how or why it happened. I told you already, that entire night is a blur, even the night before it seems to have...a few holes in it," Kevin admitted.

"How *convenient!* The only thing with holes in it is your story!" Mary said hotly.

"I don't care if you believe me or not, I know that's the truth!"

"Calm down you two! Kevin, go put some clothes on and grab whatever things you might want to take with you, I can't bring you home looking like that."

"Bring him home? Allie, you can't be serious! He's a monster!"

"So am I! So are William and Elizabeth, or did you forget?"

"Yeah, but that's different…"

"Is it? Is it really? You don't have any clue what it's like for us! How hard it is to stop ourselves from drinking until someone's nothing but a dry husk every time we're around someone living. Yeah, we don't talk about that in front of you or your dad because we don't want to scare you guys away, but that's how it really is. We're like a bunch of addicts and sure, we've been on the wagon for a long time, but that doesn't mean that the whole thing still can't just go off the rails at any moment. You don't know how close some of us have come to falling off that wagon sometimes!" she said, thinking of the other night when she'd watched Kevin's vulnerable, sleeping form, thinking of how she'd almost given into her hunger again just a few moments earlier when she was looking at his wounds. Even from across the room, the blood that was still trickling down his half naked body still called to her. *Sang* to her!

Mary ignored all of what Allison had just revealed. The idea that the vampires she thought of as being almost the same as her own family ever came close to losing control, that they sometimes contemplated making a meal out of her and her father was too horrible for her to process right now.

"Well, you know how they feel about werewolves. They sure as hell won't like you bringing one home," she countered lamely.

"And how would they feel about me if I just left this poor guy to his fate? To whatever this other werewolf, who is a *killer* has planned for him? Do you think they'd still respect me if I didn't at least try to help him?"

"Yeah, this mystery werewolf that probably doesn't even exist. And honestly, I don't think that they give a *damn* about what happens to any werewolf. 'The only good werewolf is a dead werewolf.' I have literally heard William say that - more than once!"

Kevin had just been frozen in place, watching and listening to this entire exchange with some fascination. He'd correctly deduced from the conversation that William and Elizabeth were both vampires who lived on this dairy farm with Mary and her father, who were both apparently regular, good old-fashioned humans.

"Kevin, don't listen to her. Just go and get dressed and grab your things like I asked you to, we need to get a move on. That other werewolf could show up at any moment." Allsion tried to put as much authority into her voice as she could come up with. She'd use her mesmerism on him again if he didn't obey, although she really didn't want to make a habit of doing so. She was half tempted to use it on Mary. too. She understood how distraught her friend was over losing Brittney and then almost being killed herself, but she was also frustrated that she couldn't see the logic of her arguments or appreciate the danger that they all might be in the longer they lingered here arguing around in circles.

Thankfully, Kevin rose from the floor of the tunnel to do as she'd suggested. As he got up, she caught a glimpse of his bare ass.

Not bad. Not bad at all! she couldn't help but think with a wistful smile.

"I saw that. You were totally checking out his butt," Mary chided her.

What was the point in trying to deny it? "So what if I was? Can't a girl have a little fun?"

"Is that what this is really all about? I think you just want a boyfriend for yourself. If he's dependent on you to stop him from changing into a monster then he can't ever leave you can he? How nice for you! Never mind that he might've murdered one of my only normal friends!"

"Mary, please, just stop it. I trust him that he's telling the truth. Why isn't that good enough for you? Why won't you trust *my* instincts on this? You know that I have senses that you don't have. Don't you think I'd know it if he was lying? Have I ever lied to you before? Okay, wait. Let me clarify that - have I ever lied to you about anything that really *mattered*?"

"No, but..."

"No buts! I know that you're hurting but you're taking it out on the wrong people, you've been doing it all day. You know that I love you, don't you? You have to know that I wouldn't bring him home with us if I thought he was any threat to our family. Please, just trust me on this," she pleaded.

Mary started crying, it was like a dam breaking. All of the powerful emotions she'd been keeping bottled up inside herself all day came flooding out all at once. She held onto Allison so she wouldn't be swept away by the current of them.

"Oh Al, I'm so sorry. I'm so sorry about what I said to you this morning! I saw that report about him on the news and I was convinced that he killed that girl in Shadowbrook and Brittney too! I was sure that he was a werewolf! I came here tonight because I knew you were coming to see him and I was afraid of what he'd do to you! I can't ever lose you like I lost Brittney, especially after the awful things I said to you today. I couldn't bear it if our last conversation was an argument!"

Allison patted her back with one hand and stroked her hair lovingly with the other. This girl whom she'd practically raised herself, especially after her mother passed away, part sister, part daughter, part friend. Their bond was as strong and complicated as it was unshakable.

"It's okay, it's all going to be alright. I swear," she soothed her. "It was very brave of you to try and rescue me - and foolish! Please, don't do anything like that again, okay? I can't bear to lose you either," she told her softly.

Mary nodded weakly as she wiped the tears from her eyes.

Kevin came out of the maintenance closet, fully dressed and carrying his duffel bag and skateboard.

"Okay, I'm ready," he said awkwardly as he saw the two girls hugging each other, and realized with some embarrassment that he was interrupting what his mother would probably call some sort of a "come to Jesus" moment.

"Alright, yeah. Let's get the hell out of here, Kemosabe."

Mary looked at Kevin. She realized now how awfully she'd been treating him, too, and a wave of regret washed over her.

"Hey, um...Kevin. I'm sorry about some of the things I said. I've been, sorta lashing out at everyone since Brittney died. You're obviously dealing with a whole lot too. So yeah, I'm sorry. That's all," Mary said between sniffles.

"Understandable. I mean, I guess I *did* just try to kill you, so I can't really blame you for feeling the way that you do. Uh, sorry about that again."

Mary actually laughed a little. "It's fine, I guess, under the circumstances. But she's right, we should get out of here before that other werewolf shows up, or those detectives find this place. Oh that reminds me! Allison, you'll never guess who they hired to find Kevin!"

"Who?" Allsion asked as she led the way towards the end of the tunnel.

"Matt Spike!" Mary revealed cheerfully.

"Who is that again?" a confused Allison asked.

"Oh yeah, you probably forgot his real name. His pen name is Charles Gordon Bennett."

"The dude who wrote *Dirt Nap?*"

"The very same one!"

"Get outta town!"

"It's true!"

"Hmm. I didn't think he took cases this far north of Jersey. That's pretty damned cool. Almost makes me want to hang around here and get his autograph, but I left my copies of his books back at the house," joked Allison.

Kevin paid no attention to this chit chat. His mind was still reeling from the thought that he might not really be responsible for Sylvia's death. It was a possibility he'd already thought about a little when he'd read about the DNA from two different wolves being found in her room, but he hadn't dared to hope that it meant he was exonerated. Now to find out that Sylvia didn't blame him for her death, it was too much to hope for. On top of all that, there was the revelation that not only were werewolves real, but so were ghosts and vampires too. The existence of ghosts implied the immortality of the soul, and by extension that all of that religious gobbledygook that he found so distasteful might be true, or at least have some basis in truth. The implications of all of this were mind boggling.

There was also Allison, who had come back to him and somehow stopped his transformation with just the force of her will alone. Did this mean that he might be able to have something close to a normal life now? Maybe even one with her? Finding out that she was one of the undead hadn't changed how he felt about her one bit, especially since she didn't seem to prey on other people. No, what he was more worried about was that she might only think of him as a mystery to solve and would lose interest in him once she felt like she'd figured everything out. He was also concerned over how these other vampires would react to him. They seemed to harbor some kind of a grudge against werewolves. Would she be able to protect him from them? Now that he suddenly felt that he might have a life worth living again was he about to lose it for good?

CHAPTER 12:

KILROY WUZ THERE

Once they were out of the tunnel and had walked some distance from it, Mary sprinted ahead of them towards a section of fencing.

"Follow me! There's a hole in this part of the fence. I left my bike on the other side of it," she called out to the other two.

As the trio edged nearer to the fence, they could all see a narrow slit cut in the chain link. The dark outline of the woods was visible just beyond it.

"*I* didn't know this was here," Allison said somewhat haughtily.

"You don't know everything about this place, no matter how much you may like to think that you do." Mary smirked at her as she slipped through the slit.

"I knew about it too," Kevin shrugged as he struggled to fit through with his big bag and skateboard. He got snagged on it several times before ultimately making it through.

Allison sighed as she passed through to the other side, annoyed that these two presumed to know more about the secrets of her beloved park than she did. The nerve of them! Mary picked up her bike from where it had been leaning against a nearby tree and walked with it, leading them along a narrow path between the trees.

Kevin was suddenly filled with a petrifying terror as he stepped into those woods. He hadn't felt like this since that last morning in Shadowbrook, when he'd run through the dark woods between his neighborhood and Sylvia's. He found it odd that he was now in the company of two girls that he barely knew, one of whom was a vampire who was armed with a gun and silver letter opener that could probably kill him, but he was more frightened of passing through a bunch of harmless old trees.

As he forced himself to trudge on, the feeling only worsened. He imagined these woods to be oppressively, all-encompassingly menacing. Why was he so scared of the woods all of the sudden? He'd passed through them before during the day without experiencing any of these anxieties. There had to be a reason, but his mind couldn't seize upon it. It was like trying to remember a dream; hazy images danced before his senses, but none of them made any sense to him. Was this just a case of Deja vu? Was his mind trying to protect him, and if so, from what? He had no idea, but something deep inside of him told him that he was a fool for entering these woods at night. These woods were far too much like the ones in Shadowbrook where the...where the...where the *what?*

His mind suddenly found itself fixating on that first night with Sylvia, the night before his life had become the swirling whirlpool of madness that he was presently trapped in. His last night of normalcy. He forced himself to try and remember. She passed him that note in the drive-thru. In front of his coworkers, he'd acted like he wasn't going to take her up on her offer, but of course the temptation had proven impossible to resist. She was beautiful and he'd had nothing better to do, so why not take a chance and see where the night would lead him? He'd gone home after work briefly, then ridden his bike over to her place. He'd nervously rung the doorbell and his stomach had been so filled with butterflies while he was waiting that he'd almost run away. Finally, Sylvia answered the door, wearing a bathrobe and barely anything else underneath. She'd invited him inside, they'd talked briefly as she laid out the ground rules of their arrangement. Kevin had been all too eager to agree to her terms. He'd been far too eager in general. He would've probably agreed to anything for the chance to be with her.

Then they'd spent a good chunk of the rest of the night messing around, they hadn't *quite* gone all the way, but they'd done more than Kevin had ever done before. She'd sent him home with an invitation to return for some more the next night. He recalled getting on his bike and pedaling it down Monument Drive, then off the street and onto the pine needle strewn path through the woods that would eventually spill out behind the row of townhouses that he lived in. He recalled the joy he felt as he rode home, happily lost in thoughts of his latest sexual escapades and his dreams of what might come next and then...nothing. Blackness. The next thing he could remember was waking up the next morning, feeling unusually tired and haunted by vivid nightmares from the night before. Nightmares about werewolves, of all things! He didn't even clearly remember how he'd gotten into his house, or his bed.

Kevin was mystified by this hole in his memory. Had something happened to him on the way home in the woods that night? Was he so frightened of the woods now because it reminded him of that night? It seemed likely, and the more he thought about it, the more certain he became that it *must* be so. Whatever it was, it had to be something terrible, yet what could be more terrible than waking up to find the gore streaked corpse of your lover only to realize that you were the inhuman beast that was responsible for it? He noted that his recollections of the later half of the night of Sylvia's death were as ethereal as those of his trip through the woods the night before. He'd originally attributed that to the confusion of his transformation, but now he wasn't so sure anymore. Just how much was he keeping from himself?

He remembered how he'd ruled out the possibility of him being bitten by another werewolf, believing that such an unusual experience would be impossible to forget. But he'd never stopped to consider if such an experience might be too *traumatic* to remember! He'd read about how people sometimes erected barriers in their minds to protect them from madness. Might not he be doing that? The idea that he'd really been attacked by a werewolf - a creature from folklore and movies - was certainly crazy in and of itself. Maybe it was something that his mind just hadn't been able to face? Allison seemed to think that he'd been bitten trying to defend Sylvia, but what if it had actually happened earlier than that? He concentrated. He had to remember! He *had* to!

Pictures blasted his mind now, as clear as day. In one of them, he tore off a ripped and bloodied t-shirt. He remembered feeling surprised to discover that the wounds beneath it had almost completely vanished, before tossing the shirt onto his bed and watching it tumble into the gap between the bed and the wall. In another series of images, he saw a grey-furred werewolf bounding towards him on all fours with alarming speed, yellow eyes glowing with a malice as it knocked over his bike. Kevin remembered the hot, stinking breath of the beast as its jaws snapped at him. The wet, sticky drool of the monster trickling down in rivulets onto his face. Kevin was caught between the cold, hard, unyielding ground and the gigantic man-wolf, with only the frame of the bike separating him from the monster. It didn't stop him for long, the wolf drove its snout into a gap in the bike frame and bit into Kevin's torso. Kevin felt an explosion of pain as the creature's teeth sank into his flesh and it twisted its head savagely, tearing out a chunk of his body. He screamed in agony, then, as if in answer to his cries, he saw *something* slam into the wolf, knocking it into a nearby tree with such force that the tree snapped in two like a matchstick. Kevin caught a glimpse of a rather dashing looking older man running towards the brutal sounds of snarling and barking that were coming from the direction of the now-shattered tree. He paused momentarily to look down upon Kevin and shook his head before running off. Kevin remembered painfully fighting his way back to his feet, his own hot blood pouring down his side, getting back onto his bike and pedaling as fast he possibly could, like a man possessed, far, far away from the animalistic sounds of battle behind him.

Kevin realized that he was now no longer walking, he was standing in place, shaking all over and hyperventilating. Allison noticed this too and turned back to face him.

"Whoa! Are you okay?" she asked, her voice full of concern.

"He's not starting to change again is he? Maybe what you did to him is starting to wear off?" Mary asked fearfully.

"No, it's not that. I...think I'm starting to remember some things now. Being in these woods at night must've triggered it. You asked me earlier how I became a werewolf and I told you I didn't know, but now I think I do. I was attacked one night, when I was traveling through some woods like this in between Sylvia's part of town and mine. I only got away because something else attacked the werewolf and started fighting it, and there was a man with it...they all started fighting the werewolf and I got away all in the confusion. I almost died! Somehow, I made it back home and passed out in my bed. The next day I thought I'd just dreamed the whole thing, and went to school like nothing had happened, but now I think it was real!"

Allison put a comforting arm around him. Immediately he started breathing more normally and his shaking became less pronounced.

"You said that someone fought the werewolf? Who?"

"I don't know. There were at least two of them, one that kind of tackled the werewolf when he was trying to eat me, and knocked him right into a tree so hard that it broke in half. I didn't get a good look at him, it might've even been another werewolf. And there was some guy with him who looked like he belonged on the cover of a romance novel or something. He was kind of ripped, had long hair and was dressed in old-style clothes."

Allison tried to digest this new information, but she couldn't make any sense of it. Were there *two* factions of werewolves running around fighting each other for some reason? What the hell was really going on here?

She held Kevin's hand. It felt so wonderfully warm. "We'll figure it all out. Give yourself some time and I'm sure you'll start to remember more things. There's no rush. It's going to be okay. For now, let's just concentrate on getting you home to our place."

"Okay. Thanks," he told her. Her hand was so icy, but he didn't mind. He felt that familiar, welcome sense of calm and peace that he'd felt when he first met her washing over him again. Within moments, his fear of the woods was vanquished and he felt more in control again. They continued to walk together hand in hand behind Mary.

"You're kind of amazing," he blurted suddenly, not knowing why. He was immediately embarrassed by the outburst.

"I know, it's one of my many faults," Allison smiled back at him. It felt so good to her to finally be appreciated like this. And best of all, she knew that he really meant every word of it too.

What was she going to do with this sweet, sad, broken boy? How would she explain all of this to William and Elizabeth when she didn't completely understand it herself? She hoped that none of the adults had realized that she and Mary were missing from the manor yet. They'd be even harder to win over if they were already pissed at them both for defying their orders.

"I'm sorry I ran out on you like that last night. It wasn't you, I was having a really good time playing that game. It was the first time I've had a good time in what felt like forever. It was just the crowd. I'm supposed to be like some kinda fugitive on the run now, ya know? So I didn't like all that attention," Kevin said to her.

"That makes sense I suppose. It's all good, forget about it," she told him as they finally emerged from the woods and back out onto a street

"It's funny, I'm usually not that good at that game. I think I'm only decent at it now because of how I've changed since I was bitten. It's like all my senses, my reflexes, my speed and everything are always dialed up to 10 all the time."

"Oh? And here I thought you were just doing so good because you were trying to impress me," Allison teased him, sounding a little hurt.

"Well…I think that *probably* factored into it too," he assured her a little too quickly, afraid that perhaps he'd really hurt her feelings and she wasn't just being playful with him.

She laughed. "I know what you mean though. I don't think I would've been very good at that game if it had been out back before

I became a vampire. I used to be a real klutz. We vampires have some similar powers to what you just described. Elizabeth says they're our 'gifts" - compensation for otherwise being totally screwed over by this curse. Yeah, they're cool and everything, but I'm not quite sure they balance out all the downsides of being a vampire."

"So...how long *have* you been a vampire?" Kevin asked.

"Ouch, Kevin! Never ask a girl how old she is. That's like the *first* rule, man!"

"Sooo that means you're afraid to tell me!"

"Okay, okay! I died in '89," she confessed.

"Holy shit! 1889?" Kevin gasped in astonishment.

She laughed. "No,1989, genius! Why would you think it was 1889?"

"I dunno, aren't most vampires supposed to be all gothic and Victorian?"

She laughed even harder now. "Jesus! Stop stereotyping us! Just because I live in a scary old mansion that Barnabas Collins would feel at home in doesn't mean I'm a refugee from an Anne Rice novel!"

"1989 huh? I think my mom was...maybe in her early twenties then?" Kevin mused playfully. "And I was born about a year and half later..." he continued.

"Please, *don't* do the math. Math ruins everything. All you need to understand is that I am a real teenager, physically and mentally." She said it a little sadly, hoping that this wasn't going to be a huge turn off for him.

She felt him squeeze her hand reassuringly.

"Don't worry. I'm into older women."

She rolled her eyes at being called an "older woman". Technically it was true, but it certainly wasn't how she thought of herself. Or liked to think of herself. It was easy for him to say that now, but how might he feel in a few years when he seemed to be older than she was? She stopped herself from pondering that line of thought. She was really getting ahead of herself. It was obvious that they liked each other, and they were already talking like they were a couple, but what *were* they really? This was all happening so quickly! Yet it didn't feel unnatural to her, in fact it felt more right than anything she'd felt in a long time. She just wanted to try and enjoy the moment. To enjoy being with him without worrying about what the future may or may not hold for the two of them. Then a new and somewhat disturbing thought suddenly struck her, threatening to derail her newfound happiness. She couldn't hold it in.

"What about Sylvia? I know I'm pretty fucking awesome, but wasn't she your girlfriend or something? Are you really over her that quickly?" This seemed pretty heartless to her, especially considering that she was dead now, and *how* she died.

"No, she had a boyfriend. He didn't seem to be that into her, though. He hardly spent any time with her, but he was really popular; a football player. So she didn't want to break up with him because staying with him made *her* more popular. He wasn't umm...fulfilling her needs, sexually, if you know what I mean. She suspected that maybe he was in the closet, but was too scared to trust her with that information, too worried about maintaining his reputation as a big, manly football star. So that's why she started flirting with me. It wasn't anything too serious. Purely physical. We just kind of...messed around a few times. I really barely knew her, as a person I mean," he explained.

"Geez. Modern relationships!" Allison shook her head in wonder.

She considered herself to be kind of an old-fashioned romantic. She didn't mean to be judgmental towards people who weren't, she just knew that such casual affairs weren't for her. If she was going to be with someone physically like that, she preferred for it to mean something a little deeper than just a "good time". She'd done a little (very little, actually) dating before becoming a vampire and this attitude had given her a pretty decent share of heartbreak in the past. In a way, she admired people who could separate the two things, it probably spared them a great deal of emotional pain, but it was impossible for her to do so. She wanted the whole enchilada - sex that was an expression of love and not just a way to get your rocks off. She wouldn't settle for anything less. A girl had to have her standards, didn't she?

"So you really saw her, huh? And she wasn't angry at me?" He still had trouble believing it.

"Yeah. She really scared the bejesus out of me! Like I said before, she's not mad at you at all. Quite the opposite. She wants you to stop blaming yourself for...whatever it was that happened. Maybe she'll show up again and you can see her for yourself."

"What do you mean? You can *make* me see her?" Kevin was simultaneously terrified and thrilled by the prospect. What would he say if he got the chance to really see her again? What *could* he say that would ever make it all alright?

"Sure, if you're touching me when I'm seeing her, you'll see her too. I did it once with Mary, isn't that right, Mary?" Allison made her voice obnoxiously louder so that Mary, who had been walking in silence ahead of them could hear her.

"Ugh. Don't remind me of that! It still gives me the creeps!" Mary complained.

"I used to like to do gravestone rubbings and sometimes I'd bring Mary with me. One time there was this ghost hanging around there that I showed to Mary," Allison whispered to Kevin.

"Yeah, and now she loves to torture me by bringing it up all the time!"

"That's what friends are fo–" Allison suddenly stopped walking. Kevin, who was still holding her hand, also came to a stop and looked at her in bewilderment. They had both come to a stop in front of an old church.

Allison gazed up at the huge, cathedral-like mass of bricks. Massive wooden doors guarded its interior from atop worn, weather beaten stone steps. Ivy ran up its walls, almost blotting out some of the stained glass windows. This majestic and imposing structure's decidedly medieval atmosphere was only spoiled by such modern touches as a parking lot and a sign declaring that the building was CLOSED FOR REPAIRS.

She was familiar enough with the building, it was only a few streets away from Sherwood Farm, yet tonight it seemed *different* somehow. She was getting an awful impression from the venerable structure. Her sixth sense was buzzing away, stronger now than ever before. The feeling was sickening, it was a feeling of immense evil, so complete that her mind felt like it would be drowned in it. Paradoxically, as it turned her stomach, as it disgusted her, it also appealed to some hidden darkness within herself which secretly longed to join it. This sensation was soon blotted out by another one, that of eyes watching her. She could feel them upon her, hateful, sick, hungry eyes penetrating every inch of her being. She was so frightened that she had to repress the urge to scream, and she was not someone who lost her cool easily. She shook herself out of her funk and began walking again, slightly more quickly this time. Yet still she could feel the awful sensation of those inhuman eyes following her....

The Hunter could scarcely believe his eyes, yet there he was! Kilroy would have smiled if he'd been able to do so, instead he'd contented himself with a small snarl of victory. Something was troubling him though, the boy was in human form! How was this possible? No werewolf that had been cursed from a bite could possibly resist the rays of the full moon. In the end, it was strange, but irrelevant. It changed nothing. Kilroy had been given an opportunity to correct a mistake and he would gladly take it. There was no point in wondering about the reasons behind the boy's current form.

Yes, a mistake. That's exactly what this boy was. Kilroy had been out that night last week, searching for others of their kind. It was his task to track them down for his Master, so that he could destroy them before they could join the enemy. He could feel the pull of a bloodsucker from many, many miles away. He had merely been passing through Shadowbrook on his way to investigate where his instincts were leading him next. But he'd been so hungry, it had been days since he'd last fed on fresh meat. The last thing he'd eaten was a deer, but he'd grown tired of eating animals. He'd wanted to feed on a human that night. So it was that he was soon slinking down narrow suburban streets, always keeping to the shadows, always watching and waiting.

Then he saw him, riding along on his bike. He recalled his excitement as he'd spied the child foolishly turning off of the safety of the well-lit street and down a dark path through the woods, into his world, his hunting ground. The boy would have been perfect: young, tender and so vulnerable, so very all alone in those woods. He'd been ripe for the picking, but then *they* showed up and ruined everything! *They* were probably there on the trail of the same bloodsucker he was after. Kilroy would've finished the job and killed the boy, had *they* not intervened. Kilroy had been lucky to escape *them* that night, but he wasn't the only one to elude death in those woods, for the boy had escaped while Kilroy had been preoccupied battling for his own life. Alone and outnumbered, Kilroy had been badly injured in the fight and had no time to go searching after the boy, he'd had to return to his den and lick his wounds instead.

Kilroy probably should've left Shadowbrook as soon as he could, before *they* found him again and tried to finish him off, or got to the bloodsucker he'd been after first. Yet he'd decided to linger for another day, to make sure that the boy was dealt with properly. He had to be eliminated. The Master had forbidden making any more of their kind. Now that the boy had survived being bitten, he was just like Kilroy - a werewolf. He knew all too well what would happen if *they* got to the boy first, if they convinced him to join their ranks. If the Master ever found out, he'd be *furious*, he would almost certainly punish Kilroy, and punish him *severely*. No, there was no reason why the Master had to ever know about Kilroy's mistake. If he corrected the mistake, then it would be as if it had never happened. So the next night, even though he wasn't quite fully healed, Kilroy had left his temporary den and run through the woods, feeling the earth beneath his paws, the moonlight shining upon his ancient back, and the wind whistling past his furry ears. He'd run back to Shadowbrook, dreaming of the taste of the boy's flesh in his mouth.

It has been child's play for one such as him to track the boy's path, he tracked it to a nice, big house. Kilroy was fortunate indeed, it was obvious that *they* had not found the boy yet. They must've forgotten about the boy, desperate to get to the bloodsucker before Kilroy could. Through the window, Kilroy could see the boy, lying nude on a bed, being straddled by a girl. Even through the glass, he could feel the heat of their lovemaking. The scent of it excited Kilroy.

Two for the price of one! he'd thought.

Now came the part that Kilroy loved the best, now came the killing....

Kilroy had smashed through the window and leapt towards the bed, he'd knocked the girl right off of the boy and immediately began feasting upon her. She'd tasted so sweet! He'd gotten so carried away with her that he'd almost forgotten why he was there to begin with. It was quite a shock when he found himself fighting with the boy a moment later, except that the boy was no longer just the naked, scrawny, helpless little thing he'd been earlier. The boy had already gone through the change and was fighting him tooth and claw. He hadn't expected the boy to change, the first change usually happened on the night of the full moon. The shock of his attack on the girl must've been enough to prematurely awaken the wolf that now lived inside the child.

Oh, the boy had fought well indeed. Looking back on it, Kilroy realized that he'd been too cocky. He'd assumed that he'd had all the advantages: centuries of experience and a true passion for the violence he inflicted on his prey, but Kilroy was still not fully recovered from the previous night's battle. The boy had the advantage of his youth, plus he fought to defend his woman, which perhaps gave him a kind of strength that Kilroy would never really know. In the end, he had exhausted Kilroy, and taken quite a few good chunks out of him. Kilroy had been forced to flee. He'd gotten his licks in too, he hoped that the damage he'd done to the lad was enough to kill him, that he was beyond even the uncanny healing abilities that all werewolves possessed. He just knew that he couldn't go on fighting the boy any longer without risking himself unduly. He'd fled back through the shattered window and out into the safe haven of the night. He had no more time to waste on this child. He'd already lost a day because of the boy, perhaps even lost the bloodsucker he sought to *them.* He had to get back on the trail again.

Indeed, he would eventually learn a few days later that he *had* lost the bloodsucker he'd sought because of the fiasco with the boy. By the time he'd reached its home, he found that it had been hastily abandoned. *They* had gotten to him first after all. Yet all was not lost, Kilroy could still feel other bloodsuckers nearby, *several* of them in fact. He'd doubled his efforts to follow this new signal, hoping that if he found a whole group of bloodsuckers first, and they were able to eliminate them before they could join the enemy, it would more than make up for his recent transgressions. So it was that he had come to Davenport, that he'd found the girl last night who reeked of the scent of a bloodsucker, confirming that he was on the right path. He'd spent much of the day looking for the bloodsuckers and he was certain that he'd found them on a farm not too far away from this empty old church that he'd broken into and used to take shelter in. He'd contacted the Master with the good news. He had seemed especially pleased when Kilroy had revealed which bloodsuckers in particular were to be found on that farm. He'd watched them from afar for part of that day while they'd gone about their business on the farm and he'd recognized them from the old days.

Now the Master himself was coming here with the others. They'd be here in only a few short hours. He would have to move quickly if he was to eliminate the boy before they arrived. Just one little loose end to tie up before the Master got here.

Kilroy silently slipped out of the church through the back where he'd broken in. Keeping to the shadows, he followed them, keeping at a reasonable distance. The prey seemed to be moving faster now. Did they suspect? He hoped so, he hoped they were scared, they always tasted better when they were frightened. As he observed them, Kilroy realized that one of the girls with the boy looked familiar. His keen eyes narrowed. He *had* seen her before. She lived in the manor and was a vampire herself. A Chidling created by their old friends William and Elizabeth, no doubt. He'd seen her outside today, working with the others. The other girl was unfamiliar to him, yet she had the odor of the undead clinging to every inch of her, obviously she was another resident of the manor. Odd that they had humans living with them. Perhaps they keep them as servants, made obedient by the promise of eventually being rewarded with eternal life, like in some of the stories? He wondered how they resisted feeding upon them. He certainly wouldn't have been able to resist such a constant temptation. He'd never known any bloodsuckers that he thought would be able to do so either.

They were headed back towards the farm. Why were they bringing the boy there? Were William and Elizabeth already allied with the enemy? Was he already too late? Kilroy quickened his pace....

CHAPTER 13:

THE MANOR

Randy popped open the trunk of his car. Inside was the case containing the *Vermilion Avenger* and next to that were the various pieces of Matt's suit of armor, which unfortunately did not have their own fancy storage case and had been bouncing around in the trunk the entire time.

Matt glanced around the parking lot, fortunately it was pretty deserted. Then he began looking for the cameras that covered it, trying to remember where the closest one was to the car. Finally he spotted it atop a tall lamppost.

"Hey, stand in front of me while I put this stuff on so the cameras can't pick it up clearly," he commanded Randy. Matt was a pretty tall guy, but Randy was even taller and more heavily built, so he easily blocked him. "A little more to the left. No, *my* left! Okay, that should be good, stay right there!"

Matt took off his trench coat and clearly pictured the *Vermilion Avenger* flying out of the case and hovering behind his back. No sooner had he formed the thought than the sword moved to make it a reality. Next, Matt imagined the two halves of his armor's breastplate attaching itself to his body. As they were made from the same thought-responsive, gravity defying metal that his sword's hilt was formed from, they also flew up out the trunk to obey his commands. He did the same thing with the forearm guards, the pieces that covered his upper legs, and of course the bit that protected the family jewels. The last thing he wanted was for some werewolf to bite off his dick! When he was wearing all the pieces of armor that he thought he might be able to reasonably conceal under his coat, he closed the trunk and put the coat back on, making sure to get it on over the *Vermilion Avenger*, and buttoned it up. Unfortunately, the shin guards would show - his coat was long, but not quite *that* long. And the shoulder pads were too large and bulky to fit under the coat at all.

"Well, how do I look? Do I look like one badass motherfucker that's ready to kick some serious monster ass or what?" Matt was still hoping that he wouldn't have to really face any actual monsters, especially if doing so might mean having to hurt Kevin, but he chose to hide these anxieties with flippancy as he often did.

Randy looked him over critically for a second, then shook his head. With his trench coat now completely buttoned up, the collar popped, and the bulky breastplate bulging out so much that it strained against his buttons, threatening to make them pop off, Matt looked more like an overweight flasher than a heroic monster buster. He also had to walk very stiffly because of the long sword hovering closely behind his back. Randy almost laughed at the sight of him.

"No, you look more like a total schmuck. But I suppose you won't attract too much attention."

"Gee, thanks, pal!"

"Hmph. I thought you valued my unvarnished honesty."

"Not nearly as much as I do your humility!"

"Matt, I've been thinking. Maybe I should just do a teleportation spell to get us into that older part of the park? It would be a hell of a lot faster than trying to walk back out there and the sun is almost completely down already."

Matt considered it for a moment, it *would* be much faster, but if they materialized out of thin air too close to the gate, there was a good chance that somebody would see them considering how crowded the park was tonight. They didn't need that kind of attention right now.

"Nah, someone might see us. We're just gonna have to do this the old-fashioned way, I'm afraid," he told Randy. Matt also hated the way teleportation made him feel queasy.

"Well, in that case we'd better get a move on."

"Definitely!" Matt agreed and they started moving back towards the front gate. Matt's attempts to walk briskly while at the same time having to move so stiffly because of his sword made his gait seem especially silly as they walked off.

Eventually, the pair of detectives returned to the poorly secured gate to the old park, Matt had a bit of a time slipping through it now that he was all geared up, and briefly regretted not allowing Randy to teleport them to the other side. In the end, he managed to squeeze through. The last rays of sunlight were deserting the sky and painting the rusting hulks of the old rides in deep shades of red as they moved through them, senses alert for any sign of Kevin. Soon the way ahead of them was lit only by the faint glow from the park behind them and the pearlescent light of the full moon that hung above them like a harbinger of impending doom.

Matt stopped in his tracks. He strained to hear what sounded like raised voices from somewhere ahead of them.

"So, you hear it too?" Randy asked.

Matt nodded. "Yeah, sounds like people shouting. Might be a couple of female voices. I thought I heard one of them screaming a moment ago."

"It could be from back there," Randy said, reasonably gesturing back towards the lights from the rest of the park. "Lots of rides that make people scream in there."

"*Those* rides are too lame to make most people scream like that! Besides, I think it's from ahead of us somewhere, I can barely hear the sounds from the park anymore, can you?" He was surprised that Randy couldn't tell what direction the sounds were coming from. It seemed pretty clear cut to him. He guessed that all those years of playing in his band must be starting to take their toll on his hearing.

"That's true, I...there it is again!" Randy said, holding up a hand.

This time they thought they could hear a loud, male voice shouting. It was too faint to make out any actual words though.

"I think It's coming from inside that big thing up ahead," Matt whispered. He pointed to a large, long, black mound that they could barely make out on the horizon ahead of them. He unbuttoned his jacket so that he'd have greater freedom of movement, then imagined the *Vermilion Avenger* whooshing out and hovering over his shoulder; a mere second later, what he had envisioned in his mind's eye became a reality.

Randy eyed the spectacle of the floating sword with a raised eyebrow. "What happened to the idea of not spooking him?"

"I can't run with this damned thing down my back, plus I have a bad feeling I might need it soon with all that screaming and shouting going on over there. Now let's move!" Matt explained breathlessly as he broke into a run towards the large, dark structure that he'd identified as the source of the voices. The sword followed obediently behind him and Randy was soon forced to start running too, in order to catch up.

Matt came to a stop at the entrance to the mysterious structure.

"What is this place, the Batcave?" Randy asked. He could all too easily imagine the Batmobile zooming out of its black depths.

"Let's find out, old chum," Matt quipped in his best Adam West voice as he cautiously stepped forward.

"How about a little light?" Randy asked. Matt fished a flashlight from his coat pocket.

"Seeing as how we've obviously abandoned any attempt to appear normal at this point, I think we can do a little better than *that!*" Randy said as he muttered the words

to a spell. A moment later, a small, glowing orb of light that shone forth like a miniature sun appeared in the air before them. With a gesture, he sent it hurtling ahead of them down the tunnel, making it as bright as day wherever it went.

"Show off!" Matt griped, letting the flashlight fall back into his pocket. He'd seen magic users use these little balls of light before.

Randy just smiled as he led them forwards.

As they explored the tunnel, it became obvious that they were too late. Whoever had been in here had already left. They reached a spot near the middle where there was a small room off to one side. The door to the room was hanging off the hinges as if it had been violently thrown open from the inside. Matt almost stumbled over a pile of shattered chains that littered the floor in front of it. He knelt down to examine them, lifting two broken pieces and fitting them back together.

"This doesn't look good! Something was in here that was strong enough to bust these chains and rip that door off the wall."

"From what I've read, a werewolf could easily do this sort of damage. Check these out - claw marks!" Randy pointed to deep gouges that appeared on the surface of the wooden door.

"Looks like the kid was trying to lock himself up. Why didn't he just leave town? What's keeping him here if he's so worried about not hurting people?" Matt wondered.

"I think he was sleeping in here, there's some blankets and what's left of a pillow that he went to town on after he changed. Oh! I found some cans of food he was eating out of!" Randy exclaimed as he moved deeper into the cramped room, the miniature sun following along to illuminate his surroundings.

"What's so great about a few empty cans?"

"All this stuff is soaked with his recent psychic residue. I can use it to cast a spell to track him to wherever he went off to. It will create a trail that we can follow straight to him. Oh! A ripped shirt, and it has blood on it! His blood!"

"How can you be sure that's his blood and not someone else's?" Matt asked skeptically. "What? Now you can use magic to do DNA

tests too? Hell, I shouldn't have bothered with the ABC, I should've just called you sooner!"

"No, silly! It's got the same psychic residue as the rest of his stuff. This is perfect!" Randy was squealing with the glee of a teenage girl who just got a kiss from her favorite pop star. He was so happy that he was almost doing a little dance.

"Y'know, it's downright ghoulish how excited you're getting over finding a little blood. Who gets excited about blood like that? You're kind of giving me the heebie-jeebies, dude."

"I'm only so excited because the most potent and reliable forms of magic often require at least a little blood. 'For the blood is the life.' It'll make catching up with him that much easier."

"Good, because if that's his blood, it means he's hurt, and we don't know how badly. Also, if someone hurt him, that means that they used something on him that could actually damage him, which suggests that either they got really lucky, or they already knew that he was a werewolf when they ran into him," Matt concluded grimly.

"In other words, we're probably not the only ones who are hunting him," Randy added.

"Exactly. Whoever else is after him might've just hurt him in self defense, but they could also be looking to kill him, for all we know. So if you're gonna do some kinda spell to find him, you'd better get a move on!"

"You don't have to tell me twice," Randy said as he began gathering up a few items from around the room - discarded cans of food, a blanket and the bloody shirt. He arranged them in a circle, placing the shirt in the middle, then began chanting. He removed a long, silvery ceremonial dagger that he always carried hidden upon his person from its sheath and waved it around, making a very deliberate series of gestures with it. His voice grew louder and more resonant with each new arcane word that reverberated through the man-made cavern.

Matt felt a familiar rush of wind that sometimes accompanied certain incantations; it threatened to blow the hat off his head before it died down as suddenly as it had appeared. Randy tucked his dagger away with a look of satisfaction upon his face.

"Is that it? Did it work? I don't see anything!" Matt grumbled.

"Oh ye of little faith! That's because you don't have a wizard's eyes. Here, let me give you a little peek." Randy reached out and grabbed Matt's arm.

Matt immediately saw a glowing, golden path stretching out through the air in front of him. It looked like it was made up of countless tiny pieces of glitter. Randy let go of him and it disappeared.

"Well shit. That's pretty cool," he had to admit. Matt knew that Randy was a powerful wizard, but he didn't quite know the full extent of his powers. They were partners in the sense that they divided up their caseloads, but they rarely worked on the same cases together like this anymore. He'd never seen Randy use this particular spell before, and he wondered if the wizard used this trick in his more routine investigations. He could definitely see how it would come in handy.

"Don't worry, I can still see the path. But it'll start to fade out the longer we linger here," said Randy, misinterpreting Matt's silence.

"Can't we just teleport to the other end of it?"

"We could, if I knew where that was, but I don't. I have to have a clear destination in mind for that to work. I'm afraid we're gonna have to follow it on foot. Follow me!" Randy led the way out of the tunnel. As they emerged into the open air once more, Randy said a few more words in whatever obscure tongue his spells resided, and the small sun that hovered a few feet ahead of them dimmed considerably so that it didn't cast so much light that it attracted undo attention, yet still effectively lit the way ahead.

The path led them to a slit cut in the fence, too narrow for these two large men to fit through. Matt had to use the *Vermilion Avenger* to widen it so they could get through. Randy led him down a narrow trail through the woods on the other side, the two of them jogging through them as quickly as they could manage.

As Matt followed with the *Vermilion Avenger* floating over his shoulder, he was filled with concern for Kevin. Who else could possibly be after him who knew how to successfully deal with werewolves? He guessed that such information wasn't exactly a state secret, all you had to do was watch a few cheesy movies to acquire knowledge that was shockingly accurate on the matter. But who else aside from him and Randy would be stupid enough to really believe that a werewolf was on the loose? Then he remembered that there were plenty of people back in Shadowbrook who were beginning to understand that their tragedy was the work of a werewolf. Considering this morning's grisly discovery, was it really so hard to believe that someone already inclined to believe in such things would conclude that there was a werewolf here, too?

So what was he dealing with here? Amateur monster hunters that happened to get a little lucky, or someone more deadly? Someone associated with the Guilds, like they were? As far as he knew, the Guilds were the only ones who knew for sure that there was any truth behind these werewolf legends. If Kevin had just been in a fight with someone who could hold their own against a monster that could snap chains and rip a door off its hinges, then where were they all now? Had they captured him and fled with their prize? What kind of a mess were they currently walking into, and were they already too late to save the kid?

"Wow. Is *that* where you live?" Kevin asked in awe, even though he knew that it had to be as he gazed up at the large and imposing edifices of the manor.

"Yup, welcome to the Addams Family!" Allison joked as she pushed open the big wrought iron front gate, which reminded Kevin of the high, spiked gate he'd seen surrounding a cemetery once. The manor was indeed huge. It was a colonial style mansion with titanic Romanesque pillars sitting atop a mammoth staircase that led up to a set of impassive wooden double doors. The roof was marked by several towers more typical of Victorian architecture, which Kevin guessed must've been later additions. Heavy wooden shutters covered all the windows on the first floor, yet a warm, golden glow could be seen leaking out around the edges. They stood on a cobblestone pathway bordered by a dizzying variety of vegetation. A few massive old trees dotted the grounds of the well-manicured lawn.

"Nah, we're not the Addams Family, we're the Munsters! I'm like that one normal girl who lives with them, my name is even the same!" Mary said.

"No it isn't! Her name was 'Marilyn' not 'Mary'," Kevin corrected her.

Allison was again impressed by his knowledge of vintage TV shows.

"Yeah, well whatever. Close enough!" Mary replied.

"Well, if you guys are the Munsters, I guess that makes me Eddie Munster!" Kevin joked.

"Calm down, little Eddie. You're not part of the family yet. We still need to see if Herman and Lily will welcome you into the fold!" Mary reminded him.

"Hey, but you got those names right!" Kevin said.

"Of course I did. Never underestimate the normal girl! So, does that mean I'm finally good enough to join the mutual nerd appreciation society you seem to be forming with Allison?"

She asked it with just the tiniest hint of jealousy in her otherwise playful tone. It wasn't that she was jealous because she was interested in Kevin romantically for herself. Sure, he was decent looking enough, but even if he wasn't a werewolf, he wouldn't have really been her type. No, she was more jealous of the relationship he seemed to be building with Allison, which already looked like it was moving along alarmingly quickly. She wasn't used to Allison having anyone important in her life aside from her. She realized how selfish she was by getting upset over the idea that she might no longer have Allison all to herself, and felt a little ashamed of it. Didn't Allison have a right to happiness? To a life of her own? If she truly cared about her, shouldn't she be more supportive of that? Maybe she also kind of wished that she could find someone a little like Kevin for herself. She hadn't had much luck in the boyfriend department lately.

Kevin was a little embarrassed by Mary's recognition of the bond between him and Allison. He didn't know what to say, so as he often did in such situations, he simply said nothing. Allison must have been similarly flummoxed by this, as she was uncharacteristically silent in the face of this exchange as well.

Mary led them around the building and behind it. Kevin could now see a series of rolling hills which he supposed must be pastures, along with a big red barn. It was all surrounded by a barbed wire fence. There was a smaller backyard area right behind the house which was where they all now found themselves. In this part of the grounds was an old shed that was like a smaller barn, with peeling paint and termite-infested boards. As Mary pushed open the door, she yanked on a chain hanging from the ceiling and a soft, white light chased away the shadows inside. She engaged the kickstand and parked her bike in one corner of the shed, which was filled with various tools and landscaping equipment.

Mary looked at Kevin. "I think you'd better wait here while we try and explain what's been going on to the Sherwoods. They'll freak out for sure if we just walk in with you."

"What? We can't leave him alone out here when someone might be after him!" Allison protested.

"Then you stay here and defend him, but you know I'm right. If we walk into the house with a werewolf they'll just kick him back out - if he's lucky!"

"Okay then, I will!" Allison said defiantly. Even though she knew Mary was right, she didn't have to like it. She suddenly whipped out the antique gun she'd been carrying in her purse all this time. An ugly feeling had just come over her and she gulped loudly.

"Does that old thing still work?" Kevin asked incredulously.

"Don't worry, it'll do the job," Allison said as she glanced around nervously.

"Are you okay, Al?" Mary asked, noticing the unexpected and dramatic change in Allison's mood.

"I can feel it too," Kevin told Allison. There was something terribly familiar about this feeling. He thought he was going to be sick; he had to fight the feeling back down.

She nodded towards him. "Yeah, like when we walked past that old church on the way here. A feeling of complete malevolence...."

"From a church? That's nuts! Your sixth sense must be on the fritz!" Mary said dismissively. How could something evil be coming from a church, of all places?

The other two just glared at her.

"I'm serious, Mary! There's something nearby, something *evil*! It feels like it's right outside! I'm afraid we might be in a whole bunch of trouble!" Allison said fearfully.

Waiting in the darkness outside the shed, Kilroy was pleased. He did not sense any of the enemy nearby. The other bloodsuckers were all cowering inside their mansion, leaving these young pups alone and vulnerable inside that ramshackle old shed. Now was the perfect moment to strike. To finally erase his mistake. If he was swift enough, he could destroy them and be away before the bloodsuckers had any clue what was happening. True, it would tip them off to the fact that they had enemies nearby, but from what Kilroy had seen today, with them practicing shooting, and the way the house was all shuttered up now, they probably already suspected. He could always just explain to the Master that he'd been spotted while scouting the place and had been forced to act to defend himself. The Master would be upset that the element of surprise had been spoiled, but Kilroy couldn't resist this opportunity.

He gazed lustfully at his quarry through a window in the old shed. Yes, this little upstart would pay and pay dearly for the wounds he had inflicted on Kilroy. Kilroy would show him the meaning of fear, and the meaning of pain. He would sever his head with a single swipe of his claw and show him his own body. Kilroy licked his lips in sweet anticipation and launched himself into the side of the shack.

One of the walls of the shack exploded inwards, tossing rotten wooden boards high up into the air and bringing down a rain of splinters as Kilroy smashed through it with the force of a runaway freight train.

Mary screamed at the sight of the massive, unnaturally large wolf that stood in the center of the clearing dust. She screamed even louder as it changed shape right before her disbelieving eyes. With amazing speed, it shifted into a more bipedal form glaring at them all with terrible, hateful yellow eyes before letting loose a low, guttural growl.

"Mary, run! Get help from the house! Go now!" Allison shouted to her. Out of the corner of her eye she watched as Mary ran through the still-open door and out into the night.

Allison took aim at the rapidly advancing form of the werewolf and squeezed the trigger. Inside the confines of the shed, the sound of the gunshot was deafening.

"Fuck me running!" she swore as she saw that her shot had only succeeded in clipping the wolf's shoulder. Nonetheless, it had knocked him back a little, and he was now busy howling in pain and clutching at the wound, which bought her a little time. She edged backwards and started reloading, but in the heat of the moment, her fingers fumbled and she dropped her powder horn. She watched in dismay as most of the contents spilled out onto the floor of the shed.

In desperation, Allison conceived a crazy new idea. She forced herself to look into the horrible, evil eyes of the werewolf, bringing the full force of her willpower to bear. *What the hell*, she thought, *if it worked once, it might work again.* She concentrated on the monster, trying to get him to change back into a human form, but she only seemed to succeed in confusing the beast and slowing it down. It gripped its shaggy head in both hands and swayed from side to side as it fought against her power. Then she noticed the belt made from wolf pelts that was wrapped around its midsection, which thankfully hung down low enough to shield her from the unwanted spectacle of its wolfy gonads. She remembered that William had mentioned there were some werewolves who wore magical belts which controlled their changes. She quickly realized that this was one such werewolf and that her attempts to force him to change probably wouldn't work because the nature of the source of his power was different.

However, she could *still* use her power to change Kevin back into a werewolf and try to even the odds a little bit. It was risky, of course, but she didn't believe that Kevin would really hurt her, even as a wolf. If she was wrong, she could always switch him back. Desperate times called for desperate measures, didn't they?

Kevin had been watching all of this, rooted to the spot in terror. He'd seen this beast before, he was sure of it. It was the same one that had attacked him that night in the woods, but that hadn't been the last time he'd seen him. A fresh series of repressed memories came flooding into his head, threatening to overwhelm him. Memories of *that* night. The night Sylvia had died.

"Kevin!" The urgency in Allison's voice shattered his trance. He looked at her as she gave up on trying to reload the antique pistol and flipped it around in her hand so that she was now holding onto it by the barrel. With the other hand, she pulled the silver letter opener from her jacket pocket. Their eyes locked from across the room as the werewolf recovered from the shock of its injury and her attempts to dominate its mind, and moved forwards to menace Allison once again.

"Change! Do it now!" she commanded, her icy eyes tunneling into his brain.

"But..." he tried to argue weakly. Didn't she know how dangerous that was? That there was no guarantee that he wouldn't try to hurt her, too?

"It'll be okay, I believe in you! Just do it!" she shouted, and he could feel her will overriding his own once again. He surrendered as her will shattered the mental chains that had been keeping the beast inside him at bay.

The wolf now staggered forward and lunged at Allison - she dodged deftly, thanks to her uncanny speed, but an attack from his other hand caught her unawares. One of the monster's razor-like claws ripped open a nasty gash along the length of her face, and got caught on her glasses, sending them flying through the air. She cried out in pain and swung the pistol's heavy grip at the werewolf's head, clubbing it over and over again, making full use of her superhuman strength and speed as its blood splattered onto her face and into her eyes. Still, the monster tried to edge closer to her, undaunted, its jaws snapping at her defiantly. She swung out with the letter opener as the beast came closer, stabbing at it repeatedly, plunging the weapon into its outstretched arms and paws even as she continued to batter it with the pistol grip. The bite of the silver weapon stung and burned it, finally causing it to back off for a moment.

Kevin watched in horror as Allison's beautiful face was ripped open by one savage swipe of the beast's claw. He screamed in fury as his body twisted and contorted as it underwent the change. He wouldn't let her end up like Sylvia had, now that he finally *knew* who was really responsible for what had happened to her. At this moment, all he wanted to do was save Allison the way he hadn't been able to save Sylvia and to punish the devil that had destroyed her life.

The devil that was before him right now.

With a mighty growl, Kevin, now completely changed into the vaguely bipedal form of a hulking werewolf, leapt forth into the fray, landing on the back of Kilroy just as he was stepping forward to renew his attack upon Allison. Kevin sank his teeth into Kilroy's back and tore out a chunk of his flesh while clawing at his back. Kilroy cried out in agony, and responded by spinning around several times and throwing himself forcefully into another wall, almost knocking it down. Kevin was crushed between the wall and Kilroy's body and rolled off the monster's back, momentarily stunned by the sudden move. Kilroy swiped at Kevin's chest, ripping it open with the claws of his feet. Then he turned back to face Allison once more, bounding towards her, ready to separate her head from her shoulders with a swift flick of his clawed hand.

Without warning, Matt and Randy burst into the shed through the hole that Kilroy had made in the wall. Matt saw the frightened girl standing in one corner, as a werewolf leapt through the air towards her. For one terrible moment, he thought he saw the face of Melissa Hollins superimposed over this girl's face. In an instant, any doubts he'd had about being able to fight a werewolf evaporated. He didn't know if this werewolf was Kevin or not, all he knew was that he wasn't about to stand idly by while another innocent girl got killed. Not again. Not on his watch. He sent the *Vermilion Avenger* whistling through the air and in one movement so fast that it was easy to miss, it sliced at the werewolf, hacking through its arm and cutting most of it off below the bicep before it could reach the girl. A jet of crimson spewed out of the stump, painting Allison in gore.

The wolf howled and came crashing down to the ground in front of the girl. He pawed at his bloody stump, trying to stem the tide. His malignant gaze now fell upon the newcomers and he stumbled to his feet, running towards them. Now it was Randy's turn: he intoned the words to a spell. The wolf leapt onto the two detectives, only to crash into a glowing green shield of energy that Randy had erected over them with his magic. The creature staggered back, temporarily stunned. Now Randy said a few more words and directed bolts of lightning from his fingertips at the monster. Kilroy was barely able to evade them as they came sizzling past him and singed his long, matted grey-white fur, yet evade them he did. Matt sent the *Vermilion Avenger* off to slash at the wolf again; this time, Kilroy was able to dodge the swings.

A wizard! he thought in astonishment and terror. He hadn't counted on this! Where had he come from? And that sword...he *knew* that sword! And that armor! These were Guildsmen!

Kevin was now back on his feet and staggering towards Kilroy, ready to make another attack. At that moment, William and Elizabeth came running into the shack through the front door with Mary and Charles trailing behind them and came to a stop in the door frame. Mary was held back by her father, who gripped her by one shoulder. Both vampires took aim at Kilroy with their pistols.

Knowing when he was outclassed had always been one of Kilroy's talents. It was how he'd managed to survive for this long. In this case, he was hopelessly outnumbered by a host of enemies that could easily destroy him. There was only one thing left for him to do. He jumped towards the nearest wall and smashed another hole through it, rapidly shifting into his quadrupedal form as he did so for greater speed. Even with only three good legs left to him, this would still be faster. He yelped in pain as a shot from Elizabeth's pistol ripped through his tail, but he couldn't allow that to slow him as he disappeared back into the gloom of the night from whence he'd first emerged.

"Another one!" William cried as he caught sight of Kevin across the room and lifted his pistol. Elizabeth was busy reloading.

"No!" Allison screamed as she put her body between his gun and the werewolf. "He's with us!"

"What? Are you insane? It's a werewolf! It must be destroyed! Get out of the way, girl!"

Allison swatted at the gun, knocking it from William's hand. It went off harmlessly as it fell to the ground, shooting out a pane of glass from the shack's window.

"You dare?" an enraged William accused her.

"I won't let you murder him!" she told him, jutting her chin out in defiance. She whirled around and looked into Kevin's eyes.

"Kevin, change back!" she commanded. At those words, he began shrinking back into his human form. The shock of it all caused him to fall to the ground. Allison rushed to his side and cradled him in her arms. He was now wearing only tattered clothes again, blood pouring from his new wounds, although she noticed that the injuries Mary had given him earlier had already healed completely - there was no sign that they'd ever been there.

"See, he's just a kid! Like me or Mary! And he's on *our* side! You've gotta believe me!" Allison shouted at a bewildered William and Elizabeth. They could see how strongly she felt about it and decided to back off a bit, for now at least.

"Allison, your face...I'm sorry I wasn't fast enough..." Kevin said weakly as he reached out a hand to touch the side of her face.

"Hush now. It's okay. You did just fine. It's already starting to close up, see? You're not the only one around here who heals up quickly. You did just fine. See I *told* you that you could control it!" she said proudly.

He laughed. "Normally I hate it when people are all like 'I told you so,' but in this case, I'm glad to be wrong. Thanks for believing in me."

"Anytime." She smiled at him. For a moment, he thought she might kiss him. Even though she was covered in blood, he wouldn't have cared.

"Is anyone going to tell us what in the blazes is happening around here?" William demanded. Then he looked over at Matt and Randy, who had been watching everything unfold and were still standing behind the glowing green transparent shield of energy that Randy had caused to appear. The *Vermilion Avenger* was now floating over Matt's shoulder as usual.

"And who in the hell are you two?" he added indignantly.

"Geez, you're welcome," Matt replied sardonically.

"Dearest, that was Kilroy!" Elizabeth said, placing a hand on William's shoulder in an attempt to calm him.

"I know. I recognized him too," he said darkly.

"And if *he's* here, it might mean that *you know who* isn't far behind!" she reminded him.

He knew exactly who she was talking about. Mortus Locke. Kilroy had always been one of his most devoted servants.

"Yes, I realize that, if he's even still alive..." he began.

"So I suggest that we all take this inside the manor where we might be a little safer, especially since this poor little shed looks like it's about to collapse on us at any moment! We'd do better to get this all sorted out *inside* the house!"

"You're correct, as ever, my love," he replied, then he did a double take as he took a closer look at Matt and Randy.

"You two are with the Guilds!" he said with a mixture of shock and alarm. What were Guildsmen doing here after all these years? Had they been hunting the werewolf? This was starting to get ridiculous! Who else from his past would decide to show up tonight?

"No..." Matt, who was always uncomfortable about his connection to the Guilds, started to say.

"Yes!" Randy, who was quite proud of his place in the Guilds finished.

"Well...sorta," Matt added unhelpfully. "It's complicated."

William ignored Matt's clumsy attempts to clarify things. "A wizard and a Knight of the Pendragon! I never thought I'd see your like again in my life. If you live long enough I suppose you get to see everything sooner or later. I have no quarrel with you people. I have kept the bargain I made with your ancestors, Sir Knight. We left the British Isles over two centuries ago as we were commanded to do and have not preyed on another human being since. Our covenant is intact. I beg of you to leave us in peace."

"Sir Knight? Oh! The armor! You've got it all wrong, I'm no knight! This was just given to me by them because it goes with the sword," Matt started to explain.

"He's the detective!" Mary said as she broke free of her father's arms and pushed her way into the room, walking over to Allison and Kevin. "You know, the one I told you about from the TV."

"Detective?" Elizabeth asked, now thoroughly confused.

"Matt Spike! Oh! *Cooool!*" Allison smiled, gushing with admiration for Matt.

Matt was surprised to be recognized. "Uh, yeah, that's me, Matt Spike, PI at your service. I was hired to find Kevin over there. Hi there, Kevin!" He waved at Kevin, perhaps a little too cheerfully under the circumstances. He was just overjoyed that the kid seemed to be okay (aside from being a werewolf and having some nasty slashes on his torso, that is) and was *not* the werewolf whose arm he had just lopped off.

Kevin waved back dazedly, more out of reflex than anything else.

"Your parents have been worried sick, by the way," Matt added.

"Are they okay?" Kevin asked him. He felt terrible about leaving them like he had, without any explanation.

"They will be now!" Matt beamed back at him, happy that he'd be bringing a missing kid back home alive for once, even if the kid was a werewolf now. Maybe they could correct that situation too, if this "Gooch" character was half as good at what he did as Randy seemed to believe that he was.

"Yes well, this is all very fine and good, but as my wife suggested a moment ago, let's adjourn to the house to all get better acquainted and figure out our next course of action before we come under attack again," William said sensibly.

Allison helped Kevin up off the ground. As she did so, the ripped remnants of his pants slipped down.

"*Noice!*" she commented as she ogled him. He quickly snatched up what was left of his pants and held them close to his body to cover himself.

"Good God, boy! Make yourself decent!" William complained.

"Sorry about that! I swear I'm not trying to flash everyone," Kevin said nervously, his face red.

"No need to apologize. This is the most action I've had in years!" Allison assured him.

Kevin just chuckled and shook his head. He had to admit, he was enjoying her attention.

"Let's get my duffel bag, it's got more clothes in it." He looked around the shed for it as the others filed out the front door. He was annoyed to find it covered by a pile of fallen timbers. He leaned over and quickly pulled it free, trying to keep his rear end covered as best as he could in the process. He slung it over his shoulder, freeing his hands to work on arranging what was left of his pants to cover as much of his nether regions as possible.

As they walked out, Randy leaned down and picked up the bloody forearm of Kilroy.

"This might prove useful," he smiled.

"Ugh. And you say you're not a ghoul!" Matt said in disgust.

Randy waved the forearm in Matt's face, causing the claw-covered hand to flop around loosely.

"What's the matter? Can't face your own handiwork? Get it - 'handy' work?" Randy joked, feeling far too proud of his attempt at gallows humor.

"Don't quit your day job, pal. You're not ready for the comedy clubs yet. Seriously though, what are you doing messing around with that nasty thing? It's so gross!"

"Remember what I said about blood magic? This might tell us where that werewolf ran off to."

"There has *got* to be a better way!" Matt insisted.

"I'm afraid that there isn't. Hey! That's a nice clean cut, by the way," Randy said as he continued to study the dismembered limb.

"Thanks...I guess," Matt said uncomfortably as he followed the others out of the shed.

As they all stepped outside, they gazed around themselves cautiously, expecting another assault any moment. They were able to make it to the back door of the manor and inside without any further incident.

"I guess I won't be needing this any longer, this place looks like it's built like a fortress," Randy said as he made a gesture with his hand and his green energy shield dissipated.

"It is. And for good reason; we've been expecting an attack like this for some time now," Elizabeth told him.

Randy looked at the ancient pistol she still gripped tightly in one hand.

"Yeah, I can see that!" he commented.

"Do you really think that werewolf is coming back here? We tore him up pretty good," Randy said.

"Kilroy? You can bet on it. You don't know him, he's relentless. Unfortunately, none of us dealt him a mortal blow. He'll be back as soon as he feels that he's sufficiently healed, which will be much sooner than you might think. When he does return he might not come alone, either."

"In that case, maybe I'd better reinforce your defenses a bit," Randy declared as he began chanting a new spell.

"What are you doing?" William demanded, suddenly scared by the idea of a wizard working an enchantment within his home.

"Calm down, Mac. I've seen him do this kind of thing before. He's just putting a magical force field up around your whole house," Matt told him.

This seemed to put William at ease a little. Within moments they could all see an emerald glow shining through between the slats of the shutters.

"Yes, but unfortunately the bigger they are, the shorter the amount of time they last, unless you've got a whole group of magic users working together to maintain the shield. Since it's just me, I'm gonna have to remember to put this thing back up every half hour or so. Guess I'd better set a timer on my phone," Randy informed them.

"Magical force fields? Jesus! What kind of detectives are you guys?" Kevin asked in confusion.

"Exactly the kind you need right now, kid. Exactly the kind you need!" Matt answered.

CHAPTER 14:

IT WAS A DARK AND STORMY NIGHT

Everyone moved from the kitchen through which they had entered the manor, and into a large drawing room adjacent to it where Charles had a fire already roaring in the fireplace.

"Heeeey! Swanky digs! I like it!" Matt said as he entered the room. It was the sort of thing that he typically said whenever he found himself in some kind of an upscale environment.

Before any of them could take a seat, there was a loud crashing sound from somewhere outside. They all practically jumped out of their skins.

"What the devil was that?" William demanded, as he tended to be a rather demanding fellow.

"Maybe that shed finally collapsed?" Matt suggested.

"I hope not, my bike is still in there!" Mary complained, kicking herself for leaving it there.

Randy rushed to a window and tried to peer out through the slats of the shutters.

"Calm down everybody. It was just some thunder. It's storming outside now."

"My, how cliche!" William remarked with a slight smile.

"That's odd, I can't hear any rain falling on the roof," Elizabeth noted.

"That's because it's hitting the force field instead," Randy told her.

"Oh yes. That makes sense," Elizabeth replied.

"Ummm, is there a bathroom around here where I can 'make myself decent'?" Kevin asked, gently mocking William's earlier statement.

"I'll show you the way," Charles offered, and led Kevin down a nearby corridor.

"I think I need to go to my room and get myself cleaned up a bit too. I'm sure you don't want me sitting on the furniture in this state," Allison said, indicating her face, now completely healed, but still streaked with Kilroy's blood, as were her clothes.

"Very well, but make it fast," William commanded, as he was a very commanding fellow. "There is much to discuss."

Allison nodded and dashed off in the direction of the staircase.

Inside the bathroom, Kevin ran a washcloth under some water and tried to clean the cuts on his chest from where Kilroy had kicked and slashed at him. They were already beginning to close up - they had been much deeper when they were fresh, but it still stung pretty badly. He found some antibiotic ointment in a medicine cabinet and dabbed it on, wincing as he did so, then slipped on a t-shirt from his duffel bag.

"Allison seems quite taken with you," came Charles' voice from the other side of the door.

"I really like her too," Kevin confessed. Funny, with the older man on the other side of the door, Kevin felt like he really was in some kind of confessional booth. Confession was something he'd always found difficult.

"She's a good person. Smart, funny, brave, loyal. She practically helped me raise my daughter after her mother...passed. She deserves some real happiness in her life," Charles said from the other side of the door.

Kevin didn't quite know what to say to this. He thought about a response as he dug around in his bag for a pair of jeans to put on. As he did so, he recalled with annoyance that he didn't have any shoes to wear now. He'd only brought the one pair of sneakers with him when he'd run away. He'd had the presence of mind to remove them when he'd chained himself up earlier, but the unplanned change in the shed had destroyed them. Maybe he could borrow some from this guy, who seemed to be Mary's dad? They looked like maybe they were close to the same size. He'd ask him later, now didn't seem like a good time.

"I hope I can make her happy," he finally said as he shimmied into his jeans.

"I wish you could too. It's too bad that it'll never work out."

Kevin's brows furrowed at this unexpected comment.

"Huh? What do you mean? Why not?"

"You're a werewolf. William and Elizabeth will never accept you. They *hate* werewolves. Besides, you'll continue to grow old while she stays the same."

"Where are you going with this?" Kevin wanted to know. He was kind of starting to resent this guy deciding to butt into his business like this. Who cares if her parents didn't approve? Maybe they could run away together and figure out a way to make it work somehow? She was the only one who could help him control the beast inside of him. Even if he didn't already want to, and he *did* want to, he *had* to stay around her if he was ever going to have any kind of a future.

"Break things off with her now. Don't keep leading her on like this. Nip it all in the bud before things get too far out of hand. I know it might be difficult for you, but in the end it'll spare you both a whole lot of heartache," Charles said.

Kevin could feel the anger rising up inside of him. Who was this old guy to tell him what to do with his life? Who he should love? Love? *Was* it love? He wasn't sure that he'd ever really been in love with anyone before, but this is always what he'd imagined it would feel like. He knew it was definitely different from what he had felt for Sylvia, which had been little more than lust. He had lustful thoughts about Allison too, but also a whole lot more beyond just that. He wanted to shout all of this at Charles, but decided against it - he was a guest here after all, and he would probably need to borrow his shoes to boot.

"What's it to you?" was the mildest response he could manage.

"I just don't want to see her get hurt. I care about her; she's like one of my own family."

Kevin thought that this was probably true, but he was still pretty pissed off by this unsolicited advice from a total stranger, which he had no intentions of heeding. So instead of venting his frustrations he said "Hey, what's your shoe size?"

Allison had rejoined everyone in the sitting room. Her wig was off, which drew a few surprised glances from Matt and Randy, who hadn't been aware that she'd been wearing one. In her hands she held two books (one a paperback, the other a hardcover), and a pen. She walked over to Matt.

"Would you mind signing these for me, Mr. Spike? I really enjoyed them, especially *Dirt Nap.*"

Across the room, William rolled his eyes at what he considered to be Allison's childish behavior towards their guests, but he also knew how pointless it would be to try and reprimand her for it. It would just result in an even more childish outburst.

Matt was pleased. Especially since most people preferred *Death Rattle.*

"You must've! You actually got the hardcover," he remarked.

"Oh yeah, I preordered it as soon as I heard about it. Since I liked the first one so much I figured it would be pretty good, but it was even *better*," Allison bragged.

"I'm glad you think so, it's my favorite too. Although all these books are really just fun potboilers, they're not meant to be taken too seriously," Matt said humbly as he took the pen she offered him.

"Oh I don't know about that. I thought I detected a few deeper themes running through it at times," Allison assured him.

"Nah. It was confusing sometimes, too much going on. I liked the first one more," Mary chimed in.

Matt sighed. This was the kind of response he was more used to receiving from the public. Still, he was flattered that both these kids were familiar with his work although they both seemed a bit too young to be reading it. He wasn't sure that he even wanted his own kids to read his books, at least not until they were a bit older.

"Who should I make it out to?" Matt asked, realizing that he still didn't even know most of these people's names. If they even were "people" in the usual sense of the word. He had a few ideas about what they might be.

"Allison," she told him, as he scribbled something on the inside of the cover.

"I'm kinda famous too, ya know," Randy said suddenly.

Now it was Matt's turn to roll his eyes.

Oh no, not this again! Matt thought.

Normally, Randy liked to come off as if he was above such petty emotions as jealousy or a need to compete for recognition; that he was too "spiritually advanced" for such notions (whatever that means). While it was true that he was typically much better at balancing his emotions than most people, maintaining a calm, cool, even keel and being relatively untroubled by life's many ups and downs, the truth is that despite his best efforts, Randy was still just as human as the rest of us. Occasionally, he was overwhelmed by what he considered his more base feelings, and this was one of those times. Matt figured he was still smarting from the way that reporter had dismissed him and was looking to make up for it.

"You are? That's funny. I've never seen you before in my life," Mary said.

"Oh, yeah. I'm in a band," he told her proudly

"Really? Which one?" Mary asked.

"Have you ever heard of Lung Collapse?"

"No, but it sounds uncomfortable."

Randy made a face. "Okay, then how about The Mystery Smiths?"

"I've heard of The Smiths, but not The Mystery Smiths," she answered.

"Really?" Randy sounded a little hurt. "But we had a song in the top 100 a few years ago! 'Champion'."

Allison and Mary just stared at him blankly.

"C'mon, you must've heard it! Here, I'll sing some of it for you. I'm sure you'll recognize it once you hear it!"

Randy sang:

"Find a message in bottle

which makes no sense

it gets tossed aside

condemned as useless

Along the dune comes walking the King of Nothing

Master of the Junk Castle

He spies the bottle

Reads the message

It still makes perfect nonsense

But he likes it that way

He laughs warmly

Wraps it up snugly in his cape

He consoles the inconsolable inanimate

Crying with it at its cruel condemnation

At the hands of those unable to see

That its worth was that it had no practical worth whatsoever

The bottle finds a place of honor on the mantlepiece of the Junk Castle

Now it's in a Brotherhood of Trash

Not true trash, merely that deemed as bunk by the cruel world outside

Outside of the Junk Castle

The beautiful Junk Castle

Wherein sits the King of Nothing

Who finds and treasures everything you hate or don't take the time to love

Because dammit, somebody has to"

"Oh man, I hate that song! Why're you singing that crap?" Kevin asked as he entered the room wearing Charles' shoes.

"Because I happened to write it!" Randy replied indignantly.

"Oh. Umm, sorry," Kevin said awkwardly. "For what it's worth you've got a decent singing voice," he said, trying to soften the blow of his unfiltered criticism.

Matt chuckled. "Give it a rest, pal. It looks like the people have spoken - and they just like my writing better than yours!"

"Well, 'the people' really liked it in Japan and Norway! I'll have you know that it was in the top ten in both those countries for weeks!" Randy pouted.

"Hey, at least he's heard of the song!" Allison said as she patted Randy on the shoulder. She looked up at Matt. "Thanks for the autographed copies Mr. Spike. I still can't believe that you're really in my house right now!"

"Please, just call me Matt. Mr. Spike is..."

"...my dad!" Randy finished for him.

"Geez, am I really that predictable?" Matt asked.

"Don't worry, It's one of the things I like the most about you, boss." Randy smiled at him slyly.

"AHEM!" William said loudly.

"Now that we're all finally back together and looking presentable, perhaps we can try and figure out what's going on around here and what we're going to do about it?"

"I like the new look. How did you change your hair so quickly like that?" Kevin whispered to Allison as he sat down next to her.

To one with the finely attuned senses of a vampire, Kevin's whisper was as loud as a scream. "It was a wig! *Obviously* it was a wig! Now let's all try and focus on more important matters, please!" William replied loudly and curtly. He was losing patience with all of this small talk. Didn't these people understand the danger they were all in now?

"Husband! Please, calm yourself, these people are our guests!" Elizabeth chided him.

"I'm sorry, my friends, I don't wish to seem brusque, I'm simply concerned about the gravity of the situation that we now find ourselves in. It's been a long time since we last had any visitors. I'm no longer used to entertaining - I'm afraid my manners must be a bit rusty. Charles! Please get some refreshments for our guests."

"Of course, Sir," Charles said as he dutifully headed back towards the kitchen.

"Hmm. Now where to begin? Well, I suppose I should just come out with it before we go any further. Prepare yourselves, this may be a bit of a shock! For you see, Allison, my wife Elizabeth and I are all..."

"...Vampires!" Matt and Randy looked at each other as they said it in unison. A perfectly timed thunderclap accompanying the revelation.

"So you worked it out too, huh?" Matt said to his partner proudly. The kid really was shaping up to be a pretty good detective.

"My word! Is it really that obvious?" Elizabeth asked, somewhat horrified.

"Well, let's see: you're all as pale as ghosts, live in a swanky, yet also undeniably spooky old mansion and fight werewolves with antique firearms. And don't even get me started on that highfalutin, old-fashioned way that you talk." Matt ticked off each point on his fingers, completely oblivious to the fact that his manner of speech was often peppered with just as many outdated expressions.

"And your auras are all weird. Kinda like a ghost, kinda like a zombie, yet not really totally like either one. It's been bugging me ever since I saw Allison that time in Wonderland," Randy added.

"Holy crap! Zombies are real too?" Matt exclaimed.

Randy laughed. "Please! Zombie creation is like...Necromancy 101!"

"Shit! What else are you people keeping from me?" Matt wondered plaintively.

"Hey, what do you mean by 'you people'?" Randy quipped.

"I don't mean *Jewish* people, pal! I mean magic users! *Guild* people!" Matt said defensively, afraid that he might've inadvertently insulted his friend.

Randy laughed. "Relax, Matt I know what you meant, I just like messing with you!" It was true, sometimes Matt got so serious and tended to take things so literally that he couldn't tell when people were joking with him, and Randy enjoyed taking advantage of this tendency for his own amusement.

William and Elizabeth were silent for a moment, taken aback by this bizarre exchange between the two detectives.

"You see? This is *exactly* why I don't like you going out so much! Apparently, it's quite easy for people to figure out what we really are!" William broke the silence by complaining to Allison.

"Oh, don't blame her, we're detectives! Trained observers! It's our job to figure out this sort of stuff," Matt tried to reassure them. "Besides, most people don't see auras, or really believe in vampires or werewolves. I didn't myself until recently. I'm sure you're…somewhat more convincing to regular people."

"And don't *you* worry, even though we're vampires, we don't drink human blood! That's what the cows are for!" Allison added quickly, although neither Matt nor Randy seemed to be particularly worried about the fact that they were currently hanging out in a house full of vampires. They'd been in worse situations.

"Yup, I already worked that part out too when I saw that we were on a dairy farm and your dad here told us about how he hasn't preyed on a human being in over two centuries. That was also kind of a dead giveaway that you guys were of the undead persuasion," Matt revealed.

"So now you tell me, Mr. Spike: how does a detective end up wearing the armor and carrying the sword of a Knight of the Pendragon and come to associate with a wizard?" William asked.

"And how do a bunch of vampires from the British Isles end up living on a farm in Connecticut?" Matt countered.

"No, please, I *insist* you go first," William replied.

"Hmm. Well, about 10 years ago I stumbled across the existence of the Guilds while working on a case," Matt started.

"What're the Guilds?" Kevin asked innocently.

"They're kind of like an alliance of secret societies that runs the world," Matt explained.

"*Please*! We don't *actually* run it anymore! We haven't for centuries now. At the most, we influence it for our own advantage from time to time, and that influence is waning more and more with each passing year," Randy corrected him.

"Oh yeah, that's right - the truth is that they simply don't give enough of a damn about our 'mundane' world to bother to impose any kind of order on it so long as they're still able to take whatever they want from it. I was trying to keep my explanations short and simple for the kids, so sue me," Matt grumbled.

Randy started to open his mouth to protest further, then thought better of it and started playing with the severed werewolf arm he was still holding instead.

"But I digress. After that case, the Guilds entrusted my wife and me with guarding one of their most important artifacts, and I was given this nifty flying sword to help me do it. They saw some potential in my partner Randy here and trained him as a wizard. A few years later, when the old gent that this armor belonged to died, the Knights gave me his armor since he didn't have any heirs to pass it down to and the sword and the armor are meant to go together anyways."

"Yes, I met a knight who had them both many, many years ago," William revealed. "So you're not out here to hunt us, or Kilroy?"

"No, we're only interested in bringing Kevin back home safely. I was hired by his folks. We'd already worked out that he was a werewolf and took the necessary precautions before going out to search for him."

William could tell that Matt was telling the truth due to his own vampiric senses. Fully satisfied that his family was in no danger from the pair, he now turned his stony face upon Allison and Kevin. He noted with some disapproval that they were sitting dangerously close together on the sofa and were actually holding hands in his presence - what cheeky children they were!

"And I suppose that now brings us to you, young man! I certainly hope you can explain how you came to be in our shed."

"Yeah, for the first time in a while I think I finally understand the whole thing," he said. Kevin then recounted what he'd already told Allison and Mary about the night when he had first been attacked by Kilroy while Charles returned to the room and passed out drinks from a cart that he'd wheeled in. William and Elizabeth exchanged troubled looks as he came to the part where he was saved by a mysterious group that had battled Kilroy in the forest.

"I'm sure that the werewolf that attacked me that night was the same one we just fought against. What did you call him again?"

"Kilroy," William answered grimly.

"And there's something else I just remembered, something that was jarred loose from my head by seeing him again. *He's* the one who really killed Sylvia! I went back over to Sylvia's place the next day after I was bitten. I didn't really remember being attacked the night before, I thought the whole thing had just been a nightmare. Me and Sylvia were umm...*doing it,* with her on top, when all of the sudden the window in her bedroom shattered and something flew through the room and knocked her off of me and the bed. It was that Kilroy guy! He was...eating her in one corner of the room, and that's when I started to change for the first time. As a werewolf I tried to pull him off of her. We fought each other. We really trashed her bedroom, slashing and biting at each other. It was really intense! I remember that I almost completely bit off one of his hands, it was just kind of hanging on by the skin when he finally decided to run away. I went back over to where Sylvia was...but it was too late! He'd already killed her. I guess I must've blacked out then from my own injuries, because the next thing I can remember after that is waking up a few hours later, human again and fully healed. I think he was still after me from the night before. He wanted to finish me off. If only I hadn't gone back over there! Or maybe if I'd been able to get him off of her sooner, she'd still be alive!" Kevin buried his face in his hands and began sobbing.

Even the typically stony William suddenly felt a great deal of sympathy for the lad as he recounted this part of the tale.

Allison hugged him. "Shhh. It's okay. You didn't know. None of it was really your fault, you did the best you could; it's all any of us can ever do," she whispered to him as she rubbed his back.

"Interesting. The emotions you felt when he attacked her must've been strong enough to trigger your transformation. Also, Kilroy seems to have *terrible* luck with his hands," Randy commented, waving around Kilroy's severed limb as he said the last part.

"Will you put that damned thing away already? Can't you see the kid is upset?" Matt complained.

"Er, yeah. Sorry," he said as he awkwardly tried to shove the dismembered forearm into the pocket of his own overcoat. It didn't really work - it was too big and the top of it still poked out oddly.

Kevin soon recovered enough to go on to tell them the rest; how he had tried to kill himself, then decided to leave home His arrival in Wonderland, his first meeting with Allison, his ill-fated attempts to restrain himself and how he had attacked Mary, and how Allison had willed him back into human form...

"That's really remarkable! I didn't think *anything* could prevent a werewolf from changing on the night of the full moon! You two must have a very powerful bond," Randy noted, stroking his beard thoughtfully as he said so.

"We've certainly never heard of anything like it before!" Elizabeth said.

"What I don't understand is why you came to Wonderland in the first place and decided to stay there for so long if you were really so concerned about not hurting anyone?" Matt asked Kevin.

"I don't really know. I just had a strong feeling that I *should* be here, and that I needed to stay."

"Werewolves can sense the presence of vampires from far away. They were created to serve them. I think maybe that's why he came here and stayed. He could sense that there were vampires around here somewhere. On an instinctive level, he was looking for a vampire to serve. And when he met Allison, he found exactly what he was looking for," Randy explained.

"Are you trying to say that I only...feel the way that I feel about her because of some stupid animal instinct that was driving me?" Kevin asked. He found this to be a rather depressing idea. Surely there *had* to be more to it than that?

"Well...what is any kind of sexual attraction but 'a stupid animal instinct'? It all depends on how you choose to look at it," Randy said.

Allison wrinkled her nose. "Not very romantic, is it?"

Randy just shrugged. "It is what it is. What does it matter *why* it is, so long as it makes you happy?"

Allison and Kevin didn't know quite what to make of this idea. Both of them preferred to believe that their emotions for each other had more to do with something deeper than just blindly following a set of preprogrammed instincts.

Elizabeth decided that it was time for a change of subject. "You're quite fortunate to have survived three encounters with Kilroy! He's one of the most vicious werewolves that ever lived. Back in France, in the middle of the 1700's he was known as 'The Beast of Gévaudan'. He terrorized a whole province, and the King himself was forced to send his own men after him. They only ever succeeded in killing his mate, but all the unwanted attention forced the Master and his followers to leave the country and go to Britain."

"The Beast of Gévaudan, eh? Never heard of it. I'll have to ask my wife about it some time, she's a historian. Who is this Master that you're talking about?" Matt asked.

"Isn't it obvious? She's talking about Mortus Locke!" Randy said.

"Please, we don't like to say that name in this house!" William barked.

"Who's Mortus Locke?" Kevin asked.

"What did I *just* say?" William grumbled.

"Why don't they like us saying Mortus Locke?" Matt inquired.

"Arrrgh!" William gritted his teeth in frustration.

"I read about it once. Apparently, he used to tell his followers that he could see them whenever they spoke his name. It was all bullshit of course, there's no spell that anyone knows of that works *quite* like that. It was just something he said to keep them afraid of him, to keep them under control."

"Really?" Elizabeth was surprised by this revelation. "So you're saying that it's perfectly fine to say Mor–"

"Please! Can we just *not* say it, for my own peace of mind?" William asked.

"Okay, but you still haven't explained who he is," Kevin said.

"He was an evil wizard who wanted to live forever. Wizards can reincarnate, but we usually lose most of our memories in the process. This wasn't good enough for him; he wanted to keep all his memories. So he conjured up an immortal, man-eating monster called a Grendel and drank its blood, becoming the first vampire. He created the first werewolves too, to serve him. The joke was on him though, a human brain can only hold so many memories and after about six centuries you begin to lose a bunch to make room for new ones," Randy explained.

"Wow. Naomi didn't mention that part to me," Matt remarked.

"So you used to be followers of this Mort– this, Master?" Kevin asked William and Elizabeth.

"Yes," William said sadly. "Now that the rest of you have explained yourselves I suppose it's finally our turn to tell our tale. I was born in a small village in the north of England, in the late 1760's. My mother died giving birth to my youngest sister and most of my siblings died before reaching adulthood, except for a few sisters that were married off to help settle some of my father's debts."

Mary had heard some of Williams' old stories, but she'd never heard this part before. "Ugh. Selling women off like cattle? That's seriously messed up!"

William shrugged. "It was a different time. At any rate, I only mentioned that to try and explain how it was that I came to inherit my father's farm after he fell ill and died. It wasn't much later that I began to look towards starting a family of my own, to help me out around the farm. I had my eye on the prettiest girl in the village, and eventually I won her." He looked over at Elizabeth and smiled.

"How could I resist the best looking man in the village?" she smiled back.

"Unfortunately, shortly after our wedding day, tragedy struck. One night Elizabeth went outside to fetch a pail of water from the well and she never returned. We searched and searched for days, but never found a trace. I was quite beside myself with grief."

Elizabeth told the next part of the tale. "I had been snatched up that night by a vampire that called himself Blake - one of the Master's most trusted and ruthless lieutenants. He carried me off to an old, ruined tower on an island off the coast where the Master and his group were hiding. He made me one of them. By this time, the

Master had assembled a large group of vampires and werewolves. He commanded the vampires to spread out across the land and pillage it. The attacks happened so far apart that the authorities never drew any connection between them. After some time, he had amassed quite a treasure for himself. He used some of it to rebuild the old tower into a fortress, and had tunnels dug below it where he kept his treasure. The Master's greed knew no bounds. He wanted more vampires for his ever-growing army, and I was eventually given leave to return home to recruit William."

"I was overjoyed when she suddenly returned to me one night, rapping on my window. I would do anything to be with her again. Anything! Even if it meant becoming an accursed, undead creature. I let her bite me and I drank of her blood so that we could finally be reunited. I'd rather live the half-life of a vampire with her for an eternity than spend another moment without her. Together, we went off to the tower, to serve our new Master." He paused to take a sip from a goblet of blood that Charles had set before him.

"Although I was happy to be with her again, neither of us were happy with our new 'lives' as servants of the Master. We didn't enjoy feeding on our fellow man; we were continuously wracked with guilt over the many lives we destroyed. They had a whole philosophy they'd created to try and justify all the evil they did. They said that they were a superior species, that humans were just cattle to be used by us. Did a lion feel guilt over the antelope it fed upon? No, it just did what came naturally to it, what it had to do to survive. Why should we be any different? We never really bought into it. We knew that people were not cattle, that they were intelligent beings. But what could we do? The Master had a legion of werewolves in those days, led by KIlroy. If we tried to run away, he'd set them on us and they'd rip us to pieces. We'd seen him do it to others. He made us watch, so we'd never forget or be tempted to rebel. He demanded absolute loyalty."

No wonder they don't like werewolves around here! Kevin thought.

Elizabeth took up the next part of the story. "Then one day, one of the Guilds, the Highwaymen, attacked us. They'd been upset that someone else had been plundering the countryside that they considered to be theirs. It was a bloodbath. They didn't understand what they were up against until it was too late. Only a few of them escaped alive and we were sent after them to kill them, too. William and I chased after one of them, tracking him back to his home, but we didn't kill him. Instead, we saw an opportunity to escape from the Master and we struck a bargain with him. We would let him live so that he could get help from the other Guilds in launching a new attack on the Master. We would show them a way into the tower through the tunnels beneath it. We'd even let them keep most of the treasure that was hidden down there. All that we wanted in exchange was to be allowed to live, and to leave with a portion of the treasure for ourselves. That young Highwayman, Nathaniel Peregrine, agreed to our terms and set out the next day to contact the other Guilds and tell them of the evil that lurked in the tower. In the meantime, we reported that we had dealt with the last of the survivors. Which was true...we had 'dealt' with him indeed! Nathaniel returned with an army of Guildsmen: Pirates, magic users, Knights of Pendragon, and members of Highwaymen clans that hadn't participated in the first battle. We showed them a secret entrance into the tunnels so that they could attack while most of those in the tower were still sleeping. Then we made off with our share of the treasure, rowing to the shore and escaping in a coach waiting there for us that they'd provided. One of the Knights, the same one who once wore your armor and carried your sword, Mr. Spike, had an additional condition to our arrangement: he made us swear to leave the British Isles altogether. He said that if he or any of his knights ever saw us again, they wouldn't hesitate to destroy us. So we booked passage aboard a ship bound for America the very next day."

"On the long ocean voyage we were reduced to hunting for bilge rats to suck the blood from. One of our fellow passengers, a man named Martin Lane, found us doing this one day. He realized what we really were, but instead of turning us in, he offered to let us drink from him for the remainder of the trip. In exchange, when we arrived in America, we agreed to make him like we were. You see, he wanted eternal life too. We all became friends. We bought this farm and he helped us to build this very mansion. We took on the surname 'Sherwood' since I'd always been a fan of the adventures of Robin Hood, and we couldn't use our original names any longer - the world believed we'd died years earlier. We all stayed together for some time until Martin expressed a desire to see more of the world and left us. We never saw him again. Decades passed. We were often worried that the Master had escaped the Guilds and would come for us; you see we left before the battle began and we never saw its outcome. Centuries passed. We assumed we were now safe. Charles and Mary's ancestors came to work for us and a member of their family has served us ever since. Eventually, we added Allison to our family after we found her in the wreckage of a car accident bleeding to death. The only way to save her was to make her into one of us."

"And we've all been one big, happy family ever since!" Allison added.

"Yes, quite," William said. "My concern now is that if Kilroy survived, then perhaps the Master did as well. If that's the case, they're likely still working together. Kilroy *could* just be here to eliminate young Kevin here. That certainly seems to have been his motive back in Shadowbrook. However, he could also be here hunting for us. If the Master has any inkling that *we* were the ones who betrayed him and stole part of his treasure, he'd definitely want to take his revenge out on us. And a terrible vengeance it would be, he'd make sure of it. In either case, Kilroy will definitely be returning, and the next time he might not be alone. He might've just been an advance scout for the Master."

There was silence in the room for some time as everyone mulled over what they had just learned about each other.

"How can Kilroy still be alive if he's hundreds of years old? Are werewolves immortal too?" Kevin asked.

"Technically no, in human form they age, but if they stay in wolf form, they don't. So Kilroy always remains in his wolf form to cheat death," William answered.

Kevin looked down. He wanted to stay with Allison forever, but he sure didn't want to remain a wolf in order to stop aging!

"What about those guys who saved Kevin from Kilroy in the woods that night? Who're they?" Matt asked the room.

William shook his head. "I've been wondering that too. I really have no idea, I'm afraid. Are they friends, or more enemies?"

"I wouldn't worry too much about Mort– uh, the Master, if I were you. That battle you helped make possible is called 'The Great Purge' in the histories of the Guilds. It's called that because it's believed that all of the vampires and werewolves in the world were finally destroyed in that fight, including the Master. Nobody in the Guilds *really* believes that he's still alive. We haven't seen a trace of him since then," Randy said.

"Yes, but here we all are! If we all survived, who's to say he didn't as well?" Elizabeth pointed out.

"So...where do we go from here?" Kevin asked.

Matt spoke first. "I, for one, intend to bring you back home to your folks. That's my job."

"Bring me home? In case you haven't noticed, I'm a werewolf now! And Allison is the only one who can keep my power in check. You can't just bring me back home like everything is okay. It's too dangerous! What happens the next time there's a full moon, or I get really upset about something? I need to stay here! I want to stay and help them if they come under attack again!"

Randy spoke up. "We have a plan for that! I know a guy, another wizard, who's an expert in curses; he might be able to cure you. We were gonna call him if we found you."

I wonder if that wizard could lift the curse of vampirism, too? Allison wondered hopefully. Maybe there was a way she could get her life back as well? Then perhaps she and Kevin could figure out a way that they could still be together?

"What about Allison and her family? Even if you can help me, you can't just abandon them to be killed by Kilroy or the Master!" Kevin argued. As intrigued as he was by a possible cure for his problem, he couldn't just go back to his normal life and forget about Allison. He'd always be worrying if she was okay, wondering what she was doing.

"I was thinking that maybe we could ask the UGF to send some troops over here to keep an eye on them," Matt said. Normally, he was reluctant to involve the Guilds, but he really saw no other way out of the situation.

"UGF? What's that?" Mary asked.

"United Guild Forces. It's their army. Randy here is like a Colonel or something in it. If he orders it, they'll come," Matt answered.

"I'm not a Colonel!" Randy said, clearly a little embarrassed. "I'm a Major, and I'm only a reservist. Besides, it doesn't mean much, they hand out high ranks in the UGF like they're the Rebel Alliance in Return of the Jedi!"

"Oh! I know what you mean, suddenly everyone is a General in that movie! What's up with that?" Allison chimed in.

"She gets it!" Randy said, pointing to her.

"But Matt's right. They will come if I ask them to. They should be able to handle your little problem with Kilroy. And if my colleague can't cure Kevin, we can always try to explain the situation to his parents and bring him back here, if that's okay with you?" Randy asked William and Elizabeth.

William considered it for a while. Then he finally spoke. "I suppose that if this 'UGF' is really up to the task we would be happy to have any help they can provide. And of course, young Kevin is welcome to stay here if you are unable to help him with his...condition." William had been moved by everything Kevin had been through and impressed by his devotion to Allison and willingness to stay here to help defend them all.

"Awesomesauce! It's settled then!" Matt enthused. Perhaps he really would be able to get back home in time for his daughter Autumn's birthday after all? He missed her badly, and Joe and Naomi. It had been odd being away from them all for this long.

He was feeling great satisfaction. Many of his theories regarding what had really been going on in this case had been borne out, which made him feel exceedingly clever. He also hoped that perhaps saving Kevin in some way might balance out the cosmic scales somewhat, to help make up for his failure to save Melissa Hollins. He knew that his failure to save her would always haunt him, but perhaps just a little less going forwards? He remembered the words of Allison to Kevin from just a few minutes earlier: 'None of it was really your fault, you did the best you could; it's all any of us can ever do.' Hadn't Naomi been trying to tell him the same thing for years now? Seeing Kevin blaming himself for a death he'd been powerless to prevent made him realize that he'd been doing the same thing to himself for far too long. Maybe it was time for them to both find a way to forgive themselves and find some kind of peace of mind. For the first time in a long time, he really believed that such a thing was truly possible.

He wouldn't have felt quite so good in that moment if he had realized that while they had all been engrossed in conversation, the great glowing green force field which Randy had conjured up to protect the house had just sputtered out and faded away. This had been unnoticed by everyone inside the great manor house. Randy had forgotten to set that timer on his phone - he'd been too distracted at the time by trying to prove his rock star credentials to a few skeptical teenagers to do so.

While nobody inside the house noticed the lack of a protective screen around it, others outside the house did. Dozens of shadowy forms now eagerly glided forth towards the old mansion, poised to attack....

CHAPTER 15:

THE MASTER'S PLAN

While everyone was entering the Manor and starting to get a little better acquainted with one another, Kilroy was running, as best he could with his various injuries, back towards the old church that he had made into his temporary headquarters. He enjoyed the irony of desecrating a house of God by using it in this fashion. The thought of it always made him feel a little warm inside.

He was greatly relieved to see that his enemies didn't seem to have any appetite for pursuing him to finish him off, at least not at the moment. This was incredibly foolish of them. He was more vulnerable now than he had ever been in recent memory. Their failure to take advantage of this situation would be their undoing. He'd make *sure* of it. Once he was healed, they would pay. The Master was coming to town, and he wasn't coming alone. He was bringing all of his followers with him. The war was coming to Davenport.

It was thus with a mixture of elation and anger that Kilroy saw that the Master was already here as he approached the old church. Elation that his allies were here to help him take his revenge, increasing their chances of a swift victory, and anger at the thought of the scolding he would definitely receive from the Master once he realized that Kilroy had tipped off their presence to the enemy with his latest misadventure. He had sensed them all long before he actually saw any hint of them, of course. As he emerged from the woods and onto the street across from the church, he could now see the three large black tour buses that the Master and his followers used to travel the country parked in the lot around the church.

Lightning flashed and briefly illuminated the rain-swept parking lot. He watched as a smaller box truck that they owned was opened up, a ramp lowered from the back of it, and the cage holding the Dark Mother was carefully and reverently maneuvered down the ramp by a pair of vampires. The cage had small wheels affixed to it since they had to move it around so frequently. The cage itself was ancient - it was constructed of some sort of magically forged metal created by the Master back in the days before he had forgotten such secrets. No ordinary cage would've been able to hold someone as powerful as the Dark Mother. She was now sleeping peacefully, knocked out by one of the Master's sleeping potions, otherwise it would be impossible for anyone to get that close to the cage without being torn apart. Even from this far away, he was in awe of the sight of Her. It was rare that the Master ever allowed any of his wolves to look upon Her Unholy Form. Even most of the other vampires were typically forbidden from seeing Her. None but his most trusted servants, his inner circle of vampires, the Undying Ones, were allowed to be in Her presence, to take their Unholy Communion from Her. He was spellbound by Her; even asleep, She seemed to be the very epitome of strength and terror. He looked on from the shadows as they wheeled the cage inside through a set of large double doors.

Once the cage had finally vanished inside, Kilroy loped across the street and into the lot. He shifted back to his more bipedal form, and limped into the Church on two legs. He hadn't wanted to be seen when the Dark Mother had still been around, as he was not deemed worthy enough to gaze upon Her. He would soon be in enough trouble with the Master over his recent failures, no need to add to it.

He looked at the ruin of his arm - it was already beginning to grow back, but he knew from past experience that damage this severe would take the better part of an entire day to fully heal. With a grimace he recalled the sting of the blade as it separated his forearm from the rest of his body. He'd seen that sword long ago, when the Guilds had attacked them in their tower. He knew what it could do and considered himself lucky to have escaped it with just a missing arm.

He thought about warning the Master that the Guilds were here, but decided against it. If he knew that Kilroy had inadvertently tipped off the Guilds to their presence, the Master's fury would be so great that he might just decide to destroy Kilroy altogether. He might even flee the town before trying to get his revenge. He didn't want their forces to walk into a fight with the Guilds unprepared, yet at the same time, sharing this information would almost certainly spell his own doom. No, it was far better to keep it to himself. Besides, there had only been the two Guildsmen. The numbers were on their side. If they could snuff them out before they called for help, they could triumph yet.

As Kilroy entered the sanctuary of the church, he felt all the eyes of the assembled vampires and werewolves falling upon him, some of them wearing expressions of surprise at the sorry condition he was in. There was a cluster of the Undying Ones up near the front of the room, which now parted as he approached them to reveal the dread form of the Master, Mortus Locke. He was an elegant looking man who appeared to be somewhere in his forties. Yet he'd looked much the same as this when the pyramids of Egypt were young. Only his clothing had changed in the intervening millennia (nowadays he favored a dark blue tailored suit with a matching tie and a white shirt), along with his knowledge of sorcery and his own past.

He was as much a mystery to himself as he was to those around him. He had no recollection of his childhood, his parents, or the forces that had forged him into the man he was today and set him on this course. As far as he was concerned, he had always been Mortus Locke, the first and greatest of the vampires. He knew no other kind of life. Yes, he knew some things about his past from old journals he had started keeping when he realized that he was losing his memories, but this was merely a list of dry details. They lacked the color, the flavor, the richness of detail that real memories held. It was like reading about someone else's life - he felt no real connection to those events, to that man, to that life. There was a big hole in him where there should be an identity. He often felt like he was just playing out a role that was determined for him long ago by someone else, doing what he was expected to do and *being* what he was expected to be because he didn't know any other way of being. His younger self, that part of himself that was forever lost to him, had cast him in this part for whatever his own mysterious purposes had been and he was now doomed to play it out because he simply didn't know what else to do. Because he couldn't conceive of any other kind of life for himself. So he tried to have fun with it. What was the point of being the leader of a group of monstrous beings if you didn't exploit it to the fullest? If you must be a monster, then take it to the extreme, and do it with style! That was his philosophy.

He eyed Kilroy with obvious disapproval as he grew closer. There was a man with no style whatsoever. He did at least know how to take things to the extreme, but often to their collective detriment. Still, the Master was somewhat fond of Kilroy, in that way in which a dog owner might be inordinately fond of a particularly spirited animal that was always getting himself into mischief. The foolhardy exploits of such beasts always made for such amusing anecdotes.

Kilroy was many things: fanatically loyal, dependable, and deliciously vicious. He was an excellent fighter and an even better tracker. Unfortunately he was also quite stupid, impulsive and reckless. And oh, how he *stank!* Often he delighted too much in the carnage he caused, not thinking of the consequences for the rest of them until later. Too many times in the past, Locke had had to move his entire base of operations because of Kilroy's insatiable hunger and incompetence at covering his tracks bringing unwanted attention to them all. This is why he preferred to keep him at a distance, acting as a scout and a solitary hunter rather than keeping him with the main group. From the look of him, Kilroy had failed him yet again. Luckily for him, good help was hard to find these days and Locke valued one's loyalty and capacity for cruelty towards his enemies above most other things. Kilroy had an abundance of both qualities. Tonight that might prove to be his only saving grace.

"And what, pray tell, have you been up to? Why were you not here to greet us when we arrived and how did you end up in that sorry state? Don't tell me that the Betrayer has found us here already because of your bungling?" He crossed his arms as he said it.

Kilroy shifted down to a form that was as close to human as he dared to get; he now looked something like Lon Chaney Jr as the Wolfman. In this form, his vocal chords were close enough to those of a human that he could actually speak, although his voice was very low, raspy and quite hard to understand for all but those who were used to hearing it. He got down on one knee and looked to the ground, not daring to look the Master in the eye.

"My Lord, I was spotted while keeping watch over the home of William and Elizabeth. They attacked me before I could escape, they had silver weapons! I barely escaped alive!"

"Yes, I can see *that.* By the time I'm done with you, you might wish that you hadn't!" Locke growled. He suspected that there was more that he was keeping from him. "Look at me when I'm talking to you!" he barked.

Kilroy looked up. Locke's eyes narrowed. So he *was* lying to him! He really should know better by now. It was impossible to deceive him! Still, he thought it might be amusing to toy with him for a time before dealing with his ill-advised attempts at deceit.

"I'm disappointed in you, Kilroy. You're one of my oldest servants. I expect more from you. Now, thanks to you, we no longer have the advantage of catching them unaware. If they elude me, if they join the Betrayer, then the blame will be yours and yours alone!"

"My apologies, Master. However, I have not yet felt the presence of the Betrayer or his allies. William and Elizabeth can have no idea of our true numbers. I believe that if we strike back swiftly enough, we may still be able to salvage this situation!"

William and Elizabeth! Locke thought angrily. He had been surprised that they still lived. Had they been the ones who had betrayed him all those years ago? *Someone* had betrayed him back then, he was sure of that. How else had the Guilds known how to penetrate his tower, known the best time to strike, or where he kept his treasures? They were the Childlings of the accursed Blake, who had eventually become The Great Betrayer himself. Was it so hard to believe that his vampiric offspring had been the original betrayers? Yes, he was looking forward to the conversation he would have with them soon, right before he had the pleasure of removing their heads from their shoulders!

"For your sake, I certainly hope so. Now tell me, what are you keeping from me?" You wouldn't have thought that it was possible for all the color to drain from the fuzzy face of a werewolf, but apparently it was, because it just did for Kilroy as he heard these words. Locke smiled on the inside as he watched the stinking creature squirm before him.

"Keeping from you, Master? What do you mean? I'm not keeping anything from you."

"You know, it really is quite amusing to see just how bad you are at lying to me. I suppose we'll have to do this the hard way then. I wouldn't have it any other way!"

Locke began to intone the words of a spell. There was so little magic that he remembered how to work these days without having to consult with the few spell books that he hadn't lost somewhere down the ages and could still actually read. The exceptions were those handful of spells that he found himself using on a fairly regular basis. He could no more forget how to cast them than he could forget how to walk. It was amazing how often he found an occasion to use this particular one. It was an especially nasty one. Very painful for the recipient. Naturally, it was one of his favorites.

Red tendrils of energy spread out from his head and connected with Kilroy's head. The man-beast howled in agony as the tendrils bored into his mind, ripping information from it. In his own mind's eye, the Master saw everything that Kilroy had experienced in the past week. The fury within him rose as he did so. He watched as Kilroy was ambushed in the woods by the Betrayer himself and almost killed. Not only that, but he had created another werewolf, a werewolf that was young and had proven himself capable of besting Kilroy in battle. Next, he saw that Kilroy had already lost one of the vampires that they hunted to the Betrayer and kept that failure from him! Worst of all he had run into a pair of Guildsmen at the home of William and Elizabeth. A knight who wielded the *Vermilion Avenger,* that most notorious of blades, and a wizard!

Throughout the centuries, none of the Guilds had been more relentless in their attempts to destroy him than his own people, the magic users of the Temple of the Old Gods. They were ashamed that their own ranks had produced such an endless plague of death and evil. The last thing he wanted was to tangle with them again, as unfortunately he wasn't quite the great and powerful wizard he'd once been.

He'd barely escaped from the Guilds the last time they'd caught up with him, over two centuries ago. It had taken almost that long to build his forces back up to something close to what they once had been. He'd been forced to lay low ever since, constantly moving around the world and keeping dangerous loose cannons like Kilroy far from the rest of them. Worst of all, he'd had no choice but to scale back the scope of his operations, curtailing his once lofty ambitions so that he could remain invisible to the Guilds. Circumstances had forced him to go from a world-class schemer to a penny-ante one. Mere survival had become his priority when it should've been conquest and domination of these inferior humans. Still, he dreamed that someday this would change, if he could just hang on long enough. Perhaps once this unfortunate business with the Betrayer and his rebellion he was settled? Yes, then he could refocus his attention on his old ambitions - find a way to displace the Guilds from their position of dominance over this world and rule it as he was no doubt destined to do. But in the meantime, he had to survive. He and his forces were in no condition to take on the Guilds again right now. He had a good mind to order everyone back onto the buses and get out of there while he still could.

But no, his pride was too great to allow him to just turn tail and run away like that. There seemed to be only the two Guildsmen, perhaps they were just advance scouts for the Guilds? They might even be here for the same reason that he was - to destroy William and Elizabeth. He wanted William and Elizabeth for himself, but it wouldn't be such a tragedy if the Guildsmen killed them, so long as they left it at that and didn't trace Kilroy back here. Kilroy was an overzealous idiot, but he had been right about one thing - if they struck swiftly enough, perhaps they *could* salvage the situation...if he eliminated the Guildsmen before they could report to the others.

A plan began to form in his mind. But first he would have to deal with this fool before him. Make an example of him, it was expected of him to do so. True, he was already badly hurt and in a great deal of pain right now, but it wasn't enough. Not nearly enough. He didn't want any of the others to think that he was starting to go soft on them in his old age.

He chanted the words of a different spell, another of his old favorites. Bolts of electricity sprang from his fingertips and connected with Kilroy. Unlike in the shed, this time, Kilroy didn't even try to dodge them. He knew better than to try and avoid the Master's punishments, doing so would just bring an even greater punishment - if he survived this one.

The church was filled with the smell of charred flesh and burning hair. If Kilroy had smelled bad before, he smelled doubly bad now. He didn't bother to try and cry out for mercy, for he knew that the Master had none.

In the end, Locke stopped his electrocution of Kilroy because he didn't want that awful smell to get into the fabric of his suit. If it did, he doubted that he'd ever be able to get it out. With his refined vampiric senses, he'd always be able to smell it.

"One more chance for redemption then, Kilroy. It is the will of the Dark Mother that I spare you. You can yet prove yourself worthy by joining the assault upon William and Elizabeth's home. An assault that Varney will now have the honor of leading." Locke had made a kind of religion out of the veneration of the Dark Mother, the raging Grendel that was the source of his vampiric immortality, with himself as her High Priest, the only one who could interpret her will. It was all nonsense of course. The Dark Mother was little more than a gibbering, stupid animal who knew nothing but hunger and rage, but it helped him to maintain control of his little flock.

Kilroy just nodded, mumbling, accepting his fate. With his existing injuries, and the new ones that the Master had just inflicted on him, it might as well be a death sentence.

Locke now turned to face one of the Undying Ones, his most senior and trusted inner circle of vampires. Vampires that he had personally created and who almost rivaled him in strength. This was Varney, one of the ones that had been speaking to him when Kilroy had first entered the sanctuary. He had long, shiny black hair and had sharpened some of his teeth into fangs in imitation of the fictional vampire that he took his name from. He was Locke's second in command, having moved into that position when it was suddenly left vacant by Blake's betrayal. This was another slap in the face of Kilroy, who as the one who had found William and Elizabeth would've ordinarily been put in charge of such an operation.

Varney smiled, revealing his unique, fanged mouth. "Thank you, Master! I will not fail you as this pathetic *dog* did."

"I know you won't, or you will suffer as Kilroy did. Now take half of the Childlings and the dogs. Go to the home of William and Elizabeth; Kilroy will guide you. There may be a Knight and a wizard there. If they are still there, make sure that you kill them. *Nothing* is more important than that! There is also a young dog and a young vampire there too, teenagers. Eliminate them as well. But I want William and Elizabeth brought back here to me alive, if possible. I would have words with them before I dispatch them. Go immediately, time is of the essence!" The Master was also aware from Kilroy's memories that there seemed to be a few normal humans on that property as well, but they were of such little consequence to him that he didn't even bother to mention them. No doubt, his children would feed upon them if they found them there, as was their right as the mighty apex predators that they were.

"A wizard and a Knight?" Varney asked a little fearfully. "I may need more soldiers."

"Very well, take *all* the dogs with you. Now go and do what the Dark Mother demands!" he commanded.

Varney bowed and snapped his fingers at Kilroy, who painfully got back to his feet and followed him. Varney began shouting out various names as he moved through the sanctuary. Different vampires who had been seated in the pews rose up and joined him. The werewolves, who were mostly in full wolf form, trotted behind them as they heard their names called.

Mortus Locke watched as they filed down the aisle and out of the sanctuary, confident that his army of the night would not fail him this time, not after the display he had just put on for them. Yes, if the Guildsmen were still there, they would be eliminated before they could report anything to the Guilds. This new werewolf and the Childling William and Elizabeth had created would also be wiped away before they could join the ranks of his enemies. Soon, William and Elizabeth themselves would be here, cowering before him as so many others had, and he would look into their eyes and know if they were the traitors he'd long been searching for. Even if they weren't, he'd destroy them all the same, just to make sure that they didn't join the Betrayer's forces.

Tonight was going to be a good night after all. Yes, a *very* good night!

CHAPTER 16:

SUNDAY, BLOODY SUNDAY

Allison's eyes bulged suddenly like she'd been shocked with an electric cattle prod. "Can't you feel them? My God! There must be *dozens* of them!" she shouted to William and Elizabeth.

"Huh? What's going on? What're you all talking about?" Matt asked in alarm.

"Yes, I feel them! They're right outside now!" Elizabeth said with a start as she stood up. William was on his feet now too, pulling both of his pistols from their holsters. Thankfully, he'd reloaded them while he'd been waiting for Kevin and Allison to rejoin them earlier.

"I can feel it too!" Kevin added, a sliver of fear creeping down his back.

William looked to the windows and noticed the absence of the green glow from outside. And there was more - he could now hear the persistent drizzle of the raindrops as they splattered on the rooftop. More troubling than that, he could also hear the creak of footsteps on his steps, and even on his porch! He could feel the hatred of those assembled outside the manor burning bright and hot.

"Wizard! You've failed us! You forgot to erect a new barrier!" he growled at Randy.

"Oh shit! Sorry!"

"What? I thought you were gonna set a timer!" Matt said hotly.

"I must've gotten sidetracked..." Randy explained.

"Just make a new one - pronto!" Matt ordered.

"Oh yeah, of course! Coming right up!" Randy said as he began to chant the spell once more.

But before he could finish his incantation, a dark form crashed through the nearest window. It was soon followed by another one, and another. They could hear the windows all along the first floor shattering inwards, the wood from the shutters snapping and flying everywhere. A mixed group of a half dozen werewolves and vampires were now slowly moving towards them from various directions. More of them seemed to be joining them every minute from outside.

"Kevin! Beast mode!" Allison commanded.

"Oh man, I just put these clothes on!" Kevin complained as he obeyed and his clothing began to rip and tear as his body contorted and grew in size.

"Charles! Mary! Quickly! Grab those swords from above the fireplace!" William shouted to his human charges as he and Elizabeth took aim and fired at some of the invaders. Charles ran to the fire and removed a pair of long swords and a shield that had hung over the mantle. They weren't just ornamental - William had them forged by the town blacksmith, back when the town *had* a blacksmith, in anticipation of such an attack. They were forged from pure iron. They were a little rusty, literally, but they'd still do the job. Charles gave Mary the shield and one of the swords, keeping the other one for himself.

He handed the shield to her just in time for her to use it to stop a slavering werewolf from biting her as he leapt onto her. Still, the force of his jump and the weight of his body brought them both crashing to the floor. Mary was pinned under the large shield which was almost as big as she was - from that position she was unable to do anything to defend herself with her sword. Charles hacked at the wolf's back, but it swatted him away with one arm, sending him careening across the room and into a wooden side table.

"Dad!" Mary screamed as she witnessed this.

Randy saw all of this too and decided to abandon the spell he'd been working to put up another massive barrier around the house, which was a somewhat long and complicated incantation, besides he'd only end up trapping them all inside with their attackers when he succeeded. Instead, he switched gears and said the words to a spell that, by design, had to be much shorter since it was intended to be used in the heat of a battle, when seconds mattered. A combat spell. He directed a blast of super cold air at the werewolf besieging Mary. Within moments, it was frozen solid and toppled over onto the ground, shattering into a thousand tiny pieces as it did so. Randy didn't usually make these freeze blasts so cold, but he knew that he had to amplify their power if they were going to be of any use against these kinds of opponents. He was quite satisfied with the results. Usually Randy preferred to use fireballs or bolts of lightning against his enemies, but he at least had the presence of mind to not do that right now, lest he accidentally burn down the house while they were all still trapped inside.

Mary jumped to her feet and tried to make it over to where she'd seen her father thrown, but her path was blocked by another werewolf. She swung her sword at it. It was heavier than she'd expected and it dipped low as she swung it. It connected with the monster's upper thigh, the blade burying itself half through the flesh of its muscle. It howled in outrage and slashed at her, and she barely managed to bring her shield back up to cover herself in time. Then there was an explosion of sound, bone and blood that came raining down upon her from above. She cautiously lowered her shield and saw that the top of the werewolf's head was now gone. As it fell over, she saw Allison was standing behind her, the barrel of her pistol still smoking. Allison just winked at her. From behind Allison, she could see a werewolf dressed in Kevin's tattered clothes pulling the arm off of one vampire and using it as a bat to knock away another vampire that had been advancing on the spot where her father was painfully getting back to his feet.

Matt had been using the *Vermilion Avenger* to great effect to cut off the legs of their attackers, sending them tumbling to the floor. With great dismay, he saw that this didn't completely stop them. The determined hordes of the undead and their now legless lupine allies just continued to edge closer to where Matt and Randy fought back to back from behind the sofa.

A particularly enthusiastic vampire chose that moment to jump towards Matt, who imagined his sword swooping up and barrelling right through the vampire's chest like a giant stake. The sword, as always, obeyed the pictures Matt formed in his imagination and obliged. The vampire landed on top of Matt; despite the gaping hope in its chest, it still seemed to be very much alive, and very determined to bite Matt. It brought its mouth down on his forearm, only to break some of its teeth on his armor. Matt grabbed him by the scruff of his shirt collar and tossed him off of him and onto the other side of the sofa. Out of instinct, he pulled out the 9mm pistol he always carried and blasted the vampire right between the eyes. He knew that it wouldn't kill the monster, but he figured that the force of the impact would at least knock him back a little, buying himself some more time, which it did. Now Matt mentally ordered the *Vermilion Avenger* to bury itself in the top of the vampire's skull, passing through its whole head and out the bottom of his chin - the tip of the sword stuck in the floor itself. The vampire struggled to get up, but was stuck in place, thrashing around uselessly, flailing his arms and legs.

"Why the hell doesn't driving my sword through them like a big stake work? Is it because it isn't wooden?" he shouted to Randy, who was busy freezing more of their attackers.

"No, it doesn't matter what the stake is made of! It takes more than just a stake through the heart to kill them. I guess we never really covered how to kill vampires, did we? Concentrate on beheading them! The stakes are only good for pinning them in place long enough to take the heads off. Even then, we have to stuff the heads with garlic and burn the remains later on, or else they can still be resurrected by a variety of means..."

"Okay, take off the heads! Got it! Sheesh! I didn't need a whole lecture!" Matt made the *Vermilion Avenger* lift back up into the air, freeing the vampire he'd been struggling against. It lunged at him again, but his head came off before he could reach Matt, sliced off by the sword just in time. The head fell towards Matt and he caught it with his free hand.

"Yuck!" he cried and he threw it across the room, where it hit a different vampire square in the face as it was about to grab Allison's arm as she tried to reload her pistol, knocking him over. As he fell against the wall, Kevin swiped at the neck of that vampire, tearing his head off too.

Matt saw that the various monsters whose legs he'd taken off earlier were almost to where he and Randy were standing. He made the *Vermilion Avenger* fly over to them and removed their heads too. As he did so, another vampire came flying through a nearby broken window and landed on his back.

Within seconds, Charles was swinging his sword at that vampire's neck. Charles, of course, knew all about the right way to kill a vampire from William's countless tales of the old days, which he had grown up listening to. Unfortunately, the sword Charles wielded wasn't nearly as sharp as the *Vermilion Avenger*, which could slice through virtually anything like it was made of butter. Taking off someone's head with a normal sword or axe is actually quite difficult. It usually took an executioner in medieval times several hacks at the neck to get it completely off, which is why the guillotine was considered to be a *merciful* invention when it was created. So for an out of shape, middle-aged fellow like Charles, even hopped up on a boatload of adrenaline as he now was, it was particularly difficult to stop this vampire. In the end, he succeeded though - the vampire's head was now only connected to his body by a thin piece of skin that was stretching out from the weight of the head by the time that the monster finally went limp and slid off of Matt's back.

"Thanks, man!" Matt smiled at him.

An out-of-breath Charles gave him a little salute by pressing two of his fingers to his forehead and smiled back at him. Then his expression suddenly changed completely to one of total surprise.

Matt looked on in horror as blood gushed from Charles' mouth. The man was now lifted off of his feet by a huge, shaggy arm. There was a horrid ripping sound that none of them would ever forget as Kilroy ripped the spine right out of Charles' back. Kilroy lifted his head and howled in pleasure as he raised the bloody collection of vertebrae to the sky triumphantly, with Charles' body falling forward and smacking to the ground right in front of Matt.

"Dad! No! Dad!" Mary screamed from nearby. Salty tears obscured her vision, but she continued to swing out blindly with her sword, possessed by a new kind of fury.

Kilroy flicked the spine away like it was nothing, snarled and surged towards Matt. A solid wall of scarred muscle, sinew, and matted, charred fur. As in the shed, Kilroy found himself instead coming into contact with a glowing green shield which Randy had just thrown up between Matt and the beast. Randy now directed one of his deadly freezing blasts at Kilroy, but the werewolf dodged it, leaping back out of one of the windows to safety.

"I really *hate* that guy!" Matt said angrily.

"Everyone! Get behind this shield if you can!" Randy shouted to their allies. Then he chanted a few words, making the shield bigger so that it formed into a curved, u-shaped barrier that came up to the level of he and Matt's heads. Matt and Randy tried to pick off as many of the monsters as they could that were still harassing the others so they could make it over to them.

Elizabeth and William were the first to reach them. Randy opened a temporary gap in the barrier with a gesture, allowing them entry.

"We'll never make it out of this!" Elizabeth said "There's too many of them!"

"They keep pouring in from outside faster than we can kill them!" William agreed as he raised his pistol over the barrier and fired, killing another werewolf like a pro.

"Yeah! I've noticed! Randy, buddy, now would be a *really* good time to zap us all out of here, don't you think?" Matt suggested.

"A teleportation spell? I can't! It's too risky right now!" he protested.

"So is staying here!" Matt argued. These things were all so damned fast - too many times they dodged his attempts to take off their heads with the sword.

"I can't! Not yet!" Randy replied.

Matt didn't see why Randy couldn't just teleport them somewhere else. What was the big deal? He'd seen his mentor, Wendy, save them all like that once, many years ago, when they were all trapped in a building that was about to be hit by a missile.

"Wendy could do it if she was here!"

Randy sighed. Matt just didn't understand. He remembered the incident that Matt was probably thinking of and knew that his friend didn't appreciate the differences here. For one, Wendy was then as now, the most powerful witch on the planet. Even then, she had needed the help of one of her most powerful assistants to help her teleport everyone out of that room. Teleportation spells were best done if all of the people or things being transported were touching each other. He probably *could* teleport everyone who was already behind his barrier, but what about the kids that were still fighting for their lives on the other side? If he tried to take them too without them being a part of the chain of people who were in physical contact with each other, then he'd likely grab all or most of their attackers too, and most of the other things in the room. Maybe even one of the walls! If they weren't all touching, then some of them might also get lost in *the Place Between Places* that they would briefly pass through before they rematerialized. If that happened, they'd be lost for all time!

"I'm not Wendy! We can't do it until all of us are behind this shield and touching hands! Even then, transporting seven people at once by myself is tricky!" Randy told him.

"Tricky - but not *impossible*! Staying here is suicide!" Matt said testily.

"Okay, okay! But first we need to get those kids back here with us!"

"No arguments there, pal! I didn't come all this way to get Kevin only to lose him like this!" Matt agreed as he refocused his attention on helping him and the Sherwoods to pick off the kid's numerous attackers.

Kevin, Allison and Mary had formed a rough circle, standing back to back as they battled the seemingly never ending stream of supernatural monsters constantly rushing towards them. If it wasn't for the extra help that the adults were providing, they surely would have perished by now.

"You guys, get over to us!" Matt urged again. Then he had a thought. "Hey! Maybe we can make it over to them?" He knew from past experience that this type of magical shield would move with the person who cast it.

"Yeah, it's worth a try!" Randy said. He started to fight his way across the large room, sometimes freezing the monsters, other times using a basic combat spell that allowed him to throw them around the room. He slammed them into walls or the ceiling with the kind of force that would've killed any normal person, but vampires and werewolves were many times tougher than a normal human being. This only stunned them for a few seconds, but it was long enough to get them out of their way. Slowly, he began closing the gap. The others behind the shield moved and fought along with him.

Randy froze a vampire in place just as it grabbed Mary's shield and yanked it out of her hands. Mary brought her sword crashing down on the vampire, breaking it into pieces.

Kevin, who was getting increasingly used to holding onto his humanity and controlling himself in this new form had an idea. He lifted Mary up effortlessly.

"Hey! Put me down!" she complained, suddenly fearful of him. She was kicking and squirming uselessly in his grasp.

"Kevin! What're you doing?" Allison asked. Had he lost control and forgotten who was on his side?

He paid neither of them any mind. He'd reasoned that as a human, Mary was the most vulnerable one in their group, especially since she no longer had her shield to protect her. So he threw her across the room and onto the other side of the energy barrier. William caught her and placed her down safely on her feet.

"Oh, I get it now! Good thinking, kemosabe!" Allison said approvingly as she kicked out at a lunging wolf with all her might, sending it skittering into the fireplace. It jumped out, its back on fire. Randy quickly froze it before it could set anything in the room ablaze. Matt shattered it by sending the *Vermilion Avenger* through it on its way to behead another hapless vampire that had just entered the room through a window.

Kevin now picked up Allison and threw her onto the other side. Elizabeth caught her.

"Alright! Now we just need Kevin and we can finally blow this taco stand!" Matt smiled.

Unfortunately, just as he said it, a fresh wave of creatures flooded into the room, some of them breaking down the front doors, others even coming through the windows in the upper floors and running down the steps. They split into two groups; one surrounding Kevin, and the other moving forwards to attack those behind the barrier. Randy had by now made the barrier into a complete circle of emerald energy instead of the semi circle it had started out as. Even so, some of the assailants tried to jump over it, even made it inside, but were quickly dispatched before they could hurt any of them.

With their attention now split between fighting off this new wave of attackers and trying to help Kevin, he was quickly overwhelmed. Allison's face was streaked with tears as she saw him bleeding from a dozen different places. He fell to his knees and vanished under a sea of vampires and werewolves.

"Kevin!" she shouted. She'd never felt so damned useless before.

Then, from out of nowhere - salvation! Another wave entered the fray, and just when things seemed to be at their most hopeless for those behind the barrier, just as Randy was about to give up and teleport them out, leaving Kevin behind, they watched in amazement as the latest group to enter the room began attacking the other vampires and werewolves!

Matt noticed that some of these newcomers, which was also a mix of werewolves and vampires like their attackers had been, were armed with a peculiar weapon. It was a long metal pole, sharpened to a point at one end like a stake, and the other end was like an axe. As he looked on, he saw one of the newcomers use the sharpened end to pin a vampire to the wall through its chest, then she pulled on the other end and the axe detached, still tethered to the weapon by a chain and she used it to quickly behead the vampire. In one swift motion, she reattached the axe to the shaft and yanked the weapon out of the wall. The now-headless vampire fell to the ground, and the female newcomer that had destroyed it spun around and used her weapon to trip an attacking werewolf, stabbing it with the stake end through the skull. It had all happened so quickly he was barely able to process it mentally.

"Some of these clowns are on our side! Concentrate on just fighting the ones trying to get in here with us!" he shouted to be heard over the sounds of the battle.

"What? On our side?" William said incredulously, then he watched the fight happening around where Kevin had just gone down and saw that, yes, some of the creatures out there were actually pulling the attackers off of the boy and battling them!

"Oh yes! You're right!" he said joyfully.

Allison was relieved to see Kevin rise up again, several of his tormentors sent flying into the air as he did so. He grabbed others and smashed their skulls together. He picked up one vampire and bit its head clear off and spat it out like a seed in a piece of fruit.

"Oh yeah!" she cried.

Kevin also seemed to be aware that he was now being assisted by these mysterious strangers and only attacked the creatures that kept coming at him, avoiding fighting the ones with the strange weapons.

In short order, the room seemed to have been cleared of attacking monsters. Kevin placed one arm against a wall for support, and he slid down, breathing heavily. He was losing a lot of blood from his many wounds. Allison wanted to go to him, but she was still behind the barrier. She just pressed her hands, now bloody from the battle, up against it, a frantic look on her face.

A short, rather scrappy-looking man with close-cropped brown hair now entered the room. He appeared to be in his thirties, but considering the present company, this was probably quite wrong. He was busy speaking into a cell phone. "We've established a perimeter around the house? Excellent! Okay, I'll talk to you again in a minute." He flipped the phone closed and looked at Randy.

"Wizard, I suggest you put another barrier up round this house while my people verify that all the rooms are clear. I don't think there's an intact window or door left on this building now!" he said.

William's eyes widened in recognition. "Martin? Martin Lane? Martin, is it really you?"

The man smiled broadly and threw his arms open. "One and the same! William and Elizabeth! It *has* been a long time, hasn't it?"

"Centuries!" Elizabeth beamed.

"You guys know each other?" Matt asked.

"Yes! This is the man who helped us build this house that we were just telling you about!" William said.

"It looks like I might have to help you rebuild it too, from the looks of things!" Martin added.

Randy made the barrier that had been protecting them vanish with a gesture of his hands and began chanting a spell to put up a new one around the manor. This guy was obviously a friend and he had a point, they would need to keep out any enemies while they planned their next move. As soon as he finished the spell, he made sure that he set a timer for it. He wasn't about to make *that* mistake twice!

As the barrier disappeared, Allison ran to where Kevin was sitting. William and Elizabeth rushed forwards to warmly embrace their old friend.

Mary walked over to where the body of her father lay crumpled, almost slipping on the blood-covered floor several times as she made her way over to it. She fell to her knees and started bawling.

She couldn't believe that she'd never be held by him again, never hear his laugh. Her father, who had always gone out of his way to give her whatever she needed, always indulged her oddness. He was the last of her immediate family left, now she was totally alone.

Allison told Kevin to change back to his human form. As he did so, she was even more upset to see all the cuts and scratches and bite marks covering his body. It was even worse than it had appeared when he was a wolf. She put an arm around him and cried.

"Don't you die on me! I won't have it! I won't let it end like this!" she pleaded.

He just smiled at her. "It's okay, you gave me something to live for again, at least for a little while. Thank you."

"No! Stay with me!" she kissed him then. And he kissed her back. It was an unusually long kiss which got the attention of those standing nearby. Finally, their faces separated, as Kevin needed to (reluctantly) come up for air.

"Well, maybe I'll try to stick around a little longer if there's any more of that in my future!" he laughed.

She laughed too. "I think that can be arranged."

"Oh shit! It hurts when I laugh now!" he observed, feeling his ribs. Sure enough, some of them felt broken.

A werewolf in that odd, almost human, "wolfman" kind of form had been standing nearby, watching. He carried one of those peculiar weapons and was wearing loose fitting workout clothing.

Doubtlessly it would stretch when he changed into his larger, more formidable form.

"'What wound did ever heal but by degrees?'" he commented in a deep, gravelly brogue.

"Huh?" Allison said, turning her head to look at him.

"It's Shakespeare. You know, the bard? Don't they teach you little brats anything of value these days?"

"Humph! 'He jests at scars that never felt a wound,'" Allison replied. How dare this guy assume that she was so ignorant? He didn't know who he was dealing with here! She was a book nerd and someone who longed to be an actress. She could quote Shakespeare back at him all day if she wanted to!

The werewolf laughed, which was an unusual and disturbing sound.

"Well played, girl! Don't worry about your Romeo here. He'll pull through. I've seen worse in my day. And my days on this earth have been long, indeed. 'Life is as tedious as a twice-told tale, Vexing the dull ear of a drowsy man.'"

Allison raised a quizzical eyebrow. "And you are?"

"Prospero, at your service, Lass." He held out a fuzzy hand.

She shook it and smiled. "Prospero. Yes of course, it would be, wouldn't it?" It was the name of a Shakespeare character. She was beginning to like this old crazy werewolf who had obviously spent too much time in English Literature classes.

"If I may ask, how is it that he can be in human form on the night of a full moon?" Prospero asked, a note of awe creeping into his voice.

"'That's the power of love!' Huey Lewis, 1985," Kevin answered.

Is this love? This whatever it is that's between us? Allison thought as she heard Kevin's words.

She felt like it was, like it *had* to be - no matter how crazy that seemed since they'd practically just met. The idea certainly appealed to the romantic in her.

"Eh?" Prospero asked.

"You're not the only one that can throw around a few old quotes!" Kevin smiled up at him.

"Bah! You can't compare some crappy pop song to the work of the bard!" Prospero argued.

"Crappy pop song? It happens to be used very effectively in one of the greatest movies of all time!" Kevin continued, just enjoying getting a rise out of the old guy at this point.

"Or compare something as crude as a film to a masterpiece of the stage!" Prospero carried on.

"Boys! Can't we just agree that both things can be awesome? Theatre, film, it's all just drama, all just entertainment. 'A rose by any other name would smell as sweet,'" Allison added. This seemed to quell the conflict. Prospero was obviously mollified by her use of Shakespeare to settle things. Normally she relished these kinds of arguments, but now hardly seemed the right time or the place for it. She didn't even really understand who this werewolf or any of his companions were, how they got here or why they had saved them. She was about to ask Prospero some of those questions when a group of the newcomers in the distance broke up and she saw something on the other side of the room, something that broke her heart. She saw Mary crying and pitifully rocking back and forth over Charles' body.

"Omigod! Mary! I'm such a lousy friend!" she cried out and left Kevin to run over to join her. She placed a comforting hand on her shoulder as she reached her. Mary turned and hugged her impossibly tightly.

Allison cried over Charles' body. Not just for Mary's loss, but for her own. She'd known and lived with Charles for the past 16 years. Mary was her best friend and confidant these days, but when Mary had been a small child, it had been Charles and his wife who had filled that role first. They had been the ones who had been the most sympathetic to Allison when she first came to the manor and was having so much trouble adjusting to her new life. Allison had tried to return that kindness as best she could once Mary's mom passed away by helping Charles adjust to life as a widower and helping him to raise Mary. Few people understood her as well as he did. She couldn't imagine her life without him being in it in some capacity anymore.

William and Elizabeth had noticed Allison run past them and their expressions darkened as they saw her go to Mary and recalled Charles' grisly fate. They excused themselves from Martin and joined the girls before they could really find out any of the details of how Martin had gotten there.

"I'm so sorry, Mary," Elizabeth said as she bent down to hug her. "He was like a son to us, you know? I remember the day he was born, in this very house..." she said sadly as she looked upon his gruesome remains. *Born in this house, and died in this house. Just like his father and grandfather before him,* she thought.

"I'm a fucking orphan now!" Mary blurted out between sobs.

"Don't worry, Mary. We're all family. You'll always have a home with us," William said.

This just made her cry even harder. Did this mean that with her father now gone, she'd be doomed to replace him as their servant even sooner than she had feared? That she'd never get out of here? In less than twenty four hours she'd lost a friend, her own father and maybe her chances at the kind of future she'd always dreamed about. A future far from these confining walls. She was suddenly numb with the pain of it all.

"I'm sorry. He seemed like a good man. He really saved my bacon back there," Matt said awkwardly as he wandered over to the group, Randy following close behind him.

"I'm sorry too," Randy added.

Mary snapped out of her daze at his comment. "You should be! This is all *your* fault! If you hadn't forgotten to put that barrier back up they would've never gotten in here!"

Randy's face fell and he looked away.

"I'm sorry buddy. She's just a kid, she's angry right now. Can you blame her? I'm sure she doesn't *really* mean it."

"No, she's right Matt, it *is* my fault!" he said darkly.

"No way, man! You can't believe that! You never wanted this to happen! I know a thing or two about blaming yourself for shit that you're not responsible for, believe me, that's not a road you wanna go down! You don't wanna wind up like me, or like Kevin over there always blaming himself for what happened to Sylvia. Sometimes, bad shit just happens and it's not really anyone's fault no matter how much it might make more sense if you've got someone to blame, even if that someone is yourself. We all make mistakes, we're only human..." Matt looked around the room and saw that they were probably the only *actual* humans in it and corrected himself. "Okay, so we're *mostly* only human. You know what I mean! My point is, we have to learn how to stop blaming ourselves and live with those mistakes - to move on - or we won't be much good to ourselves or any of the people we care about. You've gotta roll with the punches to get to what's real," Matt told him.

"Okay, so now you're just quoting Van Halen lyrics at me," Randy said.

"Yeah, but it's still true!" Matt argued.

Randy glanced over at Mary who was still crying and being consoled by the Sherwoods. Her life would never be the same again, and all because of one thoughtless moment on his part.

"Thanks Matt, but I can't believe it's really quite as simple as you make it sound," Randy said in a quiet voice as he studied his shoes.

"Did I ever say it's *simple*? I'm sorry if I gave you that impression. Fuck no! It's hard as hell, but it's the only way to get through it." He put a hand on his friend's shoulder and lingered there for a moment, gave it a quick squeeze, then let go and looked around the ruined room once more. A room full of beheaded corpses, said heads, and the shattered frozen remains of various monsters. The once stately room was now covered in blood, and so was everyone in it. It looked as if every piece of furniture in the room had been overturned and broken at one point or another during the fight.

"Now let's try and figure out who the heck all these jokers are!" he said, and with that he walked up to Martin.

"So...Martin. Where exactly have you been all these years?" Matt asked.

"All over the world, but these past few years in Harwinton," he answered, not sure who this inquisitive man was.

William was standing nearby, and he picked up Martin's words. "Harwinton? Isn't that fairly nearby?"

"It's south of here, yes," Martin admitted.

"It's practically down the road! You mean to tell me that you've been this close for years now and you never came to visit?"

"I...wanted to, but I couldn't bring myself to. You see, I met someone after I left you. We married, and for a time we were happy, but after almost a century together she couldn't take this lifestyle any longer. She...destroyed herself, in the end. I wandered the country for a few more decades before coming back to Connecticut and starting a small farm like this one for myself. I was afraid that maybe the centuries of isolation had gotten to you as well, that I'd discover that you'd both killed yourselves too. Or perhaps the townspeople had figured out what you were and done the deed instead, or you'd fallen off the wagon and started feeding on humans again. I wouldn't have been able to bear it if any of those ghastly scenarios had been true! I preferred to remember you all as you were. I'd never dared to hope that you'd still be here, that you'd managed to keep your secret for all these years!"

"Yes, we had a lot of help, very *good* help, with keeping our secret," William said sadly as he glanced over at Mary and Allison still hugging near Charles' broken body.

"'Oft our displeasures, to ourselves unjust, Destroy our friends and after weep their dust,'" Quoth Prospero as he wandered near.

"Prospero! You're here too!" Elizabeth said, startled.

"And still ceaselessly spouting Shakespeare, eh?" William chuckled. He'd actually kind of missed the pompous old gas bag. He was one of the few members of Locke's army that had ever shown much kindness to him and Elizabeth.

"So, you survived the attack on the tower all those centuries ago! But whatever became of your master, Blake?" Elizabeth asked. Prospero had once been Blake's most trusted and loyal "dog".

"Why don't you ask me yourselves?" a commanding voice said from behind her.

She spun around and her mouth fell open in astonishment. There stood the very man who had first stolen her away and turned her into a vampire. Blake was a handsome, long haired, youthful-seeming man who looked like he'd be very much at home on the cover of a romance novel, right down to his old-fashioned style of dress. He was wearing one of those big shirts with puffy sleeves and a plunging neckline. It was almost comical how much he looked like Fabio.

William raised his pistol and pointed it at him without hesitation.

"You *devil*! How dare you step foot in my home!"

"If I hadn't, I'm quite sure you'd all be dead by now," Blake said with remarkable indifference.

Kevin had seen the commotion and limped over to them. "Don't! I recognize this guy! He's the one who saved me in the woods that night!"

Matt was relieved to see that the kid was feeling well enough to walk. His injuries seemed to be healing before his eyes.

"Aye, and I had a little something to do with it too!" Prospero added.

"You did?" Kevin asked.

"Who do you think it was who got Kilroy off of you to begin with?" he replied with a smile and a wink.

"I care not! This is the monster who cursed us! This is the Master's old right hand man, nearly as wretched and depraved as he ever was!" William said, still aiming the gun.

"Oh don't be ridiculous! That thing can't destroy me," Blake laughed. He was right. The bullet inside, made of a pure metal and a high enough caliber could certainly hurt Blake badly, but it wouldn't quite kill him.

"A devil am I? That's a case of the pot calling the kettle black! You're hardly the angel I'm sure you'd have all your friends here believe that you are! You people should've seen this fellow back in the old days - he was full of such glorious passion, such fire! Oh, the things I've seen you do to satisfy your hunger...they surprised even me!" Blake said.

"Anything I did in the past was only because of you!" William accused.

"Oh yes, I'm sure it's much easier for you to live with yourself believing that, but the truth is a little more complicated isn't it? The blame for all your past atrocities belongs to you and you alone, I'm afraid. You are the only one who is responsible for your own predicament. As I seem to recall, I'm not the one who made you into a vampire, it was your beloved Elizabeth, who might I say, is looking as lovely as ever! You would do anything because of your pathetic devotion, your unreasonable obsession with her! Sell your very soul and degrade yourself over and over again if that was the price of being with her!"

"Please, stop it, both of you! Blake saved me from Kilroy too! Whatever your quarrel with him, it's time to leave it in the past!" Martin said forcefully.

"It's true, I'm a changed man. It took me long enough, but I eventually saw the error of my ways. You see there's been a kind of a schism in the ranks of Mortus Locke's followers, a rebellion of sorts. With myself on one side, and he on the other. This is *my* army that's just saved all your arses. We've been traveling the world, looking for vampires and werewolves to recruit so that we can take on Locke and destroy him for good. He's been doing the same, only in his case, instead of recruiting them, he kills them so I can't have them. He sees all other vampires and werewolves as potential enemies, not allies.The old boy doesn't feel he can trust anyone who isn't already on his side since I turned on him. The Great Betrayer, they call me now. I like it; it has a nice ring to it, don't you think?"

"A leopard never changes its spots!" William spat back.

"Please, William, calm yourself! Locke had Kilroy hunting me. If Blake hadn't found me first, I'd be dead now too. Now they're after you, only he's got the whole flippin' lot of them with him! We knew you wouldn't trust Blake, that's why they sent me in first, so I could personally vouch for him. If my word still means anything to you, please, lower the weapon. At least hear the man out. He *did* just save you all."

"I *do* respect the man that you were, Martin, but I also haven't seen you in almost two hundred years. A man can change a whole lot in that kind of time! Also, you don't know what this man really is, what he's capable of! What could this devil possibly have to say that I would ever care to hear?"

Blake laughed like some cheap, B-movie villain. Then he stopped short abruptly and looked William dead in the eyes.

"Only this - that I have found a way to finally end the curse of vampirism for all time. A way to turn every vampire on earth back into a normal human being!"

CHAPTER 17:

BLAKE'S CRUSADE

"**H**ot Damn!" Allison shouted, excited by Blake's promises. William shot her a dirty look.

She shrugged innocently. "Hey, he's got my vote!"

"C'mon William, end this useless charade, this silly display of machismo you're putting on for the benefit of the fair Elizabeth, whose honor you feel I besmirched when I lured her away from you all those many years ago. Poor old William, you never could quite accept the idea that perhaps Elizabeth wasn't so difficult to seduce. That a part of her preferred what I had to offer to the dreary life you could give her, grubbing around in the dirt like a common peasant until she died a wrinkled old widow, or more likely in agony giving birth to one of your welps!"

"I'm warning you!" William bellowed at Blake.

"Hey chief, If you really want William to join your side, pissing him off to the point where he's about to blow off half of your face might not be the most effective strategy. Just sayin'," Matt said, trying his best to diffuse the situation. Even if William's shot wouldn't kill Blake, he had a nasty suspicion that Blake's followers wouldn't take very kindly to such a thing.

"Yes, that's true. I suppose it's difficult for me to resist the urge to get a rise out of him. 'Tis such good sport!" Blake confessed.

"There! You see! He admits it! We're all still just playthings to him! Pawns to be used and discarded for his amusement! Nothing has changed!" William shouted.

"Husband! Please, calm down! They did just save us, and Martin trusts him. What's our alternative? If the Master truly still lives, then Blake might be our only hope of survival," Elizabeth said.

"Ah, Elizabeth! Still playing the role of the dutiful wife, the voice of reason and compassion, I see? How I've missed you and our little games together!" Blake smiled at her invitingly.

"I haven't missed you, not for a moment!" Elizabeth hissed.

"You looked into my eyes, William. You know that I speak the truth. You know that I have the cure for all our ills within my grasp," Blake said.

Finally William lowered his weapon.

"I know that *you* believe it to be so. I suppose that's good enough for now. You have my ear, but nothing else!" William conceded.

"But it *is* so! Truth be told, twas I who first discovered the secret, and convinced Blake to act upon it once he'd finally tired of this kind of life," Prospero said proudly.

"Yes, good Prosepro always enjoyed sneaking around and reading Locke's old journals and spell books while the Master slept. Most of them were lost when the Guilds drove us from the tower. But those of us who survived that battle managed to salvage a few of them. It was in one of those books that he found the answer: destroy the Dark Mother, the source of all vampirism, and you break the curse for everyone. That's why Locke brings her with him everywhere he goes, why he keeps her so well-fed and guarded. It's why he made her the object of worship," Blake revealed.

"What's the Dark Mother?" Kevin asked.

"It's what they call that Grendel that Mortus Locke conjured," Randy explained.

"A Grendel which he conjured by sacrificing his own daughter! A child he had just so that he could perform that ritual. Her flesh was used by the Grendel's spirit as...raw materials for it to build a body for itself when it manifested on this plane," Prospero elaborated.

"How horrible! I never knew that!" Elizabeth said.

"I doubt that even Locke knows it anymore! It was written in one of his oldest journals, it took me years to figure out how to translate it. It no longer exists. Most of his diaries and grimoires were lost when the Guilds attacked. But I managed to save a few of them." He patted a bag that he carried with him, its strap crossed diagonally over his chest. "I've even learned a few of the spells."

Randy's face blanched at that last comment. The unauthorized use of High Magic was considered a serious crime amongst his people in the Temple of the Old Gods. He could only imagine how dangerous the spells would be that were in a grimoire that had once belonged to someone like Mortus Locke!

"You'd better turn those books over to me when this is all over with. They're too dangerous to be allowed to exist," he said.

"You want my books? You're going to have to fight me for them!" Prospero snarled at him.

Randy was undaunted. "I hope it won't come to that, but I can't allow an amateur like you to try and practice that kind of magic."

"'Amateur'? 'Try'? I'm as much a wizard as you are, boy!" Prospero boasted.

"I doubt that! You can't learn everything from a book!" Randy said. These self-taught types who fancied themselves to be wizards were always the worst kinds of insufferable know-it-alls, in his opinion.

"Aye, but who was it that figured out how to end the vampire's curse? It wasn't you, laddie!" Prospero countered.

"You do have a point there," Randy conceded. "Your theory *does* make sense. Killing her should really break the curse. It's her enchanted blood that makes all of you vampires immortal. You all carry some of it within you. Destroy her physical body and all of her blood is destroyed too, even if it's in someone else's body," Randy mused.

"Aye, the vampires don't even really need to feed on the blood of others to survive. The Dark Mother's blood is what truly sustains them. Their bloodlust is just a kind of addiction that they've been infected with by carrying her blood inside of them," Prospero agreed.

"What? We don't need to feed? That can't be!" Allison was flabbergasted.

"It's true," Blake told her. "I didn't believe it at first either, but it really is just a habit that can be discarded with some effort. I haven't drunk a drop of blood in years."

"Unbelievable!" William thundered. He and Elizabeth were having a hard time buying all of this.

"The same is true of all of us here," one of the various vampires in Blake's army said. All the other vampires in the room nodded in agreement.

"You've got a very admirable little setup here. Feeding on cows. How clever, how humane! It's all quite unnecessary though, I assure you," Blake said.

"And what was it that made you finally turn on the Master?" Elizabeth asked. She'd been dying to know.

"How I wish I could tell you some moving, inspirational story about how I finally met a few humans who convinced me of their value as something other than food, but while that is *partially* true, it's also not as simple as all that. It was just one of many factors, but the truth is that I'd been on the fence about things for a long time. What finally pushed me over? I think it was mainly that I was tired. Tired of it all. I've lived so long that I can recall no other kind of life. I've seen everything, done everything, and I'm tired of everything. Everything but one - living as a mortal. I long to know what that's like: to grow old, to love, to have children, to die? It might be quite novel," Blake said wistfully.

"I've had my own reservations about this lifestyle for ages now. I grew weary of all the bloodshed and destruction, as well as being treated as little more than a dog by Locke. It took me the better part of a century of listening to this fool whining about things before I was finally able to convince him that we needed to *do* something about it," Prospero added.

"Yes, good old Prospero here always fancied that he saw something in me that I couldn't see for myself. Some sliver of goodness," Blake began.

"'I am as true as truth's simplicity, and simpler than the infancy of truth,'" Prospero broke in with yet another quote.

Blake smiled at his friend's eccentricities. Honestly, half the time Blake didn't really know what Prospero was trying to say through them, or if these quotations were even being used in the correct context, but they sure sounded impressive nonetheless.

He continued on with his story. "It's why he didn't just leave and go off on his own like so many others did when the Guilds attacked us. He believed in me, so he stayed to work on my conscience. When he realized that I had finally reached the breaking point, he revealed to me what he'd learned. We two, along with a few other like-minded individuals, tried to kill the Dark Mother one night, but we failed, barely escaping with our lives; and some were not so fortunate. Since then we've been searching for others like us, trying to build an army to rival Locke's before we can make another attempt to destroy her. It's turned into an arms race, with vampires and werewolves as the weapons. We seek to better arm ourselves for victory, and Locke seeks to deprive us of those weapons so he can maintain his numerical advantage. We came to Connecticut when Kilroy did, he was drawn here by the presence of Martin and yourselves, as were we. We found Martin first and convinced him to join our cause. Like so many of us, he's grown weary of eternal life. He told us about you two, so we came here to see if you were still on this farm and extend our protection to you. Our scouts came here yesterday and verified that you were here. We planned to send Martin in to explain all of this to you tonight, but when he approached your home he saw that it was under attack and called in the rest of us. And here we all are."

"You got to Martin first because Kilroy stayed behind in Shadowbrook to kill me," Kevin realized. "Why didn't you try to recruit me? Teach me how to control my powers?" he asked, feeling that they had just abandoned him. They'd seen him that night in the woods, they knew he existed. Why had nobody come to help him?

"We tried, lad! A few of the other werewolves stayed behind in Shadowbrook to search for you. By the time they figured out where you lived, you were already gone," Prospero told him.

Matt remembered Kevin's co-worker talking about people seeing werewolves in Shadowbrook. He wondered if some of them had been Prospero and his other wolves?

"Besides, you seem to be doing just fine without our help, you seem to have achieved a remarkable level of control over yourself in wolf form without any training. Such a thing usually takes more time, how did you ever pull it off?" Prospero asked.

"Thanks, I think I know how I did it. You know what they say..."

"Eh? And what is that?"

"'The power of love is a curious thing!'"

Prospero groaned at this repeated reference to such a crap song.

"So what do you say, William? Elizabeth? Will you join us, or should we just leave you and your strange new friends to your fate? We managed to beat back Locke's forces for now. But I think you know that he'll be back soon, and with a bigger army. My people tell me that even now, there are still a few of them on your property, keeping watch. Waiting for that barrier to come down again to attack. There's a good chance that if we don't leave here soon, we might have to face what's left of his whole army on our way out," Blake offered.

"What choice do we have?" William said in resignation.

"But you *do* have a choice!" Matt suddenly said. "The Guilds! We were gonna call them anyway. I'm sure they'll be *very* interested to learn that Mortus Locke is still alive. They'll probably even help you kill that Dark Mother thingy."

"That's true," Randy added. "In the Temple of the Old Gods, we always prioritized wiping out Locke. We only stopped hunting for him because we thought we'd succeeded."

"You want to bring the Guilds *here*? They'll kill all of us!" Blake said in alarm.

"No they won't, not once we explain things to them. We're pretty well-connected with the Guilds, they'll listen to us," Matt said to him. Blake studied him and could tell that he wasn't lying.

"It might not be a bad idea after all. If they'd really help us, we could finally bring this war to an end," he said.

"I think we know where they're hiding out, too!" Allison announced.

Everyone turned to look at her.

Kevin, who was standing next to her trying his best to keep what was left of his clothes covering his privates, looked at her questioningly. "We do?"

"Sure we do! Remember the old church we passed? The one with all the bad vibes? That's gotta be their base!" she reminded him.

"Damn! I think you're right!" Kevin agreed.

"We know the place! We passed it when we were following Kevin's trail. It gave me some pretty bad vibes too, remember, Matt?" said Randy.

"Yeah, I remember how spooked you were when we went by it," Matt agreed,

"There's one way to tell for sure. I could astrally project over there and find out. And if they aren't there, I could use *this* to find out where they are!" Randy said, pulling out Kilroy's severed arm and holding it up entirely too happily.

Most of the other beings in the room recoiled in disgust. Perhaps this was a little hypocritical on their part, considering that they were all standing around in a room filled with dismembered and beheaded bodies, and they were all personally responsible for a good deal of said bodily mutilations. However, they recoiled nonetheless.

"Do you normally carry around severed limbs in your pocket, lad?" a surprised Prospero asked. Apparently, such trophy keeping was considered bad form in the monster community. Who knew?

"What? No! It's just...these things come in handy sometimes for doing tracer spells. You'd know that if you were a *real* wizard!"

"Hmmph!" Prospero snorted at the insult.

"'These things come in handy?' I see what you did there, pal!" Matt chuckled.

"I wasn't trying to make a joke that time, Matt," Randy said as he found an armchair that had somehow miraculously avoided being knocked over in the chaos of the battle and sank into it. He closed his eyes and began to put himself into a trance that would allow his spirit to leave his body.

"You'd better call the UGF while I'm out," Randy suggested before he fell too deeply into the trance. Matt nodded even though Randy couldn't see the gesture, and dug his Guild Communicator out of his pocket.

Soon, Randy was out of his body. He slipped through the wall and saw that Blake had a line of his troops stationed outside on the manor's wrap-around porch. Randy effortlessly passed through the barrier of emerald energy that surrounded the house; in spirit form he could pass through it easily enough. As he moved past the house, he was upset to notice that there was indeed a substantial number of the enemy forces still wandering around right outside of the barrier. Some of the vampires in that group noticed him and hissed, trying to punch at him uselessly. He just smiled and gave them the finger as he passed straight through them. At least most of the enemies he saw surrounding the house seemed to be injured to one extent or another, although being the sorts of creatures that they were, they were also healing with typical uncanny speed.

Once he was clear of the enemy lines, Randy spied a group of cars and trucks that he didn't recognize parked in the long drive leading up to the gates of the manor. He guessed that these vehicles likely belonged to Blake's people. The enemy was camped close enough to have walked, if they truly were in the old church. Besides there weren't enough of the vehicles to have possibly transported all of the monsters that had attacked them. He picked up more speed as he zoomed down the street to the church. As he did so, he passed over the heads of some of Locke's returning forces, which had yet to reach the church. He thought he spied Kilroy amongst that group. Once at the church, he noticed the black tour buses in the parking lot, and made an effort to memorize one of the license plates just in case they tried to slip away before the UGF could get there.

He was happy to note that there was no energy barrier around the building. Perhaps Mortus Locke wasn't there, or if he was, maybe he had forgotten how to do such a spell? Basic defensive spells were the very first thing that Randy had ever been taught, so he found this hard to believe, since the spell that allowed him to erect a barrier large enough to cover an entire building was just a variation on that sort of simple spell. Was Locke's memory loss really *that* severe?

True, putting an energy barrier around the building might attract unwanted attention, but it also seemed incredibly foolish to send your people off into a battle without protecting your base like that while they were gone. Surely Kilroy had told him that there was a wizard at the manor? When they came under attack, he had felt that he and Matt had been targeted more than the others, which suggested whoever was in charge was aware of them and had prioritized them as targets. Without a barrier around it, there was really nothing to prevent Randy from teleporting Blake's whole force into the church if he wanted to. Although the thought of teleporting that many beings anywhere without the help of another wizard made him feel quite nervous, as he'd never attempted a teleportation spell on that scale before.

All of this told him that A) Locke wasn't there, B) he *was* there, but was a shadow of his former self, or C) he was incredibly overconfident and/or an incompetent strategist. He especially hoped that B and C were true.

He passed through the wall of the church. He was careful to try and keep to the shadows, as the building was likely filled with creatures capable of seeing him. He didn't want them to know that he was spying on them since it could cause them to alter whatever their plans might be. The main sanctuary was mostly vacant, but he saw a few vampires milling around. Most of them were sitting in the pews, chatting with each other. A few were on laptop computers or seemed to be texting on their phones or listening to music on iPods. To the untrained eye, they looked like any other group of bored people sitting around and trying to amuse themselves somehow. Randy felt a dark presence, an overwhelming feeling of evil, even worse than what he'd felt when he'd passed the church earlier, but it wasn't coming from this room, it was coming from somewhere beneath him. A basement? He sank through the floor to investigate further.

He now found himself under the ceiling of the basement. Inside was one of the most bizarre and disturbing sights he'd ever seen.

There was a large cage down there which looked very, very old. The door was hanging open. A few feet from it was a large, upside down cross made of the same ancient-looking metal. The cross was attached to a large, broad, stage-like base with a single step leading up to it. As Randy studied it, he saw tiny flecks of light in it and instantly knew that it was some kind of enchanted metal, forged with magical properties. The metal wasn't the most interesting thing about the cross though, the most interesting thing was what was chained to it.

A huge, hulking, hairy beast with long, matted, brown hair was chained there. Its face was disturbingly human, but the eyes were red and crazed-looking, and the mouth was unnaturally long and filled with rows of needle-like teeth. It was definitely female, he could make out the shape of breasts under the stringy, filthy, thin hairs. Its proportions were more like those of an ape than a human, with short legs and long, sinewy arms. It was chained by its feet, which rested on the crossbar of the cross, its arms were pulled up and chained above its head. There were even chains around its waist and neck. The thing radiated raw power, rage, and an unquenchable hunger while simultaneously putting out a feeling of great despair. The peculiar combination of emotions hit Randy in the gut like a sucker punch.

The Dark Mother! It has to be her! he realized.

The room was lit only by a series of candles arranged around the cross. This thankfully left most of it dark enough to conceal his astral form. Standing in front of the beast, which constantly struggled in vain against its tight bonds, was a tall, gaunt man with hollow cheeks and a beakish nose. His eyes glittered with malice. He wore crimson robes, but Randy could see a dark blue suit beneath it. He wondered if this was Mortus Locke himself. The bogeyman that had kept a thousand young witches and wizards up at night over the past millennia standing right there in front of him.

The man withdrew a dagger from beneath his robe, the blade made of the same exotic metal as the cage and the cross. The handle of the dagger was covered in precious gems and a few were even embedded in the blade itself. He raised it high above his head, chanted words in a language so obscure that even Randy didn't understand it, then whirled around theatrically and buried the blade deep in the abdomen of the writhing beast. Bright red blood gushed out. It reminded Randy, absurdly, of cherry flavored Kool-Aid. The man caught some of it in a golden goblet which was as jewel-encrusted as his dagger. He raised the goblet high over his head, said a few more words, then gulped down the entire contents of the cup, rivulets of the bright red liquid spilling down the sides of his mouth and dripping onto the collar of his shirt. A group of about half a dozen vampires who were also wearing similar robes and kneeling before him then repeated the chant. Then the tall man stepped to one side and beckoned the others to rise with one flick of his bony wrist. They all rushed forward in a wave of crimson, robes fluttering behind them like capes.

Randy was astonished as they leapt high into the air and grabbed onto the body of the beast, then bit into her flesh and drank. The creature howled in pain with each new greedy bite. It was a disturbing, unearthly sound. It was a surreal sight - as if she was covered by a half dozen, human-sized leeches.

He actually felt pity for the monster - it was such a terrible thing to behold. The Dark Mother might be terrible herself, but this was much, much worse. How many hundreds of years had this sort of thing been going on? How often did they perform this ritual? He couldn't imagine the torment that this creature must've endured. He turned his head away from the ghastly spectacle, unable to watch anymore.

That's when the man who had been leading the ceremony looked up into the corner of the ceiling and saw Randy's astral body hovering there. His attention was drawn there perhaps by Randy's strong feeling of revulsion. His eyes widened, then narrowed dangerously. That sparkle of perpetual malice that Randy had seen in them earlier only intensified.

"Spy, it is forbidden to look upon our sacraments!" he said accusingly in an impossibly deep and resonant voice. He pointed one skeletal finger at Randy and started to chant the words to a spell that Randy knew all too well. It was a standard incantation to banish unwanted spirits. Before Randy could raise a defense, it had already struck him like a Mac truck. He saw a bluish beam of energy fly from the man's finger towards him and he was violently propelled at a blinding speed back into his physical body.

Back in the manor, Matt had been watching nervously over his partner's vacant body. Then suddenly, he saw Randy convulse as the chair he was in flew backwards about a yard, then fell over as if someone had pushed it. Someone who was extremely strong.

"Holy shit!" Matt exclaimed and ran towards where Randy was now lying on his back staring up at the ceiling. Blood trickled out of one of his nostrils. In all his years of watching Randy do this sort of thing, he'd never seen anything like this happen before.

"Are you okay, man?" he asked as he offered him a hand.

Randy took his hand and slowly rose to his feet.

"I'll live," he said, and wiped at his nose, then regarded the blood that was now on his hand curiously. He tried not to be too disturbed by the hungry looks he was getting all of the sudden from every vampire in the room. He felt uncomfortably like a syringe full of heroin in a room full of junkies.

He noticed that Charles' body was now rolled up in a tapestry that had been hanging on one of the walls. William and Elizabeth were in one corner of the room with Martin, no doubt they'd been catching up on old times while Randy had been out. There was no sign of Allison or Mary in the room, but Kevin was chatting with Prospero - the boy had a cloak wrapped around him which one of them must've given him to cover himself. Blake was standing next to Matt, with an expectant look upon his face.

Most of the vampires and werewolves in the room seemed to be trying to tidy up the place as best they could. Some of them were picking up overturned pieces of furniture that were still intact. A few of them had gotten brooms out from somewhere and were busy sweeping up the shattered remains of Randy's many victims. Others were piling up dead bodies in different ends of the room. Vampires on one end, werewolves on the other. There was even a separate pile of severed heads. It was all being done with military precision and discipline.

"What the hell just happened to you?" Matt asked, still alarmed by the unusual event.

"I was spotted and violently shoved back into my body," he said in a remarkably casual way, as if this was an everyday occurrence. It *was* an occupational hazard in his line of work, after all.

"What? Who could do such a thing?" Matt said, still thoroughly freaked out.

"I think it must've been good old Mortus Locke himself," Randy said, again with his infuriating calmness.

"So he *is* there!" Blake said hungrily. "It's rare that he ever shows up for these sorts of things in person. He must suspect that Elizabeth and William are the ones who betrayed him to the Guilds all those years ago. What else did you see?"

"You were right, there are still some of them hanging around the property, waiting for the barrier to come down again." As he said the words he pulled out his phone and flipped it open to check the timer. He saw that only a few minutes had passed since he'd been out of his body, although it had felt like it had been much longer.

Such was the nature of astral travel. The barrier still had a few more minutes before he'd have to start the spell to create a new one.

He continued his account. "Most of them are headed back to the church now. There are a few inside the church that they must've been holding in reserve. And in the basement of the church I found Mortus Locke and about six others. They were all in robes, doing some kind of ritual where they were drinking the blood of the Dark Mother. It was horrible. That's when Locke spotted me and sent me back here."

Blake nodded. "That's the Dark Communion that you saw. A ritual they do to renew their strength. The ones in the robes are the Undying Ones - vampires that Locke created himself. His inner circle. They're the only ones allowed to participate in the Dark Communion. I used to be one of them." He seemed very excited by this news.

"So, both Locke and the Dark Mother are there! This is the opportunity we've been waiting for! We haven't known where he's been keeping her. Ever since the last time we tried to destroy her he's been keeping her in hiding. We have to strike now, before he takes her away and we lose track of her again!"

"I don't think that's a very good idea. Even with all the ones we just killed here, they still outnumber us by about three to one," Randy told him.

"Yeah, if you've been spending all this time trying to build up an army to take him on, you don't want to throw it all away in one reckless attack do you? Wait for the UGF to get here and bolster your numbers, that's the smart thing to do," Matt agreed. In his opinion, Blake seemed too hotheaded and passionate to make for a very good leader.

Blake didn't seem very receptive to their opinions. He wasn't used to being told what to do by a bunch of mortals. Mortals had been nothing but food to him for as long as he could recall. It was like your steak dinner trying to give you tactical advice.

"Bah! I won't lose this chance! We will wait for two hours. If they aren't here in two hours, we move out!"

Randy again brought out Kilroy's severed arm and waved it in front of Blake's face. "I still have this! I can use it to track Kilroy, remember? You won't lose them again!"

"He doesn't keep Kilroy close to him anymore. Kilroy's too wild and crazy for even Locke! Kilroy usually hunts alone and just calls the rest of them in when he comes across something that he can't handle on his own or which he thinks Locke will find to be of particular interest. So you see, knowing Kilroy's whereabouts doesn't particularly help us! What I said before still stands. In two hours we move out, you can either help us, or stay here and clean up this mess, it makes no difference to me!" Blake then stormed off towards where Martin, William and Elizabeth stood.

"What a piece of work! He's gonna get them all killed! I'm not sure I wanna go along for his little suicide mission either! And I sure don't want any of these kids trying to help him, he'd better not try to drag any of them into his damned crusade!" Matt commented bitterly as he watched him stomping away like a petulant child.

"So, I take it that you were successful in reaching the UGF?" Randy asked.

"Yeah, I called Bronson. He's sending Anne and some of her friends. She was already in the neighborhood, doing an inspection of their North American base. But I gotta tell ya, buddy, I'm not sure if they can get here in just two hours! That base is in Nebraska!" Matt told him.

"Bronson" was Bronson McDowell, the Chairman of the Inner Council of the International Confederation of Guilds, Director of the ABC, Commander in Chief of the UGF and Matt's boss and friend. Matt's original plan had been to have Randy call the UGF and use his rank within that organization to order a force of troops in to assist them, but with Randy off astrally projecting, Matt hadn't known who else to call, so he'd gone up to the very top. "Anne" was Anne Moore, Bronson's goddaughter and the field commander of the UGF.

Randy nodded, a troubled look on his face. "Yeah, it might not be enough time to mobilize and transport them here." Rapidly responding to threats had been a problem for the UGF in the past, although it was something they'd been working on improving since the last major engagement they'd been involved in back in 1997.

The timer on Randy's phone started beeping. Matt shot him an alarmed look. Before he could say anything, Randy held up a hand to silence him.

"Don't worry, I set the timer to go off a few minutes before the old force field fades away to give me enough time to do the spell. I'll do another spell now to renew it, then I'll try to call Anne myself and explain the urgency of the situation, see if I can possibly get them here any faster."

"Then I'll leave you to it. I'm gonna go check up on Kevin. Good luck, we're gonna need it!" Matt said as he walked towards Kevin and Prospero.

Randy frowned as he watched him go, then he began his spell.

Varney flung open the doors of the old church with both arms; trailing behind him was a line of mostly injured vampires and a few of the remaining werewolves. He marched up the aisle of the sanctuary, towards the stage behind the podium where Mortus Locke sat waiting on a gilded throne with a red velvet backing.

"So you have failed me and dare to return?" came the voice of the Master, in a sepulchral tone.

Varney prostrated himself before the stage.

"I beg your forgiveness, Master. The Great Betrayer himself arrived with his entire army and assisted them before we could finish them off. I left some of our people behind, to keep watch and make sure that they can receive no further help. We have them all trapped inside."

Locke raised an eyebrow. "And I see that *you* must've fought valiantly, Varney. There's not even a scratch on you. Your clothes look as tidy and impeccable as ever."

Kilroy, who stood next to Varney, laughed. Which sounded more like a bark.

"Master, this cowardly cutlet never even entered the house! He just watched it all from a hill!" Kilroy informed him, relishing each word.

"Yes, I suspected as much," the Master said disapprovingly.

"Someone had to supervise the battle from a secure vantage point, Master! To evaluate when the best moment was to send in another wave of attackers! Don't listen to this *mutt!*" Varney protested.

"This *mutt* at least took part in the actual fight!" Kilroy bit back.

"Yes, for a moment! But you didn't do so well did you? I saw you jump in there and come running back out a few seconds later with your tail between your legs!" Varney taunted him.

"Perhaps, but I alone out of all of us succeed in killing one of them!" Kilroy reminded him.

"You're really bragging about killing a *human*? And not even an important one at that! He was just one of their servants!"

"It's more than *you* did, bloodsucker!" Kilroy growled at him. Literally.

"How dare you speak to me like that, you miserable, filthy cur! I am one of the Undying Ones! You forget your place!"

Locke was enjoying himself watching the two of them bicker like this. He had half a mind to let them tear each other apart. He wasn't particularly convinced that either one of them was of much value to him anymore. At least letting them destroy one another might provide him with a bit of much-needed entertainment. Then he sighed. No, he'd probably need as much help as he could get for the coming battle. Even these two fools still had a role to play.

"Stop it, the two of you!" he bellowed at them.

They both fell silent and bowed their heads.

"You say that they are all trapped inside the house? Blake and his entire army?" he asked.

"That's right, Master!" Varney smiled his unsettling, fang-filled smile. "We have the place surrounded. We have them right where we want them! I only returned to ask for more troops to finish the job. We can end the war this very night!"

"What this leech fails to mention is that the wizard and the knight still live and are working with our enemies. The house is surrounded by an impenetrable wall of energy, we can't get in to attack them!" Kilroy said, still jockeying for the Master's favor.

"Yes, I thought as much. He paid a visit to us himself shortly before you returned," the Master said dryly.

"He was here? How?" Varney asked in a panicked tone.

"It doesn't matter. This wall of energy you mentioned is not impenetrable. If enough magical energy is directed against it, it will fall. It is within my power to accomplish such things. I will lead the troops myself this time. I shall have my revenge upon The Great Betrayer. I will rip his throat out myself and watch the light burn out his eyes. But first, we shall all partake of the Dark Communion, so that we will all have the strength to destroy our enemies."

"All of us, Master? Even the Childlings? Even the dogs?" Varney asked in disbelief. Such a thing was unprecedented Only the Undying Ones were allowed such an honor. What would even happen if you fed the blood of the Dark Mother to a werewolf? He supposed that you'd just end up with a vampire that could change into a wolf, but who could tell for sure?

Kilroy also found this news hard to believe. He would finally get to drink the Dark Mother's blood! No longer would he have to stay in this animalistic form in order to maintain his eternal life! The great honor which had long been denied him would finally be his!

No longer would he be looked down upon as a mere pet, he would finally be respected as much as any of the Undying Ones. This was a great day indeed!

Mortus Locke glared at Varney.

"Do you think I misspoke? I said that *all* of us will take the Dark Communion! Her blood will heal all of your wounds more quickly and make you all more powerful. The power that is in her blood will guarantee our victory! Now rise, Varney, and help me fill the goblets with enough of her blood for everyone. Time is of the essence. We must destroy them before they can call in more Guildsmen, more warlocks and witches to aid them! Tonight we will ride to victory!"

CHAPTER 18:

KEVIN'S NEW PANTS

Randy walked over to Matt, Kevin and Prospero. "Anne says she might be able to get here in an hour and a half. She's reluctant to push it any more than that. She doesn't want her magic users doing too many teleportation spells or else everyone will be too sick to fight for a while when they get here."

Matt nodded. It would have to do. There was something else that was bugging him. "What if Locke himself decides to come for us? Could he get through your force field?"

"Maybe. I don't know how much of his magic he remembers. He didn't even have a force field like this around his own base, which is a rookie mistake. But if he *does* decide to come for us before we get reinforcements, we could be in trouble."

Matt didn't like the sound of that. "If he doesn't have a field around the church, then *we* could teleport our people in, catch 'em with their pants down. Maybe even take out the Dark Mother and end this whole thing."

"Now you sound like Blake!" Randy complained.

"Don't get me wrong, I'm not suggesting that we do that until after the UGF gets here. I'm just saying that it might not be a bad idea once they arrive."

"That's true enough," Randy agreed.

Something else was bothering Matt. "And what about all these dead vampires? I thought you said something about burning the bodies and stuffing the heads with garlic or they might come back? Is it really such a good idea to just stack 'em all up like that?"

"You have to put the right heads back on top of the right bodies for them to get resurrected. We should be alright if we keep them separated. Besides, in a house where vampires live, I don't think you're gonna find much garlic."

"What about those ones that got broken into a bunch of little pieces that they've been sweeping up?"

"They're suffering from the Humpty Dumpty Syndrome."

"Huh?"

"Too many pieces to put back together again! We should probably burn the pieces they're collecting together in the fireplace though."

Matt made a face. "That's gonna smell *great!*" he said sarcastically.

Randy shrugged. "It's better to err on the side of caution. We don't want to have to fight them again do we? Where did the girls go off to?" he asked, noting that Allison and Mary were still missing.

"They went upstairs to get me something to wear," Kevin, who had been listening all this time, chimed in.

"Aye, a nice pair of sweatpants is a werewolf's best friend! You just loosen the drawstring before you change and you don't have to worry about completely losing your dignity when you go back to your human form, or in my case, more human-like form," Prospero added. The secret of Prospero's long life was that he, like Kilroy, stayed in a wolf-form of some kind all the time.

"When Prospero gave me his fashion tips, Mary said that her...Dad had some up in his room and Allison went with her to help her find them. Are your friends really coming to help us?" Kevin asked.

"Yeah. Hopefully they'll get here before Captain Hothead over there decides to march his army off to a slaughter," Matt said grimly.

Allison watched her friend with mounting concern as she pulled open another drawer in the chest of drawers in her father's bedroom. She'd decided to accompany her up here because she was still worried about her. She thought it might be difficult for her to go into her father's room, to be surrounded by his things so soon after his passing. She was also a little worried that there might still be some of their enemies lurking around up here too; although Martin had told them that Blake's people had cleared the building, she still wasn't about to let Mary come up here by herself.

Mary took a shirt out of the drawer and held it up to her nose. *It still smells like him,* she thought, and started crying again. Allison moved to hug her, but Mary pushed her away.

"No, it's okay, I'll be okay."

Allison furrowed her brow. "Alright, but if you ever need to talk, I'm here. You're not the only one who knows what it's like to lose your whole family, you know."

Mary's hard expression softened. She was so used to Allison being a part of her family that she had forgotten that she had once been part of a different one, that she was the sole survivor of a crash that had killed her entire family. Not for the first time, she thought about how strong of a person her friend must be. Could she ever find that kind of a strength within herself?

"Thanks. But for now, let's just worry about finding some sweatpants for your boyfriend. I guess we'd better get him a shirt, too," Mary said.

"He's *not* my boyfriend!" Allison replied reflexively.

"Ah, 'the lady doth protest too much', methinks." Mary replied.

"Oh no, not you too! Now you sound like Prospero!"

"Who?"

"You know, that weird old Scottish werewolf wizard guy? The one who suggested we get Kevin some sweatpants? He's always quoting Shakespeare like it's going out of style."

"There's so many new people in our house right now that I can't keep track anymore. Is that from Shakespeare?" Mary wondered aloud as she rifled through the contents of another drawer.

"It sure is. Hamlet," Allison informed her.

"Wow. Look at me being all smart and stuff. Maybe I can hang with you nerds after all? He totally *is* your boyfriend, by the way," she said, still not giving up.

Allison opened the closet and started looking in there. She sighed. She thought about that kiss. That long, wonderful kiss during which it had taken every ounce of her willpower to stop herself from biting Kevin. If they killed the Dark Mother, she supposed she wouldn't have to worry about such odd impulses anymore. What was the use of denying it? She and Kevin were a couple. She even thought she might really be in love with him, although she wasn't going to tell Mary *that* little secret right now. She knew how ridiculous it sounded and she didn't feel like being laughed at right now.

"Okay. You win. He *is* my boyfriend now, or something like that. We haven't really had a chance to try and define it yet with all the craziness that's been going on. Are you...okay with that? You *know* I'll always be there for you, right? I'm not gonna let some dude come between us, no matter how cute he may be." *Especially not now, with all that you've lost,* she almost added.

Mary actually laughed. It was music to Allison's ears.

"Of course I know that! And I'm happy for you, truly. I'm glad that you've got someone. You deserve it. He seems like a good guy. Even if he did try and take my head off earlier tonight."

"Jesus! Was that tonight? This has been such a long day," Allison said.

"You're telling me! And it's not over yet. Do you think we'll make it out of this alive?" Mary asked, suddenly serious again.

"I don't know. I sure hope so. Now that Blake's army is here, and the barrier is back up, I guess we'll be okay until those other Guild guys show up. And then what? Maybe they'll end this curse and I'll get to be a real human girl again, and Kevin can be a normal boy too? It seems too good to be true though, doesn't it?"

"I know one thing, if they're going after Kilroy, I want a piece of him too. After all the people he's killed today, I won't be happy ever again until I see him pay for what he's done to me!" she swore.

"Mary! No! You're just a normal human. You barely survived that last fight we were in, I won't let you risk yourself like that for revenge!" Allison said, horrified as much by what the night's events were bringing out in her friend as she was by the thought of losing her.

"Don't try and stop me, Al. This is something I've gotta do. I'll be alright. Hey, remember what I said earlier? Don't underestimate the normal girl!"

"Yeah but seriously…" Allison began.

"TA-DA! Here they are!" Mary interrupted her, holding up a pair of grey sweat pants in triumph. "Grab a shirt from that closet and let's get back downstairs. There's too many memories here for me right now," she ordered as she moved towards the door.

Allison snatched a random shirt from a hanger and frowned as she hurried after her.

The sleek black Cadillac barreled down the rain-slicked streets of Davenport at a dangerous speed. Inside, Agent Brown's heart pounded in anticipation. He was headed towards the very thing he'd been chasing for his entire career - no, for much longer than that - what he'd been after his whole life. The great white whale he'd been pursuing was finally within his sights.

Mortus Locke was back, and he was somewhere here in Davenport.

Brown hadn't been able to believe his luck when he got the call. He and his partner, Agent Grey, had already been in the area. They'd met with the local police and informed them of their suspicions about Kevin Scott having been in town, advising them to be on the lookout for the boy. They'd been somewhat less than receptive, which was understandable considering the gruesome discovery that had been made this morning. Trying to find a teenage runaway seemed like the last thing they should care about right now. Brown had almost let slip that he believed that the two things were related. True, it would have better motivated them to help, but it also would've raised too many questions, questions which Brown was not willing to provide any answers to. He'd found out from them which Medical Examiner's office had the body of the unfortunate girl who had been discovered that morning and he and Grey had taken their leave.

Brown wanted to see that body for himself, if only to confirm what he already knew. The girl has been killed by a werewolf, just like the one in Shadowbrook had been. He didn't think it was the work of Kevin Scott, although he had no doubt now that the boy was a werewolf as well. No, this had all the hallmarks of the work of a particular werewolf that he'd been tracking for some time now. The girl in Shadowbrook, Sylvia McCoy, had hardly been the first, although the wolf he was after usually did a better job of concealing his work. For whatever reason he'd been sloppier than usual with these latest killings.

Brown was obsessed with proving that these cases were the work of a werewolf. He also had a thick file of cases that he believed pointed to the activity of vampires. Practically everyone in the Guilds believed that such monsters had all perished in The Great Purge, but he knew better and had made it his life's work to prove otherwise. The monsters were still out there, they'd just gone underground. And he was the man who would stop them for good this time.

The man who now called himself Agent Brown of the ABC had come from a long line of wizards and witches. He was from what was called "the Old Families" of the Guilds. A bloodline that stretched back centuries into the foggy, shrouded depths of the various groups that made up the Guilds. He'd grown up on scary stories about Mortus Locke and his Army of the Night. From the first time he heard of him, he knew deep in his heart that he was still out there, that such evil was not so easily destroyed, that it yet lurked somewhere in the world. Unfortunately, Brown had shown little talent for practicing magic; he just couldn't quite get the hang of it, didn't have the sort of mental discipline it took to get himself into the correct state of mind to cast anything much more sophisticated than a few basic spells. He had been a great disappointment to his family in that regard, but he'd eventually found his true calling within the Guilds not as a wizard of the Temple of the Old Gods, but as an investigator for the ABC.

There, in the ABC, is where he had really shined. It was also where he could pursue his personal passion for monster hunting. With access to the ABC's extensive database of information and their worldwide surveillance network, he soon found proof of what he was looking for. However, his superiors had been less than impressed with the fruits of his side project. As far as they were concerned, Mortus Locke was history, as were werewolves and vampires. They didn't even want to look at the mountain of evidence he'd spent years carefully cataloging. That hadn't stopped him, of course. If anything, it had just hardened his resolve to be proven correct. He would show them all, the ABC, his family. He would do what no wizard had ever been able to do - he would find Mortus Locke and destroy him for all time!

This was why he and his partner had leapt at the chance to help Matt Spike when he'd contacted the ABC. Brown had been looking for an excuse to go to Davenport ever since the news of Sylvia McCoy's unusual demise had hit the media. It had all the hallmarks of a werewolf murder. It was pretty obvious to him that her death was the work of a wolf he called "W-3". It was doubly obvious to him that the boy Matt Spike was after had somehow survived an encounter with W-3, possibly because W-3 had been engaged in a fight with the wolf he classified as "W-7" at the time. He'd learned this from DNA evidence he'd discovered at the scene of the fight in the woods. Brown was aware that there seemed to be at least two major factions of these monsters now. The two groups occasionally clashed. He could only guess as to what had brought about this schism. Evidence of the second group was difficult to obtain. The vampires in that group left behind no evidence of how they fed, the wolves only seemed to feed on other wild animals, but all the signs that this was not the work of normal wolves were still there if you knew how to look.

He had considered sharing his suspicions with the detective, but he had instead stuck to doing things strictly by the book when interacting with Spike. He didn't know exactly what the detective might know, if anything, about real vampires and werewolves. It was quite likely that he didn't know anything and wouldn't take his information seriously, as so many others had done in the past. He also knew that Matt Spike was somehow well-connected with the Guilds; he was a personal friend of Director McDowell himself.

Brown didn't want it getting back to McDowell that he was still using ABC resources to investigate his little pet project. So, difficult as it had been for him to do, he'd remained silent on the subject. In the meantime at least, it gave him an excuse to be in an area where all the action had been recently and surreptitiously conduct his own investigations into the matter.

He wondered about Matt Spike himself. He was a mystery too. Nobody seemed to know exactly what his role within the Guilds was. He was rumored to be a friend of not only McDowell but Wendy Sommerdahl, the Pontifex Maximus of the Temple of the Old Gods, and Sommardahl's student, Randy Gruman, apparently also worked as a detective in Spike's agency. The woman that Spike was married to was listed as the "Supreme Archivist" of the Guilds, a position that hadn't existed prior to 1997. Spike was also rumored to have fought in the so-called "Christmas War" from that same year. It was also said that the mysterious "New Years Eve Incident' of '97 had happened at his house. However, Brown knew better than to dig too deeply into *that* rumor, it was so classified that just mentioning it would get you fired! However, there were stories of Spike from even before '97. Some say that he, his wife and Gruman were all somehow involved in what the Guilds called either "The Guild War" or the "Second Magic War" in '95. Brown had his own theories about Matt Spike. He believed that his detective agency was a cover for a deeper, even more clandestine ABC operation run by McDowell himself to pursue his own personal goals. This meant that he had to be especially careful in his interactions with the detective. However, Spike's interest in the case also served to show that McDowell might also be aware of the monster activity that Brown had dedicated himself to documenting. Spike's group might even be his way of discreetly dealing with it.

This suspicion seemed to have been born out when Brown had gotten a call from a rare, like-minded colleague in the ABC while he and Grey were at the M.E.'s office looking at the sad remains of Brittney. His ally in the good fight against the monsters had breathlessly informed him that the UGF was being mobilized and sent to someplace called Sherwood Farm in Davenport. The rumor was that they were being sent in to deal with Mortus Locke or his minions. Brown had been so surprised that he'd almost dropped his Guild Communicator. He hastily thanked the M.E. for her cooperation and he and Brown had hit the road. The M.E.'s office hadn't been in Davenport and was actually some distance away, but if they hurried, they could get back to town within the hour. Brown intended to meet them at Sherwood Farm and offer his assistance. He'd tell them that he was already in the area working on Matt Spike's case when he heard about the situation through the grapevine, which was all true enough.

There was no way that he was going to miss out on this! This was the fight he'd been spoiling for his entire life. A chance to look the thing he feared the most square in the eye and conquer it! To finally prove himself to his family and those in the ABC that had laughed at his obsession with vampires and werewolves!

Brown's partner, Agent Grey, was another matter altogether. He didn't come from an old family that had long-standing Guild connections like Brown did. He had been recruited from local law enforcement after he had an encounter with a UFO.

Most "UFOs" that were spotted by humans were not alien spaceships, but misidentified natural phenomena, or conventional or experimental aircraft. There was, however, a small number (around 5%) of sightings that were exactly what they appeared to be. The aliens were here mainly for scientific purposes. The same technology that allowed them to travel across the vast distances between stars in a reasonable amount of time also provided them with the ability to fulfill all of their material needs. Whatever they didn't have, they could easily synthesize. They had only been able to reach this level of technological sophistication because they had already achieved a stable society that was far more evolved than ours politically, economically, and spiritually. The upshot of all of this was that they had no motivation to invade our planet. They had neither a material need to do so, or a philosophical desire to.

Most races that achieved our level of sophistication tended to wipe themselves out within a few generations of learning how to split the atom. For every alien civilization that is able to send its ships to other star systems, there are thousands that have left behind nothing but ruined, burnt-out husks of planets which are now devoid of intelligent life because the so-called "intelligent life" wiped themselves out. The aliens monitoring earth tended to believe that we will eventually follow this sadly all-too-familiar pattern. They had written us off as what they called a "Dead End World". They were in a race against time to catalog as much as they could about our planet and its various life forms before we wiped it all away. They rarely came here in person, most of the ships people saw were unmanned drones or probes. Most of the "aliens" people saw were also a kind of sophisticated drone, meat puppets remotely piloted from thousands of light years away or by the AI that controlled their spacecraft. There were, of course, exceptions. Even highly advanced civilizations produce the occasional hooligan. One problem was what the ABC called "teenagers from outer space" (although in this case, some of these "teenagers" were actually many of hundreds of years old), which were basically immature aliens that sometimes came to Earth for the equivalent of a drunken joyride, to show off to their dates, or to otherwise amuse themselves by messing with the natives. This was all highly illegal, but it still happened.

Agent Grey had encountered a ship that was controlled by one such group of beings. He had responded to citizen reports of the craft, and had been able to track the craft for over an hour. When the ABC investigated the reports, they had been impressed by Grey's calm, no-nonsense demeanor during the incident, his ability to follow the ship for as long as he had, and his detailed observation of the craft. He'd picked up on many details that ordinary observers typically missed. Unfortunately, this encounter had also earned him a great deal of derision within his own police department, where they began to regard him as something of a nutcase for insisting on the reality of his encounter. Where his coworkers saw an unstable loose cannon, the ABC saw a calm, cool and especially talented observer. He was exactly what they were looking for and they wasted no time in rescuing him from a workplace environment where his talents weren't appreciated to put those same talents to work for themselves.

Grey didn't share his partner's enthusiasm for investigating rumors of vampires and werewolves. However, he also didn't have much choice in the matter. Brown was his superior and he had to follow his lead. He had to (reluctantly) admit that he had seen enough peculiar things during his time with his partner to half convince him that the man wasn't completely crazy and that there might indeed be something behind his suspicions. Now this latest rumor of the UGF being called out to deal with Mortus Locke seemed to have at long last vindicated his partner's theories. Grey had never seen his partner looking so deliriously happy. Not even when he'd visited Brown and his wife after she'd just given birth to their child. Grey thought there was something *seriously* messed up about that. He had also felt it was equally messed up how Brown had neglected to warn Matt Spike that he might be dealing with werewolves, and that he was dragging Grey into this fight. But he wasn't about to tell Brown any of that. He was his superior officer and he had to follow his lead no matter how much he may disagree with it personally.

"So, do you really think they'll let you join in the attack? We're not soldiers, we're investigators," Grey said, subtly hoping to discourage him from this course of action.

"Why wouldn't they? We may not be soldiers, but we're still both trained fighters. They'll need all the help they can get if they're really going up against Mortus Locke. Besides, I have some valuable information that might be of interest to them," he said with a confidence that Grey didn't share.

The information that he was referring to was his briefcase full of his files on the monsters which now sat on the backseat, next to a pair of iron broadswords that Brown always kept in the car. Grey didn't think that the information in those files would be of much use to them if they already knew where Locke was, yet Brown seemed keen to hand it over to them nonetheless. Grey thought that he just wanted to show off everything that he already knew. He obviously wanted to be recognized for all his work on this subject, to be vindicated. Grey figured he could understand the feeling. It must be tough to always have the subject you've dedicated your life to dismissed by everyone in authority. Grey could relate, that's very much how he had been treated by everyone at his old job after he had his UFO experience and became a little obsessed by the subject himself. The ABC had rescued him from that toxic workplace, which was why he was so loyal and obedient to Brown, even if he did often privately disagree with his decisions.

"Have you got your special bullets already loaded? Do you have your spares on you?" Brown asked.

"For the hundredth time, yes," Grey told him. Brown was referring to ammunition he'd had custom made years ago. Silver bullets that had been soaked in garlic juices. They were .44 caliber rounds because Brown figured he'd need a gun with that much power to knock back a vampire. Such a weapon would kill a werewolf, but only hurt a vampire. Most ABC agents just carried 9mm semiautomatic pistols, but both Grey and Brown carried these .44 magnum "hand cannons" on them as well. Brown had insisted on it, just as he had insisted on carrying those swords with him everywhere he went and had spent countless hours using them to spar with Grey so he'd know how to use them in a fight.

"Looks like we're coming up on the place now," Brown said, checking his GPS. Sure enough, a rather cheerful sign appeared to their right that read "SHERWOOD FARM" in big, bold red letters on a white background. Brown steered the car onto a long private road beside the sign. From their current vantage point, they couldn't see much. The manor was concealed by a series of hills and the curvature of the road. Grey could see, however, an unnatural greenish glow coming from the sky up ahead of them. It almost looked like the Aurora Borealis.

"What's wrong with the sky?" he asked.

"I don't know, but there's something very familiar about it that I can't quite put my finger on," Brown commented thoughtfully.

As they continued down the road, they next saw a long line of cars which were all pulled over to the side of the road. As they rolled by them, Grey noticed that many of them had their windows smashed in and the tires slashed. He had no way of knowing that this vandalism had been visited upon the vehicles by Varney's retreating forces.

"Looks like quite a party," he said dryly.

"Just grab your sword and get your piece out. We need to be ready for anything. We don't know exactly what we're walking into here, or why the UGF chose this place to set up camp."

Grey obediently reached for the sword in the back, accidentally hitting the back of Brown's head with the pommel.

"Ouch! Watchit will ya?" he complained.

"Sorry."

As they got closer to the manor, they could see the big iron gate hanging off its hinges and the green force field surrounding the place. Grey thought he could make out a few shadowy silhouettes standing on the porch. It looked like all the windows had been broken and the front door was missing. Inside, he could see many people moving around.

"Of course! A magical shield! That's what's causing that glow in the sky. I should've known!" Brown said. Grey just rolled his eyes.

Inside the manor, Matt's attention was drawn to the window by a bright light that momentarily shone through it. He twisted his head and saw a pair of bright headlights outside. Someone had just arrived, and they had their high beams on. The light caused little spots to dance in his vision for a moment.

"Who the hell is that?" he asked.

A second later, one of Blake's people, a female vampire that he'd seen use her weapon quite skillfully earlier, came running into the room.

"Someone's just pulled up in a car!" she told her commander.

"Great, aren't there enough people in the house already?" Mary, who along with Allison was now back downstairs asked sarcastically. Kevin was in the bathroom again, putting on his new clothes.

Matt squinted as his vision cleared and the headlights turned off.

"I know that car! It belongs to those ABC agents that were helping me out! What're they doing here?" Matt said.

"Maybe Bronson sent them to help?" Randy guessed.

"These people are allies?" Blake asked Matt.

Matt nodded. "I'm surprised that Locke's people let them through. We need to get them in here before they get torn to pieces!" As he said it, he was already moving out of the room and towards the front entrance, the *Vermillion Avenger* and Randy trailing behind him.

Outside the manor, Grey and Brown emerged from their car. Brown carried his briefcase tucked awkwardly under one arm, a sword in one hand, and his .44 magnum in the other. Grey also carried his identical gun and sword.

"How are we gonna get through that force field?" Grey asked skeptically.

Brown shrugged as he approached the house and could see the warriors on the porch, all armed with an odd weapon that he'd never seen before. "Ask very politely to be let in, I suppose."

"Are you sure those are our people?" Grey asked.

"Of course they are! This is the place isn't it? The UGF wouldn't choose a location already occupied by enemies for their field headquarters!" he replied, obviously annoyed. Grey didn't usually question him this much. True, he didn't recognize the look of these people or their weapons, but he assumed that they might be part of some clandestine monster hunting branch of the Guilds to which he had for some reason, been denied knowledge.

"We come in peace! We're here to help you! Please allow us through the barrier," he announced loudly, not aware of how absurd he looked saying that he came in peace with weapons in each of his hands.

Blake's warriors just glanced at each other quizzically.

Suddenly, there was a loud crash from behind them, and the sound of crunching metal followed by a low, menacing growl. Brown turned around to see that all of these sounds had come from a rather large werewolf that had just leapt onto the roof of his car with such force that he had cratered in part of its roof and was currently snarling at him. He had barely enough time to make sense of this unusual sight before the beast was sailing through the air right towards him.

Right before he could reach him, the creature's trajectory was violently altered. The wolf was blasted sideways in an explosion of blood by a shot from Agent Grey's gun.

Before Brown could thank his partner, he saw another wolf come flying from the shadows and land on Grey. He ran towards him, but his path was suddenly blocked by a vampire that seemed to have come from nowhere (he'd actually dropped out of the branches of a large tree nearby). Brown brought up his gun, but the vampire knocked it from his hand and pushed him back onto the hood of his car, the briefcase he had been carrying skittering across the hood of the vehicle as the vampire sank his teeth into Brown's neck and tore off a chunk of his flesh. Blood sprayed everywhere, painting the windshield red.

Agent Grey had never been so scared in all of his life. His back was on the gravel driveway, a werewolf pinning him there. The stench of its hot, fetid breath filling his nostrils. It scratched at his chest with his claws, and the only thing that saved him was the Kevlar body armor that he wore under his suit, but he knew that the armor wouldn't be enough to stop the next swipe. Pushing his fear down, Grey brought up his gun once more and squeezed the trigger over and over again.

He cursed as he realized that he'd emptied the whole gun and failed to hit his target. He closed his eyes, ready to greet the inevitable.

That's when he heard an odd whistling sound, saw a flash of light, and a moment later the head of the wolf was bouncing off of his own head and rolling onto the ground beside him wearing a shocked expression. The flash of light had been the reflection of the full moon on the blade of the *Vermillion Avenger*. Matt Spike was now standing over him, kicking the body of the werewolf off of him. He offered him a hand up, which he eagerly accepted.

"Where's Brown?" he asked in a panicked voice, then he saw the burning body of a headless vampire lying atop the hood of their car and beneath it, the lifeless form of Agent Brown. Randy had hit the monster with a fireball, and Matt had finished him off with the *Vermillion Avenger* as they had come running out of the manor.

"He didn't make it, and neither will we if we don't get to the house! Follow me!" Matt said.

Grey impulsively snatched the briefcase from the hood of the car before it could also go up in flames. It was what Brown would've wanted. Grey saw Randy unleashing more fireballs on other lunging monsters. Beside him were a few of those warriors that had been armed with those peculiar looking axe/spear combinations. They were covering for Matt and Grey as they bounded up the steps, only to run up to the edge of the energy barrier. A moment later they joined them on the steps, still fighting off some of the monsters, which now seemed to be everywhere.

Randy did a quick gesture with his hand, creating a momentary hole in the barrier. They all ran through it frantically and onto the front porch. Unfortunately, a slavering werewolf also made it through the gap, or at least it appeared to at first. Grey looked on in astonishment as he saw that the beast had been severed neatly into two pieces by the barrier closing up again behind them. As the front end of the creature flailed around on the ground at his feet, he found himself angrily hacking away at its neck with his sword until the head was off and the beast stopped twitching.

"Die, you fucker! *Die!*" he screamed at it as he swung the sword over and over again.

He hadn't realized that he was crying until Matt and Randy pulled him inside the house by the shoulders and sat him down on a blood-drenched sofa.

"I'm sorry about your partner," Matt said tenderly to the sobbing man.

"In a funny way, it's exactly how he would've wanted to die - fighting monsters," Grey told him sadly. "I just don't know how I'm going to explain this to his wife and kid."

"If *this* is the quality of the allies that you are bringing, then I think we'd better leave now!" Blake remarked as he eyed the newcomer.

"Give the guy a break! He's just been through a lot!" Matt replied angrily.

"The UGF force will contain at least several squads of magic users and assassins. Don't worry, they'll get the job done. Just sit tight," Randy told Blake, trying to keep the peace.

Blake sniffed and stormed off as he was wont to do.

"Which one are you? Brown or Grey? I can never get it straight," Matt confessed.

"Agent Grey, but you can just call me Earl if it makes it any easier."

"Hold on - is your name really Earl Grey, like the tea?" Randy asked.

Grey smiled, happy to have his mind taken off of the trauma he'd just endured. "No, my last name is really Rogers. But everyone out of the Hartford field office uses different colors for their code names, so I picked Grey as a joke. Most people don't get it."

"I do, I'm a huge Star Trek fan -'Earl Grey, Hot!'" Randy said in a commanding English accent.

"I don't get it," Matt confessed.

"Jean-Luc Picard is always ordering that kind of tea!" Randy explained.

"Exactly why I picked it!" Grey told him.

"Oh, I'm more of a classic Trek kinda guy. Never could get into the Next Generation," Matt admitted.

"That's Matt for you - so old-school!" Randy said.

Matt's expression suddenly turned serious. With a start, and little flush of shame, Matt realized how odd it was for him to think of these ABC agents, who he normally thought so dull, lifeless and robotic, as real human beings. It was strange to think of them having first names, families, personal obsessions, favorite TV shows and a sense of humor. He was sorry that it had taken such a tragic event for him to appreciate them for what they were. Just another bunch of working stiffs trying to survive like the rest of us.

"So, Earl, what brought you guys here tonight? What's in that briefcase that's so important?" Matt inquired.

"My partner, Agent Brown, was consumed with the idea that Mortus Locke was still alive. He'd been collecting evidence to back this up during his whole career in the ABC, that's what's in the case. It's also why he begged our bosses to get us assigned to help you with your case when the call came in. He suspected that the death in Shadowbrook was the work of a werewolf and he was looking for an excuse to go there and check the place out. When he heard that the UGF was sending a force here to fight Mortus Locke through one of our colleagues, he wanted to be a part of it. The man was obsessed with fighting monsters." He noticed that most of the "people" in the room were actually werewolves, and he felt safe assuming that the unusually pale ones were vampires. He wasn't too surprised to see that the Guilds had allied themselves with some of them. He was familiar with Brown's research and knew that there were now two groups of these monsters and that one of them seemed to be relatively harmless to humans.

"Uh, no offense to any such creatures that might actually be on our side," he hastily added.

"We prefer the term 'Monster Americans', laddie!" Prospero added with a wink that told Matt that this was just his somewhat lame attempt at making a joke.

"That briefcase contains Brown's entire life's work. I wasn't about to leave it out there to burn," Grey declared.

"Let's see how good he was!" Prospero said as he grabbed the briefcase and broke the lock open effortlessly before Grey could object. He studied the files inside thoughtfully for a few minutes, quickly thumbing through the pages.

"Not bad. I suppose I'm the werewolf he liked to call "W-7". He figured out a great deal of our movements around the world accurately. He even knew there were two factions fighting one another. I'm sorry to see such a brilliant mind destroyed. 'When beggars die, there are no comets seen; the heavens themselves blaze forth the death of princes.'"

"Thanks, I guess. He'd be happy to know that he got so much of it right," said Grey. He noticed a boy walking into the room, barefoot and wearing sweatpants and an unbuttoned shirt that was too big for him, the sleeves also unbuttoned. The boy looked familiar somehow. He stopped in front of Prospero.

"Are you sure this is gonna work for when I change?" he asked him skeptically.

"Aye, just mind the tail. That's where it gets tricky." He turned around to punctuate the point, showing off a bushy tail that poked out of a hole in his pants.

"I made a hole for mine since I stay in this form most of the time, but umm, you might want to let yours just poke out a wee bit from the top when you change."

"You look great, so fashionable!" Allison teased Kevin as she walked over to join them.

"Kevin Scott! So you did find him after all!" Grey said, finally figuring out who the boy was.

"Yeah, but getting him home in one piece is a whole 'nother ball game!" Matt said.

"Who's this guy?" Kevin asked.

"A friend," Matt answered.

"I've been thinking..." Randy began.

"A dangerous habit!" Prospero interjected.

Randy ignored him. "While we're all waiting around here for the UGF to arrive, I should probably go take another look at what the enemy is up to. You know, make sure they aren't trying to sneak away with the Dark Mother."

"Not a bad idea, but I think I should go this time, pal. You got whammied pretty badly the last time. I don't want that to happen to you twice in a row. It's my turn to take one for the team," Matt told him.

"Okay, but just remember to try and stick to the shadows and hide behind things. Remember, vampires can see spirits," Randy reminded him.

"Hey, I'm the one who taught you how to tail someone without being noticed, remember? I'm like a ninja - a master of stealth!" Matt smiled.

"You can astrally project? I didn't know you were a wizard too!" Kevin said.

"He's not. Anyone can astrally project if they're taught how. You've probably done it in your sleep and never knew it," Randy answered.

"Aye, all this magic stuff can be learned by anyone who takes the time to try and master it," Prospero couldn't help but add.

"That's true...*with* the proper supervision," Randy replied icily.

"Maybe you can fill in our new friend here about what's been happening while I go do my spy thing?" Matt pointed to Earl with his thumb. Randy nodded in agreement.

Matt sat down on the sofa next to Earl and closed his eyes. It took him a little longer to put himself in the trance than it had taken Randy, but soon he was out of his body and out of the house as well.

He saw that the persistent rain that night had done a good job of extinguishing the various beheaded vampires that Randy had left burning outside in the front yard, including the one who was still lying atop of Agent Brown like a grotesque lover. He soared high into the sky until he was so high up that he could see the church and he zoomed back down towards the earth in that direction. He was pleased to see that the buses Randy had described were still there and the place still lacked a force field. Matt entered through the roof. Like Randy before him, he stayed up there near the ceiling once inside, reasoning that few people ever looked up at the ceiling. It also helped that the ceiling in the sanctuary was very high. As an extra precaution, he floated over to a massive column that linked the floor to the ceiling and hid behind it.

On the stage of the church, he saw a row of various types of cups lined up. Some of them were quite fancy and ornately decorated, others were just plain old glasses and cups. The last few were actually just paper cups. Obviously, they didn't have enough of the fancy ones and had to rummage through the building to find enough. They seemed to be filled with a bright red liquid.

The pews were filled with vampires. There were only a handful of werewolves that had survived the first battle and had returned to headquarters. Matt figured this made sense since they were slightly easier to kill - at least they were if you had the right kind of ammunition. A tall man in a dark blue suit stood in front of the stage. He would call out a name, and another vampire would hand him a cup. A vampire or werewolf would rise up from the pews, take the cup and hand it back, then start shaking and convulsing for a few seconds, although in the case of the werewolves, these convulsions lasted a bit longer. Once they had regained control of their bodies, they bowed, then returned to their seats. The tall man then returned the empty cups to the stage.

Matt could see Kilroy in one of the pews, and he had both of his arms! Matt knew that these guys healed really fast, but this was ridiculous. It was as if nothing had ever happened to him.

Matt could overhear part of a conversation happening directly below him between two vampires. He slowly lowered himself down to try and hear it better.

"...can't believe that the Master is allowing these filthy dogs to partake of the Dark Communion! Are we really that desperate for victory? It's like saying that they're our equals!" one of them complained.

"Be careful! Keep your voice down! I don't like it either. At least he still didn't let them see Her. I hardly think it's necessary to do all of this either, not if he's going to be personally leading us into the next battle himself. With his sorcery on our side, how can we fail?" the other one said.

"Well I hope he gets this over with soon. I'm eager to go out there and put an end to all of this," the other one replied.

"Be patient. He's only got a few more left to do and then we'll start getting ready for the final attack."

Matt couldn't believe it. It sounded like not only were these guys planning on sticking around, but they were about to launch a new attack personally led by Mortus Locke himself! He knew that Locke would be able to knock down Randy's force field if given enough time. If they attacked before the UGF got there, they'd easily be overwhelmed. Not only that, but Locke was giving the Dark Communion to his werewolves too, which he guessed made them both werewolves and vampires at the same time? He didn't know exactly what that might mean, but he was sure that it would likely make them harder to kill at the very least.

One thing was for sure, he had to get this information back to everyone at the manor ASAP. He rose up the side of the column he'd been behind and out of the church undetected. He patted himself on the back for managing to spy on them without getting caught like Randy had. Again, he floated up extremely high in the sky until he could see the manor, then dove towards it, this time floating down through the roof until he saw his body slumped on the sofa and re-entered it.

Matt opened his eyes and looked around himself. Earl was still seated next to him, and Randy was across from him. Prospero, Kevin, Allison and Mary were off to Randy's side. He could see William, Elizabeth and Martin still chatting away nearby and Blake sulking in one corner, checking his watch. Various members of Blake's little army milled about in groups.

"Mortus Locke himself will be coming here soon," he announced as he rose to his feet groggily.

"No way! The chief shenanigator himself!" Allison said.

Everyone nearby looked at her blankly.

"Shenanigator?" Matt asked.

"It's a word I invented myself. It means 'the party which is responsible for initiating all the shenanigans,'" she explained.

"Ah, the bard was fond of inventing his own words too, lass. Although I'm not sure I'd trivialize Locke's crimes as mere 'shenanigans,'" Prospero commented.

"Still, it's a fun term. Do you mind if I borrow it for my next book?" Matt asked.

"Mind? That would be awesome!" Allison smiled.

"This is bad news!" Randy said, stroking his beard. "Locke could take down the barrier around this place. If he storms it before Anne and the UGF get here, we're done for!"

"I'm afraid that it gets worse. He's giving the Dark Communion to all his troops that are at the church. I saw it myself," Matt added breathlessly.

"What? Even the werewolves?" Prospero barked incredulously.

"Yeah, but there aren't many of them left, at least not at the church," Matt answered him.

"There's no telling what that will do!" Randy exclaimed. "It could create a kind of super monster that's twice as tough and strong as either a vampire or a werewolf, or it could just create a vampire that can also transform into a wolf, I suppose. I'd really prefer not to find out!"

"Wow, I always wondered what would happen if a vampire bit a werewolf!" Allison said suddenly.

"You did?" Kevin said, raising an eyebrow.

"Uh, sure. Yeah, but for purely academic, intellectual reasons. You know, like a thought exercise?" she said lamely, fooling nobody in the room. It was obvious that the idea of biting Kevin had crossed her mind at one point or another. Kevin wasn't sure if he should feel flattered or scared.

"It will also make the vampires more powerful," Prospero added. "Y'see, most of Locke's vampires are what they call 'Childlings' - vampires that were not created by Locke directly, and so have less of the Dark Mother's blood in them, and therefore less of her power. Only Locke and his inner circle of Undying Ones are usually allowed to drink her blood. The further removed a vampire is from someone who has drunk from the Dark Mother, the weaker they are. By giving most of his army her blood, he's just supercharged them all, boosted their power to a level that matches his own."

"Omigod! What're we gonna do? If they get here before the UGF does, we're toast!" Allison said frantically.

Randy checked his watch. "They're still not due for about another hour."

"And I heard Locke's people saying they were going to attack as soon as they were done taking the Dark Communion, and they were getting pretty close to the end when I left. We don't have much time left," Matt said grimly.

There was an uneasy silence for a few moments.

Then Matt had a sudden brainstorm. "It's more important now than ever that we kill the Dark Mother. If we do that, all the vampires go back to being regular people, right?"

"Yeah, but the werewolves won't be affected, that's a different curse," Randy said.

"Big deal! There's only a few of them left, most of his army is made up of vamps now. Listen, he wouldn't take the Dark Mother into battle with him would he? Isn't she too wild for him to control? Also he wouldn't risk exposing her to harm like that either, right? I mean, since she's the source of all his power," Matt said.

"Yes, he'd likely leave her behind with a few of his people to guard her," Prospero confirmed.

"Then the solution is simple! I can astrally project again to keep watch over the church. When I spot Locke's army leaving to attack us, I'll hurry back to warn everyone. Then we can all teleport into the church, take out the guards and finish off the Dark Mother! When Locke gets here, all he'll find is an empty house. By the time we get back here, he and all his vampires will just be regular people again and we'll be able to take 'em in a fight," Matt explained proudly, pleased with his plan.

"It could work! But our vampires will be regular people too, and they still outnumber us," Randy pointed out.

"We have more werewolves left, and we also have a few guns between us. Earl's got a gun, so do you and I, plus all of the Sherwoods. Blake's people all have those axe/spear thingies. I haven't seen any of Locke's people carrying any weapons, have you?" Matt insisted.

"Sometimes they carry swords so they can behead enemy vampires, but for the most part, they tend to depend heavily on just their own brute strength. Most of them see reliance on weapons as a sign of weakness," Prospero clarified.

"I don't know if I can teleport all of us out of here, Matt. It's a lot of people to teleport all by myself, I've never done it before with this many people," Randy admitted.

"Who said you'd be doing it all by yourself, laddie?" Prospero smiled at him.

"You know how to do a teleportation spell?" Randy asked uncertainly.

"Of course, lad! How do you think we got past Locke's people so easily earlier? I teleported some of our people onto the front porch! We attacked them from the front while others attacked them from behind. They took advantage of all the confusion this caused to break through their lines and join us on the porch," he told him.

Randy was floored. He realized with some regret that he'd been underestimating Prospero's abilities all night. He felt bad about giving him such a hard time earlier.

"I'd be happy to have your help," Randy said humbly.

"I suppose we'd better tell Commander Frowny Face what's up. He should be overjoyed to hear that we're gonna have to go into battle so soon," Matt said.

"Commander Frowny Face?" Prospero asked in confusion, then realization dawned on his face and he laughed. "Ah! You mean Blake! Yes, that name suits my moody master quite well! Leave him to me, I know how to talk to him. Truth be told, I'm the one who really runs this outfit, I just let him think he's in charge because it suits his vanity," he said and with that, he walked over towards Blake.

"I guess if we're going to be in another fight, I'd better go find my shield and sword," Matt heard Mary say as he sat down on the sofa again. He hated to be putting these kids in danger again like this, it broke his heart. But what was the alternative? If they stayed here, Locke would kill them for sure. He turned to look at Earl, who was still sitting next to him. He regarded the man sadly. He was obviously still in a great deal of shock over what had just happened to his partner.

"I'm sorry to drag you into this too. It sounds like this was more your partner's fight than it was yours."

"That's true in many ways, but I'm okay with it. We came here to help. If we can really destroy Mortus Locke for good, I can think of no better way to honor Brown's memory. I want to see this thing through to the end. Don't worry about me, I still have plenty of silver bullets left." He moved his jacket over to reveal that his belt held several clips of ammunition.

"Nice!" Matt commented, genuinely impressed.

"Brown believed in being prepared. I have to say though, if I make it out of this alive, I might be done with the ABC. I'm getting too old for this shit."

"Have you ever thought about becoming a private investigator? It's usually not quite this crazy, I promise. We could really use a guy like you at my agency," Matt offered. Then he hastily added "You don't have to answer right now, just think about it."

"Thanks for the offer, I'll consider it," Earl said, obviously feeling a little overwhelmed by the sudden offer.

Matt looked at them all. "Alright, I'm gonna go spy on them again, concentrate on getting everyone ready to teleport out of here as soon as I wake up," he said as he closed his eyes and put himself into the trance that allowed him to leave the confines of his flesh.

Just as before, Matt soared up through the ceiling and out into the still-stormy skies. He had a momentary scare when a bolt of lightning came uncomfortably close to his astral body. He didn't think it could actually hurt him, but it still frightened him in a reflexive kind of way. His spirit started to dive down towards the church, and as it did so, he was surprised to see another wispy, glowing form flying towards him. As it neared him, his eyes widened in shock. It was a young girl, covered in blood, her flesh hanging from her bones in long strips. If he'd still had a stomach, he was sure that the grisly sight of her would've made him sick.

Sylvia, he thought. It had to be. He hadn't expected to run into her. He'd forgotten that Allison had claimed to have seen her ghost.

Sylvia reached him in a matter of seconds and shot her hand out to grab his arm.

"They're all getting on the buses now! They'll be here any minute!" she told him.

"You've been watching them too?" Matt asked, dumbfounded.

"Yes, I've been watching everything, off and on. Sometimes I go off to be with my parents, other times I come back here to check on Kevin. I know you've been trying to help him. You've got to go back and warn them!" she revealed.

Matt was surprised that Randy or any of the vampires hadn't spotted her if she'd been hanging around. "Are *all* of them coming? What about the Dark Mother? Is she still in the basement?"

"What's the Dark Mother?" she asked in confusion.

"You know, the big, hairy monster that they worship?" Matt said, trying to keep it simple.

"I didn't see anything like that getting on the buses. I did see a few of them staying behind to guard the place, they weren't too happy about it either."

"How many did they leave behind?"

She made a face as if she was concentrating, which looked especially odd considering what a mess her face was right now. "Seven, I think."

"Thanks, Sylvia. You've been a big help, I mean it," Matt said tenderly.

"You can thank me by making sure that the big werewolf, the one who did this to me, gets to pay for it!" she said as another bolt of lightning tore through the sky nearby; it reflected in her eyes, briefly making them appear to shine with an unfathomable wrath.

Normally, Matt wasn't much of a fan of vengeance. He'd found that it wasn't really quite the same thing as justice. He also didn't take any particular delight in killing, it was just an occasionally necessary occupational hazard, and one that he tried to avoid whenever possible. However, when he thought about Kilroy and all the pain he'd inflicted lately, when he looked upon the ruined form of Sylvia with his own eyes, all of that suddenly went out the window. He realized that he'd have no trouble making a special exception for Kilroy. Kilroy was a true monster in every sense of the word.

"Don't worry, he'll get what's coming to him. We're all gunning for that asshole!" he told her.

She nodded her understanding. "Good luck - and keep Kevin out of trouble!" she said as she faded away.

"I will!" Matt promised. As he shouted the words into the rain, he realized that he was just talking to the storm. He could now faintly see the buses turn on their headlights and begin to move around in the church parking lot far below. He turned around in the sky and hurried back to the manor as quickly as he could possibly will his spirit to move.

It turns out that was very quickly. The next thing he knew, he was back in his body and taking a very deep breath as his eyelids flew open.

"We have to move - now! They're on their way and they're taking the buses this time, so that means that they'll get here any minute now!" The words tumbled from his mouth before he could even finish opening his eyes.

He stood up, and almost fell over. The room was spinning.

"They're taking the buses? It must be too many for Locke to teleport here, or he's forgotten how to do that, too," Randy mused.

"We're ready," Blake said. Matt saw that he was standing next to him, with Martin and the Sherwoods, who were all brandishing their ancient pistols. He saw that Mary had found her shield and was carrying both her own sword and the one that her father had used. Kevin was already in "beast mode" and looked faintly comical with his sweatpants stretched to their limit. The unbuttoned shirt he wore had still been too small to accommodate his hulking form and was torn by the transformation in the back and in the arms.

"I think I should be the one to take out the Dark Mother. I can send the *Vermillion Avenger* through the bars of her cage. There are seven guards left at the church. The rest of you keep them busy while I try to get to the Dark Mother," Matt reported.

"Just make sure you take off her head," Randy said.

"Seven guards? He's probably leaving all of the Undying Ones behind to keep watch over her. They'll be tough to defeat, but we've got the numerical advantage this time," Blake told them.

"I just renewed the barrier around the house. Knocking it out will slow them down and buy us more time to do what we have to do," Randy added.

"Good thinking, pal," Matt said approvingly.

"Several of my people have also decided to stay outside on the porch for similar reasons. If the enemy sees us all going inside at the same time, they might suspect that we're up to something," Blake informed him.

"That's suicide!" Matt exclaimed.

"It was their choice. They knew the risks when they joined our cause," Blake said a little too coldly for Matt's taste.

"Is there a room in this place with no windows? I don't want any of them to see us teleport out of here and tip off Locke," Matt said. *Especially if some of Blake's troops are willing to throw their lives away just to keep the charade going,* he thought.

"We could all go into the basement," William suggested. "Follow me."

And they did. All of them followed him down the narrow staircase off of the kitchen and down into a dark, dusty, windowless space with a dirt floor. On the way down, Matt whispered something into Randy's ear and the young wizard nodded in response.

As soon as they were all down there, Randy and Prospero linked hands. They instructed all of them to join hands as well and hold onto each other tightly. Some of them had quite a bit of trouble doing so while still holding onto their weapons. Then the two wizards began chanting the teleportation spell in unison. The magical barrier around the house prevented enemies from teleporting in, but it didn't prevent the wizard who created the barrier, or anyone he wanted to bring with him, from teleporting out. It's all about the intention behind the spell, and since it was Randy's spell, his intentions were the ones that controlled it.

Within seconds there was a brief flash of light, and the formerly cramped and stuffy old basement was empty again, populated only by spiders, moldering boxes, and the memories that they contained.

CHAPTER 19:

A FINAL RECKONING

The mixed company of humans, werewolves, and vampires spun through the *Place Between Places*, momentarily being dazzled and disoriented by the brilliant, multicolored lights that shone in that mysterious other universe before re-emerging into real space.

Everyone felt a little queasy, which was normal with this kind of travel - it would soon pass so long as they didn't teleport again in the next few hours. Matt looked around himself and saw that they were near the end of the sanctuary, by the stage. It looked like everyone had made it.

"You couldn't have put us in the basement?" he whispered to Randy.

"Hey, it's not an exact science! Just be grateful that we all got here in one piece and with all of our weapons!" Randy whispered back defensively.

Across the sanctuary, two of the Undying Ones had been chatting near the entrance to the huge chamber. Now they whipped around and looked at the small army arrayed against them with a mixture of surprise and anger.

"The Betrayer is here!" Varney shouted. They heard the sound of running feet echoing towards them from another room.

"I think now's the time for you to do that thing we talked about!" Matt said to Randy, he was no longer whispering since the enemy was already onto them.

"You got it!" Randy replied and he turned to where Kevin, Allison, and Mary stood nearby and chanted the words to a spell. Instantly, the three youths were completely enclosed in a glowing green bubble of energy.

"Hey! What's the big idea?" Allison shouted as she pounded her fists on the bubble. Kevin growled angrily and clawed at the bubble impotently beside her.

"No fair! We want to help! We want some payback!" Mary yelled.

"I'm trying to save your lives!" Matt told her.

Three other vampires came running into the room; there were now a total of five upstairs. *The other two must be in the basement,* Matt figured as he looked around for a way to get himself down there. He didn't see any obviously direct route there from this room.

The vampires now rushed towards them, with two running down the aisles on either side of the central grouping of pews.

"They're brave, I'll give 'em that!" Matt said as he watched them approach. "Cover me while I try to get to the basement!" he shouted to nobody in particular. Blake's people started to move towards the attacking Undying Ones.

"I'm coming with you!" Earl shouted as he followed Matt.

Varney launched himself into the air, flying over the pews, hoping to reach Blake. He'd been so disappointed when the Master had ordered him to stay behind, even though he had tried to spin it as a great honor, telling Varney that it was up to him to carry on their ways if anything should happen to him in battle. Varney hadn't been fooled, he knew that the Master had lost confidence in him and was deliberately sidelining him. If he could destroy Blake, though, he'd be sure to win back the Master's favor!

As Varney neared Blake, with both of his arms outstretched to grasp at him, Blake swung his weapon at him savagely, batting him to the ground. Within seconds, he was stabbing at the ground where Varney was, hoping to pin him down long enough to take his head, but Varney swiftly rolled out of the way and was back on his feet. He lunged at Blake, smacked his weapon from his hand, then grabbed him by his neck as he threw them into the raised edge of the stage.

"All those years, it should've been *I* who was second in command, not you! *I* have always been the most loyal one, but the Master couldn't see what a treacherous *dog* you were until it was almost too late! Now, you will finally pay for the glory you robbed me of for all that time, you *miserable traitor!*" Varney spat the words at him as he crushed Blake's throat. He opened his mouth wide, revealing his rows of unnaturally sharpened teeth as he moved his head closer to take a bite out of Blake. He saw the fear in Blake's eyes and he relished it. He wanted to take his time with this one, to savor every last delicious moment!

"Look into my eyes, Betrayer! And know that it was I who was the architect of your ultimate downfall! I who ended your pathetic rebellion! I, who was always the better one!" Varney continued to gloat.

Blake summoned every last reserve of his strength and jerked his own head forward with sudden, blinding speed, head butting Varney with such force that he went flying backwards. With one swift motion, Blake reached for his belt and unsheathed a pair of long, curved blades. He crossed the blades in front of his face and dove towards Varney, sliding both blades across the other vampire's neck so forcefully that his head was instantly severed from his neck.

"You talk too much!" Blake declared triumphantly as Varney's head hit the floor and rolled, a jet of crimson spraying from his neck and covering Blake's face like war paint.

As Matt and Earl ran down the aisle closest to the wall, Matt saw the first of the Undying Ones clash with one of Blake's soldiers. He watched in fascinated horror as the lead Undying One caught the weapon that was swung at him with his hand and tossed it aside, then he punched a hole right through his attacker's stomach with the other hand and swung that arm up, splitting Blake's warrior in two.

Jesus! Matt thought. *They ARE strong! And if Sylvia was right, I'm gonna have to face two of them in the basement!* Matt felt fear gripping his heart. If they could do that to a vampire that was superhumanly strong and tough, what chance did he have? He was just a guy with a flying sword and a few bits of armor. He was grateful that Earl was backing him up, but he also feared for his chances even more, all he had were some silver bullets which wouldn't really kill any of these undead bastards, it would just make them even angrier.

He shook his head and tried to banish the fear that was threatening to paralyze him. No time for that, he had a job to do. He just hoped that he'd succeed, that he'd get to see Naomi and the kids again. He wished Randy was with him, but he could see that he was too busy trying to freeze blast some of the Undying Ones, but was having a hard time getting a clear shot, and when he did have a good shot, they had an annoying habit of dodging the attacks.

Matt found a door off to the side and yanked it open. "In here!" he shouted to Earl. They found themselves in a narrow hallway that emptied into a large kitchen that looked like a cyclone had hit it. The drawers were pulled out and the cabinets were all hanging open, as was the refrigerator door.

"Over here!" Earl whispered urgently from the other side of the room, he'd opened another door and as Matt joined him, he could see a set of steps that led down into a lower level. Their eyes met as they looked at each other nervously.

"Well, here goes nothin'! Get behind me," Matt whispered.

Matt ordered the *Vermilion Avenger* forward as he took the lead, frowning as he took the first step and the wood creaked loudly under his weight.

In the basement, two of the Undying Ones, still dressed in their red ceremonial robes, glanced up at the ceiling uneasily. They could hear the sounds of battle coming from above, a variety of screams, shouts, crashes and bangs that constantly rained down upon their sensitive ears.

"The enemy is here! How?" one of them asked as he made a move forward. The other vampire caught him by the shoulder and violently pulled him back.

"No! We must stay here! We are the only thing standing between them and the Dark Mother!" he hissed.

"Yes, you're right. We should warn the Master though, so he can send help," he said as he pulled out a cell phone from beneath his robes and flipped it open.

"Good call!" the other one said as he watched his companion start to dial a number.

Before he could press send, there was a whistling sound and his head tumbled from his neck.

The other vampire's eyes widened in shock as he turned to see a shiny red sword hurtling through the air towards him. With his amazing reflexes, he smacked the flat of the sword with his forearm, knocking it off course. The *Vermilion Avenger* buried its blade in the wall instead. The vampire looked towards the stairwell and saw a pair of humans cowering there. With an inarticulate howl of fury he threw himself upon the nearest one, a man wearing a tattered and blood-stained trench coat. The weakling tried to jump to the side to avoid him, but the vampire deftly caught him by one of his arms and pulled the arm up forcefully.

Matt screamed in pain as the vampire yanked on his arm so hard that he was sure he'd instantly dislocated his shoulder. The monster continued to pull, and he feared that in another moment he'd pull it completely off of his body. With dawning horror Matt figured out that the monster was deliberately prolonging his agony.

He's just toying with me! He's enjoying this! he thought in a panic.

There was a flash of light off to his side and his ears began to ring. At the same time, his face was splatted by something wet. He'd reflexively shut his eyes, and as he opened them he now saw that Earl had shot the attacking vampire square in the face. The force of the shot had knocked him to the ground and he'd thankfully released his grip on Matt's arm in the process. The vampire had lost one entire side of his head, Matt could see exposed bits of his skull gleaming beneath his blackened flesh, smoke rising and curling off into the air from that side of his ruined face. The creature now balled his hands into fists and crouched down low as if readying to leap towards them for another attack.

Matt imagined the *Vermilion Avenger* liberating itself from the wall and taking the head off the creature. Almost as swiftly as he pictured the action in his mind, it now played itself out in reality. Before the vampire could jump at them, his head was bouncing off a nearby wall and his body was already crumbling to the ground in a lifeless heap.

"Thanks, man," Matt smiled at Earl. "I thought I was about to lose a limb!"

"How is it?" Earl asked.

Matt grimaced in pain. "It hurts like a sonofabitch, but I'll be okay. I think it's just dislocated."

"So that's her, huh?" Earl said, pointing towards a massive metal cage made of a strange, glittery metal.

Inside, they could see a large, shaggy creature that was jumping up and down excitedly, its impossibly long arms stretched out towards them through the gaps in the bars. At its feet, they could see human remains, bones that were picked completely clean. Matt recalled Naomi saying that this thing was a man-eater, he supposed that Locke had kept her well fed - he wondered with a shudder where they got the victims from.

"Yup, the real Queen of the Damned!" Matt replied. "I guess I'd better get this over with."

Normally, Matt would've felt bad about killing a defenseless creature like this, but he knew it was the only way to ensure their survival, and it was obvious that this thing would rip them apart if it could just get its hands on them, it was certainly trying to regardless, excited into a frenzy by the scent of blood in the air.

Just then, Earl tripped over one of the heads on the floor and fell forwards, clattering down next to the cage. Within moments, the Dark Mother was upon him, grasping at him with one arm from behind, her long, black claws sank into his upper chest, right below his collarbone.

"Earl!" Matt shouted.

Earl groaned in agony as he tried to angle his gun towards the beast. He emptied it into the Dark Mother's torso and it flew backwards, releasing its deadly grip upon him. He quickly scooted forwards on his hands and knees away from the cage.

Matt cursed himself for his hesitation as he regarded the creature, which had almost cost Earl his life. It was time to stop fucking around and end all of this - now. He sent the *Vermilion Avenger* sailing through the bars and aimed the point of it right at the Dark Mother's neck. It pierced it, pinning her to the wall. Her unholy, profoundly red ichor spilled out like a fountain. She clawed madly at the sword, trying to grab hold of the blade and pull it out, but succeeded only in cutting off her own fingers with the effort. Matt caused the blade to move from side to side until her head was completely severed and landed on the filthy floor of the cage, next to a human skull that she'd stripped down to the bone. He then called the *Vermilion Avenger* back out of the cage and it came to rest in the air over his shoulder as it typically did.

Earl clambered to his feet, applying pressure to the holes in his flesh made by the dark Mother's claws. Matt looked at his wound with a look of concern on his face.

"It's okay, she didn't hit any arteries," Earl answered his unspoken question.

"It's awfully quiet up above us all of the sudden," Matt remarked.

"I hope that means our monsters won," Earl said.

As if in answer, Randy came running down the steps, followed by Martin and Blake, who were suddenly not looking quite so sickly pale.

"Matt! You did it! The curse is broken!" Randy laughed and clapped him on his dislocated shoulder.

"Oww! That's great, pal. One curse down, one to go," Matt said, recalling that he still had one teenage werewolf to cure.

Upstairs, Allison was still trapped in a bubble of energy with Kevin and Mary. She immediately felt something different. She took a deep breath, and for once she could *feel* the air filling her lungs. She had a dizzying sensation of blood rushing through every inch of her body, and an almost deafening sound, a steady rhythmic beat.

It's my heartbeat! she realized. *I'm alive again! Alive!*

Tears trickled down her cheeks and she could feel the wetness of them upon her gradually warming skin for the first time in forever. There was simultaneously a curious widening and narrowing of her world of sensations as her vampiric sense receded and her human ones returned. Her world shrank at the same time that it expanded, just in completely different ways that defy explanation if you haven't experienced it for yourself.

She was overjoyed at the prospect of being restored to normalcy again, that after so long with her future looking like one unending succession of grey days that it suddenly was filled with color and possibility once more.

At the same time, a fear nagged at her that her bond with Kevin had now been ripped asunder, that now that she was just a normal human girl again, perhaps he wouldn't be interested in her any longer.

Another anxiety seized her as she realized that she could no longer will him back into his human form and she was trapped in this tiny space with him. He seemed to have been able to learn how to control himself in his werewolf form, but she wondered how much of that was really him and how much of it was due to her influence? She looked over to him and with relief saw that he wasn't making any threatening moves towards her or Mary. She couldn't help but flinch a little as he stretched out one hairy arm towards her - only to grip her in a surprisingly gentle hug.

"Thanks." She smiled up at him, reassured by his hug that his feelings for her hadn't diminished and weren't just some strange side effect of their respective curses.

Mary noticed the change in her friend and flung her arms around them both, joining the group hug. "I'm so happy for you, Al!" she exclaimed.

Nearby, William and Elizabeth regarded each other as the color flooded back into their faces.

"Are you ready to grow old with me, my Husband?" Elizabeth asked teasingly.

"There's nothing else I'd rather do, my Bride!" he said as he kissed her long and deeply.

When they finally broke apart, he looked at her with laughter sparkling in his eyes. "You know, I think a little touch of grey in your hair might just suit you quite nicely!"

She punched him in the arm and chuckled, "Not nearly as much as a few wrinkles will compliment your features!"

"I actually felt that! What a novel sensation!" William said with a note of awe. He was going to enjoy being human again.

They all turned their heads as Matt and Earl entered the sanctuary, with Randy, Blake and Martin following. Moments earlier Randy had burned the Dark Mother's body with a fireball spell, then after letting it burn for a while, extinguished it with an ice blast before it could spread.

The stench had been unbearable.

They had all hastily run up the steps to escape from the terrible odor, only to be unexpectedly greeted with a hero's welcome.

A mighty cheer went up as Blake's remaining troops surged forth; some of them shook hands with them, others clapped them on the back, Matt wincing in pain each time someone did this so on his bad shoulder.

Matt turned to Randy "Know any good healing spells to fix up this bum shoulder of mine?"

"Yeah, I'll fix you up as soon as these people get all of this gratitude out of their systems!" Randy assured him.

"Hey! Are you gonna keep us in here all night?" came Mary's cranky voice from nearby.

"Uh oh, I'd better liberate our young friends here first," Randy said as he made a bizarre gesture and spoke an obscure word or two, instantly causing the energy bubble around the kids to dissipate. Mary and Allison both ran towards the Sherwoods, who greeted them with open arms.

Prospero walked over to Kevin and looked up at him. "If you slow your breathing a bit and concentrate on the idea of becoming smaller, you can shift down to a form more like mine so you can actually talk to us again tonight. Go on, give it a try lad."

Matt watched with astonishment as Kevin's transformation reversed slightly until he was in what Matt liked to think of as the "wolfman" form that most of Blake's werewolves seemed to favor.

"Very good, boy! You're a natural!" Prospero said praisingly.

Kevin checked out his new form with some degree of wonderment. "Cool! It's nice to be able to communicate more clearly again."

"Omigod! You look just like Teenwolf now!" Allison laughed. Kevin looked a little hurt by her comments for a moment. "But it's oddly sexy, just like in the movie," she quickly added.

"Must be my natural animal magnetism!" Kevin grinned, flashing his fangs.

Matt now felt Randy's hand upon his injured arm, heard him mutter a chant, and a golden glow suffused his body. He could actually feel his torn muscles knitting themselves back together. In seconds the glow disappeared and he rotated his arm to test it out.

"Thanks, Randy, it feels as good as new. You should work some of that same magic on Earl, too. The Dark Mother nailed him pretty bad before we took her out."

Randy laid his hands on Earl and repeated the process. As he did so, they watched Blake climb up onto the stage and call for their attention. Prospero now stood beside him.

"Friends! We have scored a glorious victory! The Dark Mother is dead and those of us who were once vampires have had our long-lost humanity restored to us! It's all thanks to our new ally, Matt!" He gestured in Matt's direction and everyone clapped. Matt blushed in embarrassment at the outburst of applause and smiled his lopsided smile, waving at them rather stiffly and awkwardly like he was the Queen of England.

"Geez, all I had to do was kill one lousy monster and suddenly I'm his favorite person! I wish I'd known sooner, then I wouldn't have had to put up with all his tantrums!" Matt told Randy under his breath. Randy just smiled.

"But Prospero has reminded me that we are not out of danger yet! Locke yet lives, and is still a formidable wizard. So long as he lives there is the danger that he could recreate the Dark Mother and rebuild his forces! He suggests that we teleport back to the farm, take them by surprise from behind and finish this! Gather your weapons and join us up here on stage to link hands again! The time of the final reckoning is at hand!"

"Oh man! Another teleportation spell so soon after the last one? I'm gonna toss my cookies for sure!" Matt complained.

"I'm not happy about it either, but it *is* the best way to maintain the element of surprise," Randy sighed as they climbed the short set of steps that led up to the stage together.

They all linked hands and before they began the teleportation spell, Prospero turned to them and winked.

"'Once more unto the breach, dear friends, once more!'" he quoted with even more bombast than usual.

Locke was livid.

He'd ordered the buses to park at the bottom of one of the hills on the way to the manor and had marched them the rest of the way up to the house. Halfway there, they were greeted by the soldiers who had stayed behind to watch the manor, who joined them as they surrounded the house. Locke had unleashed a fearsome torrent of magical lightning bolts at the force field around the old house, lighting up the sky for miles around. Eventually, it finally shimmered out of existence under the weight of his persistent pounding. He'd ordered his eager henchmen forward, the taste of imminent victory upon their lips.They charged the manor, quickly overcoming the troops stationed on the porch.

At long last, Locke entered the home of his enemies with Kilroy by his side. Locke was now certain that William and Elizabeth must be the ones who had betrayed him centuries ago. How else could they afford all this land and this fine house? Why else would the Guilds be helping them now unless they had some kind of previous relationship with them? It was obvious that they had sold him out to the Guilds and stolen his treasure for themselves. He would enjoy making them pay for all the trouble that they'd caused him; he'd be sure to kill them slowly after he made them watch him kill their friends first.

Immediately upon entering the home, Kilroy knew that something was wrong.

"Master! They're not here! I can't sense anyone else here but our own people!"

"What?" He turned to the others who had followed him inside. "Search this house!" he bellowed. He knew that Kilroy's tracking instincts were the sharpest of all his wolves, but he still refused to believe that his foes had managed to slip between his fingers. It couldn't be! Not when he was this close to total victory!

A quick search of the premises confirmed it.

What a fool he'd been! The enemy had a wizard helping them; they must've teleported to safety, leaving a few guards behind to fool them into thinking that they were still there. But why bother to maintain the charade unless....

Of course! The church! The enemy wizard had seen him perform the Dark Communion, they knew that the Dark Mother was there. They'd obviously made a move to attack her, and he'd only left seven of his men behind to guard her! How had he not seen this coming? Had he really allowed his obsession with ending the war, with finally getting his revenge on Blake to blind him so thoroughly?

"All of you, with me - *now!*" he hissed.

He whirled around and stormed out of the manor. He paused on the porch and addressed those amongst his followers who had remained outside.

"We must all return to the church immediately! I will teleport some of you with me, the others will board the buses and meet us there! The enemy might be after the Dark Mother! We must stop them at all costs!" he announced, magically amplifying his voice so that they could all hear him.

Then it hit him and all the other vampires in the group, the sudden, sickening feeling of weakness, of vulnerability. For him it was completely unfamiliar, something which he had no memory of. It was terrifying.

Human! He was human again! *Mortal! Weak!* He was everything he'd struggled to escape from, everything he hated! A prisoner to the tides of time, just like the rest of the worthless, stupid people of this world! In one fell swoop, he'd been robbed of his power, of what made him so special, so feared. He was no longer Mortus Locke, the Great Immortal, Lord of the Children of the Night, High Priest of the Dark Mother. He was just another helpless, hapless mortal.

No, he hadn't been stripped of *all* of his power, he still had his magic left to him. Perhaps his knowledge of it wasn't as great as it had once been, but it was still enough to allow him to get his revenge upon those who'd done this to him. And he still had his wolves - most of them had been killed in this conflict, but he still had a few left to him that he could depend upon to carry out his dread directives. He looked over at Kilroy, who stood obediently nearby. Yes, he could yet cause a great deal of damage to his enemies with such savage servants still at his command.

"Master! What is happening to us?" one of his former vampires asked as he looked at his hands in awe at the color returning to them.

Locke snarled like some kind of wild animal and struck the man, knocking him into the muddy ground. "Idiot! Isn't it obvious! The Dark Mother has fallen! We're mortal again!"

Kilroy was also fuming. He'd briefly tasted the power he'd so long ached to share in, the power of the Undying Ones, only to have it all stripped away. True, he still had the magical belt that allowed him to maintain his werewolf form, but being returned to that familiar power level now felt unsatisfyingly weak compared to the dizzyingly Godlike surge of power he'd been enjoying mere moments ago.

There was a flash of light from a nearby hill that overlooked the house. Atop the hill, Locke could now barely make out with his inferior human eyes several silhouettes standing on its crest. One of them stepped forward. Lightning flashed, illuminating the scene momentarily.

Blake! Locke thought hatefully as the lighting revealed the form of his enemy looking down upon him, gloating, no doubt, at his newfound weakness. Blake, whom he'd once thought of as something close to a son or a brother, only to have him cruelly stab him in the back. Blake, who had been with him for so long that he didn't even know how they'd come to be together to begin with. Blake, who had now undone everything they had worked so hard to build together. Blake, who had been the last person he'd ever dared to trust. Locke bared his teeth and ground them together in rage at the sight of the man.

"The Dark Mother is dead! The Guilds will be here very soon with their armies! Surrender now, and I will ask them to grant you amnesty for your past crimes! You can all have a new lease on life, a blank slate! Continue to resist us, and there will be no chance at redemption for you, no mercy! We have more werewolves! We all have weapons, including many guns loaded with silver bullets! Your choice is simple! Stand with Locke and be destroyed! Stand with me, and live!" Blake shouted down to Locke's forces assembled below him.

"Don't listen to this *traitor*! This *heretic*! How can you trust the lies of a traitor? Have I not always fulfilled my promises to you? Have I not made you like unto the Gods? It was I who first summoned forth the Dark Mother from the Aether with my sorcery - I will do so again! I alone can restore your immortality, your power! The power that *he* stole from you! For *mine* is the kingdom, and the power, and the glory forever! *I* am the way and the truth and the life! No one comes to immortality except through *me*!" Locke screamed the words into the storm.

He looked about himself and saw that most of his followers were slowly backing away from him. Some of them were even holding their hands up in the air in an obvious gesture of surrender. Only Kilroy seemed to stand firm, still snarling and growling at his enemies up on the hill, crouched low as if to spring up for an attack at any moment.

"My children, why hast thou forsaken me?" Locke purred in a low voice, then in a flash, his face twisted into an expression of pure malice.

"Cowards! Faithless fools! None of you were ever truly worthy of what I have to offer! I see that now! So be it! I know who all of you are! I will find you again! All of you! You will all suffer my wrath! You will all spend the rest of your days looking over your shoulders in fear, and someday, you will see *me* standing there to claim what is mine! I swear it! This is *not* over!"

"Oh, but it *is* over, Locke!" Blake shouted.

"Blake! You always had such a way with words, such a silvery tongue! A new life as an inferior creature? Amnesty you say? Mercy? What fine words! And I ask you: will you render this same mercy unto me?" Locke asked mockingly.

Blake shook his head slowly and shifted his weight into a battle-ready stance, raising his weapon in anticipation, steel in his eyes and in his voice as he spoke again.

"No, your crimes are too great. For you I can offer only the mercy of death!"

Locke screamed inarticulately and in the blink of an eye, he was gone.

There was another flash of light, and he reappeared atop the hill, mere feet away from Blake. But Blake was not his target. He had seen William and Elizabeth standing to one side of Blake. William and Elizabeth who had been the *original* betrayers! He would destroy them first with his magic, then the rest of Blake's pathetic flock. Blake would see him destroy his people before his eyes and know how weak he was before Locke took his life, too. Locke's children would see his power and beg to come back to him. He'd kill them, too, of course, they'd just shown their true colors, but he'd enjoy watching them come crawling back to him before he did so. No, he'd have to start over again from the beginning. Blake had promised a clean slate and a clean slate there would be, just not the kind that he had imagined. Locke didn't really know how to create a new Dark Mother, not anymore, but he had discovered the secret once and he was confident that in time, he would do so again.

Locke chanted a spell as he reappeared, a fireball spell, and he sent that fireball spiraling out towards William and Elizabeth, a fireball big and hot enough to engulf the two of them.

Without hesitation, Blake shoved the two of them aside and jumped into the path of the screaming ball of flames. Within moments, he was burning and fell to the ground, rolling in an attempt to extinguish the intense, unearthly fire that ate away at his flesh. Randy sent a magical blast of cold air at him (not as intense as the ones he'd used as an attack earlier) to try and put out the fire.

"So noble, right up to the bitter end!" Locke smirked. From the corner of his eyes, he saw lighting streaking through the air in his direction, but this was not natural lighting. With another chant and a gesture, he erected a great, glowing force field which completely surrounded him to absorb the eldritch lighting that was being directed at him. His eyes widened as he saw that the one directing the attack at him was none other than Prospero.

"You! So, you fancy yourself a wizard now?" he laughed.

"Aye, thanks to your own spell books! Now you face a monster of your own creation, Locke!" Prospero roared the words at him as he continued to bombard him with the mystical lightning.

"It will take more than a few tricks you learned from a book to best me, pretender!" Locke said, and chanted a new spell. The ground in front of Prospero suddenly formed itself into a massive arm and a fist made of tightly packed earth and stones, which struck him savagely, sending him flying backwards and tumbling end over end down to the bottom of the hill.

"You won't find me so easy to beat! Now you face a *true* wizard of the Temple of the Old Gods!" Randy said as he also let loose upon Locke with a maelstrom of magical energy. These blasts were much bigger and brighter than the lighting that Prospero had fired. Matt had never seen Randy or any other wizard use an attack like this before, it was obviously taking some kind of toll on him. Sweat poured down his face in sheets, and it looked to Matt like he was actually slowly becoming thinner as he continued to pour it on, even his beard was slowly beginning to grey.

My God! He's channeling some of his life force into the attack to boost it somehow! He's going to kill himself if this doesn't come to an end soon! Matt realized.

From behind his barrier, Locke laughed. "That's it, fool! Drain yourself! You'll die before you ever shatter this shield!"

"We'll...se...who falls...first!" Randy said from between gritted teeth. He now understood just how badly he had underestimated Locke's wizardry. It was now obvious to him that Locke had neglected to put a barrier around his base earlier out of arrogance more than ignorance. Any ordinary wizard or witch would've had their shield shattered by this kind of attack in mere moments, yet Locke looked like he could keep this up all day. It didn't matter, sooner or later, it had to give. Randy was determined to break through it and destroy him, no matter the cost. Wendy wouldn't have been happy if she could see him doing this, he was using a kind of magic that was forbidden, that he wasn't supposed to know how to do, but as it usually did, Randy's curiosity had gotten the better of him and he had learned the secret of how to siphon off the energy of his very essence to augment the power of his assault.

Matt had never felt so helpless. He couldn't just stand by and watch his partner destroy himself like this. If only there was some way that the *Vermilion Avenger* could get through that shield! He looked down at his feet in resignation, and that's when he thought of a solution.

Locke continued to laugh. He was quite content to let this reckless young idiot blast away at him until he turned himself into a smoking skeleton. With the wizard out of the way, the rest of them would be easy pickings, lambs to the slaughter!

Locke abruptly stopped laughing as he felt a sudden, sharp, piercing pain. He never really knew what hit him, it all happened too fast. The *Vermilion Avenger* came shooting up from the ground directly beneath his feet and split him neatly in two. The bubble of energy flashed out of existence with his passing, the two halves of Mortus Locke collapsing to the rain-soaked ground with a sickening squelch. Matt had caused the sword to tunnel *beneath* the magical barrier in order to unleash it upon Locke.

Randy stopped his assault and began to fall backwards, but Matt was there to catch him.

"I've got you, buddy!"

"I know you do. Thanks," Randy said, suddenly looking a few years older.

"What the hell do you think you were doing?" Matt yelled at him. "Don't you *ever* do something like that again!"

"Don't worry. It only cost me a few years. I still have plenty of good ones left ahead of me," Randy smiled as he righted himself and stood on his own two feet again.

Kevin looked down at Allison and smiled. "It's over, it's finally over! We won!" He lifted her up and covered her in kisses.

A terrible, bestial howl suddenly pierced the night air. Everything inside of Kilroy had snapped at the sight of his Master's death. With Locke's passing, the hope of ever going back to the only way of life he'd ever known, or of tasting the blessed power of the Undying Ones ever again, had also died. Kilroy didn't want to live as a human. He *despised* humans! He'd spent so much time as a wolf that he didn't know how to live like one of these contemptible, frail little creatures. He didn't *want* to know how! He loved being a wolf, he treasured the independence that he had, he lived for the thrill of the hunt - the sense of absolute power that filled him as he stalked his prey, the feeling of complete dominance over life and death as he tore into them. No, he'd never let them tame him! His heart was wild and it always would be!

He'd rather go down fighting and take as much of this traitorous scum with him to hell as possible! He saw the boy who had been his greatest mistake up there with them. They thought they had won, but he'd show them! He'd show them that he still had a lesson or two in pain and suffering to teach these defiant little brats!

It was time to correct this mistake once and for all! He saw that the boy had a new girl already. The one who had once been a blood sucker. She was vulnerable now like the rest of those who'd once dared to imagine that they were his betters! He'd destroy her just like he had the other one! He recalled how she'd fought back and hurt him in the shed, he'd enjoy making her pay for that humiliation! He'd rip out her heart and shove it down the boy's throat, make him choke on it before he finished him off for good this time!

Kilroy bounded up the hill in a matter of seconds and launched himself into the air at the spot where Kevin, Allison and Mary stood. Kevin made himself grow back into his larger, bulkier form and charged forward.

No! You won't hurt us again! I won't let you! Kevin thought as he leapt up at his enemy.

He and Kilroy collided in the air and fell to the earth together, locked in one snarling, rolling ball of hair, teeth and claws.

Matt watched all of this unfold and cursed himself for not having Randy enclose the kids in an energy bubble again as soon as they had teleported back to the farm. He wanted to send the *Vermilion Avenger* over to take out Kilroy, but the way that he and Kevin were going at each other, he didn't dare to risk it since it seemed impossible to get a clear shot at him.

Allison, on the other hand, was much closer to the fight, so it was easier for her to feel confident that she would be able to hit Kilroy without shooting Kevin by accident. She aimed her pistol carefully, and fired a shot into Kilroy, catching him in the shoulder. He reared back in pain, and Kevin took advantage of the momentary distraction to swipe his claws across Kilroy's magical belt of wolf pelts, tearing it off of him.

As the enchanted belt fell to the ground, Kilroy suddenly shifted back into the form of a slender, pale man with a long grey beard and even longer, wild-looking hair. He was completely naked and growled at Kevin as if he was still a wolf. His bright blue eyes flashed with a deep madness.

Kilroy looked down upon his human form in shame, shame at how small and frail it was. This disgusting thing that was not his true self, that was nothing but a prison for his true, bestial spirit. No matter! He'd destroy them all the same. He'd rip them apart with his bare hands if he had to! He'd find the strength to do so somehow! These flat teeth could still bite! Could still rend and tear away soft flesh! Kilroy was not beaten! He was never beaten! He would never die, for he was death incarnate! How can you kill death itself?

Mary ran towards the man, and with a mighty roar she slashed out with her father's sword, spilling open his guts. As his steaming entrails spilled out onto the wet earth, he tried to frantically stuff them back inside. Mary twirled around on one foot and brought her other sword crashing down onto the back of his neck, nearly taking his head off. She pulled the sword out and plunged it into his back with such force that it went all the way through to his heart and came out the other side. Whipping the blade back out, she watched as he fell face forwards into the slick mud.

"Never underestimate the normal girl," she said as she stood over the murderer of her father and her friend, breathing hard. Kevin shifted back to his "Teenwolf" form, and he and Allison each placed a hand on one of Mary's shoulders. She dropped her weapons and shield and threw an arm around each of them and sobbed. The thing that had caused her so much suffering was now dead, so why did she still feel so terrible? Why did she still hurt so much?

The rain, for the first time since it had started, came to a stop and the skies began to clear.

"If any of the rest of you still want some, then come and get some! We've got plenty of death for the rest of you!" Martin Lane shouted to Locke's remaining forces, who had been watching all of this unfold from the base of the hill.

"We surrender! We surrender!" a chorus of voices shouted up to them. The war, at long last, finally seemed to be over.

Prospero now knelt down and cradled Blake in his arms, weeping openly.

"Isn't there anything you can do for him? Another healing spell?" Matt asked.

"I've already tried, he's too far gone," Prospero said quietly.

Blake was still alive, but barely hanging on by a thread. He craned his head to face William and Elizabeth. "I hope that you two will now...consider any debt I may have owed you for my past...excesses to be paid?" he croaked out hoarsely.

"Paid in full," William said and realized with some shock that he was beginning to tear up as he said it.

"And forgiven," Elizabeth added as she took one of his charred hands in her own, a single tear sliding down her cheek.

Who would he meet in the next world? His victims? Relatives and lovers from a past he no longer recalled? *Death!* he thought with some excitement. *At long last, something new!* He looked at his oldest and best friend, Prospero, who'd always dared to believe that there was some glimmer of goodness beneath all his wickedness. He'd been very blessed to be gifted with such a friend. He looked at what was left of his army, a group of people who now had a new chance at life, free of the horrors they had known for so long, and he was satisfied. Perhaps the good he had done *did* outweigh all the evil? Who could tell for sure? Who truly judged such things? All that he knew was that in this moment, all that mattered to him was that *he* felt that it did. He had helped to free the world of Mortus Locke's evil, sparing the lives of whatever victims he and his servants would've claimed in the future. He felt that his unnaturally long life had actually meant something. He was satisfied.

He smiled at Prospero. Smiling hurt. "'To die, to sleep - to sleep, perchance to dream - ay there's the rub, for in this sleep of death what dreams may come....'" It was one of his old friend's few favorite quotations that he actually felt like he understood the meaning of and knew by heart.

Prospero's eyes widened in recognition of the quote. "So you *have* been paying attention after all!"

"I've heard you say it often enough, you pretentious old windbag!" Blake laughed. Laughing *really* hurt.

Prospero laughed too. Then Blake finally slipped away, his eyes still open, staring into some unknown infinitude. Prospero closed them gently.

"Good night sweet prince," he said in a voice so low that few of the beings that had gathered around the scene could hear it.

The somber mood was suddenly shattered by a series of sonic booms from somewhere in the skies above them. They all looked up.

Several large, black jets had appeared out of thin air. They were oddly shaped, with highly angular bodies similar to those of stealth fighters. Their wings began to rotate downwards as they slowly lowered to the ground. There were no insignias to be found anywhere on them, aside from a few Roman numerals.

Randy recognized them immediately, he'd spent enough time riding in such vehicles in the past to be more than familiar with them.

"It's the UGF!" he shouted to be heard over the whine of the engines from the landing aircraft, the wind blowing his hair.

"Of course! Naturally the cavalry arrives just when the battle is over!" Allison observed wryly.

A wide ramp lowered from the back of the closest jet and a group of men and women in grey uniforms riding on small, hovering vehicles that looked like flying jet skis came roaring out of the plane. Riding in their lead was a striking woman with dark brown skin and long, honey blonde hair tied back into a ponytail that whipped in the wind behind her. She wore a black beret and her vehicle sported a large, blank grey flag on its back. Within seconds she had pulled up to where Randy and Matt stood.

"Hello, Anne," Matt said.

"Matt. Randy. I got your message, so where are all the monsters?"

"Sister, you're *really* late to the party!" was all Matt could say.

CHAPTER 20:

ENTER THE GOOCH

Matt and Randy had quickly filled Anne in on what had been going on. The UGF's first order of business had been to search the entire area in case any of Locke's werewolves had tried to sneak away to try and continue to pursue their violent lifestyles. The other remaining werewolves amongst his former followers were being detained by armed guards in a temporary camp that the UGF hastily set up on the farm. Those werewolves who owed their powers to magical wolf belts had been ordered to remove them, the belts would be sent off to Elysium where they would be studied and eventually destroyed by the magic users of the Temple of the Old Gods.

Randy had called Wendy and asked her to bring The Gooch to Sherwood Farm. It was hoped that he could find a way to cure all the werewolves that owed their condition to being bitten, or were the descendants of someone who had been. He was expected to arrive the next day.

The ABC was on its way in full force to clean up the mess at the church. They would also be creating new identities for the vampires and werewolves that had been on each side of the conflict and placing them into something akin to the witness protection program. As Blake had promised, the werewolves and former vampires, regardless of their past affiliation, were to be granted amnesty.

Matt was uneasy about the idea that the Guilds were going to give Locke's remaining people amnesty, but Prospero insisted upon it, since it was what Blake had promised them. For him, it was a matter of honor and maintaining Blake's legacy. What bothered Matt was the fact that these characters had probably personally killed hundreds or maybe even *thousands* of people in the decades and centuries that they'd spent as vampires or werewolves. How many times could you do such a thing before it becomes second nature to you? Before you acquire a strong taste for it? His fear was that these people had developed a psychological *need* for such violence, like an addiction. They might not literally be monsters any longer, but they might wind up being serial killers once they were set loose upon the public.

Prospero, however, maintained that most of their darkest desires had stemmed from the blood of the Dark Mother that had been inside of them, or in the case of the werewolves, the fiercer aspects of the Great Wolf Spirit which they had given in to. He believed that once free of these influences, they could become peaceful, productive citizens. Matt prayed that he was correct, but feared that he was being overly optimistic. He recommended that the ABC keep a close watch over them going forwards all the same.

Martin Lane had decided that he was going to move in with the Sherwoods again, at least long enough to help them repair all the damage that had been done to the manor during the night. Anne had ordered her troops to help dispose of the numerous bodies and body parts that still littered the house. They were all burned in a great bonfire that was built in one of the cow pastures. All of them that is, except for the bodies of Charles Brandon and Agent Brown, which were sent to a local funeral home.

Blake's body was cremated in an intimate ceremony held elsewhere on the farm. As they watched Blake's corpse burning upon its pyre, the old grandfather clock inside the manor struck midnight and Kevin found himself returning to his human form despite the presence of the full moon still hanging high above them.

"That is one *very* precise curse!" Allison whispered to him after checking her own wrist watch.

"Yeah, you're not kidding!" Kevin answered back, he'd always assumed that he'd have to stay in wolf form until the sun rose, not when it became the next day according to a clock. What would happen if he jumped on a plane and traveled to somewhere where it wasn't yet midnight? Would he change back into a wolf?

Magic sure was some weird shit.

Matt and Randy were going to spend the night at the manor, even though Matt still had a room booked for another night back at the hotel in Shadowbrook. Nobody felt like trying to drive all the way back there tonight, so the plan was to borrow Earl's car to return to the parking lot of Wonderland where Randy had left his car, then drive Kevin back home after The Gooch had a chance to try and cure him tomorrow.

The broken windows of the manor were swiftly boarded up by Anne's troops, and everyone tried to settle in and finally get some rest after such a long, exhausting, terrifying night. Matt called Naomi - roaming charges be damned! He needed to let her know that he and Randy were okay. When Wendy had heard that the UGF was being mobilized, she'd called Naomi to tell her the news, which had only served to make Naomi worry about her boys even more than she normally did. Matt had given Naomi the "Reader's Digest" version of events. Naomi had been astounded to learn that they had fought against Mortus Locke himself.

"It looks like I'm going to have to revise my history with some of this new information. It sounds like The Great Purge wasn't so great after all! I'd really love to talk to somebody who used to be on the inside to get their take on the events of The Great Purge and how Locke escaped from the Guilds to rebuild his organization. Do you think you could arrange for that Prospero guy to give me an interview?" she asked.

"Are you kidding me? That guy loves to do nothing *but* talk! Once you get him started you'll never be able to get him to shut up!" Matt laughed.

"That sounds perfect! Maybe we can have him over for dinner next week?" Naomi said. Listening to the stories of a being that was several hundred years old was pretty close to her idea of paradise.

"Okay, I'm game so long as you don't try to make him some haggis!"

"Aw c'mon, don't be such a spoilsport! I've always wanted to try that stuff! This is my big chance!" she teased him.

"Yuck, I think I'll pass."

"You know, some of the things that are in those hot dogs you're always eating are probably just as bad!" she pointed out, not untruthfully.

"Yeah, but as long as I try not to think about that, I can still enjoy it!"

"Well, maybe you can learn to do the same thing for haggis," she said reasonably.

"I really don't think so," Matt said firmly.

Naomi laughed. "I'm glad to see that the night's events haven't made you any less stubborn than usual. I guess you really *are* okay. I'm also happy that you found that boy." Privately, she prayed that this little victory would help him to put aside some of his guilt over the Hollins case, but she didn't bring it up.

"Yeah, well let's just hope that this goofy Gooch guy can get him back to normal, or I'm gonna have a whole lot of explaining to do to his folks."

"Wendy thinks very highly of him."

"Yeah, but Wendy also thinks that our dog is the reincarnation of the first guy I ever had to kill," he reminded her.

"And how do you know that he isn't?" Naomi countered.

Matt just grunted. "Good night, Dr. Spike. Kiss the kids for me and tell my little girl that I'll be back home tomorrow to thoroughly kick her ass in her own video games."

"Good night, Mr. Spike, I love you."

"I love you too," he said as he cut the connection, laid his cell phone down on the nightstand and turned out the light in the big, drafty bedroom he'd been given.

As soon as she saw the light go out in Matt's bedroom, Allison crept across the dark hallway, trying not to make the floorboards creak too loudly as she stepped on them. As much as she was loving being truly alive again, she was also regretting the loss of her vampiric ability to see in the dark. It was odd to suddenly find herself stumbling around in the gloom after so many years of being able to see almost as well in total darkness as she did in the light.

Allison made her way down the hall to the room that had been given to Kevin. She made a face as the door squeaked loudly as she pushed it open far enough to poke her head inside.

Kevin had been lying in bed staring at the ceiling, he looked in the direction of the door as he heard the sound.

"Oh, it's just you," he said.

"Mind if I come in?" she asked.

"I would love it!" he beamed back at her.

"I was hoping you'd say that, kemosabe!" She smiled back at him as she tiptoed into the room, shutting the door behind her.

She jumped into the bed and snuggled up to him, he put an arm around her. They just stayed like that for a while, enjoying the feel of each other. It was nice for her to be able to be this close to him without also feeling ashamed of having the strong urge to bite him and suck the life from his body.

She twisted her head up and looked into his eyes.

"What's going to become of us now?" she wondered aloud.

"I don't know," he answered honestly. "Matt's taking me back home at some point. He thinks this wizard that's coming in tomorrow can cure me."

"I know. I hope that he can."

"And if he can't? Can you handle having a werewolf for a boyfriend?"

"Sure I can. I know a thing or two about what it's like to live with a curse, to be different, remember? I'd like to be there for you, to help you cope with all that."

She was quiet for a moment, then she asked, "Is that what you are, my boyfriend?"

"I'd like to be, if you'll have me. I've never felt the way that I do about you with anyone else before," he confessed.

"I feel the same way, and of course I'll have you! But what worries me is that Shadowbrook is kinda far away and neither one of us drives yet. I mean, I know how to, Charles taught me once. I just can't do it legally yet."

"Are you online? We could always chat online or on the phone until we're able to see each other again in person. We'll find a way to make it work."

"Yeah, I'm online. I can give you my handle later on. I chat with all kinds of people," she told him.

He raised an eyebrow. "All kinds of people, huh? Should I be jealous?"

"Please! Don't go monstering out and ripping anyone's head off! I get a little lonely cooped up in here all by myself, okay? That's all. It's nothing you need to be worried about."

He chuckled. "Relax, I was just kidding."

"In the meantime, we have the rest of tonight together. Let's not waste it." She smiled at him mischievously as she slid her hand down into his sweatpants and found the hard, firm bulge inside.

If Allison seemed a little *hungry* at this moment, please try to keep in mind that she'd only had a handful of what could rather generously be called intimate encounters in her entire life, and all of these, oddly enough, happened long before Kevin had even been born. She'd spent many of the intervening years daydreaming about such things and fretting that she'd never get to really experience them. Plus she was biologically and mentally still very much a teenager with an overabundance of hormones and all of that. Under the circumstances we can't judge her too harshly, can we?

Especially considering that up until fairly recently, Kevin was just as much of a horn dog as she was in that moment.

"Whoa, slow down. Let's take things slow. Things didn't work out so well the last time I jumped into this sort of thing so quickly," Kevin said, not quite believing his own words. What was wrong with him? This girl was practically throwing herself at him, a girl who he liked very, very much, maybe even loved, and here he was discouraging her!

"OMIGOD! I forgot all about that! How could I? I'm so sorry," Allison said, feeling terrible as she quickly retracted her hand from his pants, instead placing it on his chest. The last time Kevin had been intimate with anyone, his partner had ended up dead. It was only natural that he might feel more than a little strange about the idea now. The poor guy was obviously still quite traumatized by everything he'd been through.

"I *wish* I could forget about it. It's not that I don't want to be with you, I really, *really* want to! Especially with you! With her, it was just kind of a...booty call, y'know? It was just for fun. But with you...I'd like to believe that it would be different, that it would really mean something special. I want it to be special. But I'm just gonna need a little more time I guess, before I...stop associating this sort of thing with what happened to Sylvia."

He paused and frowned, looking up into the dark depths of the room for answers, but there were none to be found within its inky recesses.

"It's crazy, I know. Maybe I'm a little crazy now. I mean now that I *know* that I wasn't really responsible for what happened to her, at least not directly, I should be able to move on, shouldn't I? But I guess I got so *used* to believing that I was responsible, blaming myself, *hating* myself because of what happened to her, that it's hard for me to really truly accept that idea. To accept the idea that I didn't murder her, that I deserve any kind of happiness, or that I can ever bring anyone else anything other than death. It's still just all too new, too raw. I can't help but think that if I do anything too sexual with someone that I'm going to change into some kind of a raging, uncontrollable monster and hurt someone. And I don't *ever* want to hurt someone like that, especially you. I couldn't bear it."

He was quiet again for a moment.

"It's so *stupid* isn't it? I know that I can control the wolf inside now. I did it plenty of times tonight already, but the fear is still there.

I'm so stupid! I'm so messed up from all of this! I'm sorry! Are you really sure that you want to be with a basket case like me?"

"Give yourself a break! I'm fine with taking things slow and just seeing where it all takes us. Really, I am. Honestly, even though I'm *technically* the older woman in this equation, I'm probably less experienced than you are when it comes to this kind of thing. I've spent most of that time cooped up in this place, just reading about life instead of really living it. I'm perfectly okay with waiting for you, no matter how long it might take for you to work out whatever issues you may have now. No pressure, okay?"

No matter how long it takes? I wonder if she really means it? he thought.

"Thanks for being so understanding."

"It's what good girlfriends do, or so I've heard." She grinned at him with those wonderful, sparkling eyes and he wanted to believe in her sincerity. He knew that he could trust her, but could he trust himself not to screw this up?

They spent the rest of that night in each other's arms, just cuddling and enjoying the warmth of one another's bodies until they drifted off into a peaceful sleep.

The next morning, everyone in the manor who wasn't already up was rudely awakened by the blaring peal of a fire alarm. The smell of something burning caused Matt to jump to his feet and burst out of his room. He bumped into Randy in the hallway.

"Something's on fire!" Randy said rather unnecessarily.

"Are we under attack again?" Matt wondered, as he summoned the *Vermilion Avenger* from his bedroom to hover beside him just in case.

Allison and Kevin came out of Kevin's room together, both looking quite alarmed. Matt noticed them coming out of the same room together and sighed. He just hoped that they'd used some kind of protection last night.

"What's going on?" Allison demanded.

"We don't know yet. It smells like it's coming from downstairs. Get behind us. We're about to go check it out!" Matt ordered.

Randy erected a magical shield in front of them which ran the width of the hallway and came up to his chin, it advanced with him as he led the way, creeping down the corridor cautiously.

Mary also came running out of her room, armed with her full complement of weapons, her shield and the two swords that were still stained with the blood of Kilroy and countless other monsters. She fell in line behind Kevin and Allison wordlessly.

Earl was the last one to emerge, his gun drawn.

"Mind if I join you?" he asked.

"The more the merrier, pal!" Matt replied.

To say that everyone was still a bit on edge after last night would be something of an understatement.

As they made their way down the steps, they followed the smoke into the kitchen. The sight that greeted them was decidedly non-threatening: Prospero, who was now in his human form as a ruddy-faced, red-bearded man in his fifties, was standing on a chair stabbing a finger at a button on a smoke detector above him. Eventually, he lost patience with this and just pulled the battery out of the device, finally ending the irritating sound that had awakened the whole house. Elizabeth was opening up a window over the kitchen sink. On the stove, they could see a frying pan filled with long, blackened strips of bacon, and on the counter beside it, several plates were stacked up with sausages and eggs. William, Martin and Anne Moore (whose military discipline dictated that she was always an early riser) sat at the kitchen table watching the entire scene unfold with some bemusement.

Prospero caught sight of the newcomers first as he climbed down off of the chair. "Do you people normally bring so many weapons to breakfast?"

Randy made the shield disappear with a wave of his hand, and everyone behind him visibly relaxed and set aside whatever weapons they were carrying. In the case of Matt, this translated into settling the *Vermillion Avenger* down into one corner of the room.

Elizabeth blushed in embarrassment as they entered the kitchen. "I wanted to make a nice, big breakfast for you all, but I'm afraid it's been centuries since I last prepared any human food. I should've paid more attention when Charles did it. However, aside from this disaster with the bacon, I do believe that the rest of the meal is...edible, if you'd care to take a seat?"

"I'm sure that your cooking will be wonderful, my love. Even if some of it is a little on the well done side," William said approvingly.

"I can't wait to see how well you do, Husband, when it's your turn to cook," Elizabeth told him.

"My turn?" he gulped.

"Sure, this isn't the 18th Century anymore! You can't expect me to do *all* the cooking, can you?" she replied.

"I suppose I *could* take up cooking as a hobby, mind you, only as a hobby! Yes, the culinary arts can be a suitable distraction for a retiring country gentleman such as myself," William replied.

Matt sat down next to Prospero and looked at him. "Prospero, what are your feelings about haggis?"

Prospero made a face. "I can't stand the stuff. I never touch it!"

"Oh, thank God for that!" Matt said, clearly relieved.

"Do you just automatically assume that every Scotsman you meet is some kind of haggis-eating, penny pinchin' machine? What kind of racist bullshit is that?"

The color drained from Matt's face. "I'm sorry. I'm not trying to offend you, I'm actually trying to invite you to dinner at my house."

Prospero laughed. "Oh lad! You should've seen the look on your face! I'm just pulling your leg! I'd be honored to come over for dinner some time."

"He's too easy, isn't he? Always so damned serious!" Randy added with a smile.

"Hardy har, har!" Matt said sarcastically at the idea of being the object of their amusement.

"I thought you always stayed in your wolf form so you wouldn't age? I didn't expect to see you looking so, so...human, this morning," Kevin told Prospero.

"Aye, well if this new wizard that's coming can really cure us of being werewolves, then I'll be a human again later on today anyhow. It doesn't seem as if the Guilds are leaving us much choice in the matter," he said pointedly, looking at Anne.

"Orders from the very top: werewolves are too inherently dangerous to remain as werewolves. Your cooperation with being cured is the price for your freedom," she said unapologetically and matter of factly.

"Precisely, so there's no sense in postponing the inevitable, is there? Besides, I'm ready to go back to aging normally anyway. I'm ready to face death again; after seeing how bravely Blake embraced it, I'm suddenly not so scared of it anymore."

Martin raised a glass of orange juice. "Here, here! To mortality!"

The others at the table raised their glasses as well and they all toasted, echoing the words, "To mortality!"

"The grim reaper's going to get all of our asses in the end, and I wouldn't have it any other way!" Martin said as he took another gulp of OJ.

The barely edible breakfast was eventually interrupted by shouts of excitement from outside. Several of the people at the table rushed to the windows to see what was going on. Kevin was astounded as a large, round area of the pasture flattened out as if something heavy was sitting on it. In the next instant, where there had been nothing but this flattened area of grass there was suddenly a silver, disc-shaped craft - a classic flying saucer.

"First werewolves, then vampires, then ghosts, then wizards, and now UFOs! Sure, why not?" Kevin shook his head in wonderment.

"Welcome to my world, kid!" Matt said. He recognized the ship, of course. It was the *Silver Bullet*, the flying saucer that belonged to Bronson McDowell. It was the only one of its kind in the world. It wasn't from an alien planet, but from an alternate reality. For years, Bronson's scientists had been trying to learn how it worked so they could mass produce them, but the secret continued to elude them.

"I didn't expect them to show up in that," Randy said.

"My Uncle Bronson feels terrible about the fact that our forces arrived too late to assist you in your fight last night, despite the fact that it was the fastest deployment of UGF troops in our history. So he took it upon himself to personally get Wendy and The Gooch here as quickly as possible. It's his way of making up for it. Of course, there is nothing on Earth faster than the *Silver Bullet*," Anne informed them in her typically flat and precise way. Bronson McDowell was not actually her uncle, he was her godfather and not a real blood relation at all, but she had called him "Uncle Bronson" since she'd been a little girl, although these days she only did so in front of friends.

"Director McDowell is here himself?" Earl said in disbelief. He'd only met his Commander in Chief once before, and the idea of seeing him again filled him with butterflies.

"He's walking down the ramp right now," Matt confirmed, as he waved at him through the window.

Bronson waved back and moved towards the little cobblestone path that led up to the back porch. He was closely followed by Wendy Sommardahl, Pontifex Maximus of the Temple of the Old Gods; a tall, willowy, pale woman with flowing, flame red hair that was always a little longer every time Matt saw her. Behind her was a man that Matt had never seen before. He wore a multicolored serape and the sort of large, conical hat favored by Asian rice paddy farmers. He carried an extremely large skateboard under one arm, which he now placed down in front of him and used to skate down the ramp of the flying saucer. As he reached the bottom of the ramp, he kicked at one end of the board and leapt off of it, catching it and tucking it back under his arm as he landed on the ground.

That must be The Gooch, Matt thought, *Every bit as eccentric as I expected! Let's hope that he knows his shit!*

Soon, Bronson was walking into the kitchen through the back door. He was a tall, thickly built black man with short-cropped, greying hair, smartly dressed in an impeccably tailored tweed suit. He appeared to be somewhere in his sixties.

"Well Matt, it seems that you've done it again, old boy! You just can't keep yourself out of trouble these days can you?" He smiled as he took a puff from his pipe.

"I didn't think I'd see you here today, Boss. Must be a slow day at the office," Matt smiled back.

"Slow day at the office? It won't be once I get back! Do you realize all the paperwork this little fiasco will have generated before it's all over? All the forms I'm going to have to sign? It's a bureaucratic nightmare!" Bronson said testily. His expression softened somewhat as he caught sight of Anne and crossed the room to kiss her on the cheek.

"Good to see you again, my dear."

"Likewise, Sir," Anne said, allowing herself a slight smile, perhaps a little embarrassed by her uncle's uncharacteristic breach of protocol in front of so many strangers, although she herself had breached it earlier by calling him uncle. The older Bronson got, the less it seemed that he cared about such things. At one time such an open show of affection would've been unthinkable for him. She attributed it all to the influence of his new wife, Denesha, who had mellowed him out considerably in the past few years. She had mixed feelings about it all. On the one hand, she was more comfortable with her uncle being more stiff, stilted and formal, as she herself was rather stiff, stilted and formal. On the other hand, she could tell that he was a far happier person than he had seemed in the past and she wanted him to be happy.

"I do apologize though, for the fact that you had to go it alone last night. I gather that you had something of a rough time of it all. Had I fully understood exactly how dire the situation was, I would've flown in as many troops as I could pack into the *Silver Bullet* myself! Still, all's well that ends well, eh? Defeating Mortus Locke - all by yourselves! That's quite the achievement! Good show, all of you! Splendid work!"

Wendy now made her way into the kitchen. "Has he been boring you all yet by complaining that he's been reduced to 'nothing but a bloody taxi driver!' By all of this? That's all we heard on the way over here!" she said, momentarily mimicking Bronson's deep British accent.

"Hey there, Granola!" Matt said to her, "Granola" being his nickname for her on account of her being such a hippy.

"Hey yourself, Beanpole!" she replied, "Beanpole" being her nickname for him on account of him being so tall and skinny, although he was hardly as skinny as he'd been when she first met him.

"Mistress," Randy said as he bowed slightly to his mentor and leader as a sign of respect.

"Apprentice," she answered with a fond smile. They still greeted each other like this, despite the fact that she had finished teaching Randy all that she intended to teach him years ago. They would always be Master and Apprentice though, no matter how much time passed between them.

She gave them both a big hug. As she pulled away she looked at the new grey hairs in Randy's beard and frowned. "It looks like you've been dabbling in things that you shouldn't be."

He opened his mouth to say something but she shushed him with one finger to his lips. "We'll talk later."

Next, The Gooch walked into the kitchen. He was of medium height with longish black hair and seemed to be in his early thirties. He appeared to be at least part Asian, and part something else. Wendy introduced him and he smiled back at everyone a little shyly.

"*That's* the guy who's gonna cure you?" Allison whispered to Kevin dubiously. He shrugged. Something about The Gooch's unassuming, extremely laid back manner didn't instantly inspire much confidence in them.

"I'm going to need to see one of these wolf belts," he said, apparently eager to get down to business.

"Of course. We're keeping them under guard and locked in a safe on one of our transport jets. I'll bring you there right away," Anne said as she excused herself and led him back out of the house.

Bronson caught sight of Earl. "Ah, Agent Grey is it?" he asked superfluously. He knew perfectly well that it was, he prided himself on being familiar with the names and backgrounds of all of his agents. "Good show last night! Bloody good work! A pity about your partner, Agent Brown. He was a good man. Don't worry, though. We'll see to it that his family is well provided for."

"Thank you, Director."

"I do believe that you are overdue for a promotion, Agent Grey! How would you like to run the Hartford field office?" Bronson asked.

"I'm honored Sir, really I am, but I'm afraid that I'm going to have to decline the offer," Earl said, somewhat hesitantly.

"Decline the offer? Are you certain? It's quite the step up!" Bronson said incredulously. Most people in Grey's position would jump at this opportunity, he simply couldn't understand what was driving the man to turn it down.

"In fact, I'd like to take an early retirement from the ABC altogether, Sir," he announced.

"Hmm. I think I understand. Last night's events must've rattled your nerves quite a bit. There's no shame in it. Happens to the best of us. I'll have everything all taken care of for your retirement."

"That's not quite it, Sir. I've just gotten a better offer, that's all," Earl said, looking over at Matt tellingly. Earl wasn't getting any younger and he was thinking of settling down and starting a family of his own before it got too late. He'd seen how his partner had to keep so many secrets from his wife because of the nature of their job, and had known that wasn't for him. He was hoping that if he worked for Matt, he'd be able to be a bit more open about what he did for a living with any future romantic partners. He was done with keeping other people's secrets and pursuing other people's obsessions. It was time to start living his own life.

"So, now you're stealing my best men away from me, is that it, Matt?" Bronson complained.

Matt smiled his lopsided grin and shrugged innocently. "Hey, I just recognize good talent when I see it. Welcome aboard, Earl." He shook Earl's hand as he said it.

"You're making a grave mistake, Grey! You *do* realize that you're going to have to move to New Jersey of all places now, don't you?" Bronson chided him.

"That's okay. I grew up in Newark and I still have some family there. New Jersey isn't all that different from Connecticut. I've been thinking of moving back anyway."

"You *are* a brave man, Grey! I'm sorry to lose you. Good luck in your new career," Bronson said earnestly and shook his hand as well.

While this exchange was going on, Randy steered Wendy over to where Prospero sat. "Wendy, I'd like you to meet the wizard I told you about. This is Prospero. Prospero, this is my friend and mentor, Wendy Sommardahl. She's the Pontifex Maximus, the supreme leader of the Temple of the Old Gods."

"Charmed, M'Lady," Prospero replied.

Wendy placed her hands on her hips and tried her best to look at him sternly, which was difficult for her to do since she was normally such a light-hearted, forgiving person.

"What are we going to do with you? Unauthorized use of High Magic is a gravely serious offense. In the past we've elevated entire religions to prominence in order to suppress it, organized massive witch hunts just to crush it. The secrets which you've been privy to are especially troubling. The spell books of someone like Mortus Locke must be filled with the darkest, most forbidden kinds of enchantments." She paused for dramatic effect. Prospero was starting to look quite worried by her words. *Good. Let him sweat a little*, she thought.

"However, in light of your service helping to defeat Mortus Locke, our most shameful rogue wizard, we are prepared to be lenient. We will see to it that you are formally instructed in the proper and ethical use of magic as a member of the Temple of the Old Gods, in exchange for whatever spell books and journals that you managed to steal from Mortus Locke." She couldn't help but smile a little as she said the last part.

Prospero looked thoughtful for a moment, then smiled to himself. "You've got a deal, M'Lady, if only because it means that this impudent fellow here won't be able to tease me about not being a proper wizard any longer! I'll go fetch the books from my room." He pushed back his chair and rose from the table.

As she watched him leave the room, Wendy turned to Randy. "Well, that was easier than I thought it would be! We're going to have to go through those books together, to see if there's anything inside of them that might help The Gooch figure out how to break this werewolf curse."

Randy nodded his understanding.

"So, you tried to defeat Mortus Locke by doing a Soul Blast spell, huh?" Wendy said, her tone dripping with disapproval.

"There's no point in trying to hide the truth from you, is there?" Randy said in resignation.

"It's as plain as the beard on your face - and in your aura! What were you thinking? You could've killed yourself! You're lucky you got away with only a few grey hairs!"

"I was thinking that I had to destroy the most evil wizard we've ever produced before he escaped and caused a few more centuries of misery and death," Randy said coolly.

"How did you even learn that spell? You know that it's forbidden!"

"I saw one of my ancestors use it during The Great Magic War when I was exploring their memories," he confessed. Reliving the experiences of their ancestors was an ability that magic users could tap into if necessary.

Wendy studied her apprentice for some time. She had great plans for Randy, she always had. She believed that he had a potential that he had yet to unlock, a special destiny. She couldn't stand the idea of him throwing his life away before he had a chance to reach that potential, he was too valuable - to her and possibly to the entire world.

"Be careful, that's how Mortus Locke began, you know? Using his ancestors' memories to recreate the lost knowledge of the past. Much of that knowledge wasn't 'lost' so much as it was deliberately buried because it was too dangerous. Just like how we're going to have to destroy these wolf belts and Prospero's books when we're done with them," she told him.

He smiled at her. "Don't worry, I'm not about to turn to the dark side or anything!"

There was a time when Wendy wouldn't have gotten that reference, as she had lived a somewhat sheltered life in some ways, but one of the first things Randy had done after he met her was insist on her watching Star Wars.

"That's not what I'm worried about. I'm worried about losing you. Think about your family, think about Matt and Naomi and Penny, and your band mates. Think about *me*. None of us could stand to lose you. I just don't want you throwing your life away like that, promise me that you won't."

"I'm not sure I can do that, honestly. Not if it's the only way I can see to save my friends." He looked her straight in the eye as he said it.

Why does he have to be so damned selfless? she thought, then she realized that she knew exactly why he was the way that he was, and that there was no way around it. He was who he was.

"Even if I made it an order?"

"All I can say is that I'll try to comply, but I can't guarantee that I always will. It depends on the situation, and who knows what the future holds?"

"Hmm. Well, thanks for being honest about it at least," she said, feeling somewhat defeated by the entire exchange.

The Gooch and Anne returned to the room, the Gooch carrying a wolf belt in one hand. With perfect timing, Prospero returned to the kitchen as well, clutching a few ancient-looking volumes that were stacked atop one another.

"Here's the books you asked for, M'Lady."

"Please, just call me Wendy," she told him, taking the books from him. "Is there somewhere more private where we can go over the contents of these volumes?" she asked.

Elizabeth had been trying to clear up the kitchen with a little help from William and Mary and overheard her question. She turned to her.

"There's a dining room right next to this room with a big old table that you can spread out all these books on. I'll show you the way."

The Gooch spied the completely charred strips of bacon that were still sitting in the frying pan and picked one up and bit into it. It crunched loudly and shattered into several hard pieces. He chewed it thoughtfully and grinned. "Delicious!" he proclaimed.

Anne rolled her eyes behind him.

Elizabeth smiled. "It's nice to see that *someone* appreciates my efforts! Feel free to have the rest of them, we were just going to throw it all out anyway."

"Don't mind if I do!" he said happily, picking up the entire frying pan and carrying it with him as she led Wendy, Randy, Prospero and Anne (who felt as though someone had to stand guard over the wolf pelt at all times) into the dining room.

Kevin and Allison watched them leave the room with great trepidation. "It looks like I'm going to be stuck with this curse forever!" he complained.

"Chin up, young man! This Gooch might be a bit of an oddball, but I understand that he's the best at what he does. We'll soon have you sorted," Bronson told him.

Kevin wished he shared his confidence, but he simply didn't.

The next several hours passed uneventfully as the magic users discussed how to break the curse in the dining room. Kevin had gone off to help Allison with her chores around the farm. At one point Matt walked into the dining room to check on their progress. He was joined by William, who was drawn to the same area by a rather peculiar aroma that he detected coming from the room.

When they entered the dining room, they saw The Gooch smoking a blunt and passing it to Wendy, who took a few puffs before passing it back to him. The various grimoires and journals were spread open on the table. Anne stood at attention nearby, looking visibly displeased.

"Hey gang, how's it going?" Matt asked.

"We might be getting closer to a solution - of sorts," The Gooch said enigmatically.

"Excuse me, but what is that you're smoking?" William demanded.

"Weed. You want a puff?" The Gooch said, taking the blunt out of his mouth and offering it to William.

"Weed? You mean that's a marijuana cigarette?" William asked, somewhat horrified.

"Yeah, duh," The Gooch replied.

"Sir, may I remind you that you are a guest in my home? I do not approve of such things under my roof. Kindly either extinguish that thing or take it outside, there are children in this house!"

"Whoa. Sorry. Mellow out man, it just helps me think, that's all. No harm no foul. I'll finish this off outside," The Gooch said as he got up.

"Yes, see that you do," William ordered.

"Wait for me!" Wendy said as she followed him from the room. Randy and Prospero remained at the table flipping through the books.

A minute later, Matt found himself outside as well. He located Wendy and The Gooch leaning up against the side of the shed where they'd first battled Kilroy the night before. It hadn't collapsed as they'd feared that it would, probably because Anne had ordered her troops to reinforce the sides of the building with several long beams of wood that were helping to prop it up, which they had gotten from someplace on the farm. Matt sauntered up to Wendy.

"Let me have a drag off that thing!" he said to her.

"Seriously?" She raised an eyebrow at him questioningly.

"Yes," he affirmed. She passed it over to him and he took a long drag off it before he went into a fit of coughing and passed it back.

"I never thought I'd see the day that I'd smoke with you, Matthew. You're usually so straight-laced," she said. Indeed, while she usually shared a few puffs with Naomi when she came to visit them, Matt had always abstained from such things in the past. He said that he didn't like to do anything that he felt might dull or otherwise alter his perceptions.

"Am I really such a stick in the mud? I used to smoke all the time back when we first met, but it was strictly nicotine. Nowadays my only vices are coffee and false modesty." She made him sound like he was such a square, but he wasn't sure that he liked to think of himself that way. Surely he could still hang with cool kids if he really wanted too?

"The fact that you're such an old-fashioned stick in the mud has always been precisely what I've appreciated the most about you," she told him.

"Yeah, well maybe I'm mellowing out in my old age? After the kind of night I've just had, I figured fuck it! I'll have one!"

"Geez Matt, don't talk like that! I'm older than you are! I wish I was still in my thirties like you."

"Please! Nobody can tell that you're in your forties now. The only thing that's different about you is that your hair is a little longer."

"You're too kind, sir. Don't tell me you're starting to feel the effects of your age? Is there a sports car in your future? You're too young for a midlife crisis in my opinion."

Matt laughed. "Well, nothing makes you realize what an out of touch old fart you are quite like spending a few days with a bunch of teenagers! They're all good kids though, Kevin and Allison sort of remind me of how me and Naomi were as kids. I'm gonna miss being around them when this is all over."

Wendy looked at her friend intensely for a few moments. "How are you, Matt? Really? I know you haven't been...quite yourself since that awful case with the missing girl a few years back. I've seen it in your aura. Your aura *seems* a little better now, closer to what it used to be, but I'm still detecting a bit too much sadness in there for my taste. Have you ever thought about getting some help? I know a really good therapist, she's also one of our best witches actually."

If anyone other than possibly Naomi or Randy had asked him something like this, or suggested such a thing to him he would've probably gotten pretty annoyed with them and shut down immediately. But even though he thought that she was pretty "out there" sometimes, Wendy was one of the few people whom he trusted implicitly and had always found it easy to confide in her. She had a way of cutting through all of his defenses and seeing through his bullshit that he found refreshing.

Also, The Gooch's powerful blend was starting to kick in.

"I *am* starting to feel a little better about the whole thing. That case has really haunted me, y'know? I don't know quite what it is that's helping me cope with it better. Maybe it's the fact that I was able to find this kid Kevin and it looks like I'll be able to get him home safely. I know that doesn't make up for what happened to Melissa Hollins, but in a way it *does* help. Maybe it's restoring my confidence? I don't know. I guess mainly what it might be is that I've seen how he's been blaming himself for all kinds of things that aren't really his fault. Like, he really believed that he'd killed a girl that he was with the first time he changed into a werewolf. Even though he knows that's not what really happened, I can tell that he's still blaming himself, asking himself what he could've done differently. It made me realize that I've been doing the same thing to myself, for *years*. Sure, maybe things would've turned out better if I'd made a few different decisions when I was working the Hollins case - and maybe they wouldn't have. Who can really tell for sure? Maybe things would've turned out even worse? Things are what they are. Torturing myself over them doesn't help anyone. The best we can do is try to learn from our mistakes and move forwards."

Wendy placed a reassuring hand on Matt's arm.

"I'm glad to hear it. I think you're getting closer to putting that whole thing behind you." She dug around in the little beaded purse that she always carried with her and produced a business card that she handed to him.

"Here's the number of that therapist I mentioned. For when you're ready. I think Kevin might need to talk to her too. She'll teleport to wherever she's needed and her rates are *very* reasonable."

Matt took the card and tucked it into his wallet. As he did so, he saw a picture of his family that he kept inside and it reminded him of something.

"I can't believe how big Celine is getting! I saw those new pictures of her you posted on your MySpace page," he commented. Celine was Wendy's daughter.

"Yes she is, isn't she? The same thing is true of your Autumn. We really need to get those two together more often, they get along so well. I think they'll be great friends someday. It's a shame that we usually only see you guys twice a year at your Halloween and New Year's parties."

"I know, but Elysium is so far away and it doesn't look like you'll be giving up your gig as Pontifex Maximus any time soon," Matt replied.

"I'm not. There's still so much work to be done. I *have* been thinking about getting a vacation house though. Maybe something closer to your neck of the woods, but outside of the magical null zone that the Orb generates, of course. That way, we can all hang out together more often," she revealed.

"Shit! All of the sudden everyone wants to move to Jersey! Who would've thunk it?" Matt laughed. "That does sound nice though."

"That's it!" The Gooch, who had been silently finishing off the blunt, suddenly exclaimed.

He looked at Matt and Wendy with a seriousness that Matt hadn't seen in him before.

"What's it?" Matt asked.

"I must commune with the Great Wolf Spirit," he announced, then he turned and marched away from them. They looked on as he strode to the top of a nearby hill and sat down on it, crossing his legs.

Matt and Wendy looked at each other and shrugged.

A half an hour later, The Gooch came down from the hill. He asked Anne to gather all the werewolves that still carried the curse within them to assemble in the dining room.

Matt, Allison and Mary were also present, as were Randy and Prospero.

"I cannot completely cure any of you," The Gooch told them. A series of groans were heard from around the room. He held up a hand. "However, I believe that I *can* mitigate the effects of the curse to the point where you will be able to live a normal life." The people around the room suddenly looked more hopeful.

"I have spoken with the Great Wolf Spirit, the God that you werewolves get your powers from. She regards you all as Her children, and Her conduit to this world. As such, She is unwilling to give you up completely. However, if I perform a certain ritual which has been revealed to me, She will relinquish, to a certain extent, the intensity of Her hold over you."

"What does that even mean? Could you be a bit more specific?" Kevin asked irritably.

The Gooch sighed. "Yes, once this ritual has been performed, none of you will be able to literally transform into wolves. But you will still retain some of your werewolf characteristics: you will continue to have somewhat heightened senses, reflexes, strength, toughness and regenerative capabilities compared to that of regular humans."

"All the benefits and none of the drawbacks?" Prospero commented, "Sounds too good to be true, laddie!"

"It is. You didn't allow me to finish. You will still find yourselves getting progressively more irritable and irrational in your thinking the closer that you get to the night of the full moon, which will be the apex of such feelings. After the full moon, these symptoms will gradually decline for a time, until they begin to build up again as you approach the next full moon."

"In other words, you're going to turn us into a bunch of lunatics!" Kevin complained.

"In a manner of speaking, yes. Although it really won't be *that* bad. You won't be crazy, just cranky. I suggest that you all start smoking a little weed to chill yourselves out as you get closer to the night of the full moon."

"You *would* recommend that!" Anne snorted derisively. She and several of her troops were also present to keep an eye on the couple of werewolves there that had been in Locke's army and were less than enthusiastic about being cured.

"Of course I would! It's all natural, baby!" He smiled at her, then his expression turned grave again. "There's more. The Great Wolf Spirit will loosen Her paw...er I mean grip, upon you, but not on your children. If any of you should have kids, there is a good chance that they will inherit the full version of the curse, complete with the ability to transform into a werewolf."

Kevin's expression darkened. He was only fifteen and in no particular rush to have any kids, but he'd always assumed that he *might* someday. He wasn't particularly happy about the idea of having the option taken away from him like this. He didn't know what Allison's thoughts on the idea of having children were, or if they'd ever even make it that far as a couple, but he hoped that the fact that it looked like having kids with him would be a *very* bad idea wouldn't drive her away from him. She seemed to sense his unease and squeezed his hand more tightly as if to say that it didn't matter.

"Now, shall we begin?" The Gooch asked, although it was really not a question.

CHAPTER 21:

PARTING IS SUCH SWEET SORROW

The ritual only took about fifteen minutes to perform all told, although The Gooch had needed Wendy and Randy's assistance to carry it out. I won't bore you with the details. All I will say is the whole affair left everyone who wasn't just watching it feeling extremely drained afterwards, as if something had been taken from them, because in fact, it had been.

The ABC had arrived and begun the tedious task of "processing" the former vampires and werewolves that were staying in the camp elsewhere on the property. They would assess their threat level and create new identities for them accordingly.

By noon, Wendy and The Gooch were saying their goodbyes and walking back up the ramp of the *Silver Bullet,* where Bronson waited somewhat impatiently inside to ferry them all home.

Randy and Matt watched the flying saucer carrying their friends lift off into the air and engage its stealth mode, which made it completely invisible. The only evidence that it had ever been there was the round depression it left behind on the grass.

Matt looked over at Randy. "I think it's time we hit the road too, pal."

"I hear ya. Let's get out of here before Elizabeth insists on feeding us all some nameless terror for lunch," he quipped.

"Amen to that!" Matt agreed, shuddering at the memory of her cold, rubbery eggs and undercooked sausages.

They began to walk back towards the manor.

Randy suddenly stopped in his tracks, his eyes as wide as saucers.

"What is it?" Matt asked, noticing the change in his friend.

"We've got a visitor," Randy told him.

"Huh? What do you mean?"

"Sylvia's back, and she's got a message for Kevin," he explained.

"Where is she?"

"Right in front of me. If you link hands with me, you'll be able to see and hear her too," Randy offered.

Matt remembered what a stomach-turning mess she had looked like the last time he'd seen her. That, coupled with Elizabeth's "cooking" would grant him a one-way ticket to pukesville for sure. He'd already done enough vomiting lately, after they'd teleported for the second time last night.

"Uhh, that's okay, I'll just take your word for it. I guess I'd better go find the kid though, so she can deliver her message to him in person.

"Yes, she says that she'd like that," Randy confirmed.

Matt hurried inside. He found Kevin and Allison up in Allison's bedroom. Thankfully it looked like they were just innocently watching some old sitcoms on TV. Mary sat at the foot of bed on the floor.

"There you are! I've been looking all over for you!" Matt told him.

"It's not time to leave yet is it?" Kevin asked a bit sadly.

"Very nearly, but before we leave there's someone waiting for you outside who wants to talk to you."

"Who?"

"Sylvia." The name hit Kevin and Allison like a ton of bricks. They traded shocked looks with one another. "Randy has a way that you can see her and talk to her," Matt continued to explain, but Kevin was already sliding off of the bed. He wobbled unsteadily on his feet for a second, still feeling a bit weak after participating in the ritual that had "dulled" his curse.

Soon, Matt, Kevin, Allison and Mary were all in the backyard where Randy and the ghost patiently waited for them.

"Take my hand," Randy told Kevin. As he did, Kevin immediately saw Sylvia standing a few feet from him, her body looking as ripped and ruined as it had when he'd last seen it, a terrible sight which had permanently imprinted itself on his nightmares. He took a deep breath as if someone had just punched him in the gut. His eyes immediately began to well up.

"Sylvia! I'm so sorry..." he began.

She actually laughed. "For what? You didn't do this to me!"

"Didn't I? Kilroy was after me. If I hadn't been there at your house that night, then he would've never had a chance to hurt you."

"You had no way of knowing that at the time, and you were at my place because *I* wanted you there. Besides, who's to say that if it hadn't happened the way that it did that he still wouldn't have gotten me? Maybe caught me outside walking from my car to the house and decided he wanted a little snack? Maybe I was always fated to wind up this way?"

"That's nuts!"

"Is it? Who knows? Anyhow I just wanted to let you know that I don't blame you for any of it. In fact, after he killed me, I watched you turn into a wolf and fight him. I know you were trying to save me, and I wanted to thank you for that."

"Thank me!" He laughed bitterly. "I failed! It's because of me that you're dead!"

"No, it isn't ! Stop saying that! I've been watching you and I've been really worried about you. You've got to stop blaming yourself for it. You're a nice guy, Kevin Scott, and I wish I'd found you a bit sooner. It was a fun ride while it lasted. I want you to be happy. You deserve it." She looked at Allison. "And so does she."

Kevin was silent for a long time, and hung his head. Then he looked back up at her. He still didn't quite understand how it was that she wasn't angry with him like he was with himself. But he was grateful that she wasn't all the same. Very grateful. Maybe it was idiotic for him to blame himself when she didn't, but that was a new idea to him, and one that would take some getting used to. It was hard for him to just let go of all his pent up anger at himself so easily.

"Thanks," he finally said as he looked up at her and smiled.

"Remember our little motto? "No promises, no regrets." I don't regret any of it. I don't want you to either," the ghost told him.

"What's gonna happen to you now?"

"Randy here has convinced me that what was keeping me here was that I was so worried about you. And now...well, I'm not quite so worried anymore. I think you're gonna be okay, in time. So I guess I'm finally ready to move on." She now looked at Randy, who could see and hear all of this and he nodded.

He started chanting a few words and a portal opened up in the sky above them. Only Randy, Kevin and Sylvia could see it. She waved at the two of them, then she turned and floated up towards the portal; as she grew closer to it, her form was stretched out like rubber and she disappeared into it. Randy closed the portal with a gesture and a few more mysterious words and it disappeared from the sky. He released Kevin's hand.

"What happened? Is she still here?" Allison asked.

"She forgave me," Kevin said in a small voice.

"See, what did I tell you? Now maybe you can stop beating yourself up about it all the time?" Allison asked.

Kevin smiled and looked at her. "Yeah, maybe I can!"

"So where did she go? Not to Old McYahweh's ambrosia farm?" Matt asked Randy. "Old McYahweh's ambrosia farm" was what Matt and Naomi called Heaven. They'd actually both been there once and didn't think much of the place. It was presided over by a being that many people thought to be God (although he wasn't THE God) who sucked up all of the psychic energy, or ambrosia as it was called, created by the praise and prayers of the people who went there when they died. Sort of like how a vampire sucked blood from the living.

"That *is* where most people who die in this culture wind up," Randy said indifferently.

"And you just *let* her go there?" Matt clearly didn't approve.

"It's not up to me, it's up to them. They go where they think they're supposed to go, you know that. Besides, it's not so bad, she probably has lots of relatives waiting for her there," Randy explained.

Matt still wasn't sure he was buying it.

Mary had been watching all of this unfold with a mixture of various emotions. One question had been nagging at her this whole time though, and finally, she couldn't hold it in any longer.

"Why hasn't my father's ghost come around?" she asked Randy.

"Not everyone hangs around on Earth when they die. In fact, most people don't. I saw him pass directly into the other side as soon as he died. The fact that he didn't stick around here doesn't mean that he didn't care about you, it just means that he's at peace now. He's where he's supposed to be," he told her gently.

She looked pensive for a moment then she looked at him. "I just wanted you to know that I'm sorry."

"For what?" Randy asked.

"For what I said to you last night. It was way out of line. I want you to know that I don't really blame you for what happened to my Dad. Well, at least not anymore."

Randy grimaced. "Well maybe you should. Maybe you were right. I fucked up, big time."

"No way! I won't have any of that kind of talk. If you and Matt hadn't shown up when you did, Kilroy might've added Kevin and Allison to his list of victims. If you two hadn't stuck around, then Locke's army probably would've killed us all before Blake's people got here. Because of you and Matt, Allison, William, Elizabeth and Kevin all have a shot at having a normal life again. Please don't blame yourself for what happened. There's been enough hurt going on around here."

"Thanks. It means a lot. I'll try to keep that in mind. So what will become of you, now?"

"William and Elizabeth are gonna adopt me. I guess I'll be a Sherwood too, now. Allison will really be my sister. We'll finally all be a real family. I always felt like I was cursed too, to follow the family tradition of serving the Sherwoods. They never felt like they could trust anyone else to keep their secrets aside from the people in my family. Now, there's no secret left to protect and I'm free. They can hire anyone to be their servant. I should be happy. But I still feel so much pain. I don't suppose you've got any magic to make the pain go away?"

Randy shook his head slowly "I'm sorry. There's limits to what I can do. I *could* make you forget what happened to him, but you'd also lose all your happy memories of him too. You can't have one without the other. I know it's not fair, but that's the way it is."

Mary considered his words. "Yeah, that's totally not worth it. It's funny, I thought getting revenge on Kilroy would make me feel better, give me some closure, y'know? But it didn't. I mean, I don't regret killing him at all. Not in any way. He was a total monster and I'm glad that he's dead. I'm glad that he won't hurt anyone else ever again. I'm especially glad that *I'm* the one who got to do it. But in the end, none of that matters. I still hurt just as badly as I did before, and I'm still angry. So *angry*."

"Honestly, you're probably always going to be angry like that, at least on some level. But in time, I know that you'll learn how to stop holding onto it so tightly, with a little help from your friends." He looked over to where Allison stood with Kevin nearby.

"You want my advice? Hold onto your friends instead of the anger, never let them go. They'll always help you get through the tough times, trust me on that."

Mary thought that what Randy had to say to her was hardly the most inspirational speech she'd ever heard, indeed it was far from that, but she appreciated that he was being honest with her, that he was treating her like an adult instead of trying to sugarcoat her pain or how hard it would be to deal with going forward.

"I'm gonna go tell Earl to get his stuff together, you'd better do the same, Kevin. I think it's time we all moved on," Matt said.

A few minutes later, they were all standing in the front yard of the manor. The black Cadillac that Earl and Agent Brown had arrived in had been cleaned off by some of Anne's troops, but there was still a large burn mark on the hood where the bodies of Brown and the vampire that had killed him had been. Matt, Randy, Kevin and Earl stood beside the car.

Anne, William, Elizabeth, Martin, Prospero, Mary and Allison had all come out to say goodbye.

"Are you sure you won't stay for lunch? My skill in the kitchen improves with each new meal I prepare!" Elizabeth said.

"That's…very tempting, Mrs. Sherwood, but we still have to bring Kevin home, then get back to New Jersey - we've got a lot of driving ahead of us," Matt said. Well, it wasn't *completely* untrue.

"Thank you Matt, for all that you've done for myself and my family. We're eternally grateful. Give us your address and we'll see to it that you've got a lifetime supply of farm-fresh eggs!" William promised.

"Thanks, William. That's very generous of you," Matt said. Naomi loved to cook and bake, she'd be very happy to hear this news, although he wondered how fresh these eggs would still be by the time they reached them.

Martin insisted on shaking all of their hands.

Matt turned to Anne. "So how long do you intend to hang around here? This is supposed to be a farm, not a military base."

"That depends on how long it takes the ABC to process the er…former monsters. Until then, we're providing security," she replied.

"Well, thanks for coming. I know you tried to get here as fast as you could."

"Damn straight we did! Fastest rapid deployment on this scale in UGF history!" she reminded him with obvious pride.

"Prospero! Looking forward to having you over for dinner soon. The missus can't wait to meet you. You've got my number, call me when you're feeling hungry."

"Aye, it'll have to be soon. These people are eager to get me over to this Elysium place so I can begin my wizard training. I suppose these fools think they can teach this old dog some new tricks," he told Matt, then looked Randy in the eyes and smiled warmly.

"Thanks for putting in a good word for me with Miss Wendy, lad. I suppose you're not so bad after all."

"You're not so terrible yourself, for an old ham!" Randy countered.

Prospero looked at them all and said "'And whether we shall meet again I know not. Therefore our everlasting farewell take: Forever, and forever, farewell!

If we do meet again, why, we shall smile; If not, why, then this parting was well made.'"

Then he took a bow. Not for the first time, Randy wondered if he'd been an actor before he'd become a werewolf - he wondered if Prospero even knew anymore?

"You stay classy, Prospero," he said.

Mary was the next to say goodbye.

"Thanks for everything, everyone. Matt, I wanted you to know that I guess *Dirt Nap* really wasn't so bad - in places."

"Gee, thanks! What a ringing endorsement! I'll have them put that review on the front cover of the next edition!" he laughed.

"Next edition? You *are* an optimist, aren't you?" she said slyly. "Just make sure you get Romeo home safe and sound. I won't be able to save you from Allison's wrath if you let anything happen to him."

"Take care, Mary," he said, little imagining that not only would he see this girl again in the future, but that she would someday become his daughter-in-law. However, I'm getting ahead of myself, and that is a story for another time.

Of course, as befits young, seemingly star-crossed lovers, Allison was the last to say her goodbyes.

"I still can't believe that you were here and did all the things that you did. Thanks for the new lease on life that you've given me. I'm really gonna treasure those books that you signed for me. It's just a pity they've got so many blood stains on them now," she told Matt.

"I'll send you some pristine, mint condition copies with new inscriptions in them once I get back home - all hard covers too!" he promised her.

"That sounds awesome, but I'll still hang onto my nasty blood-stained originals too...ahh the *nostalgia* - they're irreplaceable!" she replied.

Yup, Allison was a little weird, Matt thought, but that's why he liked her. Didn't he prefer his friends to be a little on the strange side?

She walked over to Kevin now, promising herself that she wouldn't cry. That this wasn't an ending but only a beginning for them.

"You've got all my contact info?" she asked for the millionth time.

"Right here in my pocket," he affirmed.

"I've got something else for you," she said, and removed a ring from one of her fingers. She grabbed his hand and put it on. He examined it curiously. It was a ring with a skull insignia on it.

"Pretty cool, but I thought I was the one who was supposed to be giving out the rings around here."

"Don't get ahead of yourself, hotshot. You're the one who wanted to take things slow, remember? Do you really like it? I got it at one of those Halloween shops last week. It's so you'll always remember me."

"How could I ever forget you? Forget all of this? This has been the craziest weekend of my entire life!" he chuckled.

"Just promise me that you won't," she said as she leaned in to kiss him. They kissed for a very long time, and there was more than enough tongue involved to make everyone else feel thoroughly uncomfortable. They were all quite relieved when they finally broke apart, gasping for air, and Kevin whispered that he did indeed, promise not to forget her.

"Alright! Sheesh! Enough with all the mushy stuff! Let's hit the road already! Everyone in the car! Goodbye everyone! Goodbye Sherwood Farm!" Matt shouted and waved. They all waved back. With that, they all got into the car, Earl took the wheel with Matt riding shotgun. Randy and Kevin were in the backseat, and the *Vermilion Avenger* hovered obediently in the trunk.

Kevin watched Allison's face disappear from view through the back window as they pulled away, wondering when he'd ever get to see her again in person. Whenever that might be, it wouldn't be soon enough for him.

Or for her either.

"Hang onto that one, kid. She's a keeper!" Matt said as he watched Kevin's crestfallen expression in the rear view mirror.

"I hope I can," Kevin said.

Matt didn't know if there was really such a thing as fate, that two people were ever *truly* destined to be together. Personally, he liked to believe that you made your own destiny, but who really knew? As Prospero might say "There are more things in heaven and earth, Horatio, than are dreamt of in your philosophy."

He could see that the kid could use a little hope - hell, they all could. So he decided to share a story with him from his past. A story that sometimes made him believe that some things really were meant to be.

"You never know, sometimes you get lucky like that. You know I've known my wife since we were in middle school, although to be honest, we didn't really become friends until near the end of High School. I was crazy about her, but I was always too shy to make a move. Then we grew up. She got married to someone else, even had a kid with him, but it didn't work out and she moved in with her mom in the city. I went to the city too, to go to college, and I started working part time in a detective agency while I was still in school. Eventually, I got my license to be a PI and opened up my own agency. It was a real hole-in-the wall kind of operation at first."

"That's for sure!" Randy couldn't help but add. He remembered the condition of Matt's first office all too well.

Matt ignored him and continued his story. "Then one day, out of nowhere, WHAM! I literally bumped into Naomi on a street corner. We hadn't seen each other in years. We got coffee together to catch up, and I found out she was between jobs, so I hired her on the spot to be my secretary. Fast forward a few years and we're married with a nice house in the suburbs, and she's a freakin' college professor!" Matt paused and smiled to himself.

"I guess my point in telling you all of this is this: what were the chances that we'd ever run into each other like that again? Two kids from South Jersey in a big city full of millions of people? Life is funny. Sometimes, even when you think you've lost someone for good, that you'll never see them again, they find their way back to you. Even if things don't work out between you guys now, that doesn't mean that you won't get a second chance someday. If it's meant to be, you'll find your way back to each other, even if it takes years."

Matt's story seemed to have done the trick. Kevin suddenly looked a little less glum.

"Thanks, Matt. I'll try to remember that," he said.

The black Cadillac turned off of the long, long driveway that led up to Sherwood Farm and back out onto the main road. As it zoomed down the streets of Davenport, with the autumn foliage exploding into a panoply of brilliant colors all around it, Matt Spike smiled his lopsided smile to himself and for the first time in a long time he knew, deep down in his bones, that everything was going to be okay.

EPILOGUE:

FIFTEEN YEARS LATER

(OCTOBER, 2020)

Now comes the part where I, your humble narrator, explains how it is that I came to know about these events and write them down here for you to examine. Who am I, you ask? Well, if you've read any of my other accounts of Matt's cases, you would know that I am Robert Sohl, an old high school friend of Matt and Naomi's. Matt has been amused by my retellings of some of his more noteworthy cases, and has cooperated by promising to give me access to his old case files.

When I completed my previous book in this series, *Beyond the Veil of Death,* Matt said that he would send me the details of a few other cases he'd been involved in, ones that I had no firsthand knowledge of, as I had drifted apart from him in the years that these "new" cases took place in.

The story of how I came to know about this case in particular is worth repeating.

It was a warm fall night in October of 2020. I had just finished up a late shift at the pharmacy in the nursing home where I work as a technician. As I walked to my car, I heard the sound of a car door opening and footsteps from nearby.

"Bob! Hey Bob!" an unfamiliar female voice rang out. I hadn't really gone by the name "Bob" in years. Most people call me "Robert" these days, which sounds ever so much more dignified, don't you think? So I didn't *really* think that anyone was trying to get my attention. But I looked around the mostly empty parking lot all the same, curious as to what was going on.

I saw a short, somewhat chubby (albeit in a cute kind of way) woman approaching me, followed closely by a slender man who was only a little bit taller than she was. They both appeared to be in their late twenties or early thirties. It was a little hard to tell because they were both wearing surgical masks - it was the time of COVID-19, you know. The woman seemed to be carrying a briefcase.

"Are you looking for me?" I asked a little nervously.

"Yes. I'm Allison and this is Kevin. Matt sent us. Didn't he tell you we were coming?" she asked.

"Holy crap!" I exclaimed. "I mean, he did say something about maybe sending some people down here with some of his old case files in an email a few months ago, but I didn't expect anyone to *really* drive all the way down here to Virginia. I had no idea that you were coming today."

"Well, TA-DA! Here we are!" Allison smiled. "I've got the files right here in this briefcase."

"Why not just mail them to me? Why go through all this trouble to deliver them in person?"

"These files contain lots of sensitive Guild secrets. Too important to trust to the mail or any kind of electronic methods of data transfer. These aren't the originals of course, they're just photocopies. Matt wants you to burn them when you're done with them. That's important: burn them, don't shred them, do you understand?"

I told her that I did.

By now you may be wondering how I am able to write these books if they're filled with all kinds of sensitive secrets. That's easy. For one, I change all the names. For another, the Guilds know that many of the things that happen in these stories seem too outlandish for any sane person to believe are anything other than fiction. So long as I change the names and a few other minor details, they don't care. However, as you can see, they feel quite differently about the real names and details being leaked.

She opened the briefcase and handed me the stack of files inside.

"Matt wants you to go over these files first. There's details of two different cases here. One from 2005 and another from 2013. He says that before he can explain where he and the others have been for the past few months, you need to understand these cases first. It'll all just make a bit more sense if you tell these stories first."

Matt and most of his friends and associates had disappeared near the beginning of the year, around March of 2020. I still got the occasional cryptic message from him, promising to explain everything. Apparently, a few of his associates like Allison and Kevin had stayed behind to keep his detective agency running.

"Our number is written on the top folder there. We were personally involved in that 2005 case. In fact, it's how we first met. If you have any questions, feel free to call or text. I want to make sure you get it right," she told me.

"What are you guys doing tonight? Maybe we could grab dinner or something? You're not really going all the way back to New Jersey tonight are you?" I asked, knowing from experience that it was a good eight hour drive from where I lived.

"We've wasted enough time on this nonsense for one day! We're still supposed to be working on a case, and it's time we got back to work on it!" Kevin said a little angrily, speaking up for the first time.

"Kevin! Take your medicine!" Allison admonished him.

"Fine," he said sullenly as he pulled a bottle from his jacket pocket, emptied something from inside into his other hand, pulled down his mask long enough to pop it into his mouth and chewed it.

"What was that?" I asked.

"Edible marijuana. A special blend that we get from an old friend in D.C. We came here to deliver these files to you because we were headed down to D.C. to restock. I don't think either of us realized just how far you are from D.C., though. You have to excuse my husband. He has a kind of...rare condition. He gets more irritable the closer we get to a full moon and we're due for one any day now. Well, I guess you'll read all about it in those case files I just gave you eventually. Call us if you have any questions."

Kevin looked a little embarrassed, or at least his eyes did, which was all that I could see of his face. "Sorry, man. I'm really not that much of a jerk. Thanks for the dinner invite, but we really do need to get going. Good luck with the next book. I hope you get it right, it's kind of our love story; it's important to us that you do."

"Sure, yeah, no problem. I'll do my best. Thanks for the files!" I called after them as they turned away and got back into their car.

Soon they had disappeared into the night from which they'd emerged.

So yes, that was *the* Kevin and Allison. The very same ones that were in the story you have just read. And yes, they did eventually get married and ended up working at Matt's detective agency. Matt kept in contact with them both over the years, as I would learn from texting them when I had loads of questions for them after going through the files. Matt would see to it that Kevin got the psychological counseling he needed - he ended up being a sort of surrogate father figure to Kevin, which is why Kevin eventually followed in his footsteps and became a detective too.

Allison would also come to work in Matt's office. She's a real computer whiz and tends to do more research for the firm than field work, but that's changed recently with most of the agency's staff going missing to...wherever it is that they've been since March of 2020. Lately, she's been taking a more active role in the investigations and doing more field work. I discovered that Earl Rogers, the former Agent Grey, went on to become a senior partner in the agency. He's running the place in Matt's absence, as he often does when Matt or Randy are unavailable. He also found love and started a small family for himself.

Allison did try to pursue an acting career at one point, but it didn't quite pan out for her. She did appear in a few plays and b-movies though. She still does community theatre for fun, and occasionally takes bit parts in some of the student films that are produced at Rutgers University, which is near where they live now.

Kevin gave Allison her skull ring back on the day that he proposed to her, only this time it was gold plated, with two little diamonds inserted into the eye sockets of the skull. A picture of it appears on the back cover of this book.

Allison and Kevin were married in a nice little ceremony that was held at Wonderland. The place got some new management, and it isn't as seedy and unsafe as it used to be. They even demolished the Tunnel of Love and expanded the park as had been promised for so long by the previous owners. However, both Kevin and Allison kind of preferred the older, seedier version of the park to the slick, clean and somewhat characterless version that exists today. Nostalgia is a funny thing, isn't it?

What became of some of our other players you ask?

William and Elizabeth still own Sherwood Farm. In addition to their two adopted daughters, Allison and Mary, they also went on to have a few of their own biological children, as they had both been turned into vampires before they had an opportunity to start a family, and it had always been something that they wanted. So Allison and Mary have lots of younger brothers and sisters to spoil, and spoil them they do. Especially Allison and Kevin, who can't have children of their own for reasons that should now be abundantly clear, although they are thinking of possibly adopting someday.

Martin Lane helped restore the manor to its former glory, then he returned to his own farm nearby and converted it into a winery. His wine is pretty tasty, or so I hear.

Mary went on to get a degree in electronic engineering. She works for some big government contractor, designing robotic space probes for NASA. Not bad, huh? Kevin became good friends with Matt's son Joe and one day, he and Allison introduced Joe to Mary. They hit it off, and as I let slip earlier, she ended up marrying Joe and they are expecting Matt and Naomi's first grandchild. Or at least they were. It turns out that Joe and Mary are part of the group that disappeared in March, so I have no idea, at the time of my writing this, if that baby has been born yet or not.

Prospero went on to become one of the most respected wizards of the Temple of the Old Gods.

The Gooch is...still The Gooch. You might catch sight of him someday, skating down the streets of Washington D.C. in his strange hat, riding on his longboard. He supplies Kevin and the other former werewolves with his potent blend of edibles free of charge to help manage their condition.

Matt, Randy, Naomi and Penny are all still out there...somewhere. I hope that someday soon I'll get the answers I'm looking for about where they've been since March and what they're up to. I miss them all.

Now the main thing that Kevin and Allison want anyone reading this to understand is that while it is true that they did eventually end up with each other, getting there was not a straightforward and easy path. Theirs is not one of those stories where a boy meets a girl and they ride off into the sunset and immediately live happily ever after.

It was a long and twisted road for them to find the happiness that they now enjoy together. They stayed in touch with one another throughout the years, but the physical distance between them became their first great barrier. They both inevitably became interested in other people who were simply closer in proximity to them, who were more *convenient*.

These relationships always fell apart in time, although sometimes it took years for them to do so. The problem was that nobody else could really ever understand what it was like to be them. No one else could comprehend how profoundly their respective curses had affected them. In the case of Kevin, it was difficult for his partners to deal with his irritability as the full moon approached, and the problems he continued to have with physical intimacy for the first few years after that strange weekend. In Allison's case, it was many things. From the fact that she had lost all of her original family in a tragic accident, to the reality of having to pretend that she hadn't spent sixteen years of her life stuck as a teenage vampire, she couldn't share anything about massive chunks of her life with her partners for fear that they'd think she was nuts. She also had difficulty adjusting once her clock, that had for so long been stopped, suddenly began ticking again. When she was no longer just a spectator who read about life, but someone who was actually able to fully live it again.

Then time became their enemy, their new curse. The timing was never quite right for them to get together. They always had an unspoken understanding that they would get together romantically someday, but when one of them became single, the other one was inevitably always still embroiled in a relationship. Neither of them was ever willing to hurt someone they still cared for at the time simply for the sake of being with the other. They were both too nice for that. Too classy. They had to see if those relationships would die a natural death rather than cut them short prematurely to go chasing after what they sometimes feared was just an old infatuation left over from their more impressionable years.

Once, they did get together, briefly, but Kevin got cold feet and called it off, still not quite sure he deserved the happiness he found with her. It had seemed too good to be true, and he foolishly did his best to make that into a self-fulfilling prophecy. They still managed to remain friends somehow throughout it all, even after he broke her heart that time. It would take them several more years before the stars finally aligned in such a way where they were both free of all other romantic entanglements and willing to take the journey together - when they had finally learned to love themselves enough to be able to properly love one another.

And things are still imperfect. Are they ever completely perfect? How dull that would be! There are still squabbles, sometimes there are even tears, but through it all, the curious bond that they formed all those years ago has endured, as strong as it ever was. Stronger, even.

Unbreakable.

The End

Completed in Roanoke, VA on January 18th, 2021

Matt Spike will return in
“Matt Spike Against the Amazon Saucer Women from
Venus”

OTHER BOOKS IN THE DEAD END WORLD SAGA:

The Shadow of Death

Tales from a Dead End World

Beyond the Veil of Death

Tales from a Dead End World Volume 2

Matt Spike and the Vampire's Curse

and *also Jersey Devils*

Coming in 2024:

Night of The Mothman

Matt Spike Against the Amazon Saucer Women from Venus

www.ingramcontent.com/pod-product-compliance
Lightning Source LLC
Chambersburg PA
CBHW061058210726
48294CB00001B/208